Praise fo

"Goddard increases the stakes and highlights the power of hope, faith, and trusting God in the darkest times in this rush of a series entry."

Publishers Weekly

"Goddard's second installment of her Rocky Mountain Courage series is a whirlwind adventure from the first chapter to the conclusion . . . *Deadly Target* hit the bull's-eye for me."

Life is Story

"Elizabeth Goddard pulls out all the stops in this intriguing, edge-of-your-seat suspense. It's an explosive adventure . . ."

Book Club Network

Praise for *Present Danger*

"Goddard opens her Rocky Mountain Courage series with this thrilling romance set amid an investigation into a smuggling ring. This will be a great entry point for those new to Goddard's high-octane inspirationals."

Publishers Weekly

"Readers will definitely enjoy puzzling over this story. The pacing is perfect; continuous, mind-boggling action, with plenty of time for unfinished business."

Interviews and Reviews

"*Present Danger* starts with a bang and never lets up. Goddard's fast-paced romantic suspense will have your pulse pounding as you turn the pages. Hold on to your seat and your heart as you enjoy this thrill ride!"

Rachel Dylan, bestselling author
of the Capital Intrigue series

"A plane crash, a dead body, and two people who decide that justice and love are worth fighting for all add up to a riveting read you won't want to put down. I highly recommend this book!"

Lynette Eason, bestselling, award-winning author
of the Danger Never Sleeps series

"A riveting beginning to the new Rocky Mountain Courage series, *Present Danger* takes readers on a wild ride filled with family tragedies, long-buried secrets, ancient relics, and broken hearts. Goddard has crafted a page-turner that takes off in the first nail-biting chapter, weaves through unexpected twists and shocking revelations, then culminates in a whirlwind of betrayal and redemption. I couldn't read the final chapters fast enough!"

Lynn H. Blackburn, award-winning author
of the Dive Team Investigations series

"I was captivated from the very first scene of *Present Danger* to the shocking conclusion. You can always count on Elizabeth Goddard to bring you dramatic action and adventure scenes that put you on the edge of your seat!"

Susan Sleeman, bestselling author
of the Homeland Heroes series

"Elizabeth Goddard starts her brand-new Rocky Mountain Courage series with an opening that sucks you in from page one and doesn't stop until the heart-pounding conclusion."

Lisa Harris, *USA Today* and CBA bestselling author of the Nikki Boyd Files

"*Present Danger*—another edge-of-the-seat story by Elizabeth Goddard that will keep you turning pages to the end."

Patricia Bradley, author of *Standoff*, Natchez Trace Park Rangers series

CRITICAL
ALLIANCE

Books by Elizabeth Goddard

ROCKY MOUNTAIN COURAGE
· BOOK 3 ·

CRITICAL ALLIANCE

ELIZABETH GODDARD

Revell

a division of Baker Publishing Group
Grand Rapids, Michigan

© 2022 by Elizabeth Goddard

Published by Revell
a division of Baker Publishing Group
PO Box 6287, Grand Rapids, MI 49516-6287
www.revellbooks.com

Printed in the United States of America

Library of Congress Cataloging-in-Publication Data
Names: Goddard, Elizabeth, author.
Title: Critical alliance / Elizabeth Goddard.
Description: Grand Rapids, MI : Revell, a division of Baker Publishing
 Group, [2022] | Series: Rocky mountain courage; 3
Identifiers: LCCN 2021050612 | ISBN 9780800738006 (paperback) | ISBN
 9780800741501 (casebound) | ISBN 9781493436231 (ebook)
Classification: LCC PS3607.O324 C64 2022 | DDC 813/.6—dc23
LC record available at https://lccn.loc.gov/2021050612

This book is a work of fiction. Names, characters, places, and incidents are the product of the author's imagination or are used fictitiously. Any resemblance to actual events, locales, or persons, living or dead, is coincidental.

Baker Publishing Group publications use paper produced from sustainable forestry practices and post-consumer waste whenever possible.

22 23 24 25 26 27 28   7 6 5 4 3 2 1

This novel is dedicated to my husband, Dan,
my most essential ally on this precarious journey called life.
I love you, Dan!

ONE

Her world was spinning out of control. Correction. Not her world—her *body*.

But what else could Mackenzie Hanson expect while in the grip of a colossal gyrating octopus? A cephalopod built from a jumble of plastic and metal parts, and powered by a smelly, backfiring motor. All of it quickly bolted together to be ready for patrons visiting the traveling carnival.

She imagined a tentacle flying off. How safe was she, really?

Her stomach grew queasy with the spinning and rocking motion.

Sky. People. Balloons. Asphalt. Sky. People. Balloons. Asphalt.

Over and over and over.

Mackenzie squeezed her eyes shut.

But for the brief time she'd kept them open . . .

She might have been hallucinating. Could centrifugal force cause hallucinations?

She thought she'd seen . . . No. It was only someone who looked like Julian.

Even with the mere thought of seeing him, her heart rate

skyrocketed. The ride wasn't helping. She squeezed her eyes tighter as if that would protect her from the g-force conspiring against her.

Screams erupted. Laughter too. Loud rock music pounded through her bones as her stomach dropped to catch up with her body being flung by an octopus tentacle. She clung to the safety bar that kept her secure or prevented her from escape. She hadn't decided which.

All she wanted was to get off the giant rolling octopus.

Now!

A hand squeezed her shoulder. "Are you alright?"

That William, her friend—her *date*—could even speak while the ride continued spinning added to her anxiety. Mackenzie shook her head.

"I thought it would be fun." William's voice sounded tight. "Just hang on. It'll be over soon."

But the ride wasn't over soon. In fact, it continued far too long.

Was the operator distracted? Flirting with a girl much too young for him? Had he left to use the facilities? Mackenzie recalled enjoying this crazy, exhilarating fluttering of her stomach as a kid. Things had certainly changed.

Finally, hydraulics hissed and shifted with the decrease in the motor's rumble. Her heart calmed with the knowledge that the torture by cephalopod was coming to an end. Keeping her eyes closed, she leaned back and breathed in the malodorous exhaust from the ride's overtaxed motor.

An image popped into her mind.

Glasses. Dark hair. A forest-green jacket.

Julian Abel.

It couldn't have been him. But if she'd imagined him—why? She hadn't seen him since she was sixteen, and she'd locked those memories in a vault and thrown away the proverbial key. Why was he breaking out of the crypt today?

"See, I told you it would be over soon." William's sarcasm demanded a smile.

A smile she had to force, along with an incredulous chuckle. "What was I thinking to let you talk me into this? I'm too old for this kind of thing."

William pressed his large hand over her small one, which still clung to the safety bar.

"Too old?" He quirked a brow. "I beg your pardon."

She caught him looking at her and dropped her hand from the bar, breaking free from his touch.

"Saying you're too old is the same as saying I'm too old," he said.

"Well, if the shoe—"

"Fits. I know the idiom. I've got one for you. You're never too old to have fun."

"More accurately, you mean to say that you're never too old to learn."

"To learn to have fun."

Her laugh was genuine this time. "Good one."

Now let me out of this cage.

"Mackenzie, you're young, vibrant, and beautiful, and the world is your oyster, as the saying goes." Reassurance filled William's tone. And his eyes.

Unpleasant shivers crawled over her. Was this how claustrophobia felt? Because right now, the space next to William was growing smaller. She exhaled as their turn to disembark from the car arrived. Perfect timing for an escape. The bar pinning them in released. Mackenzie couldn't get out fast enough and hopped to the ground.

And to freedom.

She headed straight for the clearly marked exit. William followed closely, his hand against the small of her back. She searched the area around the ride, hoping he didn't catch on to her wariness.

Seeing Julian had been a hallucination. Nothing more.

Music, grinding motors, screams, and laughter filled the air, along with the aroma of buttery popcorn and fried pies. Unfortunately, she also caught the pungent odor of an over-flowing garbage can as they walked.

"How about we grab a soda and cotton candy?" William asked.

What are you, seven? She smiled for his sake. He was trying so hard. Too hard. "That sounds like a plan."

"Good. No more wild rides tonight." He grinned and led her through the crowd toward the end of a long line for the food truck that featured loaded fried pickles, hot dogs, greasy fries—glorious carnival junk food.

William held her hand, and she didn't have the heart to do anything but go along with it. What was wrong with her? He was handsome and thoughtful. He was just . . . not for her.

"Agreed. No more wild rides." Calliope music drew her attention as they waited in line. "The carousel would be nice." *Then maybe just take me home.*

To make matters worse, he'd driven all the way from Lansing for the weekend, just to see her. She kept a condominium in a quaint town near Lake Michigan for weekends and summers.

"So you're heading back on Monday for the semester?" she asked.

"If I could teach something as"—he lifted his shoulders—"how can I put it . . . clandestine as you, then it would be fun teaching in the summer. But I forget, you can't really talk about your work."

She offered a smug grin. He was teasing, of course, and she could give as good as she got. "Yeah . . . it's on a need-to-know basis."

William was an adjunct professor at the university, and he had repeatedly asked her out until she finally agreed to a date.

One date. Which had somehow turned into a weekend

event since his parents supposedly owned a nearby summer lake house. *I never should have agreed to a date, much less an entire weekend.*

She was as trapped in this date as she had been riding the octopus. She had to grit her teeth to make it through and somehow let him down gently. Although . . . maybe he was feeling every bit as uncomfortable as she was.

While they moved forward in line, Mackenzie took in the carnival activities. The growing crowd was beginning to shift from adults and younger children to older teens as the evening deepened. If Julian had actually been at the carnival, she probably wouldn't even have recognized him. They'd been kids when it happened.

William cleared his throat. He'd been paying attention to her on their date, and she'd been distracted. "I admit, I'm not good company for you this evening."

He shrugged. "You don't seem to be a carnival kind of person. And to be honest, neither am I. But I thought it might be fun. I saw it when I got into town, so I made the suggestion."

"Oh, it was a great idea. We tried." She offered a grin. He really was a nice guy. Thick dark hair, clean-cut, and a boy-next-door kind of look, and as a runner, he had a lean, athletic body. But there was no emotional connection. At all. Why couldn't she get into him? She'd thought that she would be married and have at least two kids by the time she was thirty-two. Instead, she kept relationships at a distance.

They continued inching forward in the line, and she almost suggested they skip it and grab something from a drive-through.

William leaned closer. "Instead of the carousel, why don't we walk on the beach?"

Just what she didn't need to do with William. Things could get . . . romantic. More personal. More awkward. "It'll be too dark for that."

Disappointment surfaced in his gaze. Oh no. She'd hurt him.

Fortunately, it was their turn at the counter and William stepped forward. "What'll you have?" He didn't even look at her.

"Dr Pepper."

Someone bumped into her.

"Hey!" a kid yelled.

She turned to see the boy in line behind her glowering at the man in the dark-green jacket who cut through another line and disappeared in the crowd.

Julian? She had to know.

"Hey!" she said, echoing the kid as she left the line and followed the guy's path in hopes she would catch sight of him again weaving back and forth, dodging bodies left and right. She had to see for herself. Though finding Julian would prove that she hadn't hallucinated earlier on the ride, she really hoped that she'd been seeing things.

The crowd thickened as she kept her focus on the back of his head twenty or so yards ahead. He glanced over his shoulder, then turned around to walk backward and look at her. To hold her gaze.

Julian Abel.

Also known to her as 4PP3R1710N.

Or rather, *Apparition.*

He had one of those boyish faces that never seemed to age.

She hadn't imagined him, after all. He'd been watching her while she was on the ride. Her stomach dropped as if she were being tossed and turned all over again.

He couldn't be here. And yet there he was, staring at her. Why was he here? He had that knowing look in his eyes, and it stopped her in her tracks. Right in front of a young boy who barreled forward, smashing sticky caramel-covered ice cream all over her rarely used date-night blouse. Okay, her brand-new blouse.

The boy was around six, and his eyes filled with tears. His mother crouched to console him. "It's alright, sweetie. We'll get another one."

"Oh, I'm so sorry." Mackenzie hated that she'd made a child cry. She could have avoided this mishap, but she'd been too focused on finding Julian instead of watching where she was going.

The mother glared at her and dragged her son away.

William approached in a huff, somehow managing to hold two sodas and two bags of cotton candy in his large hands. She immediately relieved him of one of each item and took a few sips of the Dr Pepper while she searched the crowd for Julian.

His gaze froze on her caramelized shirt. "Mackenzie, what's going on? Besides being covered in sticky syrup." He lifted his dark eyes to her face. "You . . . you look like you've seen a ghost."

Julian had taken off. She'd seen a ghost, alright. A ghost that was very much living and breathing. And here, of all places. Here in Michigan at this carnival, and that look in his gaze left no doubt he'd deliberately tracked her down.

"Let's get out of here." Without waiting for agreement, she headed through the growing crowd toward the exit, wariness creeping into her bones. While she rushed forward, she scanned ahead, searching for the man who'd ruined her life. Correction. She'd ruined her own life. And that past had been sealed, so it was no longer in the public record.

It had essentially ceased to exist.

But Julian's appearance tonight was a reminder that her mistakes were right behind her.

She felt like she was on the ride again. Couldn't escape fast enough.

"Wait. Hold up." William tossed his drink and cotton candy in the garbage and gripped her arm, stopping her. "Please, what's going on?"

"Not here." She ground out the words. And with them, she'd said too much.

She shrugged free, pitched her cotton candy and soda as well, then took off running. She had to get away from the carnival and the feeling that Julian was watching her. He was everywhere, watching her.

And he was fully capable of being everywhere.

She weaved through the vehicles and dodged a few too. Finally, gasping for breath, she approached the shiny new Audi. William's car. Not hers. In the distance, she focused on the Ferris wheel. The lights and screams and laughter. A couple of blocks away, Lake Michigan's waves rolled against the shore. Comforting and soothing. She longed to be there.

If she'd gone walking on the beach tonight, would Julian have followed her there too? What did he want?

His face grim, William unlocked his car and opened the door for her.

"Thank you." She slid into the taupe leather seat, and he shut the door.

Once he was in the driver's seat, he started the vehicle and the quiet hum of the engine proclaimed power in complete contrast to the cranky motors of the traveling carnival rides.

"You wasted your money at the carnival. I'll make it up to you."

"You can make it up to me by telling me what happened back there. Something spooked you."

"Can we please just get out of here?"

In response, William steered slowly through the parking area, then turned onto the street. Mackenzie owed him something. Though not an explanation of what happened tonight, she definitely owed him the truth. But words failed her as images of Julian staring at her shuddered through her. A slow pounding started in her head, matching the palpitations of her heart.

To his credit, William didn't press her further.

Now that she'd had a moment to catch her breath, though, she could share at least something with him. "I saw someone I knew a long time ago. I was just surprised to see him, that's all."

"He must have made some kind of impression on you to upset you so much."

"It's complicated."

His lips pursed. At the corner ahead, she spotted a man. Glasses. Dark hair. Green jacket. He stepped into the street at the crosswalk and jogged forward to cross two lanes. A vehicle heading north in the opposite lane seemed to speed up.

Watch out!

All her muscles tensing, she gripped the seat. Julian suddenly stopped as if in shock. Mackenzie closed her eyes and gritted her teeth.

The next few moments held excruciating sounds. A thump. A speeding car.

William sucked in a breath and swerved to the side. "Did you see that? Someone just got hit by a car. It's a hit-and-run. Call 911!"

He jumped out and ran across the street, failing to close the car door behind him.

Other vehicles stopped. People rushed forward—curious onlookers and those who actually cared. Mackenzie called for emergency services and learned that someone had already called. Help was on the way.

She wouldn't jump out of the car to join the gathering crowd. She could offer no help. The two of them—she and Julian—should never be seen together. Instead, she wanted to curl into herself, but with the door wide open, the gruesome scene was framed perfectly for her to witness every minute.

Moments later, sirens rang out and lights flashed. Emergency vehicles—law enforcement cruisers, a fire truck, and an ambulance—arrived on the scene. She caught a glimpse of medics kneeling next to the body. What could she do? Nothing. Except, well, she could pray. She closed her eyes, but tears sprang up instead of heartfelt words to God.

She started to cross her arms, but her shirt remained sticky, so she thrust her hands into her jacket pockets. In her right pocket, she felt something that hadn't been there before. Mackenzie tugged it out.

A business card for Hanstech—short for Hanson Technologies—her father's brainchild. And on the back? A QR code. *What is this?*

Using her cell, she scanned the code. An animated image popped up.

Mackenzie gasped. Freda Stone, her favorite character from Knight Alliance, the MMO—Massively Multiplayer Online—game she and Julian had played together as kids, whirled around with her sword.

"You're vulnerable to deadly attacks. They're taking the stronghold!"

Mackenzie watched the short graphic again.

And again.

Dread filled her gut.

A warning. This was why Julian had bumped into her. To stick the business card in her pocket so that she would find it later.

Her father's dream start-up company had become reality, until he died. Now her older brother was at the helm. And tonight Julian hand-delivered a warning. Important enough that he sought her out in person but still kept his distance.

Important enough that he took a huge risk.

Deadly attacks . . .

She eyed the emergency vehicles, and the nausea she'd felt from the ride returned.

William climbed back in and shut his door, then stared at the steering wheel, a haggard cast to his pale features.

"Well?" she asked, the question barely a croak from her tear-clogged throat.

"He was breathing when they put him on the gurney."

She slumped with a long exhale. Julian had survived. But for how much longer? He'd communicated with her without leaving a digital trail. He was that scared. And she should be too. She shouldn't go see him in the hospital and instead should stay away.

He would want that.

William said nothing as he drove her back to the condo only a mile away and parked.

She shifted in the seat. "Listen—"

"I know what you're going to say," he huffed. "Thank you, William, but I don't want to see you anymore—at least on a personal level. I know, because that's what I was going to say, only to you."

Okay, well, she deserved that. And despite sharing his sentiment, rejection always stung. "Um . . . I was going to say that I need to get to Montana."

"Montana?" Suspicion flashed in his eyes. "Just like that?"

"Just like that. Something has come up, and I need to cancel our weekend—except, well, you already canceled it. It's okay, William. We're still friends. Colleagues. And I agree, it wasn't working."

He slumped back, and oddly, relief flashed over his features. Then he smiled. "At least now we know."

She returned his smile. Sometimes one date was all it took. "Yes, we do."

"What's in Montana?"

"Family." *A brother who warned me to stay far, far away.*

TWO

Alex Knight leaned his mountain bike against the trunk of a white pine at the Rocky Mountain Courage Memorial. He removed his helmet and hung it over the bars, then took a few steps to get a closer look at the damaged plaque honoring his father for his sacrifice.

A fist of grief pressed against his chest.

If Alex could go back in time and change one thing, he would start with the small plane crash on Stone Wolf Mountain and figure out how to keep his father home that day. And if he had changed that one day and his father had lived, maybe Alex wouldn't have ended up halfway around the world, watching others who depended on him burn in a fiery explosion.

Though he couldn't go back and fix the past, he would do everything in his power to right the wrong that had been done to the memorial—an infraction against those who died and the loved ones they left behind.

Too much crashed into him at once. The vandalism at the monument tangled up with the images flashing through his brain from the last three years spent overseas. Especially the last month.

He closed his eyes, only to see violent images burning through his mind.

The armored Suburban in front of him exploded in flames . . .
Steady, now.

He breathed in the scent of evergreens and fresh mountain air. Opened his eyes. He was surrounded by acres and acres of national forest. Montana. He was home, not on the other side of the world. Joyous birdsong sounded around him. If he listened, he could hear the Grayback River flowing nearby.

Yeah. That was better. Peace overcame the pulse pounding in his ears, and he tried to put his assignment protecting a high-risk asset in a high-threat region far behind him. That was over and done. If only he could push it totally out of his mind . . . And he would, because it was necessary. He'd come home to take a much-needed break and solve a mystery. Here at the place where his hero father was memorialized.

And that was just it. As a special agent working for the DSS, Diplomatic Security Services, vandalism wasn't the typical crime he would investigate. But as the son of a fallen hero, he was more than eager to dig in and get his hands dirty to find out who vandalized the memorial.

The same person who had taken to vandalism at the memorial months ago? Or someone new? Some kid who thought this would be funny? He took in the destruction. The violence. Each plaque was a tribute to those who'd been killed on the mountain while attempting to save the lives of others.

Hands on his hips, he walked the wide circle around the memorial, then returned to his father's plaque. Voices drifted up the trail. He glanced up in time to see two figures emerging from the trailhead. United States Forest Service Special Agent Terra Connors and her soon-to-be husband, Detective Jack Tanner.

Terra approached with a tenuous smile. "I thought I might find you here."

She was dressed in her usual khakis and button-down shirt. No uniform for her since she was an investigator. She and Alex became close friends after an avalanche killed his father and her mother fifteen years ago during a search and rescue mission. Terra and Alex, along with Erin Larson, who'd lost her stepfather. That was years ago, and they'd put the tragedy behind them, each attempting to make the world a better place in their own way.

Terra had called him about the vandalized memorial the night he got back to DC. He'd already debriefed and been told to decompress. It was as good a time as any to make a trip back to Montana and see Mom. As soon as he got back, though, he found himself in the thick of Erin's troubles. Thankfully, she was okay now, and happily engaged to Detective Nathan Campbell, her old boyfriend. Alex couldn't be happier for Terra and Erin—he thought of them as the sisters he never had but always wanted.

"Special Agent Connors." He quirked a grin.

"Hey, none of that formality needed." Terra gestured toward his bike. "How many miles have you ridden that thing so far this morning?"

He shrugged. "Only about twenty since I came directly here." He'd taken the road from the cabin he'd rented because it was the most direct route.

Jack shook his head. "You must have some serious leg muscles, dude."

Alex wouldn't admit to Jack that the last hill had almost done him in. Overseas, he didn't have much opportunity to mountain bike. "I never got to officially congratulate you on your engagement, by the way. Glad you were able to come back to Montana and stake a claim."

"Now, wait a minute. I'm not a claim to be staked." Terra fisted her hands on her hips, her smile broadening. But it slowly faded as the three of them looked toward the memorial. Vandalism wasn't necessarily a high priority, like murder or drugs or human trafficking.

Alex blew out a breath. "What can you tell me?"

"We didn't learn anything from the first incident back in October." Jack looked up at the nearest tree. "But we planted some cameras."

"And?"

"Nothing for months. We had to replace the batteries, and a camera now and then. Figured it was kids with a weird sense of how to have fun. Had almost decided it wasn't worth the time or resources and would probably not happen again. Then a few nights ago, we got this. I would have shared it earlier, but, well, we were kind of busy. So I'm sharing it now."

"That was some crazy business surrounding Erin. I'm just glad that's behind us." And they could focus on something mundane by comparison.

Jack held up his cell and let a video play across the screen. Even in the shade, it wasn't easy to see. Alex could barely make out the dark, grainy figure. But he could see enough. The headlamp on the vandal's helmet shone brightly as they bashed away with their sledgehammer, taking special interest in the plaque dedicated to Alex's father. Then everything seemed to go dark, but light caught the figure disappearing into the woods.

"Wow," Alex said. "That's not going to help you much."

Terra walked toward her mother's plaque, which was vandalized in October but received no damage this time. "We know it was someone acting alone. They dressed in black, wore a helmet with a headlamp, and brought a sledgehammer. So the act was premeditated. Our first thought was that this was just some kids, or a kid acting alone."

"But you don't know if it was the same person." Alex remained next to his father's destroyed plaque and shoved back the harsh memories—the brutal reality of lives forever changed.

Jack rubbed his neck. "We're comparing the shards of broken stone, but we concluded a sledgehammer was used in October too. It's probably the same person."

"What we're lacking," Terra said, "is—"

"Motive." Alex walked around his father's plaque.

Terra nodded. "Yes."

"What does Erin think?" The criminal psychologist in their group. He recalled that about eight months ago, back in October, he'd been in town and he, Terra, and Erin had discussed the vandalism.

Erin had suggested the violence was malicious. He offered up revenge. After all, it was the fifteen-year anniversary of when the avalanche took out his father and the other two members of the SAR team. Erin didn't think someone bent on committing an act of revenge would wait so long.

Violence. Revenge. He'd wanted to leave it all behind when he came back to Montana. When he was home with the fresh air and pristine rivers and waterfalls. This was the place he ran to when he'd had enough of the rest of the world.

Except, well, the rest of the world was encroaching on his home state, what with the murders last fall and now with what happened to Erin and Nathan recently. He accepted the painful reality.

Jack's shoulders relaxed. "Maybe you can help us with this vandalism."

"What can I do?" Alex shrugged. "You've got nothing."

"Not true," Terra said. "We can find out who bought helmets with lamps. Batteries. A sledgehammer."

"Things someone might already have in their garage." Alex wasn't impressed. "Tools everyone around here buys."

"Okay, wise guy, what's *your* plan?" Jack's brows furrowed.

"I don't have a plan. But we discussed this before in your living room, Terra, when it first happened. If it's not just some kid committing a random act of violence, then one question keeps coming back to me. Why now? It's been fifteen years, give or take. What if it *is* some kind of revenge?"

"Oh, the revenge idea again?" Terra shook her head.

He shrugged. "You asked what I thought. I admit it's out there, but Erin's the one who brought up the reasons people commit vandalism. And I'm gathering that you don't think it was just a kid out for some fun. Maybe the local news stories surrounding the memorial stirred someone up or reminded them about a past they wanted to forget."

"I agree with Alex," Jack said. "My gut feeling is that there's a reason behind this beyond a kid having some fun."

"Revenge. Something in the past. How would you go about looking into that exactly?" Terra pushed her hair back into a clip.

"I came back to see Mom and because you called and asked"—Alex noticed that Jack gave Terra a surprised look—"and yeah, I wanted to see the damage for myself. I could dig into this a little bit. I know it's not a priority for you."

"Are you even going to be here long enough to bother?" Jack asked.

Maybe Alex was overreacting, but he sensed Jack was referring to the fact that he'd left Montana at the first opportunity, and just kept going. "If you're asking if I'll be here long enough to finish what I started, I can't answer that. You've had months to solve this, and you haven't."

"Alright, boys," Terra said. "No fighting in the sandbox."

"Fighting? What fighting?" Alex smiled. She was right. They needed to dial down the tension. "We're all on the same side here."

Jack kicked at a half-buried rock. "What more would you do in terms of digging?"

What did I get myself into? He ran a hand across his jaw and the back of his neck, then angled to Jack. "I'd take a look at what's changed. Any political or environmental changes that have occurred around here. Then I might go back and look at what was going on fifteen years ago with each of the families represented here at the memorial, specifically yours, Terra's, and mine, since those plaques have been targeted."

Terra's eyes grew wide. "What?"

He bobbed his chin. "It's just a hunch, okay? The vandalism might not be related. But then again it could be. And if it is, why fifteen years later? Is someone trying to get our attention?"

He held Terra's gaze, then shifted to someone behind her. A woman hiked up the trail and stopped at the Rocky Mountain Courage main plaque. She wore Army-green cargo pants and a light jacket. Her eyes flashed around the memorial, then flicked to the three of them and snagged on Alex.

No . . .

What was *she* doing here?

Tall, slender, and athletic. Long, brown layered hair that emphasized her big hazel eyes and a dimpled grin he could never forget, though she wasn't grinning now. He took her in, but then his gaze bounced back up to her eyes. Still luminous and captivating and alluring. Scary too—when she looked at him, he got the sense she was reading his mind, even his mail. He'd last seen her in DC, and now, suddenly, she was here.

During their one day together three years ago when she'd come to DC for an interview with the DSS, she'd mentioned being from Montana too. The next day, Alex left for his overseas assignment but hadn't forgotten her.

Mackenzie . . .

How could he ever forget such a beautiful name that went with such striking eyes?

He stared . . . And she was staring back. Was Providence sending him a message? Alex took a step to make his way to her, but . . .

The earth rumbled beneath his feet—almost undetectable. Nothing unusual about that here in Montana, with up to ten small quakes a day. It reminded him of the life he'd left behind. The slight tremor passed in seconds, but not without leaving damage when a crack split the chunk that remained of his father's stone plaque.

"Ah, Alex. I'm sorry." Terra crouched and reached for the chunk that had fallen. "I barely felt that tremor, but the rest of the stone was probably already weakened."

"Leave it," he said. "It's not like you can fix it."

Using her cell, she took pictures of the cracked stone. "We'll fix it, alright. We'll find who's responsible."

He crossed his arms and glanced back to Mackenzie. She was gone. He should have approached her and said something. At least she'd recognized him too, except he had the sneaking suspicion that seeing him here was what sent her away.

Looked like he had two mysteries to solve.

THREE

With a white-knuckled grip on the wheel, Mackenzie dragged in a ragged breath and steered up the long drive toward the log cabin constructed in the side of a mountain. It blended in with the surrounding natural backwoods setting. Dad's idea. Her older brother, Rowan, had taken up residence in the house and become CEO of Hanstech after Dad's death—had it really been twelve years ago?

Palms sweating, Mackenzie parked near a copse of trees about fifteen yards from the front entrance, giving herself a chance to work up her courage and rehearse her words.

After the carnival—the night Julian delivered the cryptic warning—she packed a small duffel and hopped in her Jeep, drove north until she crossed the Mackinac Bridge to Michigan's Upper Peninsula, then traveled through Wisconsin, Minnesota, North Dakota, and finally, Montana. She'd had plenty of time to consider that cryptic message and what it could mean and prepare to take action.

But not nearly enough time to work up the courage to face Rowan, who'd repeatedly warned her away, striking fear in her when she was young and vulnerable.

Now that she was thirty-two, and in a career that she loved,

Mackenzie thought she'd gotten over the hurt of his words and pushed past the fear and dread she always felt when she saw him, but they had risen again, battling for control, especially with Julian's appearance.

She'd stopped by the Rocky Mountain Courage Memorial believing she could somehow soak up some of that courage, but instead she'd locked eyes with the guy she'd met at the DSS offices during her interview in DC. She hadn't recognized him at first because he looked so different wearing close-fitting biking shorts instead of a suit. His thick brown hair hung a little longer, not so neatly trimmed as it had been. That day in DC, Alex had shown up in a suit and tie. Handsome. Professional. A killer smile and the spark of something dangerous in his gaze.

"They asked me to show you around town. Give you the grand tour."

Then he flashed that dimpled grin of his. She wasn't going to say no, because the tour was part of the next phase in the interview package. But even if it wasn't, she would have said yes to this complete stranger. Their one day together seemed too short as he gave her the tour, and she didn't want it to end.

It had ended alright.

Seeing him today only reminded her that the DSS had passed on her after their background check. Someone had taken a peek at those sealed records, no doubt.

Her mistake just wouldn't let go. But she would face the fear head-on.

I can do this. God, help me do this.

A white pearl Lexus sped past and parked in the circle right in front of the main entrance.

Out stepped a tall, slender woman dressed in stylish professional attire but with an outdoorsy flair. Black sunglasses took up half her face, and the wind swept her long black hair behind her as she peered at Mackenzie's Jeep, which was parked away from the house but still on the drive.

Nora.

Her sister glanced between the cabin and the Jeep, hesitating before starting up the steps.

This wasn't going as planned. Mackenzie felt like an absolute fool. She shifted into gear and sped toward the front, parking behind the Lexus as her sister sprinted up the stone steps.

She hopped out. "Nora!"

Her sister was almost to the door when she whirled around.

"Mackenzie?" Nora rushed forward and met Mackenzie halfway, catching her up in a hug and stunning Mackenzie with a warmer-than-usual welcome.

It was the kind of welcome she'd always wanted. She wished it didn't knock her off-kilter.

Nora held on longer than necessary and whispered in Mackenzie's ear, "Go home as soon as you can. It's not safe here."

Not . . . *"Stay far, far away."*

Whatever. It seemed that her siblings would always have some kind of warning for her. Disappointment lodged in her gut, but what had she expected?

Nora pulled away and smiled, nothing of the warning in her expression—except her eyes. Something behind her eyes left Mackenzie disturbed.

"What a surprise." Nora started up the steps to the porch. "Why didn't you let us know you were coming?"

"I . . . I tried to call Rowan, but he didn't answer." Which was probably a good thing. He wouldn't listen to her or understand the warning she would share. Not over the phone. That's why she knew she had to come in person.

"He's been so busy lately. I'm sure he would have called you back soon."

Liar.

"Well, what matters is that you're here now." Nora led her up the few short steps. "I want to hear everything. I take it school is out for the summer. I hope you can stay with us."

What happened to her whispered warning?

Her sister bubbled on without giving Mackenzie a chance to respond. But inviting her to stay? That was a new one. Maybe the distance between them rested on Mackenzie's shoulders. Rowan hadn't repeated those words to her in years. Had she held on to them too long? Taken them to heart too deeply?

Nora's reaction went a long way in making Mackenzie regret she had ever listened to her brother. She had taken his words to heart, deep down inside, and believed herself to be a castaway. Maybe time had healed them all and given them new perspectives.

At the double doors, Nora pulled out keys from her bag and reached for the knob.

"Wait . . ."

Pausing, her sister looked at her, the smile still in place. The excitement and pleasure evident in her features. But . . . again something out of place flickered in her gaze. Nora's fear reflected her own in this moment, but what was Nora afraid of?

"I haven't seen Rowan in so long."

"You haven't seen me in as long either, and I'm glad to see you. I promise, he'll be glad to see you too." Nora's smile widened.

Why? Why would the man who had never liked her to begin with and used every opportunity to drive her away, who'd taken advantage of her mistakes, be glad to see her?

Mackenzie was walking into an alternate universe. Somewhere between Michigan and Montana, she'd gone through a wormhole. That had to be it—maybe it happened when she was on that octopus. Everything shifted then.

Nora opened the door and stepped into the foyer. "Rowan. I'm sorry I'm late. And I brought a surprise." Nora winked at her.

Setting her purse on the side table, Nora removed her jacket, making herself at home.

"Rowan!" Nora yelled again, then glanced at Mackenzie and gestured for her to follow. "I'll let you surprise him."

Mackenzie followed Nora, taking in the warm caramel colors of the logs along the way. A month before Mackenzie's eighteenth birthday, the Hanson family (everyone except Mom, who died from leukemia years before) moved from Silicon Valley to Montana, where Dad built the new Hanstech headquarters. Dad's dreams of building a successful tech company came true, with the added bonus of living in Montana where he could promote a solid work-life balance and retain his employees. Yep. But Dad lost his youngest daughter along the way during the workaholic years required to get him there, and then he was killed in a plane crash.

Nora led Mackenzie into a beautifully decorated great room containing shelves filled with books and carved bronze statues of cowboys and horses, as well as oil paintings of mountains—a few additions since she'd last been here.

"I thought he'd be here already. He left before me."

"I didn't see another car—"

"Oh, Rowan parks in the garage to the side. Let me text him that I'm waiting. He had something he wanted to talk about at home instead of at the office . . ." Nora's last words sounded shaky. She was nervous. Her gaze briefly flicked to Mackenzie, and her expression flashed unease. But it was all gone before Mackenzie could blink.

What was going on?

In fact, Nora's hands trembled as she held her cell.

Because of Mackenzie's surprise visit? "I know me showing up here is just . . . out of the blue. I don't want to mess with your plans." Of course she did. She'd come here to warn them about the threat to Hanstech—and their lives.

Now that she was more than a thousand miles from Michigan, the doubts crept in. Was she overreacting? She didn't think so, especially since Julian's actions meant that he'd taken the threat seriously too.

"I had planned to have dinner with my fiancé, Carson." Nora half-frowned at her. "You haven't met him. This is perfect timing."

"You're engaged? Wow, when did this happen?"

Nora flashed her engagement ring. "This week."

And Nora hadn't thought to call Mackenzie? But all things considered, that made sense. Still, a pang shot through her heart. "Where did you meet him? Here in the wilds of Montana?"

"Carson is Hanstech's chief financial officer."

Mackenzie's throat thickened. She was really here. Really doing this. She eased into a plush chair in the corner. Maybe it could be a new start for them.

Nora held her cell to her side. "While we wait for him, why don't we get you settled into your old room. I hope you didn't check into a hotel. You're family. Whatever happened before is in the past." Her sister's eyes brimmed with tears that disappeared with her smile. "What do you say?"

Yes. I say yes. I want this new beginning.

But it was far too complicated. Mackenzie wasn't sure she could stomach staying in the same house where she'd briefly lived before Dad died, and where Rowan now lived.

"I'm here to stay a few days, but my bag is back at the hotel. Let's wait and see what Rowan thinks."

Nora nodded. Rowan would have the last say. He always had, since Dad died.

"I'll get us something to drink."

"Sure, but Nora, what did you mean earlier when you told me to—"

Nora lifted a finger to her lips and gave a subtle shake of her head. "When Rowan gets here, we'll go out to eat together." Nora left her alone.

Fine by her. She could catch her breath—

A scream ignited the air. Heart pounding, Mackenzie raced through the house. Nora's sobs struck a terrible chord in her heart as she followed the sound to Dad's old office. Standing behind an executive desk, her sister looked down, her face twisted in grief.

She could think of only one reason for Nora's reaction.

Mackenzie moved around the desk and looked to the floor at her brother's lifeless body.

FOUR

What happened after they found Rowan's body remained a blur. After two long nights of staring at the wood beams in her old room, Mackenzie had to get out.

Too many people visiting the house.

Friends of the family.

Board members.

Rowan's ex-wife.

People Mackenzie didn't know.

Officials in and out. Medical personnel. She'd grown weary of the weeping and angst. Trying to reminisce about their family life while skipping over the part where Mackenzie messed up. Nothing was the same after that.

Funeral arrangements hadn't been made. She still needed to tell Nora why she'd come, which frankly sounded nuts when she said the words out loud, but how did she drop that bomb in the middle of a brand-new nightmare? How and when? It seemed wholly inappropriate.

"It's surreal . . . you coming back." Nora had given her a strange look on her way to her bedroom.

And there it was. The moment Mackenzie should have told Nora about the warning. Mackenzie had wanted to tell her then. After all, that had been the first real opening for her to do so. At the same time, it was no opening at all.

Oh, God, it's all messed up.

She dressed and headed down the hall to Nora's room. Mackenzie had decided to stay in the house, at least for now, because her room décor from years ago had remained in place. Even Rowan hadn't changed it. Weird. And since Rowan was gone, Nora wanted to stay at the house a few nights instead of her own home in town. Her way of holding on. They each had their ways of processing the loss and reasons for wanting to stay in the house.

At the door, Mackenzie lifted her hand to knock. She heard Nora in conversation with someone about Hanstech. Mackenzie wouldn't disturb her now, but she had to get out of this house. To get away from the pain of loss.

In the kitchen, she found a sticky notepad and scribbled a message, then stuck it near the warming coffeepot. None of those individual cups for them. A refrigerator magnet featuring a picture of Rowan, Dad, and Nora with their bikes caught her attention. Mackenzie couldn't shake the sense that she could have somehow prevented Rowan's death. She'd come back to prevent something disastrous. Julian had warned her, but she'd been too late.

A heart attack, the county coroner had said. Without an autopsy.

She definitely needed fresh air. When she returned, she would tell Nora what she had come to say. She found her old mountain bike in the garage, dusted it off, and took to the trail behind the house surrounded by four hundred acres and bordered by national forest on three sides. The acreage included a snowmobile track and an extensive network of hiking and biking trails easily accessed behind the house.

The cool morning air and exertion would do her good—and she'd feel the pain come tomorrow, because she wasn't exactly in the physical condition to mountain bike on treacherous trails. But the effort would distract her from the image of Rowan's body that was seared into her eyelids.

Her older brother had intimidated her as a child, and weirdly even into adulthood. And now that he was gone, she was surprised that part of her wasn't relieved. That the burden he'd placed on her, always holding her mistake over her head, hadn't been lifted. Maybe deep down she had imagined she would save the company from a massive computer hack, and Rowan would welcome her back into the fold.

Because she was oh-so-self-sacrificing.

Instead, her brother was gone.

He's gone. He's gone. He's gone.

No, Rowan, not yet.

She'd wasted precious years living in her own guilt and heeding his warning. Letting him intimidate her into staying away. For Dad's sake, until he died, and then for Rowan's and Nora's sakes. For what? Well, that had been another big mistake.

Life went on, even after mistakes left you scraping yourself off the ground.

The unmistakable roar of a waterfall up ahead broke through her morbid thoughts and calmed her. She remembered that the trail would take her near the waterfall and cross over a small rickety wooden bridge.

"This is what it's all about," Dad had said. Dad worked hard, but he played hard too.

She pumped the pedals to keep the burn in her lungs and legs as she aimed for the falls. The trail led her down and away, and she crossed the footbridge gingerly on her bike. On the other side of the roar and spray, she pushed on and would keep pushing until she completely left behind her torrential thoughts.

Julian at the carnival.

A DSS agent at the memorial.

She wanted off this metaphorical amusement park ride—she was absolutely not amused.

God . . . Are you listening? What do I do?

Navigating the rough and rocky terrain through the thick greenery, she pushed harder and faster. Oxygen pumping through her body, some of the tension eased. But not the grief.

Never the grief.

Her breathing almost covered up the sounds coming from behind her, except her prickling skin warned her that she wasn't alone. Because the trail was so complicated, she couldn't afford to look over her shoulder.

The obvious sounds of another biker closed in on her. Nora? No. Her sister couldn't have caught up with her. Then who?

She spotted a rise ahead and the perfect spot behind that to go off trail. She was out of practice. Accelerating, she gripped the handlebars as the bike left the ground. On the other side of the rise, she braced as the pine-carpeted earth came toward her. She hit the ground and kept going. Gaining traction, she veered off the path through the trees. Momentum was on her side.

Until her front wheel slammed into a hidden boulder—every mountain biker's fear.

Pain jarred through her. The bike stopped, and Mackenzie flew over the handlebars, landing hard on her back. The breath whooshed from her. Staring straight up, she waited for the pain to pass and for the chance to suck in a breath. Footfalls alerted her to the follower's approach. Before she could scramble away, he stood over her.

Alex Knight?

Her heart rate kicked up—even more—at the sight of him.

He wore mountain biking clothes similar to the ones she'd seen him in at the memorial, only he still had on his black helmet. His gray, searching eyes were as intense now as they had been three years ago. She wished she could have forgotten them. Wished she wasn't looking into them now.

"Are you okay?" He offered his hand as concern etched into his handsome features.

She took in the man standing above her. He had no idea he was asking a loaded question. *Okay* was a relative term. "I don't know."

Before she could know for sure, she needed to get up. But she didn't need his hand. She scrambled to her feet and slowly stretched out her body. The pain of the fall would catch up with her tomorrow, along with the abuse to her muscles from the ride itself. But this was today . . . "I don't think anything's broken."

"Except for the helmet." He frowned and stared at the right side of her head.

"What?" She pulled off the helmet and spotted the crack snaking up the back and around to the right. Oh no.

"That could have been your head." Alex took the helmet from her and examined it. "Proof these things matter."

Mackenzie glanced back at her bike. Her heart sank. The front wheel was twisted. *Great. Just great.* Rowan was dead . . . and this . . . tears threatened to spill, but she wouldn't cry in front of Alex.

"I'm surprised nothing is broken, frankly. The way you went flying, that was spectacular."

She cut her eyes to him, and yeah, he had a grin. A triple-threat grin. But she didn't miss the regret and concern behind his eyes.

Did he know about Rowan? Then it hit her. What was he doing here? "Were you following me?"

Alex handed her the broken helmet, then removed his own. He swiped an arm over his sweaty forehead and mussed his brown hair, which was a little curly at the ends. Buying time to consider his answer?

Finally, he said, "Guilty as charged. But it's not what you think."

A breeze hit the evergreens, and branches clacked together eerily. "If you mean it's not that I think I'm standing in a dark forest on private property with a creepy stalker? Then what is it?" Though she was teasing him, really, because she didn't get creepy vibes from him.

"First, let me draw your attention to the fact that I'm not the only one watching."

"What are you talking about?"

"Ever heard the phrase 'eye in the sky'?"

Mackenzie took a moment to soak in his meaning. "Are you talking about the thriller or the song?"

He squinted, looking at the treetops.

She glanced up. "You're not saying there's a drone up there watching me."

He stepped closer. "That's exactly what I'm saying."

"I'm not sure if you're aware, but Hanstech—my father's company—is a drone software company."

"And that knowledge doesn't make me feel any better."

Her sentiments exactly. She peered up through the treetops again. She hadn't kept up enough with what was going on at Hanstech—software testing on drones. Was this Nora's way of keeping tabs on her? She doubted that was the case.

Given the reason she was even in Montana, a chill crawled over her. "What kind of drone? And why? Did you see it? I don't see anything."

"I can't answer your thousands of questions, even if you ask them one at a time."

Mackenzie didn't want to see danger where none existed. After all . . . "It's probably just a hobby drone. A toy. Those things are everywhere." Though she didn't like the idea that a drone was up there—on private property. "Maybe just answer the one, then. Why are *you* here?"

"I'll answer that, but let's get out of here first. You can ride my bike, and I'll haul this one back for you."

"That's nice of you, but I can't ask you to do that. I'll be fine." Her voice cracked. "This trail is private. You know that, right?"

Mackenzie stalked up the incline. She'd come back and get the bike.

"Mackenzie." He said her name softly and with concern.

She stopped and hung her head.

"Remember the day I gave you the tour?"

She risked a glance at him. Saw the emotion in his eyes. Her throat grew tight. How could she forget? "Vaguely."

Disappointment rippled subtly over his features. She continued hiking up the hill to the trail, angling now and then, but she still didn't see any drone. He could have made it up.

"Why do you ask?"

He sidled next to her, his masculine scent wrapping around her, teasing her senses.

"After that day, I would have called you. But I left the country the next day. I haven't been back in three years. Well, briefly last fall, but I returned to the States two weeks ago."

Why was he bringing it up? "You were under no obligation to call. You were only showing me around because they asked. We had fun." The best day of her life. "I didn't expect to see you again, so you don't need to worry about it."

"Good to know. Here, take my bike." He handed it off, and she took it before she thought to refuse.

"I'll get yours." He half slid down the incline to secure hers.

Okay, then. Not like she could stop him. He lifted the broken bike over his shoulder, his biceps and back muscles bulging. Why did the guy who'd shown her one of the best times of her life have to be so heart-wrenchingly good-looking? But even more than that, why did he have to be kind, thoughtful, and caring? Because Mackenzie was at the absolute worst place in her life right now to even think about a relationship.

Once he was on the trail with her, she started forward, pushing his bike over the rough dirt. Not riding it.

He sighed, and she could almost feel the regret, the emotion in that one sound.

"I know your brother died, and I'm so sorry."

My brother's dead . . .

That's right. She'd somehow managed to block the memory, the pain of it, for a few moments. What kind of person was she anyway to even want to forget?

Tears surged. *No, no, no, no . . .*

Not here. Not now.

And then she lost it.

Alex set down the bike and lifted an arm. The next thing she knew, she was sobbing against his skin-tight shirt. She'd never wanted to be so vulnerable in front of anyone—let alone Alex Knight, of all people. A guy she barely knew.

When the tears finally subsided enough, she heard the pounding of his heart. Felt his chest and the muscles in his arms wrapped tightly around her. The heat of embarrassment flooded her. She remembered the reason she was back in Montana. Fighting the need to stay where she was a little longer, she stepped out of his arms and glanced up.

"You're vulnerable to deadly attacks. They're taking the stronghold!"

She peered up through the trees and thought she saw something. Eye in the sky? A drone watching her?

This almost-a-stranger special agent man was here for a reason—what was it? She could feel him staring at her, and she let her gaze drop from the treetops to his face. She locked onto his intense gray eyes that held her captive.

And she doubted she could free herself if she wanted to.

Mackenzie was vulnerable, alright.

FIVE

Though difficult and slow, hiking the trail with a bike across his shoulders was a great upper body workout, if he could maintain control over his inner green monster superhero for the next several miles. He plastered on a smile for Mackenzie's sake. At least he'd been there for her and convinced her to let him carry the broken bike.

She was strong and capable, but that mountain bike was heavy and awkward, especially with the twisted front wheel. There was no leaving it behind to fetch later. Plus, it gave him a good excuse to stick close.

He suspected the drone was still up there somewhere watching. He couldn't catch sight of it through the trees, which meant the drone likely couldn't see them either. Someone just out having fun with a new toy? If so, he would think that since they had spotted the drone, it would move on. There was nothing he could do about it at the moment. He hoped the thing would lose its charge, crash, and burn. Maybe he should grab his off-duty Glock and shoot it out of the sky.

"You never told me why you followed me." She followed *him* now.

At this rate, they wouldn't make it back to civilization within the next couple of hours.

"I was on the trail, and I saw the drone and then I saw you. That's all." *Partially true.*

"You're on private property, you know that, right? This trail is part of the family property."

Uh-oh. Maybe he shouldn't share what he knew about the property line, because then he really would sound like a stalker. "Um . . . maybe it was before, but this portion of the trail—across the river—is for public use now. Someone sold off most of the acreage surrounding the house."

Mackenzie stumbled at the words. Just like he thought—she hadn't known. She turned and narrowed her eyes.

Yep. "I know. I really do sound like a stalker, but it's public knowledge."

And she acted surprised, as if she hadn't known.

What are you doing, man? He wasn't entirely sure why he'd hit the trail near her home. And now he was just lying to himself. He had never forgotten that day back in DC that he spent with her. He'd wished for more time. The part of his job that took him away was the part he hadn't wanted.

Sure, the Diplomatic Security Services was an elite group who worked in hot spots and dangerous environments around the world. Because they protected VIPs, people often confused them with Secret Service agents. In general, most people had never heard of the DSS.

Not that he wanted fame or special treatment, but he was tired of living that life. Working that job. He might have had something with Mackenzie before if he hadn't left. And now, he was spying on her? Every bit as bad as that drone—if spying or invasion of privacy was what was going on.

But he wanted to see her for personal reasons. To reconnect with her. And now was his chance.

"Okay, stalker guy, you know about the land when I don't,

so aren't you going to ask what I'm doing here in Montana? Oh, wait, you already know that too, don't you?" Suspicion emerged in her already narrowed gaze.

She was sharp, or she never would have interviewed with the DSS to begin with. "Actually, I don't know. And full disclosure, I rode my bike on this trail because I"—how did he even explain?—"I was shocked to see you at the memorial, and then you left without acknowledging that you knew me. So, sure, I was thinking about you. And, sure, I chose a trail that would take me close to the Hanson family cabin." She didn't owe him anything. Maybe not even a hello. "But I had no idea you would actually be on the trail. I didn't know you had a mountain bike."

Though he should have suspected it, considering the activities included on the property. He'd been reading up on Gregory Hanson and his company.

Mackenzie stopped to maneuver the bike around a large boulder. "I didn't know I had one either. I found my old bike in the garage. Dad and I used to ride . . ." Grief twisted on her face.

He was a sucker for a broken heart and couldn't stand to see the hurt in her eyes. Alex glanced up at the evergreens, the sky, anything else. What was he even doing here, really? Was he the reason she took that fall? She'd been trying to get away from her stalker when she went off trail. Guilt squeezed his chest.

She sighed, then started forward again. "And the drone? Are you sure it was following me?"

"It seemed that way." The roar of the waterfall grew louder. Alex had come here with Mom and Dad a time or two before Dad died. Man, he missed his father even all these years later.

"It was probably some kid who got a new toy for their birthday. Don't you know that too many drones in the sky is the way of the future?"

"Maybe. I got a picture, so we can see what kind it is."

"Wow, you really are taking this seriously, aren't you?"

And why wouldn't he be? "Maybe. But people take pictures and videos of everything these days."

"You're right about that. Let me see the picture. Maybe it's just one of the Hanstech test drones."

Following her?

He unloaded the bike and pulled out his cell to find the image while Mackenzie leaned his bike against a tree. She stood next to him to peer at his cell. "Actually, I took some video too."

She gasped. "A person can't even get privacy in the woods in Montana."

"Security cameras. License plate readers. Smartphone trackers, and now, drones. If you think about it, we're being watched twenty-four-seven. But you're right." A smidgeon of shame pricked at him. "I'm living proof you can't get privacy even in the woods in Montana."

She actually chuckled and smiled up at him. Now *that* was a nice sound—and it surprised him.

"I don't know why you're really here, Alex. Maybe you're here as part of a stateside assignment or to see family, but I can't say that I'm not glad to see you."

The long way of saying she was glad to see him. "I'm not here for work. I'm taking a break."

A gunshot rang out. Tree bark exploded near them.

"Get down!" Alex shouted.

They both dropped to the ground, and he shielded her, covering her with his body. His off-duty gun was in his pack on the bike. Should he go for it? Except staying here wasn't safe. The pine needles weren't going to protect them. "There's a boulder. We can make it behind that. We'll go together."

He continued to cover her as they quickly crawled—and just in time too as another shot fired, clipping the stone. "I need you to wait here while I get my gun. Please call 911."

"What? Where's your gun?"

"Not too far." He eyed his bike that she'd leaned against the tree.

"No. You'll be too exposed."

She wasn't wrong, but they needed protection. He should have kept his recon kit bag on his back, but it got too sweaty. Inside was his loaded Glock 26, plus a twelve-round magazine.

"Just stay here and stay down no matter what happens. I don't want to worry about you." He gently pressed her to the ground. "Stay low. You can do that and make the call, can't you?"

"Okay, okay."

He peered from behind the boulder and couldn't see anyone. He considered the trees and the path he would take. He just needed to nudge the bike over onto its side, and then he could remain low and pull the kit off.

He drew in a few short, quick breaths, then crouching, dashed between tree trunks until he made it to his bike. He knocked it over, and, as expected, drew gunfire. The bullets slammed against the trunk he was hiding behind. Now, he just needed to make it back to Mackenzie. Once he got his hands on his Glock, he could send the shooter into hiding.

He pressed himself flat, then slipped his arm forward beneath the bars and felt his way around the seat and then to the recon kit buckled to the handlebars. He felt for the clasp, and after a couple of fails, he released the latch. Another bullet hit the tree, then the boulder.

From behind the tree, he could see Mackenzie covering her head as she pressed her face into the pine needles and dirt.

Now . . . to make it back.

He drew out his Glock, chambered a round, then took aim at a tree on the other side of the boulder and fired his weapon before dashing between the tree trunks. He took another shot, then crawled to the boulder where Mackenzie waited for him and pressed his back against the boulder.

"I'm glad you're back."

Heart pounding, he caught his breath. "Me too."

Her big hazel eyes took him in, measuring him. "You always pack, huh?"

"What do you think?"

"Are you working now?" She gave him an incredulous look.

What? "I already told you I'm not. But I always carry. Can we talk about this later? Someone just tried to kill you. I need to protect you."

"Given your line of work, are you sure they didn't try to kill *you*?"

"Stay here."

"Again?"

"Yes," he whispered.

He crawled to the other side of the boulder and slowly peeked around. He still couldn't see anyone.

Then a figure dashed between the trees. He glanced back at Mackenzie. "Please don't move. I'll be right back."

"Alex!" She didn't sound happy.

He dashed out from behind the boulder to another tree, pushing forward from tree to tree. Gunfire blasted the ground near his feet. He returned fire, then crawled back behind the boulder. If he was shot, then Mackenzie would be left to defend herself, but he'd wanted to apprehend the shooter.

"I couldn't make the 911 call. I get no bars on my cell. Nobody is coming to help."

"Good to know." Even if she had made the call, no one would likely arrive out here in time to help. "I'll take care of it."

"You get a signal out here?"

He glanced at his cell. "Apparently."

On his cell, he called 911. When dispatch answered, he explained the situation. Then he called Jack and left a voicemail. "We're going to hide behind the waterfall and wait for you."

He did the same on Nathan Campbell's cell. Nathan was Erin's detective boyfriend. Maybe someone would get here in time to help.

Until then, it was up to him.

When he ended the call, he couldn't ignore Mackenzie's questioning look.

"Did I just hear you tell them that we'll be hiding behind the waterfall?" She sounded incredulous.

"You heard correctly."

"Isn't that dangerous?"

"A shooter has us trapped here. But we can make it down there"—he pointed to the cascade a few yards ahead—"because we'll be protected by the water and surrounding boulders, we'll be safe. We can wait there for help."

Have you lost your mind? At least that's what he took from the look she gave him.

"I'll cover you and protect you as we climb down."

"Won't we be trapped there just like we're trapped here?"

"We'll be protected. I know some things about those falls."

Doubt swam in her eyes. He took in her smooth face shining with the heat of the day—and yeah, he admitted he wanted to know more about her.

"Don't worry. I've been there with my dad years ago. I know how to get down there."

"Okay, then. Lead on." She crouched, ready to follow him on the mad dash for their lives.

He held up his hand for her to wait and peered from behind the rock, then caught sight of the shooter aiming at them.

He fired his Glock.

"Go! I'll cover you." *Time to send the shooter running.*

Together they scrambled down the riverbank and out of the gunman's line of sight. But they'd have to hurry if they wanted to hide behind the waterfall before the shooter tried again.

He started down and realized the rocks were more slippery

than he remembered, and the way more treacherous as well. She was right—he had lost his mind.

"Be careful!" he shouted over the roar and motioned for her to start down.

Together they slowly climbed down and made their way toward the waterfall. The roar filled his ears, blocking out all other sound. He remained acutely aware of his surroundings, watching the rocks, the falls, the edge up top for the shooter, and Mackenzie as she climbed. Tension corded his shoulders, and his heart pounded. Spray from the falls soon soaked them.

He second-guessed his decision to take them into another treacherous predicament, but at the time, hiding behind the falls seemed like a good plan. He continued toward an opening between the falls and the stone.

"Okay, hurry. If we disappear behind the falls, the shooter won't know where we went."

"You hope."

Only a few more feet and he stepped into the opening, sliding in through the curtain of trickling water at the edge of the falls. Mackenzie yelped and slipped. He reached forward and caught her wrist, helping her gain traction again.

"I've got you! Just keep coming. Don't look down."

She could have plunged into the river. He kept his grip on her hand, then pulled her behind the falls. Her big eyes filled with fear as he hauled her up and over and into the gap. All the way in against him. She shivered as he held her tight.

He rubbed her arms, then he released her. "You did it. You made it."

"We made it." Surprise flicked in her eyes.

He couldn't help the smile that emerged. When he did this with his dad as a kid, it seemed both exciting and yet no big deal. Easy enough. Today, he realized how far above the river they were as they climbed down, and the real danger should one or both of them fall into the falls. They could become trapped in the vortex of water at the bottom, keeping them from rising for air. But he would keep that to himself.

Maybe hiding behind a waterfall hadn't been the best idea, but with a shooter targeting them, he'd made the decision and they were here now.

"So this is a cave. I don't think I ever knew there was a cave back here."

"It's not a true cave. The waterfall has worn the softer stone away to create this hollow. Or a rock shelter."

"I'll call it a waterfall shelter," she said.

He ran a hand over the smooth, worn, and slippery wet rocks. They were cold and wet. Her thick brown hair was plastered against her head. She shivered and hugged herself.

Stepping away from the spray at the back of the falls, he gently grabbed her elbow and led her deeper into the hollow. The space didn't go back far, but there were crevices, places she could hide. He gestured for her to step behind a ridge in the wall.

Standing close so they could trap the heat between them, he faced the opening of the hollow and the waterfall. His dad had shown him this passage, but that didn't mean the shooter didn't know about it too. Even if the shooter was aware of it, Alex would be ready, waiting and watching. He had the advantage.

He gripped his now slippery gun.

Hoped for the best.

Prepared for the worst.

SIX

Pressed against the cold, wet stone that had been washed smooth from centuries of pouring water, Mackenzie stood behind Alex. She wanted to lean into his back and absorb his warmth, but she shouldn't distract him. His clothes were soaked like hers, his hair dripping wet, the muscles in his back tense as if ready to pounce on anyone who might threaten her.

She hadn't seen him in protection mode that day in DC, but she could see now that he was definitely all about keeping others safe. After all, that was part of his job with the DSS—to protect high-risk assets.

Mackenzie didn't fall within that category, but Alex hadn't held back. Though she didn't like the circumstances that had put them here, watching him in action in his element fascinated her. Actually, more than fascinated her. The terror of being shot at and almost killed forced a rapid increase in her pulse. But she had to admit to herself and no one else—ever—that being with Alex in this scenario had also sent a thrill shooting through her.

He remained steady and protective, waiting for their pursuer to rush at them through the wall of water.

What if . . . what if he hadn't been there, hadn't found her on the trail? What would have happened? She never would have clued in on the drone, though she still wasn't sure what that was about. Was the drone connected to the shooter? Regardless, she probably would have taken a bullet and been lying facedown on the trail now.

Shuddering at the thought, she pulled her hand back and hugged herself. Her knees trembled and her heart pounded in her ears, the sound overtaking the waterfall a few yards from them. Though she'd walked in dangerous places during her previous stint in the criminal world, no one had ever shot at her before. But she'd been threatened. Fear tightened her throat, and she pressed her hand against Alex's back, causing him to shiver beneath her touch.

He glanced over his shoulder, his piercing eyes drilling into her like she would expect. "It won't be long now, Mackenzie. Help will come."

"Okay. I trust you. But will they get here in time?" Would someone step through the water and continue the rampage?

"I hope so."

"How long are we going to wait?"

He hesitated a few heartbeats, then finally said, "As long as it takes."

The way he said those words, she thought he might have experienced waiting for help. She hoped he would tell her that story one day—as if their interaction would go beyond this predicament, or even her short stay in Montana.

She leaned to the right to see around his broad shoulders. She couldn't make anything out through the curtain of water—shades of blue and white and maybe some green, but nothing specific. Would they be able to see if someone made their way through to find them?

She pulled her gaze from the water and took in the wonder of the cave—or rather, not a true cave, as Alex had explained, but a hollow created from the erosion. Amazing what water could do, washing stone away little by little over time, transforming it into something completely new.

In the same way, time affected everything in existence—chipping away, little by little, to form something new, sometimes better and sometimes worse—people too, whether they realized it or not.

That left her with a question.

How did I come to this moment—standing behind a waterfall with a special agent from an obscure agency?

She'd never considered what she would find behind the waterfall. Alex had opened up a whole new world—the drone in the sky and the shelter behind the cascade. Had he been trying to show off by bringing her here? She half smiled at the thought. No. Alex wouldn't take that kind of risk.

He remained steadfast in holding his weapon, his protective stance strong and true, and stared ahead as if he could see what was happening on the other side. The guy was full of surprises, so maybe he could see something she couldn't.

On the day Alex gave her the grand tour, she suspected he would be trouble. He was trouble for her heart, and by default that meant he was trouble for her well-kept secrets. For her honed professionalism—an attempt to always rise above and beyond the mischief of her past.

Once again, Mackenzie lifted her hand and hesitated, letting her palm hover over his back a few seconds before pressing it against his wet shirt. Energy sparked, surging up her arm. She jerked her hand away and covered her mouth as he stepped back, closer even than before. He shifted, turning toward her.

Then he leaned in, his cheek almost touching hers, and whispered, "Wait here."

What? Not again. No . . .

He pulled back to look her in the eyes, and she shook her

head. She didn't want to be left alone to shiver in the dripping waterfall cave and wonder what happened to him.

His somber expression shifted, and he offered up a confidence booster in his roguish grin. "It'll be alright."

Without another word, he stepped away and around the smallish outcropping behind which they had huddled, taking her only source of heat with him. He slowly moved toward the waterfall.

To face a shooter.

Protect her.

Lord, what is going on? I feel like my life is spiraling out of control.

She'd been on the straight and narrow for years. Why was this happening?

Alex returned to the small alcove and once again turned to face the falls, stepping back enough that the wall afforded him protection but pinned her between him and the wall. Warmth again. But at the same time, she felt . . . trapped this time.

Claustrophobic.

She wanted to escape. To be free.

He lifted his arms and aimed his gun directly at the cascade.

She held her breath.

Fear tried to take up residence in her chest, but with Alex's strong and sturdy form filling her vision, she shouldn't be afraid. Still, more than mere curiosity drove her need to know what was happening. Had they been discovered, after all?

Not wanting to give away their presence, she stood on her toes to get close to his ear. He dropped back so she could get even closer. So near to his glistening, lithe physique, his woodsy and utterly masculine scent wrapped around her.

"What did you see?" She said the words loud enough for him, but she doubted anyone near the falls could have heard them.

He didn't respond.

Dropping back to her heels, she pressed her back against the stone. How long would they have to stay here?

"Alex!" someone shouted, the sound muffled through the falls but discernible.

Lowering his gun, Alex eased away from her, opening up the space. She could breathe. Oh, she could breathe.

And think.

"In here!" Alex twisted to thrust his hand out to her. His eyes crinkled at the corners and his dimples emerged. "Help has arrived. I told you that you could trust me."

And she returned his smile. "I knew that already."

Mackenzie took his hand and allowed him to lead her forward and then out and around the waterfall, carefully stepping around the edges of the steep drop into the river. A man waited for them—the same man who had been at the memorial with Alex. Tall and fit. Sun-bleached hair and green eyes.

"Mackenzie, meet Detective Tanner," Alex shouted over his shoulder.

The frown along the detective's forehead eased as a smile formed, and he gave a quick nod, then gestured toward where they would need to climb out of the cataract. Detective Tanner climbed out first and glanced over his shoulder, giving a look that said he was satisfied with their progress. Then Mackenzie followed him, placing her hands and feet on the same stones. Alex came up behind her.

At the top of the rise, she stood tall and drew in a long inhale and breathed in the smell of rushing river water, mountain air, cedar, ponderosa pine, and Douglas fir. Water from snowmelt, rain, and maybe a few springs along the way carved down the mountain and brought a fresh scent of its own. She let that waft over and calm her.

Alex led her away from the falls to the trail where they had initially been targeted, and where the bikes had been abandoned.

He approached a dark-haired man and shook his hand. "Detective Campbell. Thanks for the help." Alex gestured to her. "This is Mackenzie Hanson."

Alex acted like he and the detectives were almost best buddies.

"And you already met Detective Tanner."

"Please just call me Jack." To Alex, he said, "No sign of the shooter, but that doesn't mean he's not hanging around. Let's get you out of here, and we can take your statement at a safe location."

"You'll need my gun for ballistics." Alex handed it over. "I gave cover as we ran to the cave."

Jack bagged it. "You have another firearm?"

"Yes. That's the main gun I use when I'm off duty. I'd like it back as soon as possible."

Mackenzie looked up at the treetops. No sign of the drone either. When she let her gaze drop, she caught Alex studying her. His gray eyes struck fear in her soul—what did he see in her? What was he thinking? And suddenly the law enforcement surrounding her, including Alex, sent her mind racing right back to the moment she was surrounded by federal agents who wanted her confession.

God, why can't I escape the memories?

"You'll get it back. In the meantime, deputies will search the woods," Detective Campbell said. "I suspect the shooter is long gone if he knows what's good for him."

"*Her,*" Alex said. "The shooter was a woman."

SEVEN

With visions of waterfalls, shooters, and Alex Knight dancing in her head, Mackenzie entered the eerily dark and quiet cabin through the garage door. Alex set her broken bike against the wall.

The detectives had driven them to a nearby gas station, of all places, to take their statements. Considering the shooter had escaped, the woods remained dangerous. After Alex and Mackenzie gave their statements, Detectives Tanner and Campbell—Jack and Nathan—dropped Mackenzie off at the Hanson cabin. Alex had refused a ride back to where he was staying and had gotten out at the cabin too. The county vehicle steered away and left him behind, along with the bikes.

"Nice having friends in high places," she said. "But seriously, Alex, I'm worried about you taking the trail. Plus, I mean . . . aren't you exhausted? How far do you have to go?"

She couldn't ride a bike anywhere right now. Her legs still shook from the trauma of being targeted by a shooter. Alex seemed to have kept his composure in the face of danger.

"A few miles. I'm staying at a cabin myself. It's nothing as fancy as this spread, though."

He gave her that look again, intensity pouring from his gaze as he stared at her as though he could read her mind. "What?" she asked.

"What *aren't* you telling the police? What aren't you telling *me*?"

"I don't know why someone shot at us, okay?" She wanted to get into the house and have a few moments of quiet before she talked to Nora. She couldn't put that off any longer. "Maybe they were shooting at *you*."

And that would make more sense—the battle she was expecting was on a different plane. The digital plane.

"Why'd you come to Montana?" He crossed his arms, which somehow made his biceps look bigger and his shoulders broader.

"I don't know. Why are *you* here?"

He arched a brow. *Touché* . . . He didn't say it, but she read his expression all the same.

"I guess we both have our secrets." A half grin split his cheek.

He got on his bike and rode around in circles on the drive next to the garage. "When you're ready to talk, Mackenzie, or if you need me for any reason, call me."

"I don't have your number."

"I put it in your phone."

Guess that meant he had hers too. "Stalk people much?" She hoped her grin let him know she was only teasing.

Sort of.

Anyone else, and she wouldn't welcome the intrusion. But this was Alex—the guy who could warm her insides with a smile. She had never forgotten that roguish grin and those brooding gray eyes.

She watched Alex's muscled legs as he pedaled away down the long drive. He would catch the trailhead down the road and cut across the foothill to his cabin. She wanted to tell him why she was here, but she had to tell her sister first. Because everything could hinge on her sister's response. Mackenzie really had nothing much to share in the way of evidence. Nothing the police could use, and they could muddy the waters for her—waters she needed to dive into and waters she needed to be clear when she took that dive.

Still standing in the garage, she stared out at the woods that would be growing dark soon. Nora had texted to ask if she was okay—after all, she'd been gone for hours. Mackenzie responded that she would return within the hour.

And here she was.

She hit the button to close the garage door and headed into the house, entering the mudroom and then the kitchen. The house felt cold and lonely, belying the warm hues of cedar and pine. She grabbed a glass of water at the sink. She had to find a way to talk to Nora. The conversation seemed unimportant in light of Rowan's death, but then again . . . it could be vitally important.

Like a stranger—an intruder, really—she crept through the house that had briefly been her home. It was big, bold, and beautiful—a testament to her father's business acumen and dream. A dream he couldn't fully experience now that he was gone, but Rowan—God rest his soul—had taken on that mantle and lifted the company to heights Dad could have only dreamed about. And those goals had been achieved partially because she had done as Rowan demanded. *"Get far, far away. If you love Dad, you'll leave him alone."*

Grief could destroy her if she let it. All the wasted time she'd spent *not* in Dad's life. Protecting him from what? Maybe if she'd stayed close to the family, been part of his business, he would somehow still be alive. But Mackenzie was grasping at blades of grass that had withered.

She thought back to when she came into the house. Nora's vehicle wasn't in the garage or the drive. Perfect. In Rowan's office, Mackenzie stared at the empty room.

He'd run her off and seemed to have no mercy to offer. Couldn't forgive her. He'd hammered her with guilt until she had to escape, so she fled and stayed far away. Dad was a workaholic—which is what had driven her to search for companionship with the wrong people—so it wasn't like her absence created a great hole in their lives.

The image of Rowan's lifeless body flashed in her mind like a press photograph.

Rowan had had heart issues at the young age of forty-two, ten full years older than Mackenzie. He'd taken medications and had a pacemaker—and had been super active like Dad. No one would have even known about his condition.

But Mackenzie couldn't stop thinking about the timing.

Deadly attacks . . . The warning she'd received made his death all the more suspicious. But she needed more information—and she needed to stop the attacker.

Whoever you are.

Now was the best time to use her skills. Snoop around someone's digital secrets. Mackenzie's cybercriminal past had driven a huge wedge between her and her family, but those same previously ill-used skills would help her now.

She pulled the office chair out and across where they'd found Rowan's body and sat down behind the desk. Ignoring the chills cascading over her, she imagined Dad behind the same desk before he died.

She booted up Rowan's desktop computer and faced the expected biometrics-required login. She could bypass it, depending on the password management software. She chewed on her bottom lip, her palms sweating.

She hadn't done anything like this since—

The lights came on, and a pang shot through her chest. She sat unmoving.

Nora crossed her arms, years of accusations and suspicions swirling in her gaze. "Just what do you think you're doing?"

Mackenzie wasn't a kid anymore, and she shouldn't shrivel under Nora's glare. "I'm logging on to Rowan's computer. What does it look like?"

"Old habits? You think because he's gone that you can just . . ."

Mackenzie stood. It was time for her to do her part in mending their conflict. "No, Nora. Please . . ."

Tears leaked down Nora's tired and worn face, and she brushed them away. "Carson is coming over soon. I don't want to fight with you."

"I need to talk to you. Can you put him off?"

"He's been out of town because his mother was in the hospital. His flight landed in Bozeman a couple of hours ago, and I miss him. I need to see him." She swiped both hands along her cheeks. Nora shook out her long tresses, primping in preparation for Carson. "This has all been too much. I'm so sorry that you got here at the worst possible time. I'm sure you're probably ready to go home."

There it was again. That fear skittering across her sister's eyes. Mackenzie's throat constricted. Trying to send a silent message that Mackenzie simply couldn't read?

"I don't want to fight either. I'll help in any way I can." Mackenzie approached her sister. She had to mend the broken relationship—if time would let her. She hugged Nora, and together they sobbed.

Dad died years ago.

Now Rowan.

It was just the two of them.

So much change was happening too fast that neither of them were ready for. Nora stepped away. "I need to freshen up. I don't want him to see me like this."

"I'm sorry I didn't check with you first before trying to log on."

Nora offered a half smile—struggling, fighting against the

grief. "I doubt you could get past his security, even with your skills."

"Maybe not. Nora . . . I . . ." Was this the right time? Would there ever be a right time? "I need to talk to you about something. It's important."

"Please, it can wait. We can talk as much as you want, but I'm not sure I would make a good listener right now."

"You don't understand. I *need* to tell you before it's too late." Mackenzie injected a threatening tone to get her sister's attention.

Nora's hand quivered as she pushed a strand of hair behind her ear. She shook her head and whispered, "Go home. It's not safe here."

"I can't go. I came here to help."

Nora stared at Mackenzie for a few heartbeats. Without words, she gestured for Mackenzie to follow. Nora led her through the kitchen, out onto the porch, and down the long steps outside.

She hadn't gotten the chance to tell Nora about the shooter.

But like Alex said, deputies were searching. The shooter had likely disappeared for the time being. Mackenzie followed her sister down to the small creek that flowed until it met the Grayback River and the waterfall. Enough daylight remained so that they could see where they were going.

Nora sat on a boulder and Mackenzie joined her, listening to the trickling brook.

"What's so important that you came all this way to help? What do I need help with?" Nora asked.

To her shame, Mackenzie couldn't say that it was to simply see her family.

"You could tell me why you keep saying it isn't safe."

Nora subtly shook her head. Mackenzie wouldn't waste another minute and showed her the business card that Julian had given her. She had kept it on her person every moment.

"A Hanstech business card," Nora said. "Rowan's card."

Flipping it over, Mackenzie scanned the QR code with her phone so the video came up. Freda from Knights Alliance spoke again. "You're vulnerable to deadly attacks. They're taking the stronghold!"

Nora stared, her eyes wide, then she burst out laughing. "Are you kidding me? This is what you wanted to show me?" She shut her eyes and shook her head.

"It's a warning! I came here to warn you and to help you. And . . . I get here and Rowan's dead, and you're scared, Nora. Telling me to go home because it's not safe. What's going on?"

"What does that message mean to you, and where did you get it?" Nora ignored Mackenzie's question.

"Where I got it isn't important."

"Oh, I think I know already. Your ghost. Your apparition." Nora's gaze drilled through her as if to search for the truth.

And if Mackenzie wanted to hold her attention, she couldn't play games. She didn't want to give him up, but her sister needed to understand the warning was serious. Although she had a feeling Nora already knew.

Mackenzie nodded. "Julian."

"What are you thinking, working with him again? You can't—"

"I'm not. He bumped into me and stuck it in my pocket. Then he was hit by a car. He's recovering in the hospital."

"I don't understand what it means. The words are like gibberish to me."

"To get my attention, he found me and must have watched for an opportunity. He's a brilliant hacker, and still, even he didn't want to leave a digital trail. He used the character from a game we loved to play together to deliver the news—knowing that would get my attention. It means someone is coming for Dad's company. They're going to hack into it and exploit data, and deadly attacks means just what it means."

She closed her eyes and thought of the game. The violence. Taking the stronghold indicated that no quarter was given, meaning when prisoners were taken, the victor showed no mercy and refused to spare lives. People were killed. She wouldn't necessarily think that translated to this situation, except . . . well . . .

She opened her eyes to use her own intimidating look on Nora. "I believe someone tried to kill Julian. Now Rowan is dead. Someone followed me on the trail today and shot at me." Or Alex.

Nora gasped. "What? Why didn't you tell me?"

"I'm telling you now. This is serious. And now it's your turn. Why are you scared? Why did you say it's not safe here?"

Because it wasn't. Nora knew that . . . how? What had happened?

What's going on at Hanstech? She preferred that Nora offer up the information. Mackenzie's heart pounded against her rib cage. Could the reason Nora was scared be related to the warning? And Rowan's death? The shooting?

"And you told the police," Nora said matter-of-factly.

"Of course. Yes. Except I haven't told anyone about what Julian shared." Sharing that would increase the amount of time she had to spend explaining herself to them.

"Because they won't believe you."

Nora said the words as if she understood firsthand.

That was part of it. "I need to find evidence first."

"What do you want me to do?"

"I want you to trust me, Nora. Trust me enough to bring me into the company to look in your system. Trust me enough to tell me what's going on."

Nora stared at the brook, the sounds of the flowing water the only noise. Why was she hesitating?

Mackenzie had hoped for a new kind of relationship with her sister. She would be the one to reach out. After all, she'd been the one to hurt them all—something she'd yet to forgive herself for. And yet she was asking that of others. And now, all that was left was her sister. Mackenzie wouldn't let anything stand between them now. Time was short. Life was fragile.

"Look, I was a kid back then. I made a mistake. You can't really hold that over me forever. Not like Rowan . . ."

She wished she hadn't brought up his name.

But she needed her sister to listen. Mackenzie needed—and wanted—Nora to work with her on this.

Nora looked up. "I know, Mackenzie. I'm glad you're back, but I wish it could have been under much different circumstances. We're sisters, and I have never stopped loving you. I never held any of that against you. Please forgive me for not being stronger. Not being able to have more influence on Rowan. He never should have said those words to you and sent you away."

Nora's searching gaze held hers again. In her sister's eyes she saw confusion and desperation. Nora was sending her mixed signals, like she needed Mackenzie's help but at the same time wanted her to leave. Nora wanted to protect her.

She glanced at her watch. "Carson will be here soon." She abruptly stood, wiped her cheeks, and fluffed her hair. "I could use your help, Mackenzie. But I can't hire a convicted criminal hacker. And I'm being watched."

That was why Nora brought them down here to talk.

"Watched. How?"

"No time to talk about it now."

Mackenzie followed Nora back to the steps. "As for bringing me on to look into your system, of course you can contract me. My past records are sealed." Never mind that the DSS passed on her because of her background. It was one thing to work for the Feds with her past and another thing entirely to work for a private company. But trust was still a factor.

"I suggest you get cleaned up. You're going to dinner with us."

"Okay, then."

Nora climbed the steps to the porch and entered the back of the house. The doorbell was ringing. "Coming!"

Mackenzie didn't appreciate the interruption, and she wished Nora's boyfriend would just go away. "You can't tell anyone what I told you, Nora. No one. Not until we've figured out a few things. Not even Carson. Look, I'm not sure Rowan wasn't murdered."

"Have you lost your mind?" Nora hissed, the fear sparking again. Nora's eyes darted around the cabin. She opened the door wide.

A tall, blue-eyed man with sandy-blond hair stepped in and drew Nora into his arms with a smile. Haircut crisp and clean, he had a boyish look about him that made her wonder if he was old enough to shave. And he appeared to be a nerd. Huh. She wouldn't have thought Nora would fall for a nerdy guy.

After quick introductions, Mackenzie excused herself and headed up the stairs to change out of her biking clothes. Seeing the obvious love between Nora and Carson filled Mackenzie with envy and emphasized that deep, gaping hole she'd ignored for so long. She was so very alone in life . . . and in love. But she had Nora now, and she wouldn't leave her sister's side.

Her sister was trapped and living in fear. Mackenzie glanced around. There were many avenues by which someone could watch and listen, especially in a smart house.

But who is watching?

EIGHT

Spending hours in Rocky Roads Internet Café in Big Rapids hadn't been on Alex's to-do list, not even at the bottom. But one couldn't easily escape the digital age, even in Big Sky Country, where lofty mountains, thick green forests, and clear streams called his name, daring him to forget his troubles. The faster he resolved the memorial vandalism, the sooner he could get back into the fresh air.

But honestly? The vandalism wasn't at the forefront of his thoughts.

Not after Mackenzie walked back into his world and their lives were thrown together—although briefly—once again. But he had no intention of walking away from her this time. Especially since she was so obviously in danger after yesterday's shooting incident in the woods.

Unlike a lot of guys he knew, he could multitask just fine. He was supposed to be decompressing. But couldn't he go somewhere without finding trouble? Apparently not. Maybe next time he would try a Caribbean island. Or Alaska. A lot of people went there to live off-grid or hide, and some went missing. He had a feeling trouble would find him there too.

He thought back to the drone following Mackenzie and

then the shooter who tried to take them out. By comparison, the figure in the grainy image at the memorial didn't seem as important. But he'd asked for this video, and he would review it. The smallish woman dressed in black dashed in and out of the camera's view, hacking away with a sledgehammer.

Such violence and . . . what? Contempt? Could he read all that into her actions?

He needed Erin to take a look at this too. She and her mother remained at Stone Wolf Ranch, where they went after their home was destroyed. Terra had offered for him to stay there too—they'd added a couple of cabins to the property—but if he was going to stay with anyone as a guest, it should be with Mom. If only he and his stepfather got along.

So instead, Alex rented a cabin a few miles outside of Big Rapids. At least there he had his own space. Peace and quiet. But he could always hang out with the gang at the ranch and spend time with Mom when she got off work from her job as a nurse at the small hospital in town. As for his stepfather, Ron, who was glad when Alex finally left home, they could at least be cordial to each other for the short time Alex was around.

And he needed to figure out the vandalism—for his father's memory as well as for the others. And for Mom's sake, he hoped to stop the vandal in their tracks. He would do what he could to assist while not stepping on the toes of local law enforcement, even though Jack had asked for Alex's help.

He reviewed the video until it replayed in his head. He wanted to make sense of it, but he couldn't. Especially with thoughts of Mackenzie taking up too much space in his head. Maybe he couldn't multitask, after all.

The county sheriff's department was handling the investigation into the shooting. But did Mackenzie need protection? He might not want to walk away from her this time, like he had three years ago, but what about her? Did she *want* him to insert himself into her life?

She'd been right in her assessment that seeing a drone wasn't unusual. In fact, far too many of the intrusive flying vehicles were encroaching into places they shouldn't go. He especially didn't appreciate seeing the drone out in nature.

Throw in a shooter, and everything was bumped to the next level. He hadn't caught a picture of the shooter, but he had pictures of the drone, and he would work with what he had. He'd given that image to the county sheriff's offices too. But that didn't preclude him from doing his own research.

He'd forwarded the drone image to his friend and tech guru Keenan Walker, who also worked for the DSS. Knowing Keenan's thoughts on the drone was imperative. Alex gave him another call and prepared himself to learn everything about drones and probably more than he wanted to know. Then he would fill Keenan in on what he had learned about Hanstech—just the basic information he could gather from their website and company brochure, and only because Mackenzie had mentioned the company's connection to drones.

"Walker here."

"You got the image?"

"Got it, but I was in the middle of a project"—he cleared his throat—"for work."

Alex heard the amusement in Keenan's voice. "You're the best, man. I wouldn't trust anyone else with this."

"You don't need to butter me up, as the saying goes."

"Are you sure?"

"I'm sure you owe me more than a compliment."

Alex laughed. "What have you got for me?"

"Just pulling it up here . . ."

Alex waited patiently, listening to Keenan typing on his keyboard for a few long seconds, then finally . . .

"The technical name for what we typically refer to as drones is UAS or unmanned aerial systems. This drone is the DJI Mavic 2

Zoom and is not something that would raise eyebrows. It's a hobbyist drone."

Alex released a slow exhale. "Then it could just be somebody invading privacy." Except the active shooter incident could be related. Regardless, aerial surveillance was ridiculously invasive anymore.

"I didn't say that."

The problem with tech gurus was they wanted to make sure everyone knew how smart they were. "I'm listening."

"In this case, it's more about the camera. Law enforcement typically uses this kind of camera to spy on individuals over distances. Let's say, over six miles for this drone, never mind US laws prohibit flying drones out of line of sight."

"I could see the drone, so it wasn't a huge distance."

"It's twofold. I'm saying that whoever was operating the drone could have been over six miles away, and throw in the camera with zoom features and video just to clarify, and you extend that distance. The camera—"

"I don't need the details on the camera."

"Did you see the drone the whole time?"

"Well, no. It disappeared at some point."

"Or so you thought. This camera is what we commonly see used to spy on and watch suspects."

"Interesting." His agency used drones in the field, as they all did. "That drone was following an individual moments before a shooter appeared."

"And you're wondering if the shooter was operating the drone? It's possible, or they could have been working with someone else. This specific UAV—unmanned aerial vehicle—isn't autonomous, so it needs a human pilot remotely controlling it."

"Okay."

"I have more . . . so much more . . ."

Alex offered up a slow laugh. "Thank you for not making my eyes glaze over. I appreciate you curating the information for me."

"What else can I do for you while you're decompressing in your home state of Montana?"

"Find out who purchased the drone."

"My grandma used the phrase 'needle in a haystack.'"

It was a long shot. "I'm familiar with it."

"The drones can be ordered online from anywhere and shipped to anywhere."

"And the camera? Are those common to the average Joe?"

Keenan sighed. "I don't think this is going to get you anywhere, but I'll do what I can. Um . . . in my free time."

Of which he had none. Alex heard him loud and clear, but he also knew Keenan would find the answer if one could be found.

"I might have some additional intel that adds a twist and maybe makes it more interesting," Alex said.

"You know I love it when you talk intrigue."

Alex fully expected Keenan to have come up with it already. Could he really surprise the guy? Well, here went nothing. "Hanstech develops what they term 'cutting-edge' technology."

"For what?"

"Initially, they developed fire threat-detection technology. AI to analyze the threat, and it looks like they partnered with a couple of other companies that major in infrared technologies. They're here in Montana. The hobby spy drone in the picture was near the Hanstech mansion-cabin." He didn't know what else to call it. "It just seems strange."

"That *is* intriguing. Okay, you got my attention. I'll dig and see what I can find. But I should at least tell you that there are many positive uses for UAVs, but possibly more negative ones. For example, drone attacks reduced half of Saudi Arabia's oil production due to toxic fires that burned for days."

Alex sighed. "I get it. In other words, in the wrong hands, drones can bring to life those far-fetched villains you see in action-adventure movies. Let's hope that's not what's happening here."

"I could send you a list of some anti-drone tech, if you'd like. You can decide what you need and get back to me."

"You'd do that for me?"

"What are friends for?"

Indeed. "Thanks for your help." Alex ended the call and stared at his cell. What just happened? Come on, he'd sent the geek a picture of a hobby drone and Keenan had planted some nasty images in his head of the potential threat.

What am I doing looking into this as if I'm on a counterintelligence task force? Which he wasn't. In fact, it was just the opposite. His SSA—supervisory special agent—Peter Lynch, had told him to take a long, peaceful break and that he didn't want to hear from him for three weeks.

Alex's greatest fear was that he would make a big mistake again like the one he'd made overseas last month, and he would have no career to return to. But the human loss . . . that was much more devastating to him.

He'd hoped Keenan would give him information that would tell him no one had been spying on Mackenzie and the shooter couldn't be connected. But instead Keenan had only confirmed his suspicions.

Squeezing the bridge of his nose, he shut his laptop and let the emotionally impacting images of Mackenzie surface again. Big hazel eyes—challenging, assessing, and then finally, trusting. Her slender body that also boasted impossibly warm feminine curves. He'd taken it all in as he caught up to her on the bike and had almost been the one to go off trail and crash. What was it about this woman? She could undo him completely, and he knew nothing much about her—only what he'd learned in one day.

That one day so long ago that left him wanting more time with her.

After being tasked with showing her around the city, he wasn't sure what he'd been expecting when he went to track her down. She wasn't the stereotypical digital genius/computer nerd. At first, she appeared to be a quiet professional—her hair pinned back. Strong handshake. Confidence. She'd been working as a college professor, so that all made sense.

But as the day wore on, she literally let her hair down. The clip had come out, and when she moved to reinsert it, Alex stopped her. Their eyes locked in that moment, and time stopped. And how he'd wanted to weave his fingers through that gorgeous hair of hers.

He never got the chance then.

He wasn't sure he should take the chance now.

God, direct me here. What am I getting into?

He was the wrong guy for her, because when he returned to his job in three weeks, he would be going into the counterintelligence unit in DC, and he'd walk away from her again, though he kept telling himself not this time. Why did the DSS, who had courted her, back off from hiring her? He wanted to find out. Any detail could be connected to what happened yesterday.

A million questions swirled in his mind, and he had his work cut out for him.

On his time off.

He blew out a breath. Emotional connections could muddy the waters of an investigation, even one he wasn't working in an official capacity.

As for Mackenzie, he'd assured her he wouldn't withhold information, so he texted her the image of the drone.

From an expert source . . . This camera is commonly used for spying. If I'm going to help, I need to know what's going on.

He left the Internet café and headed to his rental cabin to get ready for dinner at the ranch. Once he'd showered and changed out of his T-shirt and shorts and into something nicer, he stepped out onto the porch and looked into the dense woods.

He closed his eyes and listened to the sounds. The insects buzzing. A brook trickling somewhere. Birdsong. The chatter of squirrels. He could hear his cell buzzing on the table inside. No rest for the weary.

He wanted to ignore it, but he'd been waiting on a response from Mackenzie, so he went inside to grab the phone. But it wasn't Mackenzie. It was Terra, probably to remind him that they were expecting him for dinner tonight.

A knock came at the door, surprising him.

With a shooter on the loose, he grabbed his extra gun and held it at the side. He stood against the wall. "Who is it?"

"It's me."

Mackenzie.

How had she found him?

When he opened the door, he took in her determined expression and the wild look in her eyes. A breeze blew past her and brought the scent of her freshly washed hair—coconut shampoo—and the fresh Montana air filled with loam and pine.

Before he could step aside to invite her in, she rushed past him and whirled around, looking far different than the quiet professional he'd met before, or even the competent mountain biker from yesterday.

However, her chest rose and fell as if she'd biked all the way here. He fought the urge to glance outside to look for the kind of vehicle that had brought her all the way here.

And at that moment, he knew she was here to tell him what she'd held back.

NINE

Mackenzie wasn't usually indecisive, but standing in the middle of this small cabin with Alex, she wasn't sure she'd made the right decision. Last evening Nora disclosed that she was living in fear and somehow trapped, and she needed Mackenzie's help, but even so, Nora didn't respond well to the news Mackenzie shared. This morning her sister was caught up in an emergency board meeting on the heels of losing the CEO. Rowan's death had shocked them all.

Better her than me.

So Mackenzie had taken this step out of desperation and barreled into Alex's cabin. But he might not welcome the intrusion, even though he'd asked her to share the truth. Leave it to this guy to know that she'd held back.

And now, watching him, she thought of a big cat. His demeanor reminded her of a tiger ready to pounce if she made a wrong move. Another reason to second-guess her decision.

"How did you know where I was staying?" He crossed his arms, angled his head, and hinted at flashing that roguish grin. Oh, he was cute. Handsome. Enticing. Whatever. Mackenzie liked him too much. And none of that mattered exactly now.

"I . . ." Oh no. How could she explain it? Where should she start?

"Never mind." He turned his back on her and moved to the kitchen, leaving her with the distinct impression he needed to put space between them.

Or maybe she was the one who needed the space. Either way, she was grateful for it, because now she could breathe. Never mind that she'd been the one to encroach on his personal space in the first place.

He leaned against the counter, those intense eyes assessing. "I'm sure it wasn't hard to find me."

For someone like you. Had she read that thought in his eyes?

She gulped. She'd come here, so might as well dive deep. She rushed to the counter and pressed her palms against it. "I need your help, Alex. I need your help, that is, if you can keep it to yourself."

His gray eyes roamed her face in that familiar way that let her know he was watching for tells—was she lying? Deceiving? Manipulating?

He frowned. "That's hard for me to say if I don't know what's going on."

"You already know enough, don't you?" *Someone spied on me, then shot at me. At us. Isn't that enough?*

Alex came around the counter and slid onto a stool, his gaze searching hers as if he would read her mind. At the intensity coming off him, she kept her breaths even and held back the flinch begging to escape. What did he already know about her? Would he simply tell her to leave him out of it and go to the police? And she would. Once she had evidence.

Nothing could be done without evidence. He crossed his arms. "Are you saying you need my agency involved?"

"No. I'm saying I need *you* involved. You have experience. You have the skills and the connections, if it comes to that." And when.

"That's why you came to see me?"

Of course. "Why else?" Partially. How did she explain that she was desperate not to repeat the mistakes of the past? How did she explain that . . . "I trust you, Alex. Okay? And yes, your background could potentially help, but now it's more about trust."

"You hardly know me." He slipped from the stool and moved in closer.

What was it about this guy with his button-down shirt and sleeves partially rolled up? He looked out of place in Montana. But he grew up here, so there had to be a cowboy deep down in there somewhere. Didn't there?

He stood too near as he studied her, and the smell of his cologne—he'd showered and changed—teased her senses. All these reactions had been missing when she'd been with William at the carnival.

And none of that was reason enough to want Alex's help. To trust him. She was crazy. "I know *enough*." Emphasis on that last word.

She left out that she'd read everything she could about him—from his past to his present. Star quarterback on the high school football team. National Honor Society. Eagle Scout. Honors in college. Hero father. The list went on.

"I'm here to take a break." When his gaze flicked away, she caught the pain skating across his features.

"This isn't official. I've already said that. If you can't help, Alex, I—" She hadn't considered he would refuse. She was such a fool.

"I'll do what I can, Mackenzie. Make a few calls. Ask some questions. But going too deep into this without talking to someone in an official capacity is dangerous for you."

For Alex too, in more than one way. "I get it. You don't want to jeopardize your career. I wouldn't ask you if it weren't important."

"I understand. I'll do what I can." His intensity built in the way he held his shoulders, the way his gaze zeroed in on her.

She'd done her best to persuade him, yet part of her wanted to know why he would help her at all. But she didn't want him to rethink his decision. She got the strong sense that he might reach out and touch her cheek. Run his fingers through her hair. Without her permission, her body instinctively leaned forward in response. She *wanted* that touch from him. That she was so utterly drawn to this . . . ahem, stranger . . . flew in the face of all reason.

She shut her eyes, wanting to lean closer. But not now. Not here.

Opening them, she stepped back and away from the over-powering attraction and searched for an escape. Fresh air. Mackenzie moved out onto the porch and Alex followed.

"If I'm going to help, I need to know what's going on."

She drew in a breath. Where did she start?

"I'm not sure how much you know about my past."

"Nothing. Why would you think I would know anything?"

Relief swept through her. However, it was kind of disappointing that he hadn't looked into her. "Well, I interviewed with the DSS."

"They told me nothing, and despite what you might think about me, working for a federal agency doesn't mean I invaded your privacy and looked at your records."

She angled a glance and caught his half-dimpled smirk.

"Good to know." Mackenzie dragged in a breath. Might as well get it over with, though sharing the truth with this guy she liked might change the way he looked at her.

"I'm listening."

"I was sixteen when I committed a crime. A cybercrime. I won't go into how I got sucked into it, other than I was in a bad place and needed . . . I needed attention. That's no excuse, but I fell into a scheme that I thought was like Robin Hood and I could do good and help others. But it didn't work out that way and . . ." She was rambling. If she wanted his help, she needed to make sense. "In Michigan, several days ago, my former partner in crime found me and bumped into me, literally, to pass on a warning. Then someone immediately injured him in a hit-and-run."

"Go on."

Mackenzie took a deep breath, then told Alex everything, this time without showing the video in the QR code that had elicited a laugh from Nora. When she was done, she risked a glance at him. Suspicion swept across his features, but at least he hadn't asked what the warning meant. He probably understood the world of video games and cybercriminals. The warning joined both worlds with the terms *vulnerable* and *deadly attacks*.

"This partner in crime have a name? And how did *he* learn of the threat?"

She hoped he didn't see her stiffen at his question. "It doesn't matter."

She wasn't ready to give up her source yet, at least to Alex, even though she was asking him into this with her.

"Okay, then." He searched the woods. "We should get back inside."

She hadn't considered that the woods near his cabin could be dangerous. But if a drone could follow her, track her, so could the danger.

Once inside, Alex paced the small space. "The message sounds multilayered and could mean both a digital threat and a physical threat. And now the spy drone and the shooting make sense, although I haven't often heard of a cybercrime including physical violence of this nature."

He didn't say more while he continued to pace, a deep frown building in his brows and around his mouth.

Then he turned and loosely pointed her way. "*You're* a threat to whomever is behind the exploitation. *You* are their vulnerability. Such extreme measures make me wonder what's going on at Hanstech. What's so important?"

She nodded. "I agree. I'm trying to learn that from my sister. Last night I tried to convince her to let me in to help. Someone is actively searching for a vulnerability, if they haven't already found it."

"Come on, Mackenzie. With your cybersecurity skills and the fact that you teach penetration testing, you could get into the system on your own. But I get it. You want her permission."

"The Hanstech system is air-gapped. It's an intranet system."

"So *that's* why you're in Montana, and . . . here in my cabin." He stopped pacing and locked gazes with her.

Understanding passed between them, confirming that she'd made the right decision in coming to him. She needed to physically get to the company computers because they were not connected to the outside world, the Internet, or any other network or device connected to the Internet. Alex was someone with whom she could communicate. He understood even when her sister hadn't.

Thanks, God, that Alex is here in Montana too. Despite her mistakes, God still cared, and she hadn't been forgotten or discarded because of them.

"Partially. I came here to warn my brother. Now that he's gone, I wonder if his death is linked to the warning. If I was too late to stop it."

"You're saying you think he could have been murdered."

"I'm saying it's worth asking for an autopsy to find out." She pursed her lips. Should she tell him more? "He had a pacemaker."

Alex narrowed his eyes as he studied her. Did he think she was reaching?

"Someone is watching my sister. She's afraid to speak freely, and I'm running out of time."

"And you didn't go to the authorities, the FBI, with this because . . . ?" He arched a brow. "You don't have anything, really. No evidence, just a warning. So that makes me again question the source of the warning."

If he wanted to, Alex could learn the source, even with those sealed records. The news stories about kids hacking into major corporations and taking money were out there somewhere on the Internet even though she'd tried to erase them.

"You're right. I have no tangible evidence, and it would just be a waste of time, and the clock is already ticking down. But more than that, I would have to give up my source and put him in danger and possibly destroy my own career because of our connection, with nothing really to go on but a cryptic message."

And Nora's palpable fear.

Alex dropped his head forward with a sigh, then angled his face to her. "This is going to seem out of nowhere, but I have dinner plans with friends, and you're coming with me."

Not "would you like to join me for dinner?" But "you're coming with me." In the middle of this, whatever this was, she couldn't just—

Alex closed the distance and took her hand. "Please. Will you please come with me to dinner?"

Well, when you put it like that . . .

But with the way he'd cut off their serious discussion with talk of dinner, she couldn't be sure if he was taking any of what she'd told him seriously, especially since she had no evidence. Maybe she had been wrong about coming to him for help.

It wouldn't be her first mistake.

TEN

Even here at Stone Wolf Ranch, surrounded by a thousand acres of a working farm and ranch, cows, sheep and horses, equestrian therapy, and the friends he'd left behind when he fled Montana, Alex kept his protective instincts high. He wasn't sure what to do about the warning signals going off in his brain when it came to Mackenzie Hanson.

Warning signals he had no practical knowledge of, even given his extensive experience as an RSO—regional security officer, the name given to DSS agents on foreign soil—in a high-threat region. He wished he hadn't thought about that and took a few calming breaths to push those memories out of his mind. He had to focus on the here and now and be in the present.

With Mackenzie.

Protect Mackenzie.

He'd followed her back to the Hanson cabin and waited downstairs while she changed out of her cargo pants and T-shirt. When she returned, her hair was pulled high into a ponytail, the curled tresses hanging down her shoulders to reveal her long, elegant neck.

She stayed next to him as they approached the front door

of the sprawling ranch house that sat in the shadows of Stone Wolf Mountain to the west.

She stopped. "Alex . . . are you sure about this?"

He angled toward her. She hugged herself, and her eyes flitted around. Anyone could see that she was nervous and edgy.

No. Not sure at all. "Look, this is something I have to do. You need to eat too. In the meantime, I'm processing what you told me, thinking through possible questions." He stepped closer and dropped his voice to a whisper. "And I'm protecting you. You asked me to help, remember?"

And he'd told her he would make a few calls. He'd been instructed to get some rest and relaxation, and also stay out of trouble. His SSA knew him too well, he guessed. While he was supposedly "resting," the last thing he needed was to make another colossal mistake and totally destroy his career in the process.

He had a feeling he'd already stepped into this too deep.

She subtly nodded, still looking out of place.

"In the meantime, you need to relax. You look entirely too edgy."

"That bad, huh?"

"That bad."

Scared but determined, she was a woman on a mission. Making nice at a dinner with strangers obviously hadn't been on her to-do list. His fault. He gently lifted her chin, and she rewarded him with a smile.

A nice smile that he couldn't tear his eyes from.

"Better?"

"Yes, but don't overdo it." He winked.

She scrunched her face at him, then they headed for the house again. Alex glanced around at the farmland where corn, wheat, and alfalfa were grown. To the south behind the house, dense woods backed up to the national forest. He hoped he wouldn't see a drone hovering in the trees. He suddenly realized that he'd stopped in his tracks and Mackenzie had continued on and now stood at the door, watching him.

"Are you coming or what?" Her wry grin said the rest . . . *After all, this was your idea.*

He jogged forward until he stood next to her, then rang the doorbell. While they waited for someone to answer, he smiled at Mackenzie. Did she sense that *he* was the one who was nervous now? Bringing her to meet this crowd would raise a lot of eyebrows. He had moved away long ago but tried to keep up with the people who mattered most—his mom, Erin, and Terra. But he hadn't spent a lot of time with them in the last few years. While he was out of their daily lives, Terra and Erin had found love. Terra and Jack would soon marry, and he suspected it wouldn't be long before Nathan proposed to Erin.

They were couples who were meant to be together. He was glad they had found their way back into each other's lives. And in their happiness, they would look at Alex and Mackenzie and gauge their relationship. He knew without a doubt that Erin and Terra were going to ask him questions about Mackenzie he couldn't answer.

For one, he hadn't thought through how to introduce her. Friend? Old acquaintance? Girl in trouble? His only thought had been that he didn't want her to leave his side until they had both come up with a plan.

She arched a brow. "You're going to say we're dating, aren't you?"

"What? No. I hadn't—"

"Because you're not going to tell them why I'm here or that you're helping me." She crossed her arms and gave him a practiced evil eye.

"Do you use that look on your students?"

"They're in college. It doesn't work on them."

"And you think it's going to work on me?"

"Well, is it?"

He rubbed his temple. "I'm thinking. Um . . . no." The surprise in her eyes made him chuckle.

"I invited you along, so sure, it's a date. But not because you're giving me the evil eye." Maybe because deep down he wanted it to be a date, though he hadn't admitted that to himself, so he for sure wasn't going to admit that to her.

Not yet. Maybe never.

He rang the doorbell again. Knocked with the knocker.

Amusement danced in her hazel eyes. Gold flecks seemed to ignite in her irises. Oh yeah. He liked this woman. And Terra and Erin were going to see right through him whether he tried to hide it or not, so yeah, it was a date.

The door swung open, and Terra's smile grew wide. "You know you can just walk in, right?"

She thrust out her hand to Mackenzie. "I'm Terra Connors."

"Soon-to-be Terra Tanner." Alex gestured to the beautiful woman next to him. "And this is Mackenzie Hanson."

Terra extended her hand and Mackenzie shook it.

"It's nice to meet you," Terra said. "I was sorry to hear about your brother's death."

Letting her hand drop, Mackenzie glanced at Alex quickly, then back to Terra. "Thank you. It was quite a shock."

Much of her nervousness had disappeared. She was able to put on a good show, or Terra was great at making people feel comfortable. He hadn't decided which.

"Well, it's so nice to meet you. I'm glad Alex brought you." Terra turned and they followed her through the long hallway to the kitchen and then out the doors to the backyard where a fire blazed in a pit and, not far from that, a grill smoked. The aroma of sizzling elk burgers and barbecue chicken made his mouth water and stomach rumble.

Terra introduced Mackenzie to her grandfather, Robert Van

Dine, her brother, Owen, then Erin. Mackenzie also greeted Jack and Nathan, whom she'd already met.

He should ask them if they'd learned anything more about the shooter in the woods, but he would trust they would let him know if they had. Besides, he didn't want to cause more anxiety for Mackenzie. She smiled and made conversation and held her own with his boisterous law enforcement friends. He wasn't sure why he'd been so worried.

She leaned into him. "Do you still think this was a good idea?"

He edged closer. "Yes, definitely."

Those words were for him as much as for her. He almost reached for her hand, then caught himself. No need to give everyone the wrong idea or send Mackenzie the wrong signals. Or, rather, any signals too early. Before either of them was ready.

"Well, let's wrap it up soon. I'm feeling vulnerable." Her words surprised him.

And reminded him.

Vulnerable . . . deadly attacks . . .

He wasn't sure if she was sending him a coded message. Sitting at the picnic table, he had a burger and sour cream potato chips, and she picked at a grilled chicken breast and potato salad. The friends shared small talk about Terra and Jack's upcoming nuptials. Alex took the dishes to the house, and when he came back, he noticed that Owen had drawn Jack, Nathan, Robert, and, surprisingly, Mackenzie to the stables to show off one of his newer horses. Black and shiny. Beautiful for the kind of work Owen did.

Owen saddled the horse, and Mackenzie climbed on like a pro and rode around the corral. He hadn't known she could ride, but that was one of many things he didn't know about her. Admiration swelled inside. Admiration and fear. He couldn't forget the danger pressing in on her.

Terra stepped up to his right side and hung her arm over his shoulder, and Erin stood to his left. An ambush.

"I think you're smitten," Terra said.

Seriously? "What gives you that impression?"

"I noticed it the first time I saw her—that day at the Rocky Mountain Courage Memorial."

"Noticed what?"

"That dreamy look on your face."

"It's a beautiful horse. Your brother knows how to pick them, but I was under the impression this was a therapy place for wounded warriors, not a breeding stable."

"Don't try to change the subject," Erin said.

"You guys are ganging up on me."

"Not ganging up. But you're always so secretive. Hold everything close, even from us."

"I'm like your big brother. You don't need to know everything about me."

"Yeah, we see right through you. But I'm not going to tease you. I want to see more of her around here, along with you. I gotta go check on things." Terra dropped her arm, then left him standing there alone with Erin.

"I'm so happy for you," he said. "You know that."

"Thanks, Alex."

"Terra said I hold things close, but you're the one who kept a lot of secrets from all of us."

"I couldn't . . . I wasn't—"

"It's okay." He wrapped his arm around her shoulders in a protective brotherly hug. "I'm just glad it's over and you're okay, and that you and Nathan are together again. You make a great team."

"And what are you and Mackenzie?"

"I don't know yet. We'll see how it goes." He dropped his arm.

Erin lifted her cell and played the video of the vandalism.

"Not to change the subject, but this is as good a time as any. What do you think of the video?"

"It's hard to say. I'm not the psychologist, but I see hate and anger."

She nodded. "Yes. Resentment. Vengeance. I think this is personal."

Alex had suspected as much, and that chilled him to the bone. Vandalism was one thing. Would this vandal take this further? "Personal to whom? A few months ago, the vandal seemed to focus on Terra's mother's plaque, but in this recent attack, she took out my father's. How are we going to find this person?"

Erin shrugged. "I don't know. I wanted you to hear my assessment. Just be careful out there."

Alex had been trained to watch his back, so he wasn't worried. But he would need to have a conversation with his mother and get her thoughts. He should also warn her, in case this got even more personal.

He turned when Nathan approached and wrapped his arms around Erin and kissed her. When he turned away from the public display of affection, Owen was putting the horse away.

Where was Mackenzie?

Panic swelled in his chest. He thought his protective instincts were up to par, but he'd lost her. He turned slowly and took in his surroundings. He couldn't see her, so she must have gone into the house. How had she gotten past him?

He jogged forward, ignoring the curious looks from those watching. Inside the home, he paused at the kitchen counter. Terra turned from the sink. "Alex. What's wrong?"

He tried to remain emotionless, but he knew his expression gave him away. "Nothing. I was just looking for Mackenzie."

Terra frowned. "I haven't seen her."

He pushed from the counter and headed out the front door. She couldn't have left. She wouldn't.

He flung open the door, and Mackenzie whirled around, a cell to her ear. "I have to go." She ended the call.

"Mackenzie." He was breathless as he stepped forward and held out his hands, not quite touching her arms.

She was out here at the front of the house. Alone. He glanced over her shoulder at the edge of the woods, searching for any suspicious drones in the sky. A potential shooter watching. But as Keenan had mentioned—someone could be watching from a distance.

"I need to go," she said. "My sister needs me. She was upset when she couldn't find me after her meeting today."

I know the feeling. He stuck his hand in his pocket and pulled out the keys. "Let's get out of here then."

"You're not going to tell your friends goodbye?"

"They'll understand."

Once inside the vehicle, he put the ranch behind them for now. "Thanks for coming with me. I'm glad you got a chance to meet Terra and Erin, my closest friends in the world." He'd just made it sound like he'd taken her to get his friends' approval. He hadn't meant it that way. He quickly switched gears. "What did your sister say?"

Mackenzie blew out a breath. "She has postponed the funeral and asked for an autopsy, stating her reasons were due to family genetics. The county coroner didn't conduct one, just made the call based on Rowan's heart disease."

"That will tell you something." Alex hoped the man wasn't murdered. The county coroner, Emmett Hildebrand, would call on the Montana state pathologist to do the autopsy, and that would include toxicology. "But it could take a couple of months. Maybe three to get the results."

"And that's time I don't have. If this was murder, we will get justice for my brother. In the meantime, his troubles are over, as the saying goes. My sister is running a tech company now in his place, and she's walking around scared. I don't know if her fear is unrelated or if it has to do with the warning about the cybersecurity threat. I need to find out more."

This all seemed highly unusual for a cybercriminal. At what point did someone who committed crimes with their digital skills turn into a violent criminal who committed actual murder? What had she left out in her explanation to him? Like the memorial vandalism, this felt more . . . personal. He'd give her time to tell him the rest. But not much time.

"How will you do that?"

She leveled her gaze at him. "If I can't get Nora to let me into the system, then you know what I'm going to do."

Yep. "Hack into the system to stop or prevent a catastrophic attack. Just what is going on at Hanstech that's so sensitive?" He might as well get right to it. "Mackenzie . . . do you know who is behind this?"

"No." The word came out short and clipped.

Why didn't he believe her?

"Your source—whoever learned this intel—probably got it on the dark web. Maybe a hit was put out. He could have sent that warning to you because it was about you personally, Mackenzie. *You* are vulnerable to deadly exploits. Maybe it's too dangerous for you to stay at your brother's house."

She shifted to face him. "Now you know the real reason I came to you."

"Wait. You mean . . ."

"That day back in DC, you told me you were leaving the next day. You were assigned to the US embassy overseas. I figured if you were good at protecting important people, diplomats, then you should be overqualified to protect me. But you're also sharp enough to help me figure this out."

He nodded, letting the words sink in.

She had no idea about his failures in this regard. If she knew, she might reconsider. Still, he couldn't stand around and *not* protect her. Despite the disaster from his recent past, she was in a precarious position, and he knew she wouldn't ask anyone else.

"You're not hiring me. I can't work on the side. I'm here for you as a friend. I'll help get to the bottom of this too." And convince her to go to the Feds when evidence presented itself.

Hanstech. Drones. Artificial intelligence. A cybercriminal with violent tendencies who needed to be on a watch list somewhere. There was much more going on here than he could have imagined when he'd agreed to help. He got the feeling that Mackenzie knew who was behind the danger.

Alex steered around the circular drive at the Hanson cabin and parked behind a Lexus.

"Stay in the car." Mackenzie peered at him as she opened the door. "I don't need Nora asking you questions."

"But I thought you needed me for protection."

"All in good time. The house has a security system. I'll be fine for now, but I'll text after I've cleared this with my sister." She hesitated before getting out. "Are you sure about this? You came to Montana to visit family and friends. Maybe I shouldn't have asked for your help. I don't want to . . . mess up your life."

Mess up my life, please . . .

He reached across the console and squeezed her hand. "You did the right thing in asking me. You can't do this alone, Mackenzie. It's too dangerous. I'm glad I was here in town when you needed such specialized help. You know, maybe God is behind me being here at just the right time."

She angled her head, a thoughtful look in her face. "Maybe you're right. I'll be in touch." She eased out of the vehicle, then leaned in through the open door. A smile lifted the corner of her lips. "I had a nice time on our *date.*"

ELEVEN

She'd always considered herself to be smart. Above average. But jumping from a pretend date into the passenger seat of Nora's car, especially the way she sped around the curvy mountain roads with zero fear, hadn't been the best decision. Queasiness grew in her stomach.

But not just because of the way Nora steered her Lexus around the curves overlooking drops of hundreds of feet.

Because of Alex.

Like Mackenzie needed her head wrapped up in pretend dating Alex Knight. She'd had some fun teasing him, but what was she doing? That look in his eyes told her he was not at all opposed to something real between them. Even at the thought of it, her heart rate kicked up.

He was the exact right person at the exact wrong time. If only she could use Boolean logic—like a computer would—to make her decisions. Something was either true or it was false. Black or white. Uncertainty did not exist in that world. And Mackenzie was definitely operating in the gray haze of indecisiveness right now.

Someone had shot at her, and with Nora requesting an

autopsy on their brother, the dangerous stakes had become suddenly very real. It was bad enough that Julian had been hit by a car. She couldn't say without a doubt that the hit-and-run was deliberate, though she believed in her bones it was. She couldn't prove it. But Rowan . . . they would hold their collective breaths while they waited for the autopsy results, and at the same time continue forward.

"Are you alright?"

The nausea roiled again. Mackenzie pressed her hand against her stomach. "Do you have to drive so fast?"

"I'm not driving fast. The curves won't let me. You'll get used to it, Mackenzie."

"That's good to know, but what about now?"

"You could focus on the sunset. Isn't it amazing?"

Mackenzie agreed. Bright pink and orange and gold burst across the clouds, reflecting sunlight on the other side of the purple mountains to the west. The downside? It was still light enough for Mackenzie to see the big drop along the road mere feet from her as Nora cut the steering wheel deep to the right, and then to the left. Again and again.

And still, the car sped much too fast. She preferred a crawl of two miles an hour around the zigzagging curves that hugged the mountain while offering stunning views for those who dared to look.

Views that Mackenzie avoided.

"Let's talk," Nora said. "Now's good. No one can listen in."

"I'm not sure I trust you to focus on the road while we talk."

Nora chuckled. "I could drive this in my sleep. You could too if you'd stayed long enough to make this trip a thousand or more times."

Mackenzie wanted to close her eyes again but knew better. "Okay. Tell me."

"I thought about what you said, and I think you're right."

"You didn't tell Carson, did you?"

"No. I don't want to put him in danger if I don't have to. You need to get into the system and stop the trouble. Do the penetration testing or whatever it is you do. We already have a cybersecurity team in place."

Hmm. "And I suppose they're already analyzing the data using SIEM—security information and event management. It can be used for threat detection and analysis."

"Probably. I let them do their jobs."

"And they haven't seen any activity."

"Not that has been reported."

"He could be that good at covering his tracks. I would like to look through everything on my own. Eventually I could need help, otherwise it could take me weeks. But . . . Nora . . . the biggest threat, the biggest opening into your system is—"

"People."

"Yes. Insiders."

"Don't you think we know this? We've taken every precaution. No one can even bring in cell phones past the front desk."

"There are other ways." Too many.

"Well, then, it's good that you're here." Nora tossed her a warm, sisterly smile.

"Eyes on the road, please." Mackenzie focused on the road as if that would help Nora's driving. "Now, can you please tell me why you believe you're being monitored? Listened to. Maybe I can fix that too."

"Just a feeling."

Mackenzie had seen the fear in Nora's eyes, and that fear stemmed from much more than a feeling. But her sister would tell her when she was ready.

"Can I ask why Dad built the headquarters so far away from the house?"

Nora laughed. "You don't remember? He was a big fan of separating work and play."

"What I remember is that he was a workaholic."

"At first, yes. But later he realized he had to make a change." Nora glanced at Mackenzie, then back at the road.

"Please just keep your eyes on the road."

"He changed for you. You know that, right?"

Mackenzie hugged herself, then gripped the door handle when momentum threatened to throw her into her sister. "I think it was too late."

"You were busy with community service to make restitution, but you might be right—it was too late. I'm sorry for everything."

"You didn't do anything, Nora."

"Exactly. I know what Rowan said to you. He made you go away for good. And I did nothing. For that, I'm truly sorry. I hope you can forgive me."

"You're forgiven." *It's myself that I need to forgive.* "I blame him too, but really, I don't know if I would have done anything differently. He spoke the truth—my background wasn't good for the company Dad wanted to build."

"Oh, please. You were a kid. And I'm proud of what you've done with your life."

Nora took another curve, the smile on her face letting Mackenzie know her sister was enjoying the drive.

"Dad thought that by moving the headquarters here as he built the company and expanded, he could offer employees an opportunity to enjoy where they lived. Healthy bodies, healthy minds. It's a beautiful place to raise a family too. For years now, it's been a trend for tech companies to operate in such environments, especially when you factor in that the stats show Montana employers have great retention rates—people don't want to leave."

"That's one way to look at it."

"And living and working here, it's easy to incorporate adventure-based team building into the schedule. By the way, there's a team-building session this week, in fact. You're expected to join us."

Mackenzie wanted to scoff at the idea. "What's it include, zip-lining?"

Maybe she had a bad attitude, but she'd never been a fan of team building.

"How'd you know?"

Just a guess. Mackenzie wanted to roll her eyes at the question. "But, I mean . . . you're not going to participate, are you? Rowan just died. You need time to grieve."

"It would be easier to take the time if so much wasn't depending on me. We'll use the time to boost morale. Rowan would want that."

Seriously? Mackenzie felt like she hadn't known her family, or maybe it was more that she'd been born into the wrong family. Had she been adopted? As a kid, she'd wondered about that. Maybe all kids had that thought at times, especially in moments of anger or resentment or wishing for another life. All she knew was that life could change so fast, it made her head spin.

It was hard to believe that last week she'd gone to her condo on Lake Michigan and been preparing for a relaxing summer filled with meandering the white beaches.

The Lexus sped down a serious grade, and Mackenzie pressed her feet against the floorboard as if she could force Nora to slow down. "I've been living in Michigan for a few years now. You might not know, but it's flat. Very flat. I don't know how you ever got used to these mountains. I love looking at them in pictures, but that's where it ends."

"Oh, come on. You've lost your sense of adventure, Mackenzie."

At the bottom of the grade, another significant turn to the right had Mackenzie squeezing the handgrip. With the sun setting, it was growing dark down between the mountains. Trees hugged the road, but she could still see through them—for miles and miles and miles.

It was breathtaking.

But she wanted off this mountain. Right now she was trapped like she'd been on the octopus ride. She couldn't squeeze her eyes shut because that would make her motion sickness increase.

She found her cell and drew in slow, even breaths to ward off the car sickness, then realized she had a text from William.

> The news reported the hit-and-run victim has died. I'm sorry. I hope you're doing well. Call me when you can if you want to talk.

A sob rose in her throat.

"Mackenzie, what's wrong?"

Nora swerved a little too close to the edge.

"Nothing. Watch the road."

"You can't tell me it was nothing. You got a text. What did it say?"

She'd asked William to find out if the man who was struck by the car was doing well—which might have been impossible, given HIPAA—but now apparently the news had reported his death. She hadn't given Julian's name to William. He probably hadn't been using that name anymore, nor would he have wanted Mackenzie to let on to William, or anyone else, that she knew him.

Except—He was dead. She couldn't believe it.

Oh, God . . . I'm going to be sick.

"Please tell me."

"A friend in Michigan died."

"Oh, Mackenzie. I'm so sorry."

It didn't seem fair. He'd risked so much. He'd been there for her.

Why, God?

Bringing up the fact that the friend was Julian might take their easy conversation in the wrong direction. And she needed this . . . this connection with Nora. She missed her family, and now her sister was the only family she had left.

"And this happened on the heels of Rowan's death." Nora actually slowed and glanced her way. "Are you okay? Should we go back?"

She had to push past the grief of Julian's death for the moment. He'd risked so much for her. "I'll be okay. Let's keep going." She couldn't waste any more time.

"You never told me about the guy who dropped you off. Who is he?" Nora asked.

Was she ready to get into this? "His name is Alex Knight." She held back a dreamy sigh. What was wrong with her? "Considering the danger factor, I hope you don't mind that I secured a guy to protect us."

"Well, I don't need hired protection. No one shot at me in the woods. Even so, I have Carson. Is this Knight person with some sort of bodyguard service?"

"No, but he's experienced in protection."

"What do you know about him? Remember, Mackenzie, people can be part of the insider threat and vulnerability."

"He's not on the inside, Nora. And I know everything I need to know. I know you, Nora, and trust me, there's no need to hire a PI to look into him. Besides, we don't have time for that."

She needed to discover who was trying to bring down the stronghold that was Hanstech—the corporation *and* the family—before it was too late.

Nora slowed the vehicle as she steered into the valley.

Mackenzie sighed in relief. Unfortunately, they would need to go back the same way. Every day she would have to take this road. Maybe she should check in to a hotel in town. Nora steered the Lexus into the parking lot that looked like it would hold about two hundred vehicles, give or take. At one end of the lot was a modern three-story building of metal, wood, and stone. Beautiful and impressive but not overstated, it somehow seemed to blend in with the environment. Probably also took advantage of passive design strategies for heating and cooling.

Hanstech, Inc.

Dad's dream.

She released a heavy sigh. She missed him. Very. Much. She'd lost so much time with him. Another of her mistakes. But she couldn't go back. Couldn't heap more on her battered soul.

Through Hanstech, Dad had hoped to expand the ways in which drones could be used for good—like disaster relief after fires, earthquakes, or floods. Mackenzie had to wonder why Hanstech was being targeted.

Nora parked the Lexus at the front entrance next to a Mercedes. "Look. Carson's here. I didn't even tell him. He knows me too well."

Or he was keeping tabs on Nora. Though none of her business, kind of creepy.

Carson leaned against his luxury car. His arms were crossed, and he smiled at Nora as she pulled in next to him.

"No electric vehicles for you guys, huh?"

"Maybe at some point."

Before Nora opened the door to get out, Mackenzie caught her wrist. She had much more to talk about with her sister and hadn't realized Carson would be joining them. "I'm going to need to know everything about what you're doing here at Hanstech. Everything. Aboveboard and otherwise."

Nora twisted free and got out of the car.

To herself, Mackenzie mumbled, "And I'm going to need to look into your employees. Everyone, including your fiancé, CFO Carson Banks, who somehow knew you would be here."

TWELVE

n the shadow of the tree canopy, Alex perched on the stump of a fallen spruce near Hanstech headquarters and watched the facility through his night-vision monocular.

What are you doing, Mackenzie?

Her response to his follow-up text had been to simply put him off. Even then, she could have been in trouble. But knowing her, she'd find a way to tell him, even in a coded message if she had to. If there was something to tell. Considering the shooting yesterday, he wasn't going to wait around to finalize an agreement to watch out for her.

He'd followed her for now in part to be there if she needed protection, but she clearly hadn't wanted him to come along on this excursion, which seemed odd to him. By observing from a distance, he could possibly learn something—like more about what he was getting into with her.

He'd had to improvise as they drove to the Hanstech headquarters. They'd spot him anywhere he parked the car, so he'd pulled off the road and hiked through the woods to this vantage point.

From where he sat, he could watch the comings and goings.

The parking lot had been empty, except for two security vehicles parked in the front, as well as a man—not security—

who leaned against a space-gray four-door Mercedes Benz. Carson Banks. Alex remembered him from the "our team" section on the Hanstech website. Together, all three of them entered the facility. Was Carson a threat? Considering Alex was not on the inside of that building with Mackenzie, he certainly hoped not. Or did Mackenzie consider Carson's presence adequate protection?

Earlier in the evening, while Alex waited on Mackenzie to contact him, he read more information about Hanstech. Everything available to the public, anyway, which included interviews with Mackenzie's father, recently deceased brother, and very much alive sister.

Additionally, he learned about the headquarters built here in Montana and that Hanson believed the natural setting would increase productivity. But Alex couldn't help but think that in Montana . . . in a massive secluded building in the woods . . . secretive tests could be conducted in such an isolated place. Like the government conducted in Nevada or New Mexico.

After Gregory Hanson's death, his brainchild had become his son Rowan's baby. What had the son done to evoke the threats? Alex was speculating, of course, and he needed facts and evidence. He also needed to protect Mackenzie. And while he was on the outside of that building, he wasn't protecting Mackenzie or learning what *she* was learning.

He hopped off his perch, and a text buzzed through from Nathan Campbell.

> Deputy Hildebrand is calling in the state pathologist for an autopsy per Nora Hanson's request. Do you know anything? You were with Mackenzie tonight.

Yep, Alex knew something. That Hildebrand didn't know when to keep his mouth shut. That news getting to the wrong person could increase the threat. He texted back.

For genetic reasons.

Given the shooter in the woods, Alex suspected this new development regarding an autopsy had caught the detective's attention.

Time to make his presence known. He left the stump behind and half ran—not easy in the dark—and half hiked back to his car, then drove the rest of the way in and parked next to the Mercedes in the Hanstech parking lot.

No gated entrance blocked his path, and he assumed that was in keeping with the desire to blend in with nature. As if the building hadn't imposed on the landscape. Clearly the campus designers hadn't expected any physical threats, and the security guards were in place because that's what was expected to protect millions of dollars' worth of property, including the computer servers inside.

What else might he find inside? Hanstech didn't manufacture the actual drones but instead created the software to make them work. However, they would surely need to test them at this facility.

He got out of his car and leaned against it. He should have simply followed them in, but he feared if he pushed too hard, then Mackenzie would shut him out—even after *inviting* him in. He hadn't helped when he kept her at a distance with his "I'll do what I can . . ." But here he was jumping into her world with both feet.

He knew he wouldn't be getting into the building without permission, so he texted Mackenzie.

What are you doing at Hanstech this time of night?

How did you know?

Seriously? If Mackenzie wanted protection, then Carson Banks wasn't adequate. Still, Nora could have convinced

Mackenzie that Carson would do in a pinch. Um . . . a small pinch.

> I know because I'm outside. Let me in?

An angry emoji came through.

> You followed me?

> Hello. I can't protect you if I'm not with you. I don't think the CFO of the company can do the job.

Not to mention, Carson didn't have the kind of connections Alex had. Or did he? Really, Alex didn't know that much about the man. He was letting his frustration get to him.

> The man is Nora's fiancé. Wait for me outside.

Great.

He leaned against his rental vehicle. The car was completely unsexy—especially when compared to a Lexus and Mercedes-Benz. In the quiet night, a security light flickered and buzzed. A coyote yipped and howled, joined by the rest of the band. Alex should walk the perimeter, but it was at least an acre. That might draw security's attention, which was a great way to test them, but he'd wait for another opportunity. He wanted to be right here if Mackenzie needed him.

Another text came through. This time, it was Keenan Walker. Kind of late, but then again, the tech guru worked all hours.

> Got suggestions for anti-drone tech you wanted.

He opened the attached file and quickly skimmed a long list of drone detection devices, including infrared cameras. Keenan had highlighted a few on the list.

> Thanks. What about countermeasures?

What kind?

> I need to neutralize the threat, whether that's physically destroying the drone, neutralizing it, or taking control of it, I don't care. Once I know there's a potential threat, then I need to take it out.

An additional list is forthcoming.

Alex stuck his cell back in his pocket, wishing he had the tech now. Kind of surreal that he was standing at a UAV company asking for help with finding drones and taking them down while watching over a former cybercriminal while she tried to combat a dangerous cybercriminal.

A bad feeling churned in his gut about what was happening at Hanstech. He had nothing to use, no actual knowledge he could share with his agency if things escalated. Just the possibility of the perfect storm.

He walked to the edge of the parking lot and back. Though the facility had no fencing, there were ample cameras. He noticed a drive leading to the back of the building, but he would check on that later. Keenan finally responded.

> You need to know that countermeasures to take out a drone are available, but they're highly regulated, and the actual technology to neutralize a drone is illegal.

> But there have to be exceptions.

> Yes. Law enforcement and military agencies are allowed to utilize that technology, depending on the need, of course.

> Thanks for keeping me informed. Send on those recommendations.

Will do. And Alex?

Yes?

Be careful. You're not invincible.

Alex put away the cell and wanted to close his eyes, to block out the blistering images from the past accosting him.

The Suburban exploded, and flames engulfed it. He tried to save them. But he hadn't tried hard enough.

The pain of failure and grief lit through him, skewing him, searing him. He shoved the thoughts aside. Not now. Not tonight. He drew in a few reassuring breaths.

He could protect her. He *would* protect her.

THIRTEEN

"Carson, would you please let Alex in? He's at the front entrance." Mackenzie was surprised Alex hadn't found a way inside on his own.

Carson's eyes flicked to Nora. Asking permission? Then back to Mackenzie. "Will do. And who is he?"

"A friend." Maybe more. Protection. But Carson didn't need to know that just yet, if ever.

While Carson headed in the opposite direction, Mackenzie caught up with her sister, who stood by the elevators at the end of the hall. Nora had been giving Mackenzie the grand tour. She stepped into the elevators with Nora, who used her keycard to access the button to the third floor, then continued her spiel right where she'd left off.

"At Hanstech, we're very fortunate to have some of the sharpest minds working on emerging technologies. We encourage team players to work together through the design process. Our strong work ethic and creative techniques keep our company on the cutting edge of innovation."

"Cut the pitch, Nora. I read the brochures. I was here at the start, but Rowan has expanded. You have way more programmers, scientists, and engineers. What *aren't* you telling me?"

"I've told you everything."

"Are you sure you don't have a secret room where you're conducting all sorts of mad scientist experiments?" She snorted.

Nora's eyes widened a fraction, but her face remained emotionless, impassive, as the elevator slowly rose to the third floor. Her sister was definitely holding something back. Mackenzie had been joking about the secret room. Now she felt like she was in a weird sci-fi movie.

Nora turned to face her. Her sister was older and thought herself wiser. *Understandable.* She lowered her voice to a whisper. "You have a past, Mackenzie. If anyone finds out about that and what you're doing here, then we could lose everything."

"You sound like Rowan now." She sucked in a breath. "I'm sorry, Nora. I shouldn't have said that."

Nora pressed a hand to her forehead and blew out a breath. "I don't know. Maybe this isn't a good idea, after all."

Her heart jumped to her throat. Why was she trying so hard to help if her assistance wasn't even wanted? But . . . "You said you needed my help, Nora. And I'm here. I'm doing this. Your life could be in danger, don't you get it? As for the company, you could lose everything anyway. That's what I'm trying to tell you. If someone gets into your system and steals sensitive data, what happens then? And we could already be too late."

The doors opened. Finally.

The entire floor was filled with cubicles and a few completely enclosed offices on the north side. But windows all around allowed the view of the forest to saturate the space—well, during the daytime. Right now, she saw her reflection and behind that, darkness. Nora unlocked an office and opened the door. Multiple computers along with four monitors mounted on the wall made Mackenzie smile.

Nora smiled too. "I thought you'd like it here. Better for you to have privacy than to work in a cubicle where someone might see what you're up to. In the meantime, just use a different last name. How about Calhoun instead of Hanson, if anyone should ask?"

"Okay."

"And try to blend in and don't do anything to stand out or draw attention. We have people working on groundbreaking projects, some of which are disclosure projects, so—"

"I get it. Shrouded in secrecy."

"Yes. They're kept under wraps, so it's unlikely anyone will ask you what you're doing."

"And if they do, I'll just say it's a tented project."

"Yes. Good."

"You don't have to worry. I'm usually invisible to others, and I'll be in this cave working for the most part."

"Good. I'll take care of human resources. Oh, and here's a keycard for you." She pulled another one out of her pocket and handed it over. "You'll need it for the stairwells and elevators. I'll need to get you a key for your office. This is a master key, so I'm keeping it. Oh, and you must leave your cell phone with security. They have assigned lockboxes up front. You log in the cell, and the front desk staff takes care of it."

"To keep someone from inadvertently creating a Wi-Fi connection to the air-gapped system."

"Right." Nora tugged her shirt down and stood tall. Her smile was tenuous at best. "I imagine finding the issue won't take too long."

Oh. It could take weeks. But she would hope for the best. "That depends on what I find, and if you get me access to *everything*." Otherwise, this could be a colossal waste of time.

Or she could be hunting someone who had already come and gone. Someone who could already be selling Hanstech secrets or proprietary software on the dark web. She needed more information from Julian, but he was gone now. A fist squeezed her heart. She wouldn't let his death be for nothing.

Mackenzie dropped into the ergonomic chair and booted up the computers. Nora leaned over her and logged in. She scribbled the login information and password on a sticky note. "I'll have HR come in to set up your biometrics tomorrow."

"Will HR want me to fill out employment paperwork?"

"I said I would take care of it."

"Okay, just making sure. Whose office was this? Looks like it hasn't been unoccupied that long."

"This is the programming floor. An AI specialist, I think. With around a hundred and fifty employees, I can't keep up with everyone."

Mackenzie started typing on the computer.

"I need to run down to my office on the first floor, then I'll be back up to get you. So that'll give you a few minutes."

"I can't stay through the night?"

"No. We don't want to draw unnecessary attention."

"Let me at least look at your security programs to see if any threats were detected." Then she could go hunting for security breaches.

"Do you want to talk to the cybersecurity department to-morrow?"

Mackenzie shrugged. "Not yet. Your program could stop a majority of threats, but those are known threats. I'm looking for an unknown threat, except, well . . . I know about it. It would be like, say . . . a zero-day threat. You've heard of that, right? It's a vulnerability that isn't known yet."

Nora's blank expression said it all.

"How could you not know this stuff working at a software company?"

"I have employees for that."

Whatever. "That's fair." But explaining the details was not going to happen.

"I just need to run a few analytics system tests. I'll be looking at the usual OSINT—"

"English, please."

"Oh, open-source intelligence. It's what criminal hackers use to get past security." Mackenzie glanced at her sister. "Your eyes are already glazing over."

"No. I find it fascinating that someone could hack into this system. Tell me how that could happen. We're not connected to the outside."

"Think of a home burglar. A hacker is like that. They watch the house. Figure out the best way and time to break in. In hacker terminology—exploit the system. Let's say you have a window that you left unlocked. That's a vulnerability—and that's the way the burglar gets in. Then the real damage begins. They steal your jewelry. That said, we know that the biggest cybersecurity threats come from the inside."

She watched Nora's reaction, hoping her sister was following.

Nora nodded slowly. "So we might be looking at someone on the inside who has left that window unlocked?"

"Exactly."

"Do you know what you're looking for specifically in *our* system?"

"Right now, I'm hoping the hacker has only found a vulnerability but hasn't actually taken advantage of it. Considering the message—'You're vulnerable to deadly attacks. They're taking the stronghold!'—and the fact that actual physical attacks have already happened, I could be too late." And she probably was. She needed to learn more about the stakes. If this wasn't a ransomware attack—which it didn't seem to be, otherwise they would've received a "ransom note"—then sensitive data was being stolen.

Nora subtly shuddered. "I'll leave you to work for a few minutes, and then we'll head home."

Nora shut the door, leaving Mackenzie alone. Though she wouldn't have expected her sister to remain by her side the entire time, that Nora left her alone somehow felt surreal—after all, some part of Nora must have still considered Mackenzie a security risk because of her past.

No. Nora needed her help. That was clear. And Mackenzie would earn Nora's trust through this. Maybe she could even find a way to redeem the past and . . . forgive herself? *Lord, help me.*

She closed her eyes with the silent, heartfelt prayer. Why was it sometimes easier to forgive others than it was to forgive oneself? She drew in a calming breath and opened her eyes to stare at the monitors.

Time to hunt for the threat, the attacker who could be lurking in the system without being detected. There were entire armies being raised up—hacking armies. Cyberforces created to run schemes and steal billions of dollars. Countries like China, North Korea, and Russia were working to attack infrastructures. She mumbled to herself as she perused the system and strategized how to check for vulnerabilities and exploits, and how to protect Hanstech.

And her sister.

She needed to look at anomalies in the data. Weird log-in times. An IP address moving through the network in unusual behaviors or going somewhere it wasn't supposed to go. She set up the available cybersecurity tools to run analytics. She created queries to search the data, the activity, and even company emails. Because . . . she needed to know the real hidden treasure Hanstech held. Someone wanted something. What was it? And why?

Mackenzie was grateful Nora hadn't returned yet. That would give Mackenzie time to get all the needed queries running so she would have data to look at in the morning. While the initial analytics were running and before Nora returned, Mackenzie needed to explore to see if there were actually additional floors that Nora hadn't shown her. Something about

Nora's reaction to Mackenzie's joke about mad scientists left her wondering. And since no other employees were here—except for the two security guards—there would never be a better time.

Mackenzie grabbed her bag and the new keycard and headed for the elevator. She left the office door unlocked. Nora hadn't given her a key yet. Inside the elevator she used the keycard and pressed the button for the first-floor level. Once there, she could look for exits to another level. Maybe try the stairwell. If she knew more about Hanstech, if she knew what Nora was hiding, then Mackenzie could know how best to help.

Lights flickered. Gears ground as the elevator stopped suddenly.

Huh?

She pushed down the panic. This wasn't a skyscraper. But if she had to guess, she was stuck between the second and third floors. She could definitely suffer an injury if the elevator dropped. In the meantime, how did she get out of here?

An alarm went off. The elevator? The building? Was there a fire somewhere?

Her heart rate jumped. She gulped for air. What about the elevator fail-safe, where the battery kicked in? *It's going to be okay.* She wouldn't panic yet. Using her cell for light, she spotted the alarm button, but there was already an alarm blaring somewhere. She pressed the red button on the emergency elevator phone. Not really a phone but the image of a phone, a speaker and instructions that read "push to talk."

She held it down to speak. "Help! Anyone there? Hello? I'm stuck in the elevator. Please get me out!"

She released the button and heard nothing. No static. No response. Her breath hitched, and she repeatedly pressed the button as if that would make a difference.

Do not panic.

Remain calm.

Just wait.

Right. That wasn't going to work. Panic flooded her despite her determination. She pounded on the door. "Help! I'm in the elevator. Help me out!"

Mackenzie looked at her cell. No reception.

I'm in a small box in the dark. There's no reason to be afraid.

A facility like this should have backup generators.

Unless. Was someone already in the system and messing with them? With her? Could this be a cyberattack? This was a smart building with a lot of vectors for attacks, including—a chill swept through her—an elevator. Building codes required real-time voice and video in every elevator car. And yet no one seemed able to hear or see her.

Please, no. She was letting fear get the best of her. Still . . . using the light from her cell since the elevator fail-safe had so profoundly failed, she glanced up and spotted the camera. That terrified her more.

Was the cybercriminal watching her even now?

The air in the small car suddenly grew stuffy. She yanked off her jacket. Sweat beaded at her brow.

Think, Mackenzie.

She positioned herself so she could try to pull the elevator doors open, but they didn't budge. She glanced up at the top of the elevator to the emergency hatch. That provided a way in and out of the box, but there was no way she could reach it.

"Mackenzie? Are you in there?" Through the elevator doors, the familiar voice was muted, but it sent relief flooding through her.

"Alex? Alex! Yes. Please, can you get me out?"

"Hold on. You might want to stand back."

Why? Was he going to press C-4 against the doors and blow them open? Her wild imagination certainly wasn't helping. But she wouldn't question his advice, so she stood against the far corner and covered her head—just in case.

She heard Alex groaning. Actually, she heard two men grumble. A flashlight beam shone from behind the legs of two people as the doors slowly began to separate. With the doors pried open a good distance, she could see the car had stopped between floors. Alex crouched to look down at her. Relief surged through her, but she wasn't out of danger yet. His expression told her that he was concerned as well.

He thrust his arms through the space they'd opened up—apprehension in his eyes, concern carved across his features. "Come on."

"You don't have to ask me twice." She rushed forward and let him pull her through the opening. Dim lights flashed in the hallway. Then the power came back on, and lights flickered bright in the corridor. The elevator doors closed, and the car sounded as if it were going down to the main floor.

What would have happened if she had been climbing out and the elevator started again?

Alex pulled her to her feet and gently gripped her arms. He peered at her, distress exploding from his intense gaze. "Are you okay?"

Now that you're here. She was terrified moments ago. A ridiculous, unreasonable terror. Seeing Alex's face had surprised and relieved her, but there was another, more powerful emotion that she couldn't put her finger on as he held her gaze for far too long.

Heart pounding, she found her voice. "Yes . . ." The word came out in a whisper. "Now that I'm out of that terror box, I'm fine." She glanced around the corridor, where emergency lights still flashed. The alarm had been shut off, though. "Can someone please tell me what exactly happened?"

Tilden, one of two security guards Mackenzie had met when she'd entered the facility earlier, finished speaking with his night shift partner over his radio, then waved them forward and down the corridor toward the stairwell.

"Some kind of catastrophic power failure," he said. "I'm going to get to the bottom of it." They followed him down the corridor as he continued talking. "The elevator runs on a battery and should have safely taken you to the main floor."

On the first-floor level, they pushed through the stairwell door into the main foyer. Tilden turned to Nora. "I'll let the fire department know we got her out. They were on their way."

"And you didn't wait?" Mackenzie looked between Tilden and Alex.

"He wouldn't wait." Tilden gestured at Alex.

"Thank you." She would still be waiting in the elevator for the fire department if Alex hadn't decided to intrude into her night at Hanstech.

My hero.

FOURTEEN

Outside in the dimly lit parking lot, Alex stood next to his rental car and studied Mackenzie as she watched her sister drive away. Carson followed in his luxury car. Though Alex didn't know enough to understand their family dynamics, he sensed a strong combination of tension and love connected the sisters.

A security light flickered and buzzed, holding back the darkness that seemed eager to close in on them.

Was someone watching?

Aiming to shoot?

"We should get out of here." The high-tech facility seemed oddly unprotected, but maybe the rugged natural landscape, along with cameras, was protection enough.

When she didn't respond, he leaned in. "Earth to Mackenzie."

She startled, then looked at him, blinking rapidly. "Oh, right."

He opened the car door and waited for her to get in, then he jogged around to the other side and climbed behind the wheel.

Buckling in, he said, "I don't feel comfortable protecting you at your brother's cabin."

He felt this way for a thousand reasons, not the least of which was that her brother might have been murdered there. He started the car and steered out of the parking lot. "What possessed you to want to stay there instead of going with your sister?"

Nora had made the abrupt decision to stay at her condo tonight. She'd invited Mackenzie, who refused.

"I need more time at the house. Maybe I could look around and see if there's anything that might hint at what's going on."

He sensed that her reasons went much deeper. The family dynamics again. Or . . . "You mean search your brother's computer."

"Yes."

"You do know that *if* he was murdered, his computer could be taken into evidence. It's better to stay away. In fact, I don't think it's a good idea to go back to the house at all."

When she didn't answer, Alex gave her space. He needed to concentrate on the drive and think about what he'd seen tonight at Hanstech. When the power went off, he followed Carson in search of Nora and Mackenzie. Dread had gripped him.

She tensed as he took the curves on the mountain road. He slowed to make her more comfortable and said nothing more until he steered the car right up to the home that was set against a mountain. All the lights were off.

"I would think a timer would be set to turn the lights on," he said. "I'm assuming it's a smart house." Every tech company CEO should have a smart home, right? Everything from speakers and cameras to security systems and appliances all connected.

"It is, but I don't know about the lights. My guess is it has to do with keeping things as natural as possible for the animal life." She reached for the car door.

"What about personal safety?"

"I have the security code to get in." Mackenzie hopped out, but not before he saw her brief hesitation. Oh, brother. He left the vehicle lights on. Then he grabbed his flashlight, monocular, and gun all in one fluid motion and followed her up the steps.

Something felt off, and personal experience warned him never to ignore that feeling. Maybe it stemmed from the fact that she'd been attacked on the trail not two miles from this house. Or it could be that he sensed she was hiding something. He needed to learn everything she knew. If he came on too harsh or pressed her too hard, she might back away completely.

Alex inwardly groaned. What had he gotten himself into? She was stubborn.

Brilliant.

Gorgeous.

I shouldn't be making a list.

At the door, she lifted her shoulders and offered a sheepish grin. "You were right. I shouldn't stay here since Nora isn't here. I'm sorry to make you bring me all the way. I guess you think I'm afraid of the dark now."

"Of course not. After what happened tonight, you're understandably shaken, and I think you're making the right decision." Relief swept through him as he started to turn around. "Wait. I left my stuff up in the bedroom. I need a change of clothes and my laptop."

She inserted the key, unlocked the door, then flipped on the lights—both outside and in. Mackenzie then disarmed the security system, only to rearm it once they were inside with the door closed.

She glanced at him. "What?"

"Can't you just *tell* it to do this stuff?"

"My voice isn't in the system yet."

Interesting. "What about cameras?" he asked as he moved

through the house, clearing it of potential bad guys. Looking through every room, every closet.

Mackenzie kept close to him. "What about them?"

"If you have security cameras, those could tell us something about what happened to your brother."

"Good idea. But I don't think they'll tell us anything about his death."

"Because?"

"The cameras would show him collapsing, and that's all."

"But how do you know someone wasn't here with him?" Alex held his weapon ready, flipped on lights, and searched the next room.

"That's a fair point." She shivered behind him. "I had planned to get into the security cameras, just so you know."

He cleared the kitchen. "How hard would it be to hack into a pacemaker?"

"That's not my expertise, but I have a friend in cybersecurity whose job is to hack into medical devices to test their security, and I can ask her."

Interesting. Next room—the library. "The fact that there is such a job is worrisome."

"Exactly."

He paused at the bottom of the stairs to the second floor.

She stared at her cell and typed. "Sending her a text." Then she looked at him. "I don't know when I'll hear from her. Looking at it from my limited knowledge, the hacker could insert malware into the system and then when the device connects to the internet to send or receive data, the malware is—"

"Downloaded and can cause a malfunction. The same way it happens to any electronic device."

She nodded. "But it's really unheard of—at least that we know about. That kind of news getting out would cause panic. Besides, hackers are usually more interested in identity theft."

"But you think it could happen."

"Yes. His pacemaker could be associated with an older system that wasn't updated with patches or a new system with a zero-day vulnerability. If someone wanted to commit a murder that would be hard to discover, this would be it."

His gut tightened at the idea. "What would a cybercriminal do, exactly?"

"Deplete the battery? Alter pacing? Even if the hacker couldn't gain access to the hospital intranet system, he could hack in by proximity to the medical device or the home transmitter."

"You mean kind of like hackers use RFID skimmers to get credit card numbers and personal information by just sitting next to you at the airport."

"Yes." She held his gaze and rubbed her arms.

"Meaning, his killer could have been close." Could still be close.

Her face paled. "Let's see what the pathologist tells the coroner, assuming the pacemaker is even examined as part of the autopsy. In the meantime, I'll find out what my friend has to say." She smiled, then glanced at her cell. "And here's her answer."

She read for a few seconds, then said, "Basically what I just said to you is correct, but to know for certain, she would need more information regarding the exact device. I'm just going to thank her." Mackenzie blew out a breath after she finished the text. "I don't have that information yet."

"Then I think starting with the cameras is a good idea."

"Honestly, someone who would hack into a pacemaker is not going to let security cameras take him down."

She had him there. "Well, it's clear on the first floor. You can wait here, and I'll make sure it's safe upstairs."

"I'll go too. My stuff is upstairs in my old room."

"I can grab it for you."

"That's okay."

Was she afraid to be alone? "Suit yourself."

He led the way upstairs and cleared the rooms as he moved down the hall. Pushing through the last door to the left, he cleared it, then paused to take in the figurines on a shelf, as well as the posters of mountain bikers and movie stars on the wall. "This is your old room."

"Dad kept it like it was when I left for college. Then after Dad died, for some weird reason, Rowan never changed it. He was probably too busy or maybe he felt too guilty after everything else. I don't know."

What did that mean?

She waltzed into the room, stepped around him, and quickly stuffed a few personal items into a duffel bag. Now he understood why she hadn't wanted him to grab her much-too-personal stuff.

"Or he couldn't bear to change it because he cared about you." He had no business offering up a psychoanalysis of her family.

She huffed. "Hardly."

Yep. Family issues. He understood—he had them himself, except he'd never considered Ron family because he wasn't Alex's biological father. Just his stepfather—a guy he never got along with. Maybe the bad attitude was all on Alex.

After packing her laptop in a tote, she lugged the duffel over her shoulder. "I didn't bring a lot."

"Nothing wrong with traveling light."

Once downstairs, Mackenzie headed for the back of the house instead of the front door.

"Where are you going?"

"I need a moment . . . I have a few good memories of my father here. Give me this, okay, Alex?"

She flipped on the lights to the deck, disarmed the security system, opened the French doors, then stepped outside. Alex followed her out onto the balcony that overlooked a small stream. The sound of trickling water met his ears.

She eased into an Adirondack chair.

"Mackenzie," he said, keeping his voice quiet. "We can't stay long." He'd prefer they didn't stay at all, but she'd invoked the memory of her father, a request he couldn't deny.

"I know." Pain edged her whisper.

He stood back against the walls in the shadows created by the soft lights. She obviously needed time to process with the recent events. Her brother's death. Still, she wasn't thinking about her brother.

She was thinking about her father.

He watched the woods, peering through his night-vision monocular. He saw no heat signatures, except for an animal or two.

And if a drone was out there, watching, spying . . .

What exactly could he do about it?

I have to get my hands on that drone-neutralizing tech.

She sighed deeply, sounding like she held on to a hundred years of regret. He understood her melancholy but wished they were in a safer place.

"Tell me about him."

Another sigh, then she said, "I was born in Sacramento, but when I was twelve, we moved to Silicon Valley. Dad was my best friend. We spent a lot of time together and used to mountain bike in the Sierra Nevada mountains."

He heard the pain in her voice. Something had happened to strain their relationship. If he shared his own pain, then she might open up. And he wanted to know more about her. Personally, that was. Still, learning more could also help him discover the truth behind what was going on.

"I felt the same about my dad. He was my hero. I wanted to be just like him. He and I worked on an old '67 Mustang together. And then he died in a search and rescue accident."

In the end, he died for someone who turned out to be a criminal. Dad wouldn't have let that stop him, though. Alex had struggled with the fact that Dad seemed to put others before his family. What about Mom? What about Alex? He needed his father. But deadly accidents happened in life—whether one was volunteering to save another or for a million other nonsensical reasons.

"I'm sorry, Alex."

"So what happened to your father?"

"Oh, he didn't die in anything as heroic as an SAR mission. He was killed in a car accident. Years before that, when we were all kids, Mom died of leukemia. But this house, the company . . . Dad had been working so hard to build something. Creating a legacy for us, he'd said. The only problem was that all his work took him away from me. He spent less and less time with me until . . ." Her words trailed off with an incredulous chuckle.

Alex's skin prickled, and he peered through the monocular again. He couldn't see anything in those woods, but he could hear something.

Someone.

She stiffened and sat up, alert. She heard it too.

"We've stayed too long," he whispered.

They hurried into the house, pausing only once they were inside so Mackenzie could flip off most of the lights. Then at the front door, Alex froze. Mackenzie gasped.

The front door was wide open.

He had closed it. She had secured the alarm. But then she'd disarmed it to step outside onto the deck.

Someone was in the house.

FIFTEEN

Stay close to me." Alex held his gun, ready for any threat coming at them.

He never should have brought her back here. Alex gritted his teeth and shut the door behind them, then he stood in front of her on the porch. They had both sensed that someone had approached—but that had been when they were outside on the deck. Maybe what they had sensed was someone entering the house.

"Hurry." He led her quickly down the steps, and they got in the car. He started it, then headed away from the house. "I'm getting a safe distance away."

He steered along the long drive, then onto the county road, where he turned around and parked at the end of the drive, leaving the engine running. Relief washed through him that they'd made it without incident.

"What are you doing?"

"I'm calling 911." He made the call and explained that someone had broken into the house. The dispatcher told him a deputy would arrive soon.

Not likely. The county was big. This road long. But he would wait for whoever showed up while he protected Mackenzie.

"I feel kind of silly. Are you sure we didn't just leave the door open?" she asked. "I mean, I turned the alarm off, then opened the French doors. Maybe a vacuum caused the front door to open too."

"We were being watched. I could feel it."

They sat in eerie silence for a few long moments, during which time he searched the darkness with his monocular.

"What about your detective friends? Jack and Nathan?"

"I'm not sure who will show up tonight, but it's worth sending a text." Though at the same time, he hated to disturb them at almost midnight.

Alex started a text, but before he could send it, lights flashed in his rearview mirror. Friend or foe? He would remain cautious until he knew who was approaching the house. It seemed too soon for a deputy to arrive, but he thought he recognized the vehicle and the man behind the wheel. Tension eased out of his shoulders.

He decided to head closer to the house, then stopped near the entrance. Nathan Campbell parked his vehicle behind Alex and stepped out. Then a regular county vehicle pulled in behind Nathan, and a deputy Alex didn't recognize stepped out.

"Wait in the car," Alex said to Mackenzie. Then he got out and shook hands with Nathan. "What are you doing here?"

"I asked to be informed of anything happening at the Hanson cabin. While Henry . . . er . . . Sheriff Gibson is out of town, I'm in charge. Plus, I was heading away from Stone Wolf Ranch, so I was close enough. You still have an intruder?"

"I'm not sure," Alex said.

"You wait here with Mackenzie, and Deputy Weeks and I will check out the house."

"We closed the door behind us, so it could be locked. Let me at least get you inside."

Alex ran to the car and grabbed the key from Mackenzie,

then the three rushed to the house. He unlocked the door. Mackenzie hadn't reset the security alarm when they fled, so he didn't need to disarm it. Then he flipped on the lights— he'd never been a fan of the low-light tactics used by some in law enforcement.

"Go back and stay with Mackenzie," Nathan said.

While Nathan and the deputy cleared the house, Alex decided instead to stay at the door, blocking that exit as he watched the vehicle where Mackenzie waited. The lights flicked on all through the house as the detective and deputy cleared each room, communicating as they did.

Alex took a few glimpses through his monocular at the woods surrounding the front and sides of the house. If the intruder was the same person who shot at them on the trail, then they were definitely armed and dangerous.

His skin prickled again, sensing the danger. He glanced at the French doors down the long hallway from the foyer. Another exit. If someone was still inside, they could go through a window, the front door, the French doors, the exit to the deck, the kitchen exit into the garage . . .

The lights flicked off.

He tensed and gripped his weapon. Now the intruder had the advantage. And help—if Mackenzie's cybercriminal had been the reason the lights went off.

Holding his gun ready, he peered through the night with his monocular.

Gunfire rang out from upstairs, shattering the silence.

Adrenaline surged as he took cover and prepared to return fire if needed. A figure bounded down the stairs, hopped over the rail, and ran toward the French doors. Flashlights beamed on the stairs as the deputies followed. Alex dropped the monocular to give chase.

"Stay here!" Nathan shouted from behind as he passed Alex and ran to the back of the house. Weeks rushed after him.

"He fled through the French doors!" Alex called after the deputies. He? Or she? He hadn't been able to tell this time.

The two deputies disappeared through the doors.

Mackenzie! Alex turned and raced through the front door and back to the vehicle where she was focused on her laptop, a flowing beacon in the dark night.

He slid into the driver's seat, breathless. "What are you doing?"

The house lights suddenly came on.

"I got the lights back on, at least. Someone was messing with the smart-house technology. I'll have Nora change all the codes—or better, drop the technology completely. I would have done that already since someone has been watching her and she didn't feel free to speak while in the house. But she has been too scared to tamper with it—so I want to be careful too. I won't do it without knowing more."

"Someone broke into her house. What more do you need to know?"

"I need to know what Nora hasn't told me. I have to tread carefully. My interference could escalate the threat to her. Plugging a hole here at the house could cause the dam to break elsewhere."

Alex would have to trust Mackenzie on this because she was the one with the expertise in cybercrime.

Nathan and Deputy Weeks stepped into view around front and jogged over to the vehicle.

"Hold on," Alex said to Mackenzie before climbing out to meet the men. "What happened back there? Who fired the shot?"

"I did." Weeks frowned. "When the lights went out, he rushed me."

And you missed? Alex bit back the words. He didn't need to make enemies.

Nathan squeezed the man's shoulder. "No one was hurt.

Unfortunately, not even the intruder. In the meantime, the house is a crime scene now."

"Good." He didn't want to betray Mackenzie's trust, but he could make a suggestion. "Take all the computers too, including Rowan's."

Nathan narrowed his eyes. "I don't have probable cause."

"Don't you?" Alex didn't look away from Nathan's scrutinous stare.

"The autopsy isn't for genetics, is it?"

"I'm not saying one way or another. Find a reason to get forensics on the computer. The security cameras." He glanced back at Mackenzie. "Everything."

She didn't want to tamper with the technology because of the hacker, so she might not agree. But the sooner they gained control over this situation, the better.

Nathan took their official statements and then released them to get somewhere safe while Weeks secured the scene. He had requested crime scene techs in hopes they could find DNA that would lead them to the intruder and possibly connect the intruder to the shooter in the woods once they gathered all the evidence.

Once he was back in his vehicle, he punched the gas, wishing he'd rented something entirely more elegant and sexier. Fast. As he sped away from the cabin, he peered in the rearview mirror. He needed a better handle on the situation. Knowledge was power.

"Before we were rudely interrupted by an intruder, what were you going to say?" He hoped she heard the levity in his tone. "Your father spent less time with you until . . . what . . . he was killed in the accident?"

"The accident happened after I had already left home. Before we moved to Montana, he just didn't have time for me anymore. He was building up the company, getting investors, though Hanstech remains privately held. You know, the whole corporate America thing. He believed he was doing all of it for us kids. He loved me, but it still hurts if I think about it too much. Right or wrong, I don't know. I reacted badly. I was just a kid. Young and stupid. I guess part of me was angry at my father. But I spent too much time with the wrong friend. We thought we were going to change the world. Again, I was stupid."

"You told me a little about the Robin Hood scheme, but I'd like to hear more about it. Was it some kind of ransomware?"

"Nothing as extravagant as that. Basic malware attacks. The plan was to move money from wealthy, profitable companies with bad reputations and give it to the poor—to charities, actually. Small charities."

"And this scheme took place via your hacking skills? What went wrong?"

He whipped around a curve a little too fast and the car veered into the opposite lane. Thankfully no cars were coming his direction.

"Um . . . please slow down, and I'll answer your questions. This road makes me queasy."

He pressed harder on the brakes. "That better?"

"I'll be better when we're in the valley. To answer your questions, we felt like we were doing something good, like my father. He was accepting money from wealthy people to build his company."

"Without their permission?" Alex said.

"Oh, I agree. I know I made a terrible mistake. I already paid the price. A big price."

"Okay. No judgment." He should have kept his mouth shut.

"My friend had hooked us up with someone else who ended up calling the shots. And things got messed up. We were both scared. Too scared to go against him. We moved money, and it no longer felt like we were being Robin Hood. My original partner agreed we were getting in too deep. And then we went to the FBI Cybercrimes Division and turned ourselves in. We were more scared of . . ."

"Who?"

Mackenzie didn't answer for a few seconds. "I don't know who he was."

"Then why were you so scared?"

"Because of what he could do. He became increasingly belligerent and threatening. I didn't have enough experience to stand up to him. I never should have allowed him to pull me in to begin with."

"Like you said, you were young. Everyone makes mistakes when they're young."

"Not necessarily on such a grand scale."

"You might be surprised." He focused on taking the last snaking curve in the road. "How did your family take it?"

"Dad was so disappointed. Devastated, even. Here he was trying to get investors for his computer tech company, and he has a 'notorious' hacker child." Her voice grew thick with pain. "I was a juvenile delinquent sentenced to community service. Eventually, we moved to Montana for the Hanstech new headquarters, but I didn't live there long because I left for college."

Alex pulled over to the side of the road and shifted toward her. He took her hand. "Mackenzie, you don't have to tell me, but I think it might help me to assist you if I knew what happened when you left."

"I don't see how." She wiped at the tears, looking so much younger than she was. Young and vulnerable. But he knew that childhood memories could often keep people vulnerable for decades.

"Humor me."

"Before I left for college, Rowan told me if I cared about Dad and what he was trying to build, I would go far away and stay away. I was a criminal, and that would affect all of them. I already felt guilty, but Rowan drove the point home and never let me forget. I went off to school and got my degree and built a life away from them. So, see . . . I paid a price. And it was much too high."

Alex searched his heart for the words that would comfort her and take the pain away.

"Mackenzie"—his heart palpitated with the weight of her story—"people leave home and build lives away from their families every day, and not because they've committed a crime. Life has a way of coming up on us fast until we look back and realize we failed to treasure every moment. I'm saying, I have regrets too. Sure, you left, but did you have zero contact with them?"

"Oh, of course we talked on the phone or video chatted. When Dad had time. I came home for the holidays. But at some point, I became overwhelmed with learning about cyber-security, focusing on getting that degree that took away the pain. Then Dad died. He had been headquartered in Montana for two years—I had just turned twenty. Then when Rowan and Nora were running the company, I knew how my brother felt about me."

He steered from the side of the road and headed toward *his* cabin in the woods. "And your sister? Were you close?"

"Not like you might think. I don't believe she held the same sentiment as Rowan about my presence, but she didn't stand up for me either."

And that had to hurt. "You never came back?"

"We tried a few holidays together after Dad was gone. I came back, but our relationships were always strained—and then the last several Christmases, everyone had their own plans. I hadn't been back in years until this week."

"Right, because you got the cryptic message. And your thoughts went immediately to Hanstech and your family."

"What else could I think?"

"Do you still have the message? I'd like to see it when we stop again."

"Where are we going?"

"If it's okay with you, let's crash at my cabin. There's no technology whatsoever, so we're safe from that threat. You can take the bed, and I'll take the sofa. I have an idea of where you can stay that will be safe, and I'll arrange for that tomorrow."

Yawning, she said, "Sounds good. All I need is sleep."

He finally steered up the dirt road to the cabin, where he'd left on a porch light and one small light in the kitchen. Once inside, he cleared the place to make certain no one was waiting for them there—doubtful, but he would take no chances— then he holstered his gun.

"Let's see the message."

She nodded and pulled out the card. "There's a QR code on the back. You'll need a cell signal."

"I have one." He hovered over the code, and the video character appeared and gave the warning.

Interesting. "And this is all it took to get you here?"

"More than that. My friend risked his life to get me the message. A friend in Michigan told me my friend died from his injuries from the hit-and-run. The police are still looking for the driver."

"You never told me he died. I should have asked."

"I knew it was serious, because he never would have gone to the trouble to warn me, or in the way he did, unless it was."

"Meaning?"

"Finding me. Physically stalking me and bumping into me but not meeting with me—because that could have ruined us both."

He scratched his jaw. He could see how that could happen. "And the game he chose to deliver the message . . ."

She angled her head. "What about it?"

"Tell me about that game. Maybe that's part of the message too, so what's the theme?"

"I mean . . . he used the character because that was my created character, my avatar, from the game. I would know it was him. I hadn't considered the game itself. Knight Alliance is about war." Her face paled with those words.

"War . . . Have you considered this cybercriminal is the person from your past you betrayed by going to the Feds?"

SIXTEEN

No."

Mackenzie palmed her eyes. *Please, no . . .*

She'd worked hard to put the past behind her, but the words he'd spoken long ago now haunted her.

"I'll come for you when you least expect it."

Nebulous 2.0's words had driven fear all the way to her bones—back then.

The Feds never pinpointed whether Nebulous 2.0 was a person or a group masquerading as a person. But she'd always thought the cybercriminal was just an individual working alone. Regardless, she'd been told repeatedly by agents that they would find and incarcerate Nebulous 2.0 or shut the group down. Told not to be concerned about the threats ever again. It was all out of her hands. Believing them was the only way she was able to move forward with her life.

She was warned not to communicate with 4PP3R1710N— Apparition—ever again. Julian. To move on, she'd had to push both Julian and Nebulous 2.0 out of her mind.

They were no longer her concern.

But given the lengths Julian had gone to reach out to her, she should have suspected the past had caught up to them. And if that was the case . . . her greatest fear—that she could never escape the mistake she'd made, the crime she'd committed—had chased her back to Montana.

"Mackenzie, did you hear me? Who's behind this? I think you know."

"I don't know!" Her pulse rose with her panic.

"Breathe, Mackenzie. Just calm down. We need to figure this out."

She drew in a long breath, then another . . . Of course he was right. She couldn't let fear control her.

Dropping her hands, she looked at Alex and steadied her voice. "Even if it's him, I don't know his actual name." *God, please don't let it be him.* "That was so long ago, and the FBI agent who initially handled the case told me not to worry about him. Not to be scared anymore."

Alex studied her. "I can see why the agent tried to remove some of the burden and fear. He wanted to reassure you that they would find the person or persons behind the cyberattacks. The question is—"

"Did they? Is he locked up somewhere, unable to access the Internet to commit crimes?"

"I'll see what I can find out through my connections."

His intense gaze remained locked on her. What was he thinking?

She'd kept so much from him already, and she was the one who'd asked for his help. "I thought you weren't going to get too involved."

He barked an incredulous laugh. "We both know I'm already in deep. In fact, I'm in it up to my neck."

But his eyes held warmth, not contempt or resentment. As if he wanted to be in this with her and, in an inexplicable way, enjoyed every minute of it. She was imagining things and had to admit that exhaustion was making her irrational.

Still . . . should she tell him the rest? Since Alex had come this far with her, she shouldn't hold back. "The cybercriminal told me he would come for me when I least expected it." A chill crawled over her, and she hugged herself. "Now I wish I hadn't said the words out loud. It makes it seem too real. I don't want it to be him."

"And you certainly didn't expect this to happen. Even if it's him, this has to be about more than personal vengeance. What did you cost him before?"

Mackenzie cleared her throat. "Millions of dollars." Nausea erupted at the confession, the reminder. She pressed her hand against her midsection. "I had to end it, and I convinced my friend that we should go to the Feds, and he agreed. Things had taken a wrong turn and gone too far."

Actually, they'd gone too far the moment she illegally hacked. Alex eased into the chair at the kitchen table. Yeah, now it seemed like he was getting it. She was accepting what she hadn't wanted to think about.

"He went by Nebulous 2.0," she said. "We used leetspeak to spell our names. His is complicated, so I won't bother."

"I know enough to know that leetspeak is a coded language. And you guys didn't think you should stay away from someone who called themselves Nebulous 2.0?"

"We didn't choose to work with him. He forced us into letting him join because he found us and threatened to expose us. So we didn't have a choice."

"It's obvious he thought you were good, because he brought you into his grand scheme. And I'm leaning toward his involvement. I can easily understand why he doesn't want you blocking his efforts now."

"We don't know it's him. I hope it's not." Mackenzie feared the cybercriminal could mess with her records. Get her arrested somehow. She didn't know what to expect with this guy. "Because if it's him, he wants his money while destroying my family."

Alex scraped a hand through his hair. "That's what worries me the most, given the nature of the warning . . . that game . . ."

"I know where you're going with this. You're worried about what he might want from Hanstech that could earn him that kind of money. But we don't know anything yet. That's why I'm here. To find out."

"It could be too dangerous." Alex stood and started pacing.

She stepped in front of him, effectively stopping him in his tracks before he could wear a path on the old wood floor. "This is my family's company. Who better to get in than me?"

"There are other avenues we can take."

"Or we can take this more expedient one. I'll search the Hanstech systems for his signature. I should be able to recognize some of his code if he's already been in the system. More than that, I'll keep working on Nora. She knows something."

"Thirty-six hours."

"What?"

"I'll give you . . . us . . . thirty-six hours, and then I need to make contact with my agency."

His statement felt more like a threat, and she lifted her chin. "I thought I could trust you. Why don't you just step away now?"

He showed her his palms as if in surrender. "And you *can* trust me. I have your best interest at heart. And I'm not stepping away. I care about you, and I want you safe. But you do realize this is bigger than either of us, don't you?"

And more important than her career.

She slumped. She was too tired to argue with him, and he was right, of course. "Just show me to the bedroom. I'm exhausted."

"Good idea. We both need to sleep on it."

Alex showed her to the room and then shut the door behind him. She pulled the quilt back and crawled under it.

Beneath the covers, Mackenzie rolled around the somewhat

lumpy mattress—what had she expected?—to get comfortable. Sleep should overtake her.

Any minute now.

Soon.

She felt totally and completely safe here with Alex. She could picture him standing guard at the bedroom door, or even outside the cabin. Even though she didn't appreciate his threat to go to the authorities, asking for his help had been the right thing to do.

When this all started, she hadn't wanted to go to the authorities because she would have been forced to reveal Julian's identity. That could have destroyed him after they had both spent years climbing out of the hole they had dug for themselves. But Julian was dead, and his worries were over. A pang ignited in her heart.

Oh . . . God . . .

He was dead. Gone. With a clock ticking down, she didn't have time to process his death. But she wouldn't let it be in vain. He'd taken the risk for a reason. Had his message to her been not only a warning but also an invitation to communicate with him in their game like they had years ago? Had he been trying to ask her to get on Knight Alliance? If so, he was dead, and it was too late.

Her lids grew heavy, and she closed her eyes.

Freda Stone raced toward the castle walls on her black steed, hanging on for dear life. Behind her, a thousand hooves thudded against the ground, sounding like thunder as an army of marauders gave chase.

One armored knight guarded the castle.

Even if he made it inside the walls, one knight could not hold off an entire horde of raiders. Suddenly someone gripped her tighter. A woman rode the horse with her and grabbed for the reins around her to slow the horse. Freda fought for control and urged the horse faster—through the dark woods, over the drawbridge, and past the castle walls to the keep. She hopped from the destrier. The other woman dropped to the ground too, and her hooded robe fell away. Long hair fell to her shoulders. Nora with blond hair instead of black.

A heavy rattling noise drew her attention to the portcullis—the metal grill had dropped to protect the main entrance, but the drawbridge had not been raised.

Freda rushed forward.

The knight rattled the gate, demanding entrance. Behind him, pillagers on horses closed in. He removed his helmet as if he wanted her to know his identity and to look her in the eyes.

Alex.

She stumbled back. Wait. This wasn't right. What was he doing here? He didn't belong here. She had to help him. Even if she tried, she wouldn't be able to open the portcullis in time to let him in.

He looked at her—sharp and true. Turned to face the onslaught. Freda had to try. With Nora's help, they worked the winch that pulled the chains and raised the portcullis. Freda dashed through, and Nora released the winch, dropping the portcullis as planned. With the metal grill of the gate at her back, Freda stepped next to Alex, who'd been prepared to face the raiders alone.

"What are you doing? You'll be killed."

"I can't let you do this alone."

"Then you'll have to use your majuk, or we'll both be slaughtered."

What majuk?

"I don't know of what you speak!"

"You have to use it. Now!"

He gripped and shook her. Those piercing eyes, now pleading, held her captive even as the marauders bore down on them.

She jerked awake and gasped, her heartbeat racing much too fast. A man stood over her, gripping her arms.

Mackenzie screamed and fought.

"It's me, Mackenzie. It's me . . . Alex . . ." He loosened his grip on her arms as she relaxed.

Dim light spilled through the door and revealed his twisted, concerned features. "You had a bad dream. Or a nightmare."

He still gripped her but finally slowly released her, and she immediately missed the warm touch of his hands. Her breathing still erratic, she pushed to sit against the pillow and tried to calm her racing pulse.

"You want to talk about it?"

Rubbing her eyes, she realized her palms were sweaty. Not just her palms. Her forehead. Her entire body. Alex had been in that dream with her, and he was going to die, was prepared to die, to save her. Only, he wanted her to . . . what was it? She couldn't remember.

"No. It was nonsensical. I can't remember most of it." She stared up at him—emotion building in her chest.

In the shadows, she couldn't see the gray of his eyes, but she could feel the intensity of his gaze on her. His musky scent wrapped around her.

"Are you going to be okay?" The tenderness in his voice curled around her heart.

No. "Yes." The word came out breathy.

He remained by her side for a few more heartbeats, then eased away and stood as he scraped a hand through his hair. "I'll leave you to get back to sleep then."

At the doorway, he hung his head and hesitated as if he wanted to say something else or return to her side, but then he simply walked out and pulled the door shut behind him.

She fluffed her pillow and laid down again, doubting sleep would find her. That dream had left her troubled and with a rising sense of doom.

SEVENTEEN

The sun peeked over the mountains with the promise of a blue-sky kind of day, but that promise didn't reach all the way into Alex's troubled soul as he left Mackenzie at the Hanstech facility with her sister. Nora had met them at the entrance where two security guards stood. He was uneasy leaving her, but Nora assured him that Mackenzie would be safe. No visitors were allowed in the facility over the next two weeks, and everyone in the building was employed by Hanstech.

Though the power company claimed the cause of the malfunction had to do with equipment failure, Mackenzie had suspected a cyberattack, and her suspicion remained. His too. And he couldn't wait for the moment he could come back and pick her up—whether two hours or ten, the day would feel long and arduous.

Before he started his vehicle, his cell rang. Keenan. He'd texted him last night after Mackenzie's nightmare. Keenan definitely knew more than enough about drones, and probably cybercriminals as well, to fill a book. Diplomatic Security Services was considered a global leader when it came to international investigations. Alex was well informed in threat analysis, cybersecurity, and counterterrorism, but he didn't feel like he understood their adversary in this situation. He wanted to know more. To understand. Getting in the head of Nebulous 2.0—and he had a strong gut feeling that was exactly who they were dealing with here—could help him strategize.

He answered his cell. "Knight here."

"Alex. We're becoming regular buddies. I don't think you ever talk to me so much, even when you're working."

"Funny."

"Think like a hacker."

Alex rubbed his forehead. "That's your answer to my question?"

"That's my answer to the question you didn't ask."

"You got me. I'm confused."

"You asked what I know about cybercriminals. Dude, that's a terrifically vague question."

"That's fair. But why tell me to think like a hacker?"

"We'll get to that. Why are you asking about cybercriminals, aka bad hackers? Black-hat hackers versus white-hat hackers? You know—all that spaghetti western terminology."

"Spaghetti western?"

"Come on. The good guys wear white hats, and the bad guys wear black hats."

Oh. "I got it."

"Well, why are you asking?"

How much could Alex say without offering too much information? Mackenzie trusted him. She also knew that at some point, within thirty-six hours—tomorrow afternoon, actually—they would be sharing everything with a cybercrime division at a federal agency. First, though, he would call his SSA.

"Just tell me about the cybercriminals, hackers, as people in general."

"Hmm. Key philosophies. Let's see. Hacking is in the very nature of a hacker and also a culture. Take a kid who gets his kicks out of hacking into the local school records. First, he's curious and gets a taste of what he can do. What he can change. He gets a taste of the power. And then he tries something bigger just to push the boundaries of what's possible. How far he can reach. And that excites him. He's all-powerful. No one can stop him. I'm getting chills myself. Maybe deep inside, I'm a hacker."

"That's comforting."

"Indeed."

"But really . . . why do it?" Alex asked. "Why hack into a computer?"

"And there's the question you didn't ask. If you were to think like a hacker, then you would understand." Keenan chuckled. "But in answer to that question—it depends. An ethical hacker also enjoys the game and beating the odds just like an unethical hacker. For either type of hacker, it's addictive. One method happens to be legal and the other way is not. But an unethical hacker does it for mischief and yes, sometimes . . . a grudge."

"What about a cause or an ideology?"

"Hacktivism is a different beast. Two groups come to mind. WikiLeaks and Anonymous. Their goals are usually political in nature, and the attacks are used against governments or big corporations."

Alex closed his eyes and processed the information.

"Does any of this answer your vague question or enable you to think like a hacker?"

What about a hacker who did it for his own cause *and* the money? "I'm not sure. What about violence?"

"What kind of violence?"

"Extreme violence. Murder."

"Give me context. Do you mean hacking caused the loss of life?"

Maybe. The elevator fail could have been injurious, if not deadly, to Mackenzie. If Rowan's pacemaker had been hacked, then yes. "In combination with physical attacks."

"I'm no profiler, Alex. Are you working undercover? I thought you were taking time off."

"I'm helping a friend who's in trouble."

"That makes sense. Trouble kind of follows you. I feel moderately better about our conversations now. Let me know what else I can do to help."

"You can find out everything about Hanstech. What is the company doing that I can't read about on their website? And a cybercriminal who went by the name Nebulous 2.0."

"Dude. I just got goosebumps. Okay. I'm late to a meeting already, but I'll do what I can."

Ending the call, Alex stared at his cell, then set it in the seat next to him. Now he was dragging Keenan into Mackenzie's private investigation, but he had no doubt that he would need help when the thirty-six hours were up.

Tomorrow.

Mackenzie might be the only person who could stop Nebulous 2.0 or find him, and quickly. He'd give her that chance. But he feared what the cybercriminal would try to do with drone technology. In the meantime, Alex would trust that Mackenzie was safe inside Hanstech. She had sworn off elevators for the foreseeable future.

Alex steered from the parking lot and drove down a side road next to the building to check out all the exits. A possible back entrance. A security vehicle coming from the opposite direction flashed its lights, and Alex stopped. The vehicle slowed next to him, and the security guard lowered his window. Alex did the same.

"This area is off-limits," the guard said.

"I was just turning around."

"Please just back up."

"Okay." The security guard's reaction made Alex suspect there was a back entrance used for testing or delivering drones.

After leaving Hanstech, he headed to the Rocky Mountain

Courage Memorial, a diversion he could use to keep him from obsessing over Mackenzie and constantly texting to check on her. She couldn't focus with interference, and they didn't have much time.

Keenan would find a few answers for him, and the county sheriff's department was looking into the shooter and the break-in last night. Alex would step back from Mackenzie's cybercriminal to get perspective—and focus instead on the vandal's identity.

He parked at the trailhead and hiked up. At the memorial, two men wearing helmets and safety jackets worked to replace his father's destroyed plaque, thanks to an anonymous donor, which he knew to be Terra's grandfather.

He wouldn't be alone. He hadn't thought he would be the only one here, but the noise of the men working was too distracting. He moved off trail and headed up an incline into the woods, where he found a nice flat rock, perfect for sitting and watching the activity below. Who knew? Maybe he would get lucky and see a suspicious individual approach the memorial. A small woman who acted and moved like the vandal on the video. If she carried a sledgehammer, that would be even better. But that would also be too easy.

The day was breezy, wrapping the thick scent of evergreens, pine needles, and earthy loam around him. A gust whipped over him, bringing a chill that clawed under his jacket even though it was almost summer. If he hiked up the trail, he could see the snow still clinging to the top of Stone Wolf Mountain and the surrounding peaks.

After the busyness of living in the city and the chaos of his travels, the fresh mountain air and quiet of the forest soothed his nerves. *Clink, clink, clink.* At least the stone plaque hammering was distant and could melt into the background noise in his mind.

And he heard Mackenzie's voice in his head. The sound of

pain fracturing her words as she spoke of her father. Everyone makes mistakes, especially when they're young. How could her mistake have cost her so much? She made it sound as if she'd been banished from her family—all so they could build the company.

In the end, what had any of it mattered? The wealthy and successful died the same as anyone else. Mackenzie had missed out on being with a family that had seemed to love her. Then again, she'd made her own choices too. College and career often dragged people away from home.

An insect buzzed, and he swatted it away. Why was he thinking about Mackenzie's choices? He'd made plenty of his own mistakes.

Her screams in the night rocked through him again. His heart rate jumped at the memory, and he dragged in the wild forest scents with a deep breath. He recalled the feral look she'd given him after the dream, and a million emotions exploded in his chest.

He stood and shook off the craziness. Brushed off a few pine needles that had fallen from the trees onto his shoulders and jeans.

Twenty minutes, and only a couple of hikers had passed on the trail, but no one had stopped to look at the memorial. To many of the locals, the memorial had probably become invisible. Most people didn't much care about those who'd given their lives for others in the years gone by.

But at least one person cared. Why had she taken a sledgehammer to the plaques?

He shifted forward, listening to the hammer hitting wood and stone below him. The sound pinged through him and again reminded him of his reaction to Mackenzie's pain, which was quickly becoming personal to him. He couldn't seem to shake it.

He remembered what Erin had said about the person who had vandalized the memorial . . .

"It's personal."

On that note, he had some questions for his mother. He needed to spend time with her too, but he would prefer to do so when his stepfather wasn't around.

He texted his mother.

> How's your day looking?

> I work the evening shift. How about lunch?

> I'll be there.

He glanced at his watch. Just enough time to stop by Stone Wolf Ranch and see about arranging for Mackenzie to stay in one of the new guest cabins. With Jack and Nathan visiting Terra and Erin frequently, there was often a contingent of law enforcement at the property, and he couldn't think of a better, safer place for Mackenzie to stay while he helped her work through the deadly exploits or vulnerabilities or whatever else she called them. Someone would have to be a complete fool to try anything at the ranch.

He wasn't sure which of the detectives had been assigned to the shooter case, but it seemed both Jack and Nathan were invested. On the way down the trail back to his vehicle, he called Nathan.

"This is Alex."

"I had a feeling you were going to call. Don't know anything about the intruder yet."

"What about the shooter on the trail?"

"We have casings. We've matched a few to your gun. Two that are no match and could belong to the shooter. If you want to swing by, you can pick up your gun."

"I'll be at the ranch later. Can you bring it to me there?"

"Sure enough."

"I don't suppose you have automatic license plate readers installed anywhere that could help us in this situation."

"A bi-county drug task force got awarded a grant to pay for the camera, but it was placed in an area suspected of trafficking—far from here. So no readers in place locally that can help us."

Yeah. What he suspected.

"What about wildlife or security cameras along that mountain road to the house? Anything?"

"I've requested the security feed from a gas station and a small grocery along the highway. You're talking hours of video, and if you didn't see the shooter, it's not like you're going to recognize her. It's possible she hiked a few miles down and caught another trail. I'm working on getting possible feed on all the roads that could connect to trailheads. But I wanted the footage in case we want to cross-reference a tip."

"I appreciate all you're doing. I got a glimpse of the shooter, enough to know it was a woman, so it's possible I would recognize her. If I get the chance, I'll come by to review whatever you get."

"I'll have someone cull it down so you only need to look at relevant footage."

"Sounds good." Ending the call, Alex climbed into his vehicle. *Lord, what am I missing? What else can I do?*

Stone Wolf Ranch wasn't far from the trailhead but was about twenty miles from Hanstech. After a stop at the ranch, Alex could lunch with Mom in Big Rapids, then head to the tech company to wait on Mackenzie.

At the ranch, Alex spotted Owen working with a client and waved, though he doubted Terra's brother had seen him. Maybe he should have called first, but he knew he'd find at least Erin here, and he wanted to get her input. At the porch, he paused when he heard a vehicle pulling in. Terra steered her forest service SUV right behind his rental car.

He waited for her at the door.

She approached, her demeanor telling him she was clearly

still in special agent mode. "And to what do I owe this pleasure?"

"I could ask you the same." He smiled. "What are you doing here in the middle of the day?"

She arched a brow. "I was working a couple miles away and thought I'd stop in and check on Erin. Actually, *Nathan* called to ask if I could check on her."

"Oh? Everything okay?"

She shrugged. "She could be in the middle of her podcast. But she didn't answer when he called or texted."

"Well, by all means, let's go. I'll follow you."

Terra headed for the door. "How's Mackenzie doing?"

"Actually, that's why I'm here. I know Erin's staying here with her mother for the time being. I wanted to ask what she thought about me putting Mackenzie up here too."

"And you didn't think to ask me?"

"You already offered use of the cabin, remember? Well, you offered it to me, personally."

"And you think by extension, Mackenzie."

He shrugged. "You have a problem with that?"

She smiled. "You know I don't."

"I thought to talk to Erin because she's here more than you are."

"And you know she won't have a problem either." Terra opened the door, and he followed her inside.

Erin stood at the counter sipping from a cup of tea. "Hi, you two." She put her palm in the air. "Don't tell me . . ."

Terra lifted both her palms in surrender. "Okay, I won't tell you."

"You're checking up on me for Nathan, aren't you? Seriously, guys, I'm alright. Of course, I'm good. I'm fine." Erin shoved her blonde hair behind her ears. "And did he call you too, Alex?"

Alex stared at his cell. "Nope. I can't imagine why he would."

Oh, he could imagine why. Nathan didn't want Alex making any moves on Erin, as if he would actually do that. Erin was like a sister to him, but Nathan was protective in a normal male jealous kind of way. Alex didn't fault him for that. "But I did just talk to him a few minutes ago."

Erin's eyes widened.

Alex pursed his lips, then a smile finally broke through. "Not about you, Erin. But really, give the guy a break. You should be glad he's so protective of you, especially after everything you and your mother just went through."

"I know, you're right." Erin sipped from her teacup.

Terra moved to the fridge and looked inside. "Do you want some tea or coffee? Or something for lunch?"

"I'm having lunch with Mom," he said. He directed his next words at Erin. "I'm thinking of moving Mackenzie out here for a few days. You're staying in one of the small guest cabins, right?"

Terra's brother, Owen, and their grandfather added the cabins as a convenience for Owen's equestrian therapy guests who had to travel long distances. Alex could see this ranch being completely transformed in the future, moving completely away from growing crops.

"Sure. It would be nice to have another neighbor." Erin stared at him over the rim of her cup, one brow arched.

Terra studied them both, then settled on Alex. "What's going on? I thought you brought her to the ranch on a date. It's easy to see you like her. But there's more, isn't there?"

He nodded. "I don't know how much more yet."

"Someone shot at her on the mountain biking trail," Erin said. "I was at the county offices and heard Nathan, Jack, and Trevor talking. Someone had followed her with a drone."

Maybe Alex was making a mistake, but he didn't have many options. "I don't want to bring danger to the ranch."

"I think it's a great idea for her to stay here." Terra smiled.

"We practically have a detachment of law enforcement here on most days."

"My thinking exactly," Alex said.

"We could add someone official, though," Terra said. "Oh, wait. You're her protection, aren't you?"

"Not officially, no."

"Do you know who or why someone would try to shoot her?" Terra asked.

And stalk us at the cabin last night.

"Not yet." Alex crossed his arms. "But keep your eyes out for anything suspicious."

Terra lifted a finger. "I might have something already."

He followed her outside and back around to the barn. She opened the old barn door and gestured. "Owen shot it out of the sky the day of the party. You guys had just left."

A mangled drone with a camera lay in the hay.

EIGHTEEN

Mackenzie had feared she would struggle to stay awake after the night she'd had.

She remembered now. In the dream, Alex told her they would die if she didn't use her magic, which she translated to mean special skills. It was only a dream, after all, but she was using her special skills right now, searching for anomalies in the data, weird log-in times for users, IP addresses, and open ports. Sniffing data packets. Malicious code injected into a good vulnerability patch that had come from a known and trusted source.

All of it.

And coming up empty.

If Nebulous 2.0 was behind the threat, then it could take her weeks without help. She would keep looking for his digital signature, though it could have changed significantly over the years. Still, she should recognize his intrusion.

God, please let it not be Nebulous 2.0.

She hadn't even considered the possibility until Alex brought it up, though she should have known. After all, Julian probably wouldn't have been scared enough to warn her otherwise. She continued skimming the results of the queries so far, and nothing snagged her attention.

She was also searching emails for suspicious activity. People really had no idea just how much cybersecurity professionals saw. Or what they could do. Like right now. She started digging into her keycard access. Maybe she could give herself greater access in case she came across a lower level in the building, after all, or other rooms with limited access. But she couldn't seem to expand the access and permissions on this keycard. Strange. There must be a master keycard.

She'd only been at it for a few hours when the phone at her desk rang. Oh. Was she supposed to answer that? Nora hadn't given her much in the way of instructions other than to keep her real purpose here to herself. No problem. Finally, the ringing stopped, only to start up again.

Okay, she should answer it then. "Mackenzie here."

"Can you come to my office?" Nora sounded short.

Great. Just what she hated about any corporate America job. Except she wasn't actually employed here. She grabbed her iPad to take notes on, opened the door to her fake office, and stepped into the short hall that opened up into the expanse of cubicles. She tried not to make eye contact with any programmers even though she wanted to. After all, any one of them could be the insider. A few programmers huddled around a computer screen at one cubicle. She was invisible. Good. She didn't need them asking why she, the new girl, got an office of her own with multiple monitors. She made a beeline for the stairwell at the end of the hallway. After last night's experience in the elevators, she wanted to make sure she wouldn't be caught again in the small dark space between floors.

On the first floor, she noticed someone exiting an office that was actually a hallway and then caught sight of another stairwell at the end of that hallway. And another set of elevators.

Bingo.

What she'd been looking for last night.

Okay, Nora, you'll have to wait.

Mackenzie entered the doors unnoticed. Though she had no intention of taking this set of elevators, which were disconnected from the main elevators, they reminded her of her words to her sister.

"Are you sure you don't have some lower level in the building where you're conducting all sorts of mad scientist experiments?"

Her sister's reaction made sense now, and she *was* hiding something. Hiding something and wasting Mackenzie's time. She pressed the elevator button and peered inside. Just one more level. A lower level.

She stepped inside and tried her keycard. Nothing. Then she headed for the stairwell, but she couldn't open that door either without the right keycard to give her access. Nora had to have one.

Mackenzie peeked out the office door. No one was watching. Actually, cameras were watching. She had to take the risk and hope no one questioned her actions. She exited through the doorway designated for authorized personnel only and then headed for her sister's office.

She walked right by the big desk behind which sat a young, hip woman—Nora's administrative assistant. The nameplate on the desk read MACI SANDERS. With her spiked black hair—a little blue at the sides—and multiple piercings along her earlobes, she didn't look anything like a stereotypical administrative assistant as she spoke on the phone using an extremely professional voice. Her big brown eyes widened as Mackenzie waltzed by her, through Nora's door, and into her expansive office.

When Mackenzie glanced back, she spotted a child coloring on the floor behind Maci's desk. What a cutie. Brown curls. And he must have sensed her watching, because he looked up at her at that moment with his momma's big brown eyes.

Mackenzie stepped back to the assistant's desk and crouched. "Hey, buddy. What's your name? My name's Mackenzie."

Maci hung up the phone and scooped the child into her arms. "This is my son, Cleo. He's nonverbal."

"He's precious."

His eyes grew wide, and then he pressed his face into his mother's shoulder as if he were super shy.

Maci gave Mackenzie an apologetic look. "The babysitter fell through. That's what I love about Hanstech. Miss Hanson assured us we're getting onsite day care soon."

"I'm so glad to hear that." Though she didn't have children of her own, she hoped her smile was understanding. "I didn't mean to disturb you."

The phone rang, and Maci answered as her son crawled out of her lap and back to his coloring book. Maybe she should be more social with other employees and could learn something that way, though it was doubtful. Plus, she didn't need them asking questions, and she certainly didn't want to tip off the insider. Though it would seem the cybercriminal behind the threat already knew she was here.

Mackenzie left Maci and Cleo and entered Nora's office again, only to find her sister on the phone. Nora was now the acting CEO. Honestly, she wasn't sure what position Nora held before. Regardless, Nora had to be feeling the pressure. The proverbial changing of the Hanstech guard seemed to be happening so fast. Rowan hadn't been dead even a week.

Why had Nora called her into her office? Unease crept up Mackenzie's spine as she lowered into a chair.

Nora ended the call, clearly on edge.

"How long will searching for hackers take? Per your request, I haven't alerted our cybersecurity team about possible intrusions. It seems to me you would want to work with them."

"I do at some point. Without their help, it could definitely take too long."

"Then why not ask for the help?"

"Though Hanstech isn't connected to the Internet, there are a few other ways someone can get into your system, but it's usually always someone on the inside or someone who gets to someone on the inside to facilitate the breach. It could even be one of your cybersecurity people. I want to rule that out before we bring them on, if it comes to that." Mackenzie scooted to the edge of her seat and leaned forward, putting on her experienced professional face in case Nora only saw her as a lost, confused little girl. "I have the skills to do this, and I won't let you down. But I need to know the *real* stakes here." At the moment, she could only guess.

"What have you learned so far?"

Ah. Avoid the question by asking one of your own. Good one, Nora. "I doubt you would understand half of what I told you."

"Talk to me like you would talk to a client." Nora was on edge. She was a stressed-out CEO today. Not Mackenzie's sister. Make that a scared, stressed-out CEO.

Mackenzie hadn't been working on it long enough to say for certain there was no evidence of an attack. But she knew enough to tread carefully. She sighed. "You're wasting my time."

"What are you talking about?"

"You asked for my help, but you're not letting me in. You haven't told me everything I need to know so that I can help. I can save Hanstech." *And protect you from facing the same fate Rowan suffered.* "Please."

"I've told you all I can tell you."

Mackenzie rubbed her forehead and bit back her frustration. Letting her this far into Hanstech had been a big step for Nora, especially if she was afraid because she believed someone was monitoring her actions. Or perhaps even controlling her? Blackmailing her? How did Mackenzie help Nora beyond what she was trying to do here?

She studied Nora's expression. *What are you thinking?*

Fear sparked in Nora's gaze before she narrowed it. There it was. She still didn't trust Mackenzie. "Please, learn what you can with what I've given you." Nora held her gaze, her eyes filled with an emotion Mackenzie couldn't read.

Is there a hidden message in her words? Or was Mackenzie reading too much into her expression? She was seeing cryptic messages everywhere and having weird dreams to top them off.

Before she could say more, Nora continued. "In the meantime, remember that this afternoon is team building."

No. Oh, please, no. She loathed those activities. "Is it really necessary? I don't want to lose my focus."

Nora nodded. "Remember your need to blend in and not stand out? Besides, if I'm not here, you're not here."

"What do you mean? Are you saying you don't trust me?"

"I trust you. But I don't want any questions later, in case this all goes wrong and your past comes up."

The vault of emotions—regret, anger, and hurt—burst open, and Mackenzie bolted from the chair. She stepped closer to Nora's desk, unwilling to back down. Even if Nora stood right next to her looking over her shoulder at the computer screen, she wouldn't know what Mackenzie was up to, so her request was absurd. But Mackenzie wasn't about to bring that up. "You do know that I was a kid. Those records are sealed. The past shouldn't come up. It's those same skills that can help you. Help us. Tell me who you're trying to protect."

Nora's shoulders sagged, and she averted her gaze to the panoramic window displaying a vast rich green forest and, beyond, snowcapped mountains. Her sister moved to the window and released a long breath.

"I'm sorry," Nora said. "You can't understand what it's like to try to live up to Dad's reputation, and now Rowan's. The legacies they left behind. Both had powerful, dynamic, and explosive personalities."

That's not me . . . Mackenzie thought she heard what Nora wasn't saying.

Compassion flooded her, and she stood next to her sister. "What are you talking about? You're every bit the powerhouse as either of them. You can do this. That is, if you want to. But more than that . . . tell me what more is going on."

Nora squeezed Mackenzie's hand in warning. Mackenzie squeezed it right back, reassuring her sister.

I'm back, and this time I'll take the chance to right the wrongs. Try to build a connection that was lost along the way with what family she had left. "Look, sis, when this is all over, I'd love to just hang out with you. We could get away for a day, a week. I don't know. But I do know that I'm in this with you. Let me help. You can trust me."

"Yeah?" Nora angled her head, a teasing grin on her lips.

"Sure, you can. I'm all grown up now. A professional. I teach ethical hacking at a university. I'm a trusted individual. In the summer, I do pen testing for charities."

A smirk lifted Nora's lips, and she stood taller. "Really?"

"As a way to make up for my mistakes."

Her sister turned and faced her, then took her hands. "I'm sorry I made it sound like I doubted you. Of course, what happened before isn't who you really are. I'm glad you're here to help." Nora brushed her dark bangs from her face and revealed the shadows under her eyes that she'd tried to hide with makeup. "In the meantime, please come with me this afternoon. It'll give us both a fresh perspective. Dad was big on this. Rowan too. I can't let them down. The employees will lose morale if I cancel."

Was Nora scared to go? Mackenzie could let the tests and algorithms run while she was gone. And maybe she would build more trust, more of a connection so Nora would share what she hadn't shared yet.

"Okay. I'll be there. About Rowan—I don't suppose there's any news yet?"

"The state pathologist will be doing the autopsy tomorrow. I've been told it could be sixty days before we get all the results back. If a drug caused a heart attack, the tox reports are going to tell us."

Mackenzie feared that his pacemaker had been hacked, but if so, Nebulous 2.0 would have made his tampering difficult to discover.

How can I live with myself if he was murdered?

A knock came at the door, and Carson stuck his head in. "You ready for lunch? You should join us too, Mackenzie, if you have time."

"Actually, this needs to be a working lunch, and we have some things to discuss. I hope you understand, Mackenzie." Nora had turned all professional again.

"Sure."

Mackenzie followed her sister out of her office to join Carson. While they got on the elevator, Mackenzie used the stairwell and made it to her office without running into anyone.

Glancing out her office window, she watched Nora get in the car with Carson, relieved that her sister decided she trusted her enough to leave her at the company, after all. Either that or with Carson's appearance, she'd forgotten her dictum.

Just where did they go for lunch around here besides the small onsite cafeteria? Mackenzie should grab lunch too before this afternoon's team-building adventure. Instead, she checked analytics and, as expected, spotted nothing out of the ordinary. Her chest constricted with frustration. This was a colossal waste of time. The cryptic message delivered via Freda Stone was ridiculous. And now, she was seeing secret coded messages everywhere.

She thought back to her sister's words. *"Learn what you can with what I've given you."*

What have you given me? Nothing except an air-gapped network that's completely separate from whatever you're doing on that secret lower level.

Mackenzie stepped out of her office and eyed the elevators she did not want to get on. She couldn't get down to that level without a keycard, but she had a plan. She had left her iPad on Nora's desk as an excuse to get back into her office while she was gone. Maybe she could find the keycard she needed. She headed down the stairs to Nora's office and stopped at Maci's desk.

"Hey, I forgot my iPad."

On the phone again, Maci waved her through. Maybe all the phone calls had to do with Rowan's recent passing. Whatever they were about, they distracted Maci.

Rushing around to her sister's desk, she tried the drawers. Locked. Nora really didn't trust anyone. Mackenzie stood and searched the room. Nora probably had the keycard on her. Mackenzie was stupid to even try. She grabbed her iPad from the desk—and just in time.

"Did you find it?" Maci stood at the door.

"Yes."

Mackenzie glanced behind the woman. "Where's Cleo?"

"My ex came and got him."

Mackenzie embraced her iPad to hide her shaking hands. She wasn't meant for this clandestine stuff—unless, of course, it was on a digital plane. She'd snooped around in computer systems, but she couldn't physically snoop around.

She moved to the large window and took in the expansive view.

Maci stood next to her. "It's gorgeous. Listen, I won't tell her you were looking for something in her office, if you won't tell her that I let you walk right in."

Mackenzie angled her head. Smart girl. A new ally perhaps? Except she and Nora weren't enemies. But they would be if Mackenzie lost her sister's trust. "What's on the lower level?"

"I don't know."

"You've never been down there?"

"No."

At least she hadn't denied the existence of a lower level.

A sound drew her attention around. Nora blew into her office like a whirlwind. "What's going on?"

"Mackenzie asked to wait for you in your office. We were admiring the view."

Nora's face brightened with expectation. She thought Mackenzie had something to report.

"Thank you, Maci."

"I'll leave you two alone now." Maci tossed Mackenzie a subtle smirk, then left, shutting the door behind her.

"That was a fast lunch."

"Carson got called away. A family emergency. So you learned something?"

"We both know this isn't about this network. It's about the *other* system that you've been keeping from me." That all-too-familiar fear surged in Nora's eyes again. Acid churned in Mackenzie's gut. "This whole time you've been letting me play around, knowing I wouldn't find anything."

"You shouldn't be here," Nora whispered so low Mackenzie barely heard her.

"But I *am* here." *In this mess with you.* "Now, let me into the other system."

Nora sighed deeply, painfully. "You need security clearance."

Mackenzie stared at her sister for a few breaths. "You mean clearance to get into Hanstech's restricted areas? Or do you mean *federal* security clearance, giving access to classified information?"

In that case, this could be about much more than Hanstech or saving her sister.

"Hanstech secured government contracts for a classified project."

"This whole time you've known. Why didn't you tell me? You wasted my time."

Nora stepped closer and lowered her voice to a whisper. "I told you to go home, didn't I?"

"And you also need my help. You want me to help. You're sending me mixed signals."

"My hands are tied."

"Then get me security clearance. Get me into that other system, and I can stop this . . . whatever it is, and whoever is doing this."

"I can't. Even with sealed records, your particular background would come up in the vetting process. It takes months anyway."

Nodding, Mackenzie pursed her lips. "And . . . we don't have that kind of time."

"No, we don't." Nora chewed on her lip. "Look, if you're going to do this, then you have to find your own way in."

Nora had clearly hoped Mackenzie would do that on her own without even asking about the other system. So it was like that, then. Mackenzie had thought as much, but she wanted to hear Nora say it so that she wasn't second-guessing what her sister truly wanted from her. What Nora suggested was illegal, and Mackenzie wasn't a criminal anymore. Though she didn't want to go that route, she didn't see another way. Unless . . .

"Then let's go to the Feds today. Let's get help—"

"No. We can't. You don't understand."

"Then help me to understand."

But Nora slowly shook her head. Someone had a chokehold on her. Mackenzie recognized that she wouldn't get anything more from her terrified sister.

She took a step closer. "Okay, Nora. I'll find my own way in. You do your thing and don't worry about me."

Looked like she would have to become a cybercriminal—again—to fix this.

NINETEEN

Alex pushed his thoughts of the drone Owen had shot down out of his mind, at least for the next hour. He wanted to look into it more, but he'd needed to head to Mom's for lunch. Besides, he'd confirmed that Keenan was sending him both drone detection and countermeasure devices. Keenan had also texted him regarding Nebulous 2.0. He'd been able to quickly discover that the cybercriminal remained at large. The Feds never identified him or made an arrest, though they had assured Mackenzie they would.

Had Nebulous 2.0 returned for revenge? Alex was leaning toward yes.

He pushed those thoughts away and cleared his mind for what came next.

Mom.

He stared at the wreath of lavender and pine hanging on the sage-colored front door. Mom and Ron purchased the small-frame house with yellow vinyl siding after Alex left for college. After he left, he just kept going and never looked back.

Like anyone that age, he'd been anxious to get out on his own, but it had felt more like he was running from his stepfather. The guy had never liked him and had always been hard on him. Looking back, Alex had to be honest with himself. Maybe it was more that Alex resented the man for trying to take Dad's place. Alex had still been grieving his father's death on that mountain when Mom married Ron.

Lifting his hand to knock, he pushed the remaining resentment down.

Mom opened the door and offered a wide smile. "Oh, hon, just come on in. You don't need to knock. My home is your home too. How many times do I have to tell you?"

"Probably every time." Alex stepped into the warm and cozy home, sunlight spilling through the windows to nurture a bazillion potted plants. "It's a jungle in here."

And reminded him of the home he'd grown up in. Memories, good and bad, rushed over him.

He smiled and drew his mother into a hug as if he hadn't seen her since he first got back to Montana. She squeezed him long and hard. Afraid he would slip away and stay gone for another year or two?

Finally releasing him, she patted him on the arm, then led him through the house. In the kitchen, she grabbed a couple of bowls. "I hope you don't mind that we're having leftovers. I warmed up last night's chili."

"Of course I don't mind. We could have a bowl of Cheerios and I'd be happy. It's not about the food. It's about the company." He grabbed glasses from the cabinet, added ice, and poured tea into them, then set them on the table. "Anything else I can do?"

Amusement filled her eyes. "Just chips or crackers to go with the chili. I'll get the small salad from the fridge."

Alex grabbed both items from the pantry. With the table ready for lunch, he pulled out a chair for his mother to sit.

"My, my." She took the seat he offered. "You know we're not so formal around here."

He leaned over and kissed his mom on the cheek. "It's not every day I get to have lunch with you."

"That's by choice." She flicked a look at him. "You know you can stay here while you're in town, and then you'll get breakfast, lunch, and dinner on the house."

Hurt edged her tone. He wished he could take it away, but there wasn't anything he could say that wouldn't make him feel more awkward. He grabbed her hand and said grace.

He had always loved Mom's chili and took a bite before diving into a conversation he'd wished to avoid. "I appreciate the offer, Mom. But it's not necessary. You and Ron have your routine, and I don't want to be a nuisance."

"You're never a nuisance. You're family."

He avoided her gaze and bit back the words he wanted to say—that Ron might have different thoughts about him staying. "At some point I might take you up on the offer, but right now . . ."

"I know, I know. You need your space."

From Ron. "I think this is your best chili yet." He grinned and kept eating.

"Aw, you're so sweet. You might think something different if you knew this isn't my chili."

"Not yours?" A neighbor's? A friend's? By the amusement in Mom's eyes, he realized he'd walked into a trap of sorts.

"It's Ron's." She snickered.

Alex almost choked. He chugged a few swallows of tea, then stared at his empty bowl. At least he was done.

"Would you like another bowl?" Mom asked.

"I'm good, thanks."

"You know, you never really gave him a chance."

"That's fair. It was just a rough time in my life, without losing my father on top of it."

"And you and your father were so close." She pressed her hand over his on the table. "I know that. And I'll be the first to admit, I didn't think you and Ron could get along anyway. At least back then. But you're older now, as we all are. All that to say, I hope you'll try a little harder."

Alex nibbled on crackers, fully aware she had pursed her lips and was staring at him, waiting, hoping for a response. He didn't live in Montana and saw no real point in trying harder to get along with Ron, except he hated to be the one to put that hurt in Mom's eyes. "I'll try, Mom. I'm cordial, and I laugh at his jokes. In fact, I'll take you both out for dinner while I'm in town."

"Oh? We'd love that. When?"

"Give me a few days to arrange it. I'm in the middle of helping a friend through something."

"What kind of friend?"

"I'll tell you more another time. Let's talk about you. What have you been up to?"

Fortunately, she was more than happy to share her plans for the backyard garden and a greenhouse she'd ordered. Then she moved on to talk about her job at the clinic and the fact that Ron would retire from the fire department in two years.

She pushed her empty bowl aside and stood. "Come on. I want to show you something."

He took one last sip of his drink, then followed her through the utility room and out into the backyard. She headed toward a large building separate from the house and the attached garage.

Alex took in the well-tended backyard and the foundation for the greenhouse on the far side as they approached the metal building. "This must be Ron's workshop."

"Yes, and no." She opened the side door and stepped in. He followed. Workbenches, sawhorses, and tools were neatly organized along the walls. A boat sat to one side, and it looked like Ron was repairing it. On the far side, a big tarp covered another vehicle.

Mom led Alex over to the tarp and pulled it back.

He gasped at the sight.

"Dad's old '67 Mustang." Cherry red.

Alex helped her heave the tarp all the way off the car.

"Not your father's. Yours."

He and Dad had spent countless hours restoring the classic, and his heart lurched at the memories. "I'm surprised you kept it when you moved."

"Ron wanted to sell it, but I kept it for you. Your father wanted you to have it. You should have taken it when you left."

But he'd been angry with Ron and told him off during his grand, drama-filled exit. He also hadn't wanted the memories of his biological father to drag him down, so he'd left the "Stang" behind, going so far as to tell Ron he could have the car, a mistake he'd regretted ever since, to go with all his other mistakes. "I don't know what to say, Mom."

His heart pounded, and emotion constricted his throat.

"A simple thank-you will do."

He caught her up in a long hug. "Thanks for being such a good mother."

Tears welled in his eyes. Seriously? He was going to cry over his mother keeping the Mustang for him? He released her and walked around the car, pushing down the nostalgia so she wouldn't see just how much her thoughtfulness had affected him. How much he appreciated it.

"Catch."

He glanced up in time to grab the keys she tossed him. He couldn't find the words to express his appreciation, but there would be time. He would make the time with his mother.

She smiled. "You want to take it for a ride?"

"I do, I do. But I'm in the middle of some . . ." No. He couldn't tell her about what was going on at Hanstech with Mackenzie. "I'll return the rental car and come back for this. Get a friend to bring me. Thanks again, Mom."

Her smile was huge, and he didn't miss the tears of joy welling in her eyes. "Dad would be so proud of you, son."

"I hope that's true."

Silence hung between them as he stared at the Mustang, then again at his mother. He'd come here to talk to her, to ask her questions, but he wasn't sure now was the time.

"What's new with you?" she asked.

He got the feeling she was trying to move the conversation along so she wouldn't full-on sob. He was glad for the distraction too.

With her question, she'd opened the door to talk, and since Ron wasn't around, he shouldn't put off his own questions. Or again, maybe Alex needed to adjust his attitude toward the man. Let the past stay far behind him and try for something new. Still, Mom had waited until they were alone to show him the Mustang and officially hand it over. He wondered if Ron would have agreed with her decision.

"Well, you know I'm taking a short break. Vacation time, but not really a vacation. I wanted to see you, of course, but I'm looking into the vandalism at the memorial, unofficially. The county is working on it. But they'll take my help."

"I'm sure it's hard to come back here after living in DC and then who knows where around the world. You probably need to look into the vandalism to keep from getting bored out of your mind." She chuckled. "What have you learned?"

"Actually, I wanted to talk to you about that."

Subtle frown lines formed between her brows. "I'm listening."

"Fifteen years ago, around the time of the accident, before the accident, let's say. What do you remember?"

"Well, you were there, son. What do *you* remember?"

Why had she suddenly turned defensive? "I know what I remember. But I'm asking you. I'm working the angle that this vandalism is somehow . . . personal."

Mom was quiet for a few seconds, then said, "No. It's been fifteen years. If it was personal, why wait so long?"

"I can figure that out if I know why someone might have an issue with the plaques commemorating those who died on the mountain."

"Others have died on the mountain. Not just the SAR team that day."

He scratched his head. "True. But so far, two plaques, two members of the team have been targeted." Which could mean something, but he wasn't sure what. Or it could mean nothing and this could be a colossal waste of his time, or as Mom put it, a way to keep from getting bored. But helping Mackenzie left him anything but bored. He'd been told to rest his brain, as if he had some sort of traumatic brain injury and solving a mystery would slow his healing.

Mom closed her eyes. She drew in a breath, and her lips quivered slightly. Oh, he hadn't meant to hurt her. Had bringing back the memories of that time caused her pain?

"Mom, if this is too hard. . ."

"It's okay. You're right to ask. You were a kid, and there were things you didn't know about. Adult things." He was seventeen, almost eighteen, at the time, but apparently that still hadn't been adult enough for the much "older and wiser" adults.

He leaned forward and pressed his hand over hers. "What *adult* things?"

She pulled her hand away and her frown deepened. "I don't see how it could have anything to do with the vandalism."

"Just tell me."

"No. It doesn't matter. I can't." Tears welled in her eyes. This wasn't how Alex had hoped their conversation would go.

"Can't tell him what?" Ron stepped into his workshop and crossed his arms.

TWENTY

*E*nd Hunger Games"?

Of course her father would have come up with something so creative and inspiring that would end with employees delivering the nonperishable items won at the event to local food banks. But Mackenzie was no archer and missed her target in this sort-of tag challenge incorporated into a rigorous boot camp–style obstacle course.

But maybe this wasn't a waste of time and participating would help her find the insider who'd facilitated the gateway to cybercrime at Hanstech. Beyond that, Nora's life could be at risk, and Mackenzie didn't like the idea of her sister running around in the woods. She thought she and Nora would do the course together, but that hadn't happened.

Where are you, Nora?

Alex would be furious with this turn of events since he believed she was safe inside the building—the only reason he was willing to leave her.

Just make it through.

The activity would end at some point. Right? Well, maybe not soon enough. Sweat poured from her as she climbed a rope and swung across a small creek, then fell onto the other side, her head barely missing a rock. The two-mile course had been created to start about a mile from the Hanstech campus. She'd guess all these people participating were in shape, had practiced many times. A woman ran past her.

Red team.

Mackenzie was on the blue team.

Another red team member ran past—a guy this time. His Nerf archery gear was attached to his back. You had to keep all your gear throughout the obstacle course. He didn't stop to offer a hand and help her up. Of course—it was red against blue. Why would he?

She pushed up onto all fours, pulling her face from the well-beaten path of the obstacle course where many a shoe had roamed.

"You okay?" A man thrust out his hand.

He was on the blue team too. "Thanks, but I'm good."

She hopped to her feet as if she had all the energy in the world. At least when she finally returned to Michigan, she knew to up her physical fitness game.

On her feet, she dusted off the dirt. "You must do this a lot."

Drenched in sweat, he shrugged. "You get used to it. Too bad we couldn't have done paintball today. I prefer that to the archery."

"Me too." Um . . . not really.

He turned and continued jogging down the trail. More participants passed her.

Mackenzie would hike the rest of the way. She was done running the course like everyone else. What about people who couldn't participate for health reasons, or refused?

"On your left."

Mackenzie slowed and turned to watch her sister—on the opposing red team—jogging toward her.

"I'm surprised to see you pulling up the rear of your team," Mackenzie said.

"You're last too. So whichever one of us is faster is going to win for our team."

Nora passed her.

Mackenzie would walk the rest of the way, so she wouldn't be catching up to Nora. She wasn't accustomed to this kind of daily activity, though she had been at one time. She gasped for breath but emerged from the trees in time to see the red team cheering Nora on when she hit the target with her last Nerf arrow, then ran past the stone markers.

At least this was over.

And oddly, the blue team, who had lost because of her, cheered her on, then clapped her damp back when she practically dragged her feet—one foot in front of the other, that's all she had to do—over the invisible line. Everyone was pumped, except for her. She could see the smiles and the camaraderie. No one was in pain.

Except Mackenzie.

Everyone else seemed exhilarated by the challenge. Dad had been right. Team building helped coworkers get to know each other even better over time. But she hadn't learned anything that could help her discover who inside the company had helped the cybercriminal get into the system.

"Let's end this day right!" someone shouted. "The zip line is ready to go."

Another round of cheers.

Still catching her breath, Mackenzie frowned and watched as all the crazy fitness and outdoor enthusiasts cheered and walked in the same direction. She had only *imagined* she was an outdoor enthusiast.

The outdoor activities and fresh air brought new perspectives. She needed to look deeper into what she thought she could be missing. But first, she had to zip-line across a canyon with the Grayback River flowing along the bottom.

She hobbled forward to stand at the end of the line and

glanced behind her. Maybe she could follow the trail back to the facility. Then again, she didn't want to draw attention. Did they do a head count on the other side to make sure they weren't missing anyone? She stared at the setup again.

Two men who wore T-shirts with a zip-line company emblem—Cross-Country Zip—assisted individuals into the harness. *Oh, Lord . . .*

"Have you ever zip-lined before?" the man behind her asked, startling her.

Where had he come from? She thought she was the last person in line.

She turned as she stepped to the side, offering him a view of the line and the canyon. It was the same guy who had helped her on the trail.

"No." Maybe. A long time ago. "I'm accustomed to flat farmland. Flat cities. Flat everything."

"Well, you'll get a good view of the canyon." He shifted forward and thrust out his hand. "I'm sorry, I don't think we've met. I'm Chad, by the way."

"Mackenzie, and I really don't think I can do this." She watched someone traverse the zip line. "But how does everyone get back?"

"Oh, there are buses on the other side."

Huh. "Tell me, Chad. Do you think all this outdoor activity is appropriate? Doesn't it keep you from getting your work done?" She thought of all those queries she'd created to hunt for a cyberattacker.

"I can't see the harm in getting out of the office for an afternoon."

"But this isn't everyone."

"Right. Just a mix of people from every floor and division. That way we can get to know people outside of our circle."

Interesting.

"What circle are you in?" The lower-level division, perhaps? She kept her smile in place.

"Programmer."

"What programs are you working on?"

"Cybersecurity."

She thought her breath might have visibly whooshed out. There was so much she wanted to ask him.

Whoa, girl. Slow down. Don't scare the dude off. "How long have you worked at Hanstech?"

"I came on a few months ago." He inched forward toward the zip line, standing next to her.

The line was going entirely too fast. She should turn back before it was too late. She glanced behind her—she could hike back to the Hanstech offices. No one was forcing her to use the zip line.

"Where'd you move from?" she asked.

"Who says I moved from anywhere?"

"Come on. You're not from Montana." She hadn't meant to sound so blunt. "I mean, most people working in this tech sector come to work at Hanstech from out of state."

"Don't kid yourself. The Montana universities are meeting the local tech sector demand." He laughed, but it sounded forced. "But you're right. I'm not from Montana. I moved here from Virginia."

"Maybe we could have coffee sometime."

His smile faltered.

Oh. She hadn't meant to scare him off. She wasn't coming on to him or anything. "I mean . . . just hang out and talk shop."

He studied her. Measured her. The atmosphere and the tension around them shifted. "Sure. We could do that."

Another thrill seeker's scream made her shudder.

"For Rowan!" someone shouted. Others repeated the shout.

The team building, the competition, and the excitement all seemed entirely inappropriate to her. Mackenzie rubbed her temples. Still, she could see Dad in the middle of this, making it work. Making it all worth the effort. But somehow today just felt wrong. Creepy. Maybe it was just her. After all, she was here to find a dangerous criminal. And Nora was trapped and scared.

"And you're Rowan and Nora's sister, right?"

A breeze blasted over her from the mountains, but it didn't hide the cold chill that crawled down her back. "Um . . ." How did he know? Nora had told her to use Calhoun as her last name if anyone asked. Maybe it wasn't so hard to know Nora had a sister, though they didn't look anything alike.

What did she say? Caught by surprise, she stared too long. She wasn't cut out for this undercover business, unless it was across cyberspace.

He stepped closer, leaned in, and pointed to something across the canyon as he spoke under his breath. "I know why you're here."

Her heart jumped to her throat. Was he threatening her? Warning her?

Pulse pounding in her ears, she couldn't move. Couldn't speak. Just waited for what he might say next. He drew in a breath to say more—

The guy manning the zip line clapped his hands to get their attention.

"It's your turn." He gestured for Chad to strap into the harness.

Chad turned to her. "Ladies first."

"I . . . uh . . ." She glanced over her shoulder at the trail back through the woods. She should have run when she had the chance.

"It's fine. I'll go." Chad gently squeezed her arm and stepped forward to get into the harness.

He was offering her this—a sort of lifeline. So that was it then . . . he knew something. He wanted to connect with her. He glanced over his shoulder. The look he gave her seemed to confirm just that.

They would need to communicate. She and Nora weren't in this alone. Someone else knew there was a danger—an abstract, undefined danger. The worst kind.

Nebulous 2.0?

She watched him slide across with ease, and then the zip line stalled. His harness seemed to snag on something. He just hung there.

A snap echoed. Then he shouted, "Help!"

He plummeted, flailing and screaming, into the canyon.

TWENTY-ONE

The sky darkened with an approaching storm to match the fear that stirred inside his gut. Alex slammed on the brakes, and the vehicle skidded across the pebbled back road that ended at a viewpoint overlooking the canyon. He couldn't scramble out of the car fast enough, and then he had to weave through county sheriff's department vehicles, including a couple of fire trucks and an ambulance.

Search and rescue team members geared up to scale the canyon, but he suspected that with the river at the bottom, they could end up searching farther down. But he was making a lot of assumptions. Maybe the man who'd fallen in the freak accident had somehow survived the fall and the rushing river.

And maybe it wasn't an accident.

On the drive over, he'd asked Siri to give him the percentage of zip-line incidents across the country and world. No central repository of data had been collected, and no federal or state restrictions or safety measures were in place. Incidents involving severe injuries or fatalities were rare, but they existed.

A couple of shuttle buses idled on the side of the road. Hanstech employees. He suspected they had all been questioned—another assumption—and headed for the buses in search of Mackenzie.

God, please let this incident have nothing at all to do with Mackenzie or the company. Regardless of his silent prayer, the fear in his gut ramped up. Mackenzie was in danger.

While others were already on the buses, Mackenzie stood in between two county sheriff's vehicles speaking with someone official. His heart jumped to his throat. Alex weaved between the cars, rushing toward her.

Nathan stepped into Alex's path. "Give them a minute."

"Who's she talking to?"

"Trevor West. He's a county detective too."

Another detective? "How many detectives have you got?"

"Three." Nathan arched a brow.

"It wasn't an insult, man."

Alex focused on Mackenzie as she spoke to the detective.

"I know you prefer to be with her," Nathan said, "but let her finish first."

Yeah. Whatever. Alex exhaled slowly. He could show some gratitude. Nathan had called him, after all.

"Was she the last one he interviewed? Or did she witness more than the others?" He wanted details.

"My understanding is that she was talking to the man who died in the accident right before it happened. But most all of them saw him fall."

"So now they all get to go from a day of team building to therapy."

"Something like that."

Alex had questions. Many more questions. Especially for Mackenzie, who supposedly wanted him as protection, then didn't want him—at least with her at Hanstech—and hadn't called him. No, instead, he'd heard about the accident from Nathan. That call had, fortunately, been perfect timing in terms of pulling him out of an inquisition with Ron. He'd left his mother to tame the beast and rushed right over. As for Mackenzie not contacting him . . . he didn't know what he thought about that. Hurt and anger both twisted together and tangled around his heart.

"Thanks for calling me."

"I thought you'd want to know, given the events in the woods. It's understandable that she's shaken up. They all are. Erin shared that Mackenzie would be staying at the ranch. You're protecting her then?"

Nathan held his gaze, and he thought he caught a hint of accusation in his eyes—if Alex was protecting her, he wasn't doing a very good job. Or maybe he was only imagining that vibe coming from Nathan.

"I'm trying. But she's not making it easy."

He held back the anger, the frustration that he hadn't been here with her. It was one thing to be inside the facility, with security guards around. But it was another to be out in the woods. They needed to have a serious discussion about the level of protection she needed.

"Well, it's clear that she's been targeted, with the shooting in the woods and the break-in. And she's asked you to be a bodyguard of sorts. Do you know who's behind it?"

"No."

"Any ideas or rumors?"

"I'm working on it. I appreciate you asking. As soon as I have something to tell you, I'll let you know."

"Are you sure about that?" Nathan had crossed his arms. His stance was wide. He looked intimidating and official.

"I'm sure."

Across the way, Mackenzie nodded and looked distressed. The urge to go to her nearly undid him. But he would find out more from Nathan before he made that move. "The zip line gave way? What really happened? How is that even possible?"

Nathan rubbed his jaw. "Exactly. We're looking into it."

"What can you tell me? I know I'm not an investigator or with the county, but I'd appreciate learning anything you're willing to share."

Nathan appeared to measure his words. Unsure how much he should share with Alex? "Apparently the zip line was installed by a company out of New Jersey. As a matter of precaution and per their insurance, the zip-line company employees check the line and assist to make sure the harnesses are attached properly."

Alex shook his head. "Do you think it was an accident?"

"I'm leaning toward accident. But we'll look at all angles. Forensic techs will examine the harness when we find it. But as far as I know, it's still attached to the man. In the meantime, they can examine the clasp that remained on the zip line."

Alex pursed his lips. "You said Mackenzie was the last person to talk to him. So that means she was next in line?"

Nathan's frown deepened, and he pulled out his pad, then flipped through his notes. "Says here she could have gone next but hesitated, so Chad Hastings took her place."

What did that mean?

Nathan closed his pad and fixed his eyes on Alex. "I get the strong sense that you're not telling me everything."

Not yet. "I'm just worried about her."

"Has something else happened?"

"Nothing."

"It would be better for her if you told us *why* she needs protecting."

Nathan would keep pressing. Alex understood. "Look, as soon as I know something, I'll tell you. Let me know what the forensic tech says about the harness. Was it cut or weakened in some way? I don't see how this could fall under operator error since there are two guys put in place to manage it."

"We're interviewing them too."

"So is the man who plummeted presumed dead?"

"Witnesses saw him land in the river. He could have hit the bottom and been knocked unconscious or killed. No one saw him come back up for air."

Before Nathan could say more, Detective West ushered Mackenzie forward. She appeared dazed, and by the look in the detective's eyes, he was concerned for her. He seemed to be handing her off to Alex as the designated caretaker. Had she indicated to him that she wanted to speak with Alex?

He was here for her, after all. What about Nora? Where was she during all this? Alex hadn't thought to ask, and it was too late now.

He bent until he was eye level with her and hovered his hands over her arms, afraid that if he touched her, she might break. Though he knew she had to be strong to have already endured so much.

"Mackenzie," he said softly.

She blinked a few times, then tears spilled over. "Alex."

He said nothing else. Simply pulled her to him and wrapped his arms around her. She cried against him, soaking his shirt. He felt her wet tears against the skin on his chest. The deep anguish spilling out of her bore right through to his heart, drilled down to his bones. His knees shook, but he stood strong for her.

He had to be there for her next time.

He couldn't be too late for her . . .

He couldn't fail her too like he'd failed on the other side of the world.

As her tears became sniffles and hiccups, he glanced at the bus that remained idling. The other had already pulled out. Everyone at the event would probably need counseling after watching someone fall from a zip line, likely to their death. Next to the bus, a grim-faced Nora glanced at him, then climbed up into the bus. It shifted gears.

Mackenzie eased back from his arms and then stepped away.

She swiped at her wet cheeks and red-rimmed eyes. "I need to go. The bus is going to leave without me."

She turned to dash away. He snagged her wrist. "Mackenzie, I'm taking you."

Angling back to him, she blinked up at him. "I should stay with the group. I could . . . I could learn something."

Not in your current state of mind. He stepped closer and leaned in. "Mackenzie, I'll take you home."

"Home?"

"I made arrangements for you to stay at Stone Wolf Ranch at one of their new cabins. It'll be safe there."

She swiped at her eyes again, shoving her thick brown hair back behind her ears as the wind picked up and blew the strands across her face. "My stuff is back at Hanstech, so let's stop there first."

They started for his car, but she veered away from him and toward the viewpoint. He kept pace with her, his hand ready to grab her, steady her, if needed. She stopped at the edge of the canyon and glanced down, a little too close for comfort.

"What are you doing?" He gently took her hand and pulled her back from the edge a few steps.

"I need some space. I need to think."

He gave her a few moments.

When she finally looked at him, he could see the gears tumbling in her head. She glanced around them. "Let's get out of here."

Once they were inside the car and buckled in, he maneuvered around the emergency vehicles and steered over the bumpy unpaved road to the farm road, then connected with the long driveway into Hanstech. The spring storm had blown in cooler air, so he flipped on the heat. At the Hanstech facility, employees spilled out of the buses, some heading back into the building and others directly to their cars. Alex left his cell in the car so he wouldn't have to hand it off and received a visitor's badge from the security guard at the front desk so he could accompany Mackenzie into the building. They stopped by her office to get her briefcase containing her laptop, then headed to the lockers near the women's showers where he waited outside the door while she grabbed her purse and clothes.

They didn't converse but moved in silence through all the tasks. At the front desk, she retrieved her cell phone. She said nothing as he drove the twenty minutes to Stone Wolf Ranch. He didn't want to question her or push her for information. She needed space to process the events of this afternoon, but Alex had a feeling she knew something she wasn't sharing.

What was new?

He switched on the radio, and Paul Simon sang "Koda-chrome"—a happy, upbeat song to hopefully lift their moods. But somehow, even Paul Simon wasn't changing the atmosphere in the car.

Raindrops appeared on the windshield as he turned onto the drive that would take them to Stone Wolf Ranch. Instead of driving toward the main house, he took a small road through the woods to the new cabins in the back.

She shifted in the seat, and he could feel the tension rolling off her. "Where are you taking me?"

She didn't trust him? "Terra's grandfather is adding guest cabins in the back for those who have a long drive or come from too far to make the drive in a day. They can stay for a week or more at a time."

He sounded like a regular infomercial. Alex parked in front of the quaint cedar log cabin, shut off the car, then turned toward her and took in her grim features. He hated seeing her like this.

Lord, hasn't she been through enough already? Please help me keep her safe.

"The cabin is all set for you to stay here."

She sat quietly for a moment, just staring straight ahead. "Thank you. For everything. I . . . I didn't think when I asked for your help that . . . I thought that, well, you kind of speak my language. You know what I mean usually when I'm talking about cybersecurity issues. And you have the resources and—"

"It's okay, Mackenzie. I know why you asked, and I'm glad you did. And in fact, I have more resources than you probably thought." He gestured at the cabin. This opportunity had surprised him as well. "God was looking out for you."

"You mean the cabin?"

"I do. Are you ready to go inside? Or do you want to wait out the rain?"

In answer, she shoved open the door and ran to the front porch. He jumped out and caught up. They were soaking wet by the time they made it under the covered porch.

Soaking wet and cold.

He dug around in his pocket and held up the key for her. If she unlocked the door, she would feel more in control. More *at home.* She snatched the key and then tried to unlock the door, but her fingers kept slipping.

"Let me help," he said.

He reached for the key, but she didn't step away, and his fingers got tangled up with hers. The key fell to the ground, and they both bent down to grab it, bumping heads. He gripped the key, then stood and found himself much too close, her face inches from his.

The same longing that rose in his chest was reflected in her luminous eyes. Pulse pounding in his ears, Alex tried to remember to breathe. Attraction raced through him. She blinked as if to somehow break the connection or hide that she even felt a connection with him.

Raindrops clung to her cheeks, and she shivered.

His only intention had been to warm her when he cupped her cheeks and leaned close, then without any thought at all, his lips were gently pressed against hers. Soft and tender. A thrilling warmth flooded his belly, and though he took a step back, she clung to him and pressed her lips harder against his.

But now . . . now wasn't the time.

She was vulnerable. Hurt. Only a jerk would kiss her when she was struggling.

The crunch of tires signaled an approaching vehicle and interrupted the moment, breaking the spell. Mackenzie stepped back. He keenly felt the absence of her lips, her passion, and it took him maybe two seconds too long to compose himself as she stole the key from his hands.

She opened the door to the cabin while Alex shook off the moment, then turned to see Terra hopping out of her vehicle. She quickly closed the distance, her left brow arched. High.

Mackenzie had already stepped inside or, rather, fled—embarrassed that someone had seen them kiss?—but she'd left the door open.

Terra paused at the porch. "Looks like I got here just in time."

"I guess that depends on your perspective." But he couldn't agree more.

She grinned wryly and handed over his gun. "Nathan left this for you." Then she waltzed by him into the cabin.

"Welcome, Mackenzie." Terra's voice echoed back to him. "I just stopped by to show you around and make sure you know where everything is."

Good that Terra was here to reassure Mackenzie. In the meantime, Alex hiked around the cabin to look at the surrounding area. Stone Wolf Ranch was safe—even though Owen had shot down that drone. He'd sent images to Keenan, but it looked like the drone that had followed her in the woods the day of the shooting. Even so, there was no better place for Mackenzie to stay at the moment.

He and his friends would keep her safe.

Keenan was sending him a radio-frequency analyzer, anti-drone technology that he could use while here if necessary. Ignoring the now-misting rain, he hiked into the woods so he could peer at the cabin. A drone would have to fly pretty low to see into any of those windows, but he would be sure to tell her to keep the blinds drawn. Even a long-distance camera couldn't see through the thick trees surrounding the cabin, and in that case, the drone would need to move in closer—that is, if someone planned to watch Mackenzie.

Fury crawled over him at the thought of someone watching. Stalking. Of course, with all the new UAV technology coming out, someone could go so far as to attach heat-sensing technology to see right through the walls.

Bring it. He almost wanted the chance to detect the drone and drop it. He hiked all the way around, then entered the cabin. Mackenzie glanced from Terra to him, her face flushed.

And the memory of that kiss warmed him again.

Kissing her couldn't happen again. He was here to protect her. Not blow past her defenses and break her heart.

Or his.

TWENTY-TWO

Mackenzie shifted on the sofa, nursing her aches and pains from a day of activity to which she wasn't accustomed. More than that, her heart was bruised and her mind traumatized from watching her new acquaintance, Chad, fall to his death.

Exhaustion pressing down on her, she struggled to appreciate Alex, the man who was not only protecting her but also watching out for her. She'd showered and changed into comfy sweats, grateful that Alex had brought her duffel from his cabin. She appreciated that he'd arranged for her to stay at this ranch—like he said, he had more resources than she could have imagined. Here at the ranch, she hoped to stay out of reach of the ghosts from her past, present, and maybe even future.

And that kiss . . . her desperate emotional need for physical connection. But she knew it was so much more than that—when it came to Alex Knight. She'd liked him, really liked him, that very first day she spent with him. So throw them both together into a crucible and let the pressure build and heat up, and yeah . . . that kiss was bound to happen. Or was she making excuses for her own weakness?

Whatever the reason it happened, it couldn't have happened at a worse time. She didn't want to associate a man's death with the first kiss she shared with Alex.

She pressed her palms over her eyes. *Listen to me, I'm thinking about first kisses as though there will be more.* She let out a soft groan.

While sitting here, she certainly wasn't making progress on hunting for a cybercriminal, but on the other hand, she couldn't make progress until she found a way into the real target at Hanstech.

Alex shut the door. He'd been on the porch talking to Terra, who'd brought them barbecue, and he was supposed to explain to Terra that Mackenzie didn't feel up to hanging out with a bunch of strangers at the main house. Of course, Alex would word it better. She definitely didn't feel up to handling questions about what happened today. Or smiling. Or tolerating the gentle treatment. She couldn't be around people.

But if she was staying at the ranch where Alex's friends and their significant others frequently congregated, she would have to show up once in a while. Still, she couldn't seem to pull her gaze from the soothing green forest or the sound of rain dripping from the needles and leaves. She'd opened the window to listen to the rain, and when that stopped, the dripping slowed just enough to ease the tension in her neck and shoulders.

She glanced up to find Alex setting a plate with a barbecued chicken quarter, corn, and potatoes on the coffee table.

"You need to eat."

She recalled her first "date" with Alex. They'd eaten delicious grilled elk burgers at the ranch house. "It looks good. Your friends have all kinds of culinary talent."

"It's takeout. Erin picked it up in town." Alex came around to sit on the edge of the sofa.

"You need to eat too," she said.

"I will, if you will." He smiled, directing that entirely too-roguish grin at her, the grin that had probably broken too many hearts.

If she wasn't so gutted over today, her heart would be pounding—because, oh yeah, she liked his smile. "Why are you doing this?"

"What exactly am I doing?" Elbows on his thighs, he shifted forward. Alex had pushed up the sleeves of his shirt. One of his endearing habits, though she had no idea why she liked it so much.

"You're taking care of me." *I don't need to be taken care of.* If he wasn't here, she would survive. She'd survived on her own for years, long before he showed up. Not just survived but excelled. Succeeded. "When I asked you to help, I hadn't intended so much."

Except . . . someone had shot at her. Someone wanted her gone. And she still hadn't figured out what today was about. But a man was dead.

An accident?

Intentional?

Because of her or unrelated?

"I would be here anyway. Don't you know that?"

Yes. I do.

She shouldn't look so long into those deep gray eyes, because, really, what was she searching for? What did she think she would find?

"Mackenzie . . . about that . . ." His hesitation told her he was thinking about the kiss.

"About what?"

He rubbed his hand over his lips and chin. Something . . . untamed . . . sparked in his eyes. Her heart jumped. Yeah, he was thinking about that kiss. And right now, so was she. Was he going to apologize?

Mackenzie sat forward and stared at the barbecue. Eating

would be a distraction from this awkward moment. Time to redirect. "You said you would eat too."

He left her and headed to the kitchen, then came back with his own plate. He cut into the chicken, apparently unwilling to use his fingers. "Mackenzie . . . I . . ."

Again with the hesitation? "I don't want an apology for the kiss, okay?" There, she'd said it.

He grinned, and his gaze roamed her face and made her blush. Fortunately, he turned his attention to the food. Around bites, they talked about her job at the university. A safe enough topic.

Eating and talking about what happened today or anything else revolving around cybercrime would cause her to lose her appetite. She struggled as it was. He kept his questions light and simple. And she was more than happy to think about how much she enjoyed teaching kids to use their skills for good in the world of ethical hacking and cybersecurity.

"And I have a condo near Lake Michigan in a little town called Frankfort." She closed her eyes and sighed. "I usually spend summers walking the beach. I do some pen testing for charities on the side. My way of giving back."

He smiled around a mouthful of barbecue, admiration swimming in his gaze. She hadn't been looking for that from him. But seeing it warmed her down to her toes.

"Enough about me. What about you? Tell me about your assignment overseas. What have you been doing for the last three years, Alex?"

His expression immediately shifted to something entirely too dark, then flattened. As if he'd caught himself and schooled his features for her benefit. "What do you want to know?"

She smiled, hoping the question wouldn't bother him. "Oh, if you don't want to talk about it, that's fine. I told you a bit about my job and my life in Michigan."

"So you thought I'd want to share about mine."

Uh-oh. "Not if you don't want to." She'd caught him a time or two with a pained look in his eyes. She sensed that something bad had happened.

She couldn't take that searching stare—his questioning eyes piercing through her. Mackenzie grabbed their plates and headed for the kitchen sink.

"Hey, wait a minute. You don't need to clean up. I'll get it." He followed her into the small kitchen and reached for the plates.

She held them out of his reach, then stuck them in the sink.

"I'll do the dishes," he said. "You just relax."

"I'll make a deal with you. Tell me something about your life. Your job. It's no fair you know so much about mine. Tell me and you can do the dishes."

He laughed, and the sound sent tingles over her. "You know how to drive a hard bargain."

"Do we have a deal?"

He turned on the water. "Next time, let's use paper plates."

Next time. How long would she be here in Montana? How long would they be in this cabin? "Agreed. How about you wash, and I'll dry?"

"There's only two. I got it."

Leaning against the counter, she crossed her arms and watched him. Studied his profile. Would he share a piece of himself? Tell her about his job? She wouldn't press him. Wait. Oh, yes, she would. "What about our deal?"

He put the two plates away, then placed what remained in the takeout containers into the fridge.

"I was hoping you'd forget."

"Was it that bad?"

He grabbed her hand and led her back to the sofa. He took a chair across from her and leaned back. His gaze bored into her. "I'll tell you my story, if you'll tell me what you learned at Hanstech today. What you're holding back."

"You can't renegotiate."

"Oh, I can, and I just did."

"Okay, fine. Though I wasn't holding back. I just haven't found the right moment to talk." She closed her eyes and pressed her hand against her midsection. Nausea swirled at the image. The man's screams.

"I know it's been a rough day. But you're running out of time."

She sensed she was running out of time in other ways. Someone else could die.

Had Chad died because of—

"Alright." He pinched the bridge of his nose. "I'll tell you about my last assignment. The one that brought me all the way back to Montana. I'll share as much as I can, anyway."

That got her attention, which she imagined was his point—to save her from the trauma of today. She opened her eyes and watched him lean forward. Elbows against his thighs, he hung his head.

Whatever happened to put the pain in your face, that defeated demeanor across your shoulders, I'm so sorry, Alex.

Maybe she didn't want to hear it, after all, but she wouldn't back out now. She might never get another opportunity.

"I was on a temporary assignment in a small country you probably haven't even heard of."

Seriously? "Try me."

"You don't need to know those details. This isn't public knowledge, so don't share with anyone."

Mackenzie sat forward to focus on this story only a privileged few knew.

"I was an RSO on a PSD."

"Excuse me, English please."

"Right. RSO stands for regional security officer. Here in the States, we're called DS SA—diplomatic security special agent. Overseas it's RSO. We're assigned to US embassies and consulates all over the world on a PSD—Protective Security Detail team. Regardless of where we serve, we have atypical assignments."

"You mean, you do regular special agent stuff plus more than a regular federal agent?"

Surprise lit his eyes, and he rewarded her with a crooked, dimpled smile. "Exactly."

Alex sat up and angled his head as if listening to a noise in the house. Or outside. Mackenzie heard nothing except for continued dripping and a few buzzing insects. He relaxed. False alarm. Then he focused his attention on her again.

"I was assigned a team, the AXLE Team 3-5. All teams were designated AXLE with numbers assigned."

"Is that the real name?"

Half his cheek hitched again. "No. I'm changing the names to protect the innocent. To protect you. I ran high-profile missions into what I'll term an unsecured zone."

She almost wished she hadn't asked, because it seemed that by telling the story, the pain in his eyes had increased. If only she could comfort him in some way. She longed to reach over and cup his cheek, somehow wash away the pain.

"High-profile details took us into high-threat regions."

"The unsecured zone."

"You're listening."

"Of course."

"It means driving an armored Suburban mounted with large ECMs—"

"Wait. What's an ECM?"

"Electronic countermeasures—it's used in presidential and vice-presidential motorcades, or in the case of transporting high-profile assets. It should counter any IEDs or rocket-propelled grenades—anything that's a guided attack, it'll jam and can change jamming frequency depending on the range."

His frown deepened.

What had happened? And why was he choosing to share this specific story with her? But she wanted to know more. "I didn't mean to interrupt. Thanks for explaining."

"You're welcome." He shuddered slightly. She might have missed it if she hadn't been so focused on him.

"Our teams included just one DS agent or RSO, and the rest were a mix of military guys and private security guys, who were usually ex-military. Marines. Army Rangers. All experienced in combat. Oh, and a medic. I'm getting ahead of myself. As the AIC—agent in charge—I had the sole responsibility for the protectees, the high-profile passengers. I gathered all the details, coordinated all the points of contact. Everything. I didn't like transporting people into unsecure regions. No one did. But sometimes it happened. Those were the most intense trips. I reviewed and rereviewed the routes. Instructed the protectees how to get into the Suburban and where to sit."

"So what happened?" She wished she had kept her mouth shut. Let him tell his story. He was great with details.

He drew in a long, shaky breath.

Wow. Whatever happened still affected him. She wished he had sat next to her. Wished she was brave enough to reach across the distance and pull him closer.

"During an intel brief before our assignment, we learned that vehicle-borne improvised explosive devices had been used to attack a nearby hotel."

"In the unsecured zone?"

"Yep. There had been more attacks, and the area was increasingly volatile."

"Couldn't you just say no?"

"Not to these particular individuals. But the news meant our usual routes were impacted. And we had to move around the areas of recent explosions."

"And US motorcades were probably targets."

"Always. Or at least prime targets."

"I mean . . . by the locals?"

"Yes, especially during periods of unrest. We were on the move, but some of our planned routes had been shut down. I radioed the TOC—tactical operations center—for an update. Some of the other teams had to return without completing their missions."

"And they wanted you back?"

"Our mission was deemed critical, and we were required to complete it. We drove quickly through the streets in our four-vehicle motorcade. I already mentioned the lineup. The last vehicle held the shooters. Machine guns and sniper rifles."

He looked at her as though deciding if he would continue and how much to share and how much to hold back, then hung his head.

"We kept changing our route, but finally, we had to stop at a checkpoint. We slowed to a complete halt. Something we never wanted to do in a motorcade carrying a high-profile asset. Jacobs, the TC—tactical commander—got out to go talk to them and the situation escalated."

Mackenzie imagined she could see the weight on his shoulders. She wasn't sure if he would lift his head again, and her breath hitched. She knew his next words would reveal a mission gone wrong.

"Everything that happened next replays in my mind over and over."

She so got that. She was guilty of that kind of mental torture, but now wasn't the time to speak. She needed to listen. Apparently, he needed to tell her.

"It's like it all happened at the same instant, but in slow motion." He closed his eyes. "I don't want to relive this over and over."

And I'm making you . . .

"It was an ambush. Jacobs was gunned down. A massive explosion rocked the Suburban in front of me. The blast destroyed the engine and set the vehicle on fire. The cab maintained integrity and protected the passengers from the blast, but they still had to escape the fire. Then a machine gun from an approaching vehicle started in, trapping them. We were trained to protect, but that protection starts with not getting into these situations. I radioed for the HIRRT—the US embassy's Helicopter Insertion Rapid Response Team.

"I tried to save them. I tried . . . but team members held me back, thinking I would only die too. In the end, two of our guys died. Two of our guys plus . . . our protectee. The mission was a failure all around. I lost people. I lost Jacobs. He was a friend. He had a wife and a kid."

He pressed his face into his hands.

TWENTY-THREE

lex blew out a breath and lifted his gaze to meet Mackenzie's beautiful eyes, so filled with concern. And tears. For him? She suddenly jumped up and rushed around the couch. But he caught her wiping at her eyes. He hadn't meant to add his pain to her burden. Alex got up and followed Mackenzie, who had moved past him and stepped out onto the porch. He waited a breath or two to regain his composure after what he'd just shared, then joined her.

She leaned against a pine post, and he did the same against the opposite post.

She sighed. "Would you look at that? They set up the cabins to have the perfect view of the sunset, didn't they?"

"Looks like it." Bright purple and reddish-pink colored the billowing clouds that remained after the storm had moved out. He drew in the fresh scent that came after a drenching rain. The pines and spruces and cedars.

Memories of his past life in Montana rushed over him. He missed this place so much, but everything had changed. He'd learned too late that he couldn't go off for a few years and come back and expect to find things the same. Of course, he knew he wouldn't. Dad was gone from his life before he'd even left. He might have stayed otherwise. Then he wouldn't have met Mackenzie. Not that anything would come of meeting her, but why had their paths crossed twice—and this second time in such a spectacular way?

God working all things for good, as Dad used to paraphrase from the Bible.

While Mackenzie stared at the sunset, Alex took the opportunity to look at her. Her thick brown hair was a jumble of long curls, and he thought back to the kiss they'd shared.

"It's beautiful, isn't it?" she asked.

"Yes." His throat constricted with that one word so that it came out too husky.

She turned to look at him, and he knew she hadn't missed his tone. Her expression could undo him.

She averted her gaze. "But . . . we're not staying here to enjoy the scenery."

He couldn't help the half grin that emerged. "That's too bad, because it's pretty amazing from where I'm standing."

She stared at the ground. And he'd made her blush again. He wasn't making this easy for either of them. Mackenzie was right. They weren't here to enjoy the moment, but it was so tempting. How much life had he let pass him by already? He needed to make the hard choice here—life was filled with hard choices. Why couldn't they explore this connection they had with each other? Enjoy the time together—short or long?

But no. They were caught up in danger that neither of them had asked for. And after this was over, then what?

A horse whinnied in the distance, snapping his attention back. Alex pushed aside the errant thoughts, held out his hand, and led her back inside to sit on the sofa. She didn't resist.

"Are you ready to talk about it?"

"Talk about what?"

"You learned something today while at Hanstech. What is it?"

"I learned two things. First"—she rolled her head to look

at the ceiling and sighed—"the guy who died. He knew why I was there. He was going to tell me something."

"What do you mean he knew?"

"We were standing in line, waiting to take our turn on the zip line. We started up a conversation. He knew I was Rowan and Nora's sister even though I had been using the name Calhoun, which Nora had asked me to use."

"Come on, she had to know that wouldn't work around a bunch of brilliant people."

"It could work for a while. The point is that I wasn't supposed to draw attention. Knowing I was a Hanson would make people ask too many questions."

She was right. "So what happened next?"

"He leaned close and spoke so only I could hear him and said, 'I know why you're here.'"

Alex sat back. "What did he mean?"

"I didn't get the chance to ask. I had no idea if it was meant as a threat, but honestly . . . I don't think it was. He seemed like he wanted to help. Like he knew something. Now I'll never know what he might have told me."

Alex wanted to question the zip-line company workers about the incident, but he knew the local detectives would do that. But it could have been Mackenzie who fell. Had she thought of that?

He didn't want to scare her, but . . . "Were you supposed to be next in line?"

"I don't know. I don't remember. Chad tried to give me the chance to go, but he saw my hesitancy, so he stepped up to the zip line instead."

Mackenzie closed her eyes and shuddered.

Alex got up and went to the kitchen. Grabbed them a couple of sodas from the fridge, then returned and popped the tops. She opened her eyes at the sound.

"Thank you." She took the soda from him.

"Now, let's hear the second thing you learned."

"There's a lower level at Hanstech with servers, another system for which a security clearance is needed."

Wow. Alex suspected that might be the case. "That makes sense. There's the commercial side of Hanstech where they're developing the software for drones—what we read about on the website."

"And the other side with government contracts. They could be developing something for the military."

And he would need to communicate the threat to his superior. He rubbed his hand over his mouth, then dropped it. "Your thirty-six hours might be up sooner than expected. Someone needs to know about this."

"Please, Alex. I understand and I agree, but . . ." She pursed her lips.

"Now isn't the time to hold back. Tell me."

"I've told you that Nora is scared and claims someone is watching her. She's too scared to tell the authorities and ask for help. It could just be that the cybercriminal has her terrified. But I've wondered if Rowan had planned to go to the authorities when—"

"Okay. I hear you. Rowan could have been killed to prevent him from reporting the cybercrime potentially involving the theft of trade or military secrets." What more did Nora know that she hadn't shared with Mackenzie?

Alex moved to sit next to her and took her hands. "Mackenzie . . . this has moved into seriously dangerous waters. Possible espionage on what seems to be a high-value target. I can only guess at what Hanstech is up to."

Nausea roiled in his gut.

"I'm so close, Alex. Let me find a way to protect my sister."

"And you. I'm not sure that zip-line incident wasn't meant for you, if it was more than an accident."

"Or Chad was killed because of what he knew. Maybe he was the intended target."

He wished he could whisk her away from the danger, but she'd been pulled in, and he was grateful he was here to help.

God, direct me. What do I do here?

Again . . . hard choices. Going to the authorities could destroy her trust, the reason she'd come to him in the first place. And doing it at the wrong time—too soon—could also sabotage their chances of catching the criminal. If it was just one guy and not a cyberattack facilitated by a specific country. Russia. China. North Korea.

Alex rose and moved to peek out the window. They'd closed the mini blinds to protect against prying eyes—or, rather, spying eyes. The woods were quickly growing dark and the shadows long.

"What is it?" Mackenzie stood.

"I need to check the perimeter. Make sure all is well. In the meantime, you need to get some rest."

Would a hotel in town have been a better place to protect her? US Marshals most often used hotels for safe houses. A shadow moved, and he palmed his weapon, his heart rate ticking up as he took in a breath. Then an elk dashed away, and he slowly released his breath.

"In the morning, we'll make plans for the day. I need to be with you inside Hanstech." He turned to face her. "No more standing on the porch until we get to the bottom of this, okay?"

"Sure."

"Why don't you go lie down?"

"I can't rest. Not yet."

"What are you thinking?"

"That I'd like to go back to Hanstech after hours and explore unimpeded."

She wasn't at all deterred by the thought of a military-grade security on those servers. She'd been courted by the DSS, after all. He couldn't forget her skills were top-notch. Still . . .

"I thought you didn't want to do anything illegal, so why not ask your sister?"

"I've already asked her. She's hoping I will do what I need to do to save Hanstech and protect the both of us from Rowan's fate. At the same time, she suggested I go home. Essentially, she's too paralyzed, too terrified to make a real decision. The irony. The thing that estranged me from my family is the very thing that could save what's left of them now." Mackenzie released an incredulous bark. "If this is Nebulous 2.0, he'll make sure I pay whether I stay or go. So I'm staying. If I can get into the other system, then I can confirm whether it's him. I would recognize his code."

"What if that's how your friend realized this was a threat against you? He recognized the code. He knew he needed to deliver your message in person . . . all of that because he knew your old Nebulous 2.0 friend would be watching."

"It makes sense."

Alex thought through the warning she'd received. "The card with the warning, do you still have it?"

"Sure, I'll grab it." She scrambled off the sofa and dug out her wallet from her bag.

But she couldn't find the card. She dumped the contents of her bag onto the table. Alex wanted to tease her about all the stuff she carried around. She shoved most of it back inside, searching until she found the card, which she handed to Alex.

Alex flipped the card over to the QR code. "I think your friend sent you a message, but he sent you more. It's hidden in plain sight."

She absorbed his words, then realization dawned. "Data hidden in the image? Steganography? Why didn't I think of that?"

Alex scanned the QR code again with his cell, expecting to see the video game character. "Oh no."

"What is it?"

"It's a dead link. The message is gone." A pang of frustration burned in his chest. Then an idea hit him. "But is there a way we could retrieve the message by accessing the Internet archives?"

Mackenzie leaned in close to peer at his cell and the now-defunct link. "I doubt it would have been accessible to the automated crawlers, and it would have been password protected and inaccessible. My friend would have made sure of that."

"Then why did he take it down?" Alex asked.

"He didn't take it down. He's dead, remember? He could have set it up for a limited time, though."

"We'll never know if he sent more information." Alex worked his jaw. Why hadn't he thought of it earlier? "The game. Knight Alliance."

She chuckled. "Yeah?"

"Maybe he left a message in the game too. I think it's worth a look, don't you?"

His cell dinged with an alert, surprising him.

"What's that?" She stepped back. "What's going on?"

"Hold on." He pulled up the camera. "It's just a motion detector. I set up some cameras of my own near the memorial. Problem is that animals can set it off, and they do. It's probably nothing."

He peered at the dark images, barely discernible at night.

"That doesn't look like an animal to me," she said. "Could just be someone on the trail. But I don't think so."

"Me either."

"Let's go, then." Mackenzie grabbed her bag.

"Go where?"

"To check it out."

Heart pounding, he glanced up at her. "Mackenzie, I need to protect you."

"Come on. You're helping me. I'm helping you. You can tell me about the memorial on the way." She moved to the door and turned back around to face him. "Are you coming or what?"

"I don't know what I'll find there. It could be dangerous."

"I'll be safer with you there than here alone at the cabin. And if you set up cameras, then I figure it's important to you. Let's do this."

He followed her out and locked the door behind him. Once inside the vehicle, he called Terra to let her know what was happening and left a voice mail when she didn't answer. Then he did the same with Jack, who'd been working the case.

He handed off his cell to Mackenzie as he sped out of the drive and onto the highway. "Even though we're close, I doubt we'll make it there in time. It could be nothing."

"What's going on with the memorial? I saw that it had been damaged. But I don't know what happened."

Alex filled her in on the facts, then added, "Now I'm looking into the past."

"The past?"

"I talked to my mother and asked about the past. Fifteen years ago. She got upset and wouldn't tell me anything, claiming it wasn't related. Maybe it's not, but she clammed up when my stepfather showed up."

Mackenzie didn't respond but stared at the live camera footage on his cell.

"We're almost there. What do you see?"

"Nothing. It's dark and quiet."

After a few more minutes, he finally steered into the trailhead parking lot. "You should wait in the car."

"Not happening. I need the distraction, so don't waste your time trying to stop me."

He hopped out, and she joined him. Moonlight dappled through the damp forest. "The path is slippery."

When they were up the trail a ways, he thought he heard

the sound of a vehicle by the trailhead. Someone escaping? Someone approaching?

They continued up, slowly and quietly.

"Alex." The hissed whisper drew his attention from behind.

Palm to his gun, he turned to see a figure coming up the trail behind them.

"I got your message," Terra whispered. "Let's go."

When they could see the memorial through the trees, Alex stopped. He motioned for them to wait. Terra stepped off trail behind a tree to watch, and Alex did the same, Mackenzie at his side. The cameras didn't alert him on his cell to any movement.

Stepping back on the trail, Terra started toward the memorial, Alex and Mackenzie on her heels. She shined her flashlight into the woods, then around the memorial. "What did you see?" Terra asked.

"We got movement on my camera. Jack might have a better look on the cameras he set up."

"I don't see any new damage here. Honestly, I don't know why someone would bother with this. Or how someone intent on vandalizing a memorial in the woods could be caught."

"Maybe I should camp out." Alex laughed.

"For months at a time?"

Mackenzie wandered over to Alex's father's plaque. "I have an idea."

Alex moved to stand next to her, and Terra followed.

"I'm listening," he said.

"Why not hold a special ceremony to rededicate the memorial? That could draw out this unstable person. Around that time, someone could be out here hiding and watching."

Terra blew out a breath. "I appreciate the memorial commemorating my mother, your father, and Erin's stepfather, as well as others, but that seems like a lot of effort on our part. I can't speak for the county, but my guess is they don't have the resources."

Mackenzie moved around the plaques. "Wait a minute. Only two plaques have been destroyed." She looked from the plaque for Terra's mother to the one for Alex's father. "That could mean something."

Alex looked at Terra. "I agree. We talked about this. It seems I'm not the only one to see the obvious. You could ask your father about that time. He left after your mother died. Maybe there's more to it than we already know."

Like him, maybe Terra wasn't sure she wanted to know. Stirring up the past was never good for anyone. But perhaps that's what the vandalism was all about.

"I'll see what I can find out," she said. "In the meantime, I'm heading home."

"We should go too." He dreaded unearthing secrets best left buried.

He glanced at Mackenzie. In her case, he was pretty sure someone had already stirred up the past, and he and Mackenzie had to walk the path through the valley that held more than shadows of death.

TWENTY-FOUR

While Alex steered away from the trailhead, Mackenzie couldn't ignore the sense of urgency that weighed on her.

"Take me to Hanstech."

He slammed on the brakes, and the car slid across the gravel of the parking lot. "What? Why?"

"I need to see what's on that lower level."

"You already know. Servers. Another system that requires security clearance."

"My sister's in trouble. I'm in trouble. I need to get into the servers. Maybe I shouldn't have shared this with you. You could get into a lot of trouble, assisting a known criminal as she hacks into sensitive data." He didn't respond. *What does that mean?* "Alex, I need to know what you're thinking. Please . . . If you need out, want out, then tell me."

Glancing around at the darkness surrounding them, he accelerated, steering onto the paved road and in the opposite direction of Stone Wolf Ranch. So he was taking her to Hanstech, after all, and that was answer enough.

She slowly exhaled her relief, but it was short-lived. Anxiety prickled her skin. Physically breaking into this restricted area was pushing the danger and risk to the next level.

"I'm in this with you to the end, Mackenzie. How about we spin this tale another way. How about I'm a hero who helps you save the day."

She laughed. Actually laughed. "I like the sound of that, but is that realistic?"

"Let's not worry about it yet. Besides, how are you going to get into that system?"

She gave him a look, but he was focused on the road. "Really?"

"You need to think about this. What about your career? This could tarnish your reputation, and this time, it won't go into a sealed vault or be expunged."

"I've been thinking about it since I left Michigan. Why do I care about that when we're not safe? Nora is being held hostage by an invisible force, and I'm going to free her." *And myself.* "This is about cyber*security*, Alex. No one *with* security clearance—the cybersecurity group—has caught the threat. I'm the person to do this, and there isn't time to wait for permission."

He didn't respond, and she wondered what he was thinking, but she let him focus on the curvy mountain road until he approached the drive into Hanstech.

He slowed to a stop near the entrance and sighed. "What about the game? Let's check the game before we do this."

"We're here. Think about it, Alex. It's almost as if this door has been opened for us. But if you don't want to go . . ." *To sneak into a sensitive area.* A small thrill coursed through her. The same thrill she'd gotten as a kid when she held power over others through criminal hacking. She banished that thrill into the recesses of her mind.

Lord, help me. I don't want to be that person. I'm not that person.

Guilt and shame from her past invaded her thoughts and heart.

No, no, no . . .

But she needed to forgive herself.

Alex drove into the parking lot and headed for the front of the building. "If anyone is going to see what's down there, it's going to be me."

"And you can't get down there without my help, so I guess we're good to go, then."

He parked and turned off the car. "I want to see what Hanstech is actually doing—you know, the stuff they don't publish in their brochures or put online for the public."

He stared straight ahead and squeezed the steering wheel. Was he having second thoughts? "I get it. You work for the State Department. And you feel like you're getting in over your head." Mackenzie reached for his hand, still on the wheel, and covered it with hers. "I love hearing your positive attitude and spin on the story—that your part in this will be seen as heroic. We're all heroes for saving the day. When I went to the FBI with the cybercrime I'd committed and turned over all the information I had on both my partners, I didn't get any free passes. Maybe a couple of nods of approval that I'd done the right thing. I wasn't tried as an adult, but I was considered a delinquent and sentenced to community service." Julian too. They had both felt that Nebulous 2.0 was taking them to dark places they didn't want to go. Her throat constricted at the thought. What did the cybercriminal have in mind? What secrets was he stealing? "Hero status aside, the reality is that you could get into serious trouble."

He dropped his hands from the wheel but quickly grabbed her hand again and squeezed. She loved the connection she had with him, the feel of her fingers in his strong grip. Why did they have to go through this? Why couldn't they have met by chance again or through God making it all work out for them? Like normal people. But really, neither of them was normal.

"Mackenzie, I won't let you do this alone. I'm in this with you, no matter what. I hope I don't have to tell you again."

Brave man.

"You might." She sent him a wry grin.

But hearing the sincerity in his voice made her wonder how he could choose her over his career when he hardly even knew her. Mackenzie didn't want to be responsible for destroying anyone's life or future, like she'd almost done her own.

"So how do we get in? Security isn't going to let us walk in without a good reason, especially since it's past ten o'clock."

"It's been a rough day, so it's reasonable that I might need to get into my locker tonight since I left my iPad behind." The iPad was proving useful in brand-new ways. "Besides, it's night security. Probably Tilden. He's more likely to trust us and let you come with me this time on protective duty."

"You hope."

Yes, she did.

They scrambled out of the car, and she bounded toward the glass doors to peer inside. They were locked. Tilden approached, looking surprised, but unlocked the door.

He opened it but also blocked their path. "Miss Calhoun, is everything alright?"

She allowed the grief she truly felt to show on her face. "I left some stuff in my locker that I need."

"And you couldn't wait until morning?"

"Come on, man," Alex said. "It's been a difficult day."

Tilden nodded. "I didn't mean to give you a hard time. We're all shocked about what happened. I'm glad you weren't hurt too." His gaze moved to Alex. "Good to see you again."

"I didn't want her coming here alone."

"Good thinking. Seems like too many strange things are happening around here lately."

Mackenzie wanted to ask him more, but she wouldn't push.

Maybe after she looked at the lower level and got into the servers down below, she would ask Tilden what he'd seen.

He opened the door wider to allow them in. "Please drop your cell phones in the security box. I'll log that you left them but won't lock them away since you'll only be a minute."

Mackenzie lifted her empty hands, though her bag was on her shoulder. "I left mine in the car."

"Mine too." Alex held up his palms.

Nodding, Tilden gestured for them to continue forward, and he radioed to the other security guard that Alex and Mackenzie were headed to the lockers.

Once inside the foyer, Mackenzie realized her sneakers were squeaking. Alex's shoes made no sound at all. Figured.

"I'll be here at the desk if you need anything," he called. "Danny's checking the perimeter."

"We'll be fine," Alex said.

"Oh." Mackenzie whirled around. "I don't have my keycard for the elevator." Or the stairwell.

Tilden frowned slightly, and she held her breath and headed back to him. Mackenzie shrugged. "I'm not thinking clearly today."

He unlocked a box and then handed one over. "I'll need it back when you're done, but that'll take you where you need to go. I'm glad you're willing to use the elevators after your experience. I'm so sorry about that."

"They seem to be running fine now. Thanks, Tilden."

She took the keycard from him, then she and Alex headed to the elevators. She glanced over her shoulder, and she couldn't see Tilden. Good. She passed the elevators.

"You forgot your keycard?"

"Yes, actually. I dumped my purse looking for the card to scan the QR code, and I left it on the table. We were rushing out to the memorial, remember?" She hadn't thought she'd be coming here. But the advantage was that the keycard from

Tilden, with its black matte finish, looked different from hers and might be a master keycard with more permissions—one he didn't often hand out.

"The security guard trusts you," Alex whispered. "Does he know your true identity?"

"Yes."

Mackenzie led him to the end of the hall and through the office door. As she closed it behind them, relief washed over her that the door wasn't locked but probably should have been. "See, elevators here. Stairwell there," she said, pointing.

"And a sign that says AUTHORIZED PERSONNEL ONLY."

"Uh-huh." She moved to the elevators and tried the keycard. Nothing.

"What's wrong?"

"This keycard doesn't work. I thought it would." Mackenzie's heart rate kicked up. This was no time to panic. She took a deep breath. "It was worth a try."

"Your attempt could have triggered an alarm." Alex paced the small room.

"It could have."

"And what about cameras?"

"Yes. That too. Time for plan B."

"Glad you're not giving up so quickly."

"Never. I've come too far for that." She was all in, and there was no going back now.

"I'm just along for the ride, but we should hurry."

She led him back to the main elevators. Alex said nothing on the ride up to the third floor to her office. He followed her, and she closed the door and sat at her temporary desk.

"Care to share your plan B? If we don't return quickly, he's going to look for us."

"I know. So shut up and let me work."

"Are you hacking . . . I mean, using cybersecurity methods to—"

"Access the lower level with this keycard? Yes. And to fine-tune the cameras—loop them—for a few minutes. We have ten minutes before they loop back. I hope that's more time than we need, but I didn't want to take longer, or Tilden will come looking for us. My regular keycard wouldn't work on the lower level. I already tried. But this keycard is different. If I'm right, and this is a master. I have to try to add permissions."

"You seem to know a lot about the cameras."

"It's something I teach in class. Not how to hack into one but that security cameras are notoriously easy to hack. And the irony is that the cameras are intended to catch people committing crimes, but with the addition of the Internet and the software to run the cameras, cybercriminals can break into the camera itself."

And here we are . . . breaking all the rules to find a dangerous rule-breaker.

"Now to tweak this keycard."

"So why doesn't the company use biometrics instead?"

"I wasn't part of that decision-making process. But no matter the access method, credentials data—biometric or otherwise—is sent for authentication in the same way. Keycards are easy to manage. Now, let me work."

"Okay, okay."

"Come on . . ." she mumbled, willing her codes to work. "There. I'm in the system and just gave this keycard the ability to take me to the lower level. Now, let's go. We have one shot at this."

And for Mackenzie to gain access to the air-gapped system. She could be using the exact same technique that someone else had used to allow a cybercriminal access. Nothing had been revealed to the cybersecurity team, and that made her even more nervous. If she was the hacker, if she was Nebulous 2.0, she would steal all the sensitive data and then set the system to crash before anyone was the wiser. He'd done it before.

She had to find out if it was him. And if it was Nebulous 2.0, he had to know she was here. Alex had brought up the idea at the start—she was a threat to his plans. That's why she had been attacked.

They raced to the elevator and took it down to the first floor. Mackenzie hoped Tilden wasn't waiting for them. The door whooshed open, and she peeked out. She didn't see him. She and Alex hurried through the office doors to the second set of elevators. She pressed the button to open the door, and they stepped inside. Though the keycard should work, she held her breath as she thrust it in, then pressed the lower-level button.

The doors closed and the box started moving.

Down.

She hadn't wanted to get on a Hanstech elevator again. Maybe she should have used the stairwell instead, in case the cybercriminal was watching and wanted to mess with her again. Prevent her from getting into the servers below deck.

She had to work quickly, gather what intel she could.

To save government secrets. To save Nora.

She mentally prepared herself to commit a crime.

Forgive me . . .

TWENTY-FIVE

Alex braced himself for what came next.

He woulda, coulda, shoulda called his superior before heading into the bowels of Hanstech to reveal—no, wait, *protect*—secrets requiring security clearance. They were the good guys here. Everything was moving forward much too fast, and he couldn't stop the momentum. He just hoped his agency saw it that way too, and he and Mackenzie didn't lose everything.

Maybe that's what Nebulous 2.0 wanted. Destroying her reputation and career and landing her in prison could all be part of his plan. Except Alex knew that the cybercriminal at play here—Nebulous 2.0 or someone else, a country-sponsored network even—didn't want Mackenzie to disrupt their plans, and so they attacked her.

As the elevator took them to the lower level, the slowness of the ride left him too much time to second-guess his decision to go forward in this unsanctioned op. He reminded himself that he had no choice, really. He was in a position to find out more, to help stop this before things went too far. To that end, he would go forward and risk everything.

Lord, what have I gotten myself into?

Trouble found him everywhere he went.

Alex palmed the gun in his holster hidden under his jacket. He was sure Tilden had noticed, but the guard hadn't stopped him from entering the building, and he appreciated that the man had common sense enough to allow Alex to protect Mackenzie.

His muscles tensed as the elevator stopped. It only had to go one floor, but that seemed to take an eternity—maybe the lower level was deeper than the elevator indicated.

"What can we expect on the lower level? Please tell me no one is working down there."

Mackenzie shook her head. "We didn't see other cars in the parking lot, but I also looked at those cameras before looping them. I didn't see anyone."

He braced himself for what lay on the other side of the elevator door. The elevator dinged, and the doors whooshed open to reveal the dark lower level. Dark except for a few lights—white, blue, and some red—spilling from racks of servers behind glass walls.

Mackenzie exited the elevator and motion-detector lights popped on. Alex stepped out too but held her back.

"I'll go first."

"Make it quick," she said. "We have seven minutes before the cameras flip back."

He held his gun at his side. They passed the server room and found cubicles with desks and monitors, and beyond that, another glass wall.

No lights on behind it.

Mackenzie rushed forward and opened up the door to the server room, then slipped inside. He followed behind her. She walked through the tall racks as if searching for one in particular.

"What are we looking for?"

"You know the system is air-gapped. There's no network

interface. No Wi-Fi or Bluetooth. Nothing that could be used to send the data outside the machine."

"So how will you get in?" He had an idea but enjoyed watching her in her element.

"A method called Air-Fi. Think a MacGyver type of hack. I'll create an Air-Fi covert channel, via encryption keys and credentials, to start exfiltrating the data. These servers emit electromagnetic radiation, and anything with a Wi-Fi interface will pick up the exfiltrated data. Basically, Air-Fi mimics Wi-Fi. You just have to know how to plug into it. Once I'm in, I'll inject code to allow me to encode and read signals—exfiltration. Find the malware and deploy anti-malware code. It's slower than actual Wi-Fi but hard to detect."

"I suspect there's much more to it."

"I don't have time to explain."

He admired her skills. Her brain. Her smile and those bright eyes that flashed at him. She dug in her bag and pulled out a cell.

Alex arched a brow. "You told Tilden you left your cell in the car."

"I did. This isn't my cell. It's a cheap one I picked up on my drive to Montana. I've encoded it with the necessary information to allow me to gain access to the air-gapped system, just in case." She handed it to Alex. "And this is where you really get your hands dirty. I need you to set it on top of the server. I'm not tall enough."

He took the cell and could barely reach the top. "Once this goes up there, it's not coming down. And it's incriminating."

"And untraceable. The code will crash in forty-eight hours."

"We need to go to the authorities with this soon."

"Timing is everything, and we were out of time when I got that message. I'm afraid he's going to go for Nora. She brought me in. At the very least, she needs to be free from the threat."

Cyberwarfare used to be the way of the future but was now a present reality as well as a threat level on the scale with biological warfare. Companies were already being crippled via ransomware. In this case, no ransom was involved.

Alex headed toward the back end of the server room, opened the door, and stepped down. Across a short corridor, a glass-encased room remained in the dark.

Mackenzie followed him. "We need to hurry, Alex. What are you doing?"

He stood at the door, itching to get inside and take a look. He couldn't see inside the dark room because the dim lighting in the server room created a mirror effect.

"Have you ever considered that Nora could be behind everything?" He hadn't wanted to bring it up and hoped Mackenzie had already thought about it.

"No. She's too scared." Mackenzie stood next to him.

"It could be an act. Or she could be working with the person behind it, either by choice or because she's been threatened."

"I know my sister. She's not that good of an actor."

"Your emotions could be clouding the truth. You don't want her to be behind it."

In the reflection, Mackenzie shivered. He should have waited to bring up the possibility.

"It's impossible to see," she said.

Redirecting the conversation?

"Can you get us inside?"

"We have three minutes. And you can see that this time, a biometric handprint is required."

"I was hoping you would have a workaround."

"Nothing I can do in three minutes."

He removed the night-vision monocular from his jacket.

She arched a brow. "Really?"

"Aren't you glad I'm resourceful?" He peered through the monocular. "Looks like a large, disassembled drone on the table closest to the door. Lots of drones in various states of assembly. Looks like a test facility."

"Well, that makes sense. The software is tested here even though manufacturing is done elsewhere."

"I've seen enough. Let's get out of here," he said. "You get into that system, stop the attack, and find out where it's coming from. That's how we're going to save our skins."

When they turned around, he noticed a red light flashing on the far wall. "A silent alarm."

Mackenzie gasped. "What?" Fear edged her words.

"Come on." He grabbed her hand, and they ran toward the elevator.

"Wait. No. We should use the stairwell in case the elevator is compromised again."

His thoughts had been tracking that way as well. Perhaps Mackenzie wasn't the only person invading the code at Hanstech.

At the stairwell, Mackenzie used her keycard and headed up the steps. How much longer would it work before someone caught on?

"We need to head to the locker room. If anyone finds us, it needs to be at the lockers."

They entered the second floor. "Hurry," she gasped. She led him down a long hallway and pushed through a door. "This is the women's locker room, but you can come too since no one is here."

She quickly rushed down the long set of lockers, found hers, opened the combination padlock, and grabbed her iPad.

"You really did forget it?"

"I left it for just such an occasion." Then louder, she said, "Okay, I'm ready to go."

Tablet in hand, she slammed the locker door, then locked it.

Tilden stepped into view. "I was getting worried about you. The alarm went off."

"I didn't hear an alarm," Mackenzie said. "What's going on?"

"It's a silent alarm. Nothing showed on the cameras, though."

Tilden gave her a curious look. What did the man know about her skills and her reason for being here at Hanstech? Alex didn't like concealing their actions from the guard, but then again, the less Tilden knew, the safer he would be. And he had the feeling Tilden didn't miss anything.

"You should follow the protocol. Did you call for security backup?" Alex asked. *Listen to me. Telling the guy how to do his job.*

"They're on the way." Tilden studied Alex. Measuring him. Had he looked into Alex's background?

"Maybe we somehow set something off." Mackenzie handed Tilden the keycard.

Tilden glanced between them, his expression unreadable.

Alex wanted—no, *needed*—for his actions to be sanctioned. He couldn't wait the full thirty-six hours. This had gone too far, and he had let it. Too many questions grappled for space in his brain. Guilt suffused him. He didn't want the man to come to harm because of their actions.

"I have a law enforcement background. Do you need assistance?"

The man's cell buzzed, and he glanced at it. "My backup is here. Nothing's been breached that I can see on the cameras. Thanks for your offer, but it isn't safe at the moment. I'll escort you to your vehicle."

"Thanks, Tilden," Mackenzie said. "I can let Nora know about the alarm."

"I'll let her know." Tilden escorted them out of the locker room, down the elevators, then through the front door as two additional guards entered. Tilden stopped to brief them as he watched Alex and Mackenzie climb into the car.

"That was weird," she said.

"Obviously we set off an alarm." At least they were out now and had completed the mission.

"I don't know that it was us. I'll look into everything once I get into the system. We don't have much time. I only gave myself twelve hours to see what I need to see."

Alex started his vehicle and got on the road to Stone Wolf Ranch, then he sucked in a long breath. "Whatever happened back there, that was close, Mackenzie. Much too close."

"You need to pull over."

"What are you talking about?"

"I need to access the network and restore that keycard as well as remove any trace of the loop on the cameras."

Alex pulled off onto a side road and into the trees. He turned off the headlights.

Another vehicle whizzed past. Nora's Lexus. "There goes your sister. Are you sure the guard didn't know what we were up to?"

"I don't know, and right now, I don't care. I'll talk to Nora in the morning." Mackenzie had opened her iPad case, which included a keyboard.

He remained quiet and listened to the tapping keys and her breathing—pinched breaths and long exhales. A gasp or two, reflecting success. He smiled to himself—he never could have imagined this scenario.

She closed her iPad. "Okay, that's taken care of. Now, unless you want to sit here all night, get me back to the ranch—and fast. I need to find out what's going on and take down the cyberthreat before I'm shut out."

"I'm good with that." Alex steered them toward Stone Wolf Ranch, thinking about the huge risk they'd taken tonight. *God, please let us find the answers we need before it's too late.*

He drove the car right up to the cabin and insisted that he clear the place first, ignoring Mackenzie's obvious impatience. Back in the cabin she sat at the small table and focused on her laptop. He didn't think she was going to have enough time to find anything because it could take days, weeks, or months without a whole team—according to her. Except in her case, she thought she knew the potential cybercriminal suspect.

He itched to call his superior or Keenan.

"Quit pacing," she said. "You're nervous, and you're making me nervous."

She was on to him. He eyed his cell and looked at his boss's number.

These actions he'd taken with Mackenzie could break him or make him, but of course, it wasn't about him. Sometimes the door God opened for a person to walk through had more to do with the greater good.

"I'm going to go outside so I won't disturb you."

"I can imagine who you're calling at this hour, so don't. Besides, I already know stuff."

That got his attention. He stopped pacing. Did he want to know? "Like what?"

"DARPA."

The Defense Advanced Research Projects Agency. "I could see them working with Hanstech. Drones. AI. But what's the project?"

He moved to sit next to her and looked at her screen. She turned it away. "You can't call your people, Alex. You call them, the cybercriminal will find out, and I don't have a handle on this yet. I need to shut this hacker down before he can hurt anyone else."

Alex tucked his cell away—for the moment. He would learn as much as he could first. Then . . . *Sorry, Mackenzie, I have to inform the authorities.* Why did it feel like he was using her instead of helping her?

She would hate him when this was over.

TWENTY-SIX

t is *you* . . .

Mackenzie rubbed her arms and stared at the code rippling across her laptop. Waves of nausea rolled through her at the thought of what she'd done—breaking into the system, through the security parameters even after she gained access via her covert connection.

She wasn't part of the company. Not on the board. Not an official employee. But she was a Hanson, and, in a way, this was her company too. Her sister, her family, had been threatened. She didn't need to keep justifying her actions for saving the family name. Saving lives.

But she'd had to know, and now she could confirm that her past had risen up to attack her personally. Her family and . . . friends. She glanced at Alex. She had to stop Nebulous 2.0 before he could harm anyone else.

Hadn't she known, deep down, that this attack was him all along?

"I'll come for you when you least expect it."

And she *hadn't* expected it. She'd been counseled not to worry about him. She should have known better. And now he wanted to inflict his own personal brand of revenge. Payback for the money she and Julian lost him years ago—and much, much more. She admitted she'd been terrified those days would come back to bite her.

And Julian had been scared at the carnival. He'd known who the threat was from. The hidden message must have said as much, and she'd been too stunned to recognize he'd left a hidden message for her.

Alex leaned in close and peered over her shoulder at the laptop. "You said I can't call the agency because he'll know. Does that mean . . ."

"Yes. It's him." Her palms slicked, and she wiped them on her pants.

Alex moved to sit next to her, scooting the chair closer. "How do you *know* it's him . . . or her?"

"I'd always thought of Nebulous 2.0 as a man—the way he 'talked' to us before. The aggression. I could have been completely wrong, of course."

"Right, but how do you know it's actually Nebulous 2.0 and not someone else? If he's as skilled as you say, wouldn't he write self-erasing code? Fake his web addresses. Route his attacks through other people's devices?"

"He does it all. But I have the advantage in this case." She closed her eyes and drew in a calming breath. "You know when you hear someone speaking . . . you know their voice. Or a song on the radio, you know who's singing. I can recognize his voice."

"You're kidding. Even in boring code?"

"He has some tells. An extra parenthesis here and there. Certain styles. His previous attacks were what we call advanced persistent threats that build over time. I started there. I knew where to look, and that's where I found him. His tactics are sophisticated, but they haven't changed. He pursued me because he saw the skills I already had, then built on those and taught me . . . um . . . well, if I can say that."

Alex gently squeezed her shoulder. "You definitely can. You're one of a kind, Mackenzie. I'm surprised you're not part of the national response team of ethical hackers." He left his warm hand on her shoulder, and she soaked up his assurances.

"Who says I'm not?"

"Are you?"

She laughed. "If I were, this entire scenario would be different."

"So you found malicious code. And he's attacking Hanstech because he wants revenge."

"He's invaded the system, but his code isn't set to run yet. He's been here for a while. Exfiltrating information. I need to find his rogue access point and shut it down."

"Rogue access point. You mean an unauthorized rogue access point created by a malicious attacker as opposed to a well-meaning, unauthorized hacker, like what you did tonight?"

She flicked her gaze to him. "Yes. Mine is still also a rogue access point. The cybercriminal also could have gained access via Air-Fi through a well-placed smartphone, router, or even a fire alarm. I need to find that and shut it down before my access point is found and shut down."

Alex dropped his hand and paced again, which she tried to ignore. "He's stealing secrets. I need to—"

Make a call? Was that what he was going to say? She lifted a finger, signaling to Alex that she wanted quiet. "Tomorrow, while I'm at Hanstech, I'll search for the access point. I can physically walk through the place, and the amplitude should get stronger the closer I get. I'll work it that way, now that I know he is definitely in the system. In the meantime, I'm deploying my own countermeasures to stop his attacks."

Mackenzie spent another hour working to counter Nebulous 2.0's planned attack. A sense of purpose filled her, and even the feeling of victory that she'd found him. But it was short-lived, considering she alone was the reason he was in the Hanstech system.

A code name intrigued her—D-Swarmbut—but the data would take too long to go through. She searched the code name in another window, and after digging deep, found a short video clip. Tiny robots crawled along the street of a small town while drones swarmed above them—all working in tandem.

Alex was back, leaning over her shoulder. "Swarming drones?"

"One of DARPA's experiments. It's just like a sci-fi movie."

"Robots and all. Well, tiny ones."

"Gives me the creeps to think it's real."

"But they're good tiny robots that will assist in military missions." He sighed and moved away from her laptop. "UAVs are part of our military now. We know that."

"Alex, I know about drones. Dad wanted to use them for good, but there's a dark side to all this."

"They can be used against us." He crossed his arms and lifted his hand to his mouth in thought.

Alex was handsome and brilliant. Under these precarious circumstances, she couldn't believe her thoughts actually went there. But she couldn't stop them or the admiration she had for him, along with something warm that fluttered through her. She took a deep breath to clear her mind and waited for what he would say next.

"You mentioned the rogue access point. You're using a smartphone. What if he's doing the same thing, only he's accessing the information with a drone?"

She pursed her lips, pressed her fingers against them. "Hmm. The servers are underground, but there could be another entrance to the building. Maybe at the back. A tunnel. Something. I don't know. But you could be onto something."

Mackenzie rewatched the video with the drone and tiny

robots. It was a couple of years old, but because she found the code name reference on the secured servers, it left her to wonder what role Hanstech had played. Had Hanstech assisted in creating these drones? Was their current project along the same lines as what she saw in the video?

What if Nebulous 2.0 was putting additional code in for use later when the most damage could be done? That thought sent a chill down her spine.

Drones could be hacked. Code could be changed.

Her legs shook.

Maybe it was time for Alex to call his people. She was in over her head. Who did she think she was to take on Nebulous 2.0 all by herself? If only she had Julian to help. Maybe he'd planned to help. The message had been in the hidden data. If only she hadn't been an idiot.

"Alex . . . I think—"

Her cell buzzed with a 911 text from her sister. Mackenzie snatched it up.

> HELP! I'm trapped in my car. Someone hacked my car!

Mackenzie bolted off the sofa. "Oh no, Alex . . ."

"What's happened?" He rushed around to read the text as she typed her response.

> Where are you? We're coming to get you.

> It's not safe.

> Well, can you get out?

> No. He locked the doors. I have nothing to break the glass with.

"He?" Alex asked.

> I can't get out. I'm locked in.

Mackenzie gripped her cell too hard as she repeated her question.

> Where are you?

> Some forest road off the main road between my house and Hanstech.

> We'll head that way. Try to remember which forest road.

> I'm scared. Help me. But please don't call the police. He'll know!

Mackenzie looked at Alex. "We have to help her."

She grabbed her bag, along with her laptop, and rushed out the door, Alex following. He brandished his gun, a protective and determined expression on his face.

"I don't know what you think a gun is going to do against a hacker working through technology," she said as they got into his rental car.

"Protect you against a shooter in the woods. How about that?"

"Or since this is Montana, a bear."

"Seriously, can Nebulous 2.0 control her car like this?"

"Where have you been, Alex Knight? Surely a DSS agent knows the dangers."

"I've heard of a few incidents, but it's hard to believe."

"I have a friend who is an ethical hacker for the automobile industry. Nebulous 2.0 obviously found his way into Nora's Lexus. Hers has the latest and greatest technology. I hope your rental car is older. Less technology will keep us safe from his interference."

Alex accelerated, spinning out across the grass as he steered away from the cabin.

Alex Knight, you're quickly becoming my hero.

"Just head toward her house, and we'll backtrack and try to find her."

"Do you know how many forest roads are along that drive?"

Think. "Maybe I can hack into her GPS system and find her, except I don't want to trigger Nebulous 2.0 to hurt her even more." Fear for Nora curdled in her gut. What was he up to? Would he drive her car into a ravine? "We have to hurry before it's too late."

"I have an idea."

"Wait, where are you going?"

"Just a quick detour. I promise it will be worth it."

Mackenzie tried to text her sister, but they were in a dead zone, and the text wouldn't go through. Ten minutes in and her nerves had her wanting to crawl out of her skin. "This is taking too long. I'm going to call one of your county friends."

"I did already."

"What? When?"

"While you were grabbing your bag and computer. I texted Terra to let the gang know."

"The gang?"

"Yep. Easier that way."

"But she said whoever was controlling her car would know."

"Not likely. This isn't going through regular police channels."

He steered through a neighborhood and parked in front of a house. "We have to keep quiet."

"Where are we?"

"I'll explain later." Alex led her around between the houses. A dog barked nearby. He unlatched the gate and headed into the backyard. She assumed this was his family's home.

He headed to a big workshop at the back. Alex lifted a padlock on the door and groaned.

"What?"

Lights came on in the backyard and a man rushed out, cocking his shotgun.

"Great," Alex said. "Ron, it's me, Alex."

"What are you doing, sneaking around my house?"

A woman rushed around the man, pulling her robe tight. "Alex?" She continued forward. "Ron, what are you doing? It's your stepson. Alex is here for his car."

"*His* car?" he said, lowering the shotgun. "I didn't give him that car."

"You're right, you didn't. It wasn't yours to give. It *belongs* to him. You know he never meant those words back then. Wait here." Alex's mother stepped into the house for a moment and came out jangling keys on a key ring and handed them to Alex. "I'm sorry, son. I didn't know he would try to lock you out. He never locks this."

Mackenzie hated the tension she sensed between Alex and his stepfather.

"I'm sorry I didn't knock on your door first, but it's late and I didn't want to wake you. And it's an emergency."

Alex's mother glanced from Alex to Mackenzie and thrust her hand out with a smile. "I'm Alex's mother, Carol."

"I'm Mackenzie."

"It's nice to meet you. I hope Alex will bring you back during the day for lunch."

Alex unlocked the padlock and, inside the workshop, flipped on the lights. His mother pressed a button that opened the garage door. Alex yanked off a big tarp to reveal an old car.

A convertible Mustang.

What? She came here for . . . Oh. Now she got it.

He hopped in and started it. "Are you coming, or what?"

"Alex Arthur Knight. That's no way to treat your date."

"Oh, I'm no date." Mackenzie opened the door and sat in the leather seats.

No. I'm much more than a date.

What exactly she was when it came to Alex, she hadn't figured out. But she did know something about Alex. "Smart, getting this car."

"Old. No tech to break into."

"I like it."

And she liked Alex. A little too much.

His stepfather had lowered the shotgun and opened the wide gate so Alex could exit. He saluted the man as they drove by, but it was clear no love was lost there. She'd have to get that story from him, like he'd gotten part of her story from her.

But right now, Nora was in trouble. Mackenzie texted her again.

> Nora, we're on the way.

Mackenzie stared at her phone, waiting for a response. She tried not to panic. Nora could have lost the signal. She could have escaped. Terra and "the gang" could be there now helping her. She tried calling instead, but only got Nora's voice mail.

She squeezed her cell phone. They'd taken too long. "There's no answer, Alex. I'm scared. Can we call your friends again?"

He handed over his cell. Mackenzie found the contacts and called Terra.

"Alex," Terra answered.

"This is Mackenzie. We're on the way. Have you found her?"

"No. She could be anywhere. There are a lot of forest roads between her house and Hanstech, and they encompass hundreds, if not thousands, of acres."

Mackenzie's hands shook.

"What's going on, Mackenzie?" Terra asked.

"Someone hacked her car."

"But what can the hacker really do?"

"Microprocessors control practically everything in modern vehicles. He could accelerate. He could disable the brakes. Use your imagination."

"Oh . . . wait . . . I have an incoming call. Hold on."

Mackenzie waited while Alex accelerated until they found the main road Nora said she was near.

"It's not a self-driving car. So it's not like he could take over her steering wheel, right?" Alex tried to sound reassuring.

"He could change the destination of the GPS and control the vehicle that way. So, yes, the vehicle would seem to have a life of its own."

"Mackenzie!" Terra came back on the line, her voice excited.

"Jack found her car."

"Oh, thank goodness! Where?"

"On Old Camp Road, almost a half a mile from the main road." Mackenzie repeated the words so Alex could hear.

"But she's not there."

TWENTY-SEVEN

Alex was glad he'd contacted Terra immediately. Fortunately, he remembered where Old Camp Road was, and he accelerated.

Mackenzie groaned. "I lost the call. And she's missing. They found the car, but she's not in it."

"I'm heading over to Old Camp Road."

"You know it?"

"Yes." He put more confidence into his words than he felt and steered the Mustang around the mountain road.

"Where could she have gone?" Mackenzie leaned toward the window.

Dread curdled in his gut. "Given the scenario . . ."

"You think he would actually take her?" She blew out a ragged breath.

"Don't you?"

She didn't respond at first, then said, "It seems out of character."

"Does it? We need to be prepared for that strong possibility. Why else would he send her car into the woods?"

"To mess with her. To threaten her and keep her terrified."

"I hope you're right."

"Let's pray I'm right, and that Nora found a way to escape the car and fled the area because she was afraid."

He prayed under his breath, hating the additional possible scenarios that flashed through his mind. Bear or another dangerous animal. Falling into the nearby ravine to her death or the river and getting washed away.

"Don't worry, Mackenzie. We'll find her." Putting worry aside was easier said than done.

Mackenzie opened her laptop. "I'm going to . . . never mind. We're in a dead zone. I'm not going to do anything."

"Makes you wonder how he could control her car in a dead zone."

She sat up. "Maybe . . . maybe he got control but lost it because of the dead zone."

Hope poured from her gaze, and she reached over and squeezed his upper arm. At her touch, electricity raced up his arm. He focused on the road and tried to shake off the effect she had on him even in the direst situations.

This was the absolute wrong time for those kinds of thoughts about chemistry, attraction, emotions . . . Mackenzie.

A figure stepped out onto the highway directly in their path.

"Alex!" Mackenzie shouted at the same time he slammed on the brakes, and the squeal of tires ripped through the night, along with Mackenzie's scream, as the Mustang skidded forward until it finally stopped.

A woman stood in the road, waving them down.

"Nora!" Mackenzie jumped out and ran to her sister.

Heart pounding, Alex shook off the sheer panic that had engulfed him. He gulped a few calming breaths, then steered the Mustang off the road so it wouldn't become the victim of a late-night driver who wasn't paying attention.

He hopped out and joined the two sisters. "Let's get out of the middle of the road."

Mackenzie nodded, and they ushered Nora out of the road and over to the Mustang.

"Are you hurt?" he asked, glancing between her and Mackenzie.

Trembling, Nora sniffled and shook her head. He wasn't so sure about that.

"Come on, Nora," Mackenzie said. "Get in the car, and we'll go *somewhere safe.*"

Mackenzie glanced to Alex and held his gaze. She'd emphasized those last two words. She wanted him to take Nora to the Stone Wolf Ranch cabin?

She tried to urge her sister into the car, but Nora refused to move. "I can't. I can't get into the car. I can't. He—"

"Can't hack a '67 Mustang." Alex hadn't intended the note of pride that escaped.

Her eyes widened. "What?"

"You're safe," Mackenzie said. "Get in. You're safe now, Nora. I'm going to fix this. Fix it all. He's not going to hurt you."

Nora climbed into the back seat, and Mackenzie got into the passenger seat. Alex glanced around them. How far was she from Old Camp Road? Where were his friends?

He rushed around the Mustang and got into the driver's side.

"Carson will be worried about me. I need to call him. He's out of town, and we were talking when my cell went dead."

Alex steered onto the road. "Did you lose your cell?"

"I left it behind in the car." Nora's voice shook as if she was going through the terror of her experience again.

"Tell us what happened."

"It was like a prison. I was heading back from Hanstech and suddenly my car had a mind of its own. First it stopped. Then it turned down this road. I couldn't get control, then suddenly it just stopped. Of course, I wanted out and tried to open the door." Tears choked her words.

Alex and Mackenzie didn't push her. Just gave her the space she needed.

"Sorry. I feel like a sniveling idiot."

"You've been through a terrifying experience," Mackenzie said. "It's okay, Nora. Cry. Scream. Whatever you need to do. Just tell us what happened."

Quiet filled the cab of the Mustang for a few heartbeats, then . . .

"I tried to open the door . . . and nothing. It's just too automated. All of it. Stupid electronic car brains. I texted you. I tried to call Carson again, but I couldn't get a reliable signal."

"How did you get out?"

"I kept banging on the window and trying the door, and then suddenly I was able to open it. Just like that. My car was dead. I couldn't even turn it on, but I could open the door. Whoever had control either lost it or allowed me to open the door. Honestly, I'm not sure which thought scared me more. So I ran."

Well, that answered the question about why she hadn't stayed with the car.

"I was freaked out and took off running. But I didn't know if he was there waiting on me. Now it seems ridiculous to have thought he would be. I feel like an idiot. A driveling idiot."

"You're nothing of the kind, Nora. I'm just glad you're okay." Mackenzie handed her cell back to Nora. "Let Carson know you're okay, but nothing more."

"What do you mean 'but nothing more'? You think the hacker is listening to our calls?"

"You've said that you felt like you're being watched. You can't tell me you haven't thought of someone listening in on your calls. Regardless, I think it's better to be safe and limit the information we share."

While Nora left a voice mail for Carson, Alex headed for Old Camp Road, where his friends had found Nora's car. Maybe one of them was still with the vehicle, or if nothing else, he could finally get a signal on his cell.

"Where are you going?" Nora gasped. "Please don't take me back to my car. Not tonight."

"Relax, Nora, please." Mackenzie twisted in her seat to face her sister.

Alex adjusted the rearview mirror. "I need to let them know you're okay."

They would want to take her statement as well.

Mackenzie touched his arm. "You can call Terra and let her know. Please just take us back to . . ."

She didn't finish. She didn't have to. Nora was in a bad frame of mind, and she would be more upset if he took her back to the scene. His law enforcement friends would just have to be okay with it. He turned around and returned to Stone Wolf Ranch while he called Terra to let her know that Nora was safe and where they were headed.

One of the detectives planned to stop by the cabin to talk to Nora. Alex wasn't sure how much Nora would share and how much she would hold close.

Relief washed over him when he steered the Mustang up the long drive to Stone Wolf Ranch, and as he took the short drive back to the cabins, he noticed the lights were off in the cabin across the way where Erin and her mother were staying. Alex was relieved Terra hadn't woken Erin.

He stopped in front of the cabin and climbed out, then helped Mackenzie assist her sister. Nora's jacket, blouse, and pants had a few smudges and one rip near the hem of her slacks, but she looked psychologically traumatized more than physically harmed. Still, one could be as bad as the other.

"What is this place?" She glanced at Mackenzie.

"I . . . uh . . ." Mackenzie looked to Alex for help. "I'm staying here. Nora, I'm sorry. I guess I didn't mention that someone broke into Dad's—I mean, Rowan's—house. Alex took me there to gather my things after we were at Hanstech the night the elevator stalled. I hadn't intended to stay, and while we were there, someone broke in."

Nora speared Mackenzie with a look. "And you didn't tell me?"

"Let's have this conversation inside." After what she'd been through, now probably wasn't the best time to break that news to her. He ushered them forward toward the cabin.

"Why wasn't I informed?"

"I'm sorry." Mackenzie's demeanor seemed to change when she was around her sister. "We'll talk about everything once we get inside."

Alex nearly tripped over a box at the door. FedEx had found the cabin. Wait. Not in the middle of the night. Maybe it had been delivered to the main house and Owen or someone had brought it over.

He wouldn't complain. He'd been expecting a package and quickly examined the sender's information to make sure it was legit. He unlocked the cabin door, flipped on the lights, and cleared the two bedrooms. That was the best part—the cabin was easy to clear. The blinds were already drawn. Nothing smart about this cabin.

Mackenzie got Nora a glass of water and took it to where she waited on the sofa, face in her hands. Nora dropped her hands on Mackenzie's approach.

"You can stay here tonight, Nora." Mackenzie handed her the glass.

"Someone from the county will stop by later to talk to you and get your story," Alex said. "I suspect they'll be here any minute now."

A knock came at the door.

"It's Nathan." Alex eyed them. "He's going to take your statement, Nora."

"I . . . I don't want the police involved." Her forehead crinkled.

"They were there to help tonight."

He opened the door and stepped out to speak with Nathan. "Nora doesn't want you involved."

"And we aren't, officially. We're here to help as your friends, off-the-record, like you said."

"I know that, but can you convince *her*?"

"Let me try."

Alex opened the door for Nathan to enter and introduced Nora. For someone who hadn't wanted to involve the police, Nora spilled the sordid tale easily enough to Nathan. When she was done, Nathan gestured for Alex to follow him out. Alex glanced back at Mackenzie.

"Come on, Nora," she said. "You can have my room. Let's get you cleaned up."

Alex stepped outside onto the porch with Nathan, who leveled his gaze. "What do you know about who is behind this?"

"Not a lot." Which was true.

Nathan shook his head as he stalked out to his vehicle.

"Nathan, wait." Alex followed him out. "I'll tell you as soon as I can. I might need your help."

The words didn't seem to appease Nathan, who got in his vehicle and drove away. Alex sighed and grabbed his cell. His palms slicked against the smooth surface.

Think, Alex. Think. How did he explain everything succinctly and make his SSA understand?

Heart pounding, he made the call. The next few moments would alter his life forever. For good or for bad, he didn't know. He only knew he had to make that call, and he might have waited too long already.

Mackenzie would shut him out completely once she knew.

TWENTY-EIGHT

Mackenzie ushered her sister into the bathroom.

Nora gasped when she saw her reflection in the mirror. No mascara ran down her face, but a few small sticks had nicked her cheek and forehead. Her hair was tangled, and her eyes were red and puffy.

Grief squeezed Mackenzie's heart, but she was still grateful. Nora could have been seriously injured or killed.

Nora . . . the last of Mackenzie's family.

You are not going to take her from me, Nebulous 2.0, whoever you are.

"Let's get you washed up." Mackenzie gave Nora a quick shoulder hug. "I'll dig out some of my clothes if you want to change. They'll fit you."

Mackenzie glanced at the glowing red numbers on the side table in the bedroom—1:45 a.m.

Though she already suspected the reason, Mackenzie wanted to hear Nora's explanation. "Why were you going to Hanstech in the middle of the night?"

"I got a call about the alarms going off. I had asked Tilden to inform me about anomalies."

Either they had triggered it or Nebulous 2.0 set it off. He wanted to stop her from messing with his plans of revenge.

Nora splashed her face, then used a towel to wipe it dry. "Let me take a long, hot shower, okay? I need it."

"Sure." Mackenzie handed off the clothes.

Nora took one look at them and scrunched up her nose. "I suppose these will work in a pinch." Tears welled in her eyes. "Never mind me. That was rude."

"Well, this is a pinch if there ever was one." Mackenzie smiled for her sister's sake.

Nora laughed through her tears.

"I'm sorry, Nora. It's been a tough night for you."

Heart aching for Nora, Mackenzie pulled her into a hug. She held her sister for a few moments, then released her and stepped out of the bathroom.

Nora shut the bathroom door, and Mackenzie dropped into a chair to wait. Exhaustion threatened to overcome her, but she was determined to get answers from Nora tonight, despite the late hour.

When Nora finally stepped from the bathroom, Mackenzie stood and took her hand, then led her to the corner chair.

Nora eased into it and eyed the bed. "Are you going to let me sleep?"

"Could you?"

She rubbed her eyes. "If I could, I would hope that when I woke up, this had all been a nightmare."

Mackenzie sat on the edge of the bed. "To which nightmare are you referring?"

Nora stared at her. Deciding what she would tell her?

"We haven't had a real chance to talk since I got here," Mackenzie said. "I know you're scared. Someone is holding you hostage. I want to know everything. This isn't the time to hold back."

Nora glanced at the closed door. "What about *him*?"

"Alex? What about him?"

"Oh, come on. He's a federal agent. I saw right through your little secret."

"And we could use his help."

"Okay." Nora closed her eyes, her lip quivering. "Dad wanted our Montana facility to be secluded and private because of government contracts."

"In a relatively isolated environment, no one would see the tests you conducted."

"Right. But after Dad died, Rowan garnered contracts for sophisticated artificial intelligence and GIS—geographic information systems—mapping integrated with our drones. Next-level stuff. He said the future is now, and we need to be part of that big push."

That's why working with DARPA made total sense. "This is nothing I couldn't find out on my own or read in the news."

"I don't know what I should say. I don't know what I *can* say."

Frustration boiled. "With tonight's attack, I think we're past the point where you should hold anything back. Tell me what I need to know to fix this."

"We were working on a prototype when someone started sabotaging our efforts."

"A prototype that does what?"

"The list is long, but think Israel's Iron Dome kind of stuff." Nora covered her face.

Mackenzie thought her sister might hyperventilate. She rushed to her and knelt, grabbing her hands. "Nora, it's okay. It's going to be okay. Take steady breaths."

Nora's shoulders bobbed up and down as if she was dry sobbing. Mackenzie didn't know how to comfort her. When Nora finally dropped her hands, the fear Mackenzie saw in her eyes knocked her back on her seat.

"It's all about war. AI and cyberweapons. UAVs. Dad wanted to use drones for good to help people. I know he wouldn't have gone in this direction. Of course we have to keep our military prepared for the future, but that was never the Hanstech mission."

"Until Rowan."

Nora nodded. "A few months ago, Rowan said he suspected espionage."

Frowning, Mackenzie shook her head. "I'm confused. Sabotage and espionage are two very different things. Why would someone sabotage your efforts if what they really wanted was to steal your secrets?"

Distress lines grew in Nora's face. "I've given this a lot of thought. Rowan kept so much from me, but I think he discovered someone had infiltrated our system first. Then the sabotage happened to show who had the upper hand and to coerce Rowan into participating in the intellectual theft."

"At some point, he'd had enough and planned to report it," Mackenzie added.

Nora squeezed her eyes. "He was warned that if he communicated with the authorities, he would die . . . along with his company."

Mackenzie sucked in a breath. "So you knew . . . you *suspected* he was murdered to begin with, before I told you about the warning I received."

"I was scared. Too scared to talk. We can't even talk in our own home. I took a risk having an autopsy. But this cybercriminal, whoever he is, could probably change those results if he wanted, except he didn't change them."

"What . . . what are you talking about?"

"I heard earlier today after connecting with the pathologist, Dr. Sylvan. The pacemaker lost power." She stared at the floor and shook her head as if denying all of it had happened. "Now . . . finally, we can make funeral arrangements."

Seriously? That's what Nora was thinking about at this moment?

But not Mackenzie. Instead, all she could think about was that Nebulous 2.0 had terrorized her family so much that they couldn't even reach out to anyone to help them. She was one to talk, although she had reached out to Alex. Still, Mackenzie couldn't imagine that a hacker could inflict as much terror as she saw in her sister's eyes, even after causing Rowan's death. And Julian's. Mackenzie shivered. "What else, Nora? What aren't you telling me?"

"He physically threatened me."

"Wait . . . you mean . . . you're not talking about the car tonight."

"No."

"You *saw* him?"

"I woke up in my bed, and a man's hand was at my throat. I couldn't breathe." Nora's nostrils flared to go with the angry tears welling in her eyes.

Mackenzie's hand reflexively went to her own throat. Nora had been a prisoner in her own home.

"When was this? Did you get a good look at him?"

Nora closed her eyes. "Two nights ago. And no, it was dark. I couldn't see anything."

"Did he say something?"

"He didn't have to. I think he simply wanted me to know how very close he was, and he could kill me in any way he wanted."

Mackenzie was finally beginning to understand. "I'm so sorry, Nora. About everything. Have you told Carson?"

"No. I can't lose him too. Telling anyone puts them in danger." She lifted her gaze to Mackenzie. "That's why I wanted you to go home."

Rising from the bed, she paced—just like Alex. A shiver started in her belly and crawled over her. So Nebulous 2.0 was here in Montana? Was it really *him*—the guy the FBI couldn't get their hands on before? The man who had twisted Julian and Mackenzie's efforts on their Robin Hood scheme? Was this about the money they'd taken? Or something more?

But she'd had no contact with Nebulous 2.0. The FBI had kept tabs on her for years, waiting and watching for him. Why was he suddenly back in her life, targeting her family and the company? Was it solely to get to her?

She had the feeling that her being here was actually part of his plan. She would feel the most pain if she was involved and in the middle of it. Had Julian been part of a ruse to get her here? Or had Nebulous 2.0 simply played him, suspecting he would warn Mackenzie and set things in motion? She needed to learn if the hit-and-run driver had been found. The less cybercrime she committed through this ordeal, the better it would go for her on the other side.

Nora sighed, the sound bringing Mackenzie's thoughts back to the present.

"I know who's behind this. I recognized the code of the cybercriminal while hacking into the network at the lower level."

"You what? No wonder he tried to kill me tonight! You don't know what you've done!"

"He *wanted* me in the system." Or did she have it all wrong?

Nora rose and fisted her hands. "Are you saying it's the same guy you were in cahoots with years ago? And he's back now? Because if you are, then . . . then you brought this down on us. We're being punished. Rowan is dead because of—"

"Stop it," Alex said as he stepped into the room. "Mackenzie isn't to blame. We have a mad hacker on the loose. We need to report this."

"We can't. We'll lose our contracts. I can't be the reason for Hanstech's downfall."

"You won't lose your contracts unless you handle this cybersecurity breach poorly," Alex said.

It could be much too late for that.

"The security threat is only part of what's at stake," Nora

said. "Our lives are too. Then there's the prototype drone lost somewhere in the Montana wilderness."

Mackenzie climbed to her feet. "What *kind* of drone? You mentioned the Iron Dome, but I need to know details."

Nora pursed her lips as if she feared saying more, but then finally said, "I . . . I shouldn't be telling you, even in this situation. But our enemies are using autonomous lethal drones powered by artificial intelligence to engage soldiers. Our government and military are falling behind in this technological landscape, and this lethal threat is only going to grow over the months and years. It's an unacceptable risk level for our military forces, and for civilians right here at home."

Nora hadn't exactly answered the question.

"So Hanstech has built a weaponized drone with special capabilities?"

"No. It's next-level threat detection technology that will protect against explosive attack drones. It's not a matter of *if*, it's a matter of *when* those attacks will occur, and we're running out of time."

Alex's tone was somber. "And if someone gets their hands on the technology, they could develop the countermeasures, taking out our defense system against the weaponized drones."

Nora nodded. "And like I said, our prototype is missing. At first, I thought Rowan had died of a heart attack because we lost it."

"Then you absolutely have to tell someone," Alex said.

"And lose our contract and all future contracts—that is, if I even still have my life?"

Mackenzie squeezed her fists. "Don't worry. We'll find the missing drone."

And she wanted to meet this man face-to-face—and end this, once and for all. With Alex by her side, of course.

Nora yawned.

"We'll talk more tomorrow." Mackenzie headed for the door.

Mackenzie and Alex left her sister in her bedroom and shut the door. She turned to him. "I need to get back on Knights Alliance and see if Julian could have left a message there. You were right—this is about war. That's why Julian picked the game we used to play. It all connects and makes sense. And in fact, maybe there was no hidden message, but he expected the QR code to send me back to the game instead." She pressed her hand to her forehead. "Why didn't I think of that?"

"You're exhausted. That's why. Have you gotten a decent night's rest since this started?"

Mackenzie shook her head.

"Okay, just listen. Don't react. But what if Nebulous 2.0 *is* Julian, and thanks for that by the way. You never actually told me his name."

"And I didn't mean to this time. And no. There's no way. The FBI would have figured that out if he was. Julian is dead."

"Or he faked his death, Mackenzie. This cybercriminal has the ability to change up records. You haven't physically seen a body, so you can't know."

What? No. Julian was dead, and he hadn't faked his death. He couldn't be Nebulous 2.0. "I'm exhausted, and I can't think straight."

Mackenzie stepped forward, getting closer than she should have. But this guy . . . Alex. "I don't know how I can ever thank you for what you've done. Helping me. Protecting Nora and me." Why would he risk his own safety and career for her? Regardless of the reasons, she was grateful he had. "I knew I could trust you."

Alex's gaze—the intensity of his gray eyes—held her in place. What was he thinking? Then . . . pain flickered before it was shuttered away. He cleared his throat and gestured to his room. "You need to grab a few hours of shut-eye."

His abruptness startled her, though what had she expected? And she was so drained, she should sleep before she said something she regretted on a more . . . personal level. "Right. Okay. See you in the morning."

She headed for the bedroom and admired the beautiful handmade quilt on the bed. She'd already changed into sweats earlier that evening. Her duffel was in the room with Nora. So she simply pulled back the covers and climbed into the crisp sheets.

A soft knock came at the door, and she sat up. Nora couldn't sleep? "Come in."

The door opened wide, but it wasn't Nora. Alex's broad-shouldered silhouette filled the doorway.

"What happened?" She started throwing the covers off, grateful she slept in sweats.

He stepped forward. "No, stay."

"What's wrong?"

He approached the bed. "The timing is just . . . all wrong. I'm sorry, Mackenzie. But I can't wait any longer. I need to tell you."

She touched her feet to the area rug. "You're scaring me."

He sat next to her on the bed. "I'm sorry if this makes you uncomfortable, but I couldn't talk to you in front of Nora. I didn't want her to overhear either."

"Just spit it out." A million terrible scenarios ran through her mind.

"I told you I would help you, Mackenzie. But at some point, you had to know that I couldn't keep this to myself."

She stood and skewered him with an accusing glare. "You betrayed me?"

"No . . . no, no." He stood too and shook his head, stepping forward.

He'd pinned her between the bed and the wall. Light spilled from the main room into the bedroom, but his face was still in shadows. Even so, she felt those intense eyes on her. Imagined the stern set of his jaw. Her heart palpitated at his nearness.

"Betrayal is a strong word." His voice sounded breathy. Desperate.

He could probably hear her pounding heart.

"It's not like that," he added.

Her breathing had kicked up, and emotions choked her throat, her words. She found them, though. "Then what is it like? Tell me who you told. What you did."

"Alright, I'll tell you what you already know. You're in over your head. We're in over our heads. We can't keep it to ourselves when other lives could be in danger. This could be a matter of national security. I called my SSA to let him know what's been happening. I'm pretty sure I crossed a line last night. Still, I've been given permission to continue while he makes his own calls."

Pressing his hand against the wall, he leaned even closer, hung his head and sighed. "Me calling someone doesn't mean I betrayed you. I'm with you until the end, no matter what. You know this guy like no one else, and no one . . . *no one* could have found him already. And you're the person to stop him. I can . . ."

"Make it sound like we're heroes. I know, Alex. You said that earlier tonight. Now I understand." She stepped around him, leaving him to hold up the wall. "I trusted you, Alex."

"And you can still trust me!" he said a little too loud and turned to face her. Anguish edged his tone.

Why was he pleading with her to trust him? He obviously didn't care if she trusted him or not. Except the way her heart was beating at his nearness, the emotion pouring from him, she wanted him to care, and . . . she wanted to trust him. Still . . . "We should have made that decision together. You don't know what you've done, Alex. Now, please get out of my room. I mean . . . your room. Whatever. Get out."

Mackenzie maintained her composure as Alex turned and walked out. Then her entire body shook.

TWENTY-NINE

The next morning, Alex sat on a stool at the kitchen counter, listening to Terra and Jack's discussion about jurisdiction issues between federal government lands—national forests, for which she investigated as a special agent—and state and county. Nathan nodded and added his two-cent opinion that he probably thought was worth a dollar. Erin's mother, Celia, dumped biscuits into a bowl. Terra's brother, Owen, crunched on bacon and watched his sister and Jack as if entertained.

Erin chatted with Nora and Mackenzie about all things Montana.

And Alex breathed a sigh of relief, though he remained on edge.

"You don't know what you've done, Alex."

Yes, he did. And no, he didn't.

Mackenzie's words had chiseled through his armor and eaten away at his heart. Hammered his bones. The words had multiple layers. Maybe Nebulous 2.0 would ramp up his schedule now—Alex didn't know. That meant Mackenzie and Nora could both be in imminent danger.

He suspected that Nora had shared much more with her

sister in the bedroom before he'd heard her raised voice, accusing Mackenzie. Then he'd stepped in.

But he could forget about Mackenzie sharing anything with him now. Unless he could somehow earn her trust again.

Mackenzie hadn't looked at him this morning, but at least she hadn't run. She still needed him for protection, or maybe it was more about him protecting Nora. Perhaps Mackenzie would have left the cabin, left Alex behind, if she were on her own. But she hadn't let on to Nora that she was upset with Alex, and Nora seemed too caught up in the traumatic events to notice Mackenzie's attitude toward him.

He'd tried to start the day right—like any good Montanan—to set the stage for a better day by bringing Nora and Mackenzie up to the big house for a hearty Saturday morning breakfast and some perspective. And fresh air, mountain views, and the presence of his law enforcement friends, both old and new.

He was beginning to realize how grateful he was for Jack and Nathan. At first, years ago, he hadn't liked either of them. Erin and Terra had been like sisters to him, so why should he like the guys who'd broken their hearts? Though in Erin's case, she'd been the heartbreaker. But Alex had come to respect and trust both men.

He was counting on hanging out with this crew to help Mackenzie and Nora relax. Maybe even trust. Nora was wound much too tightly, and he feared she was going to stab Alex and Mackenzie in the backs—betray them in a devastating way.

He cringed as he recalled the sound of those harsh words on Mackenzie's lips last night. Maybe she was right, and he should have talked to her before making that call. Persuaded her. But she had wild ideas and operated in a different world from most, and he had this overwhelming fear that she was about to crawl into that world and he would lose her forever.

Like he ever *had* her.

Sure. He could admit that he *wanted* her in his life. Or maybe he wished she wanted him in *her* life. Either way, he had the urge to rush into something deep and profound with her, because, well, he had hoped he could have something lasting. But he'd blown that chance.

He stood from the counter and carried his plate over to the sink. He hadn't slept, and he struggled to know what he should do next, especially if Mackenzie was shutting him out. But one thing he knew—he needed to make another call to his SSA, Lynch, who'd requested Alex call him today. Alex especially needed to find out what Lynch had learned on his own calls. Alex remained uncertain about his standing, and he needed reassurance that his unofficial observation could continue. His boss would know more today about the reaction of his superiors to Alex's role in Mackenzie's hacking into Hanstech's servers.

Things were about to ramp up on all sides, and Alex braced himself. Admittedly, *he* was the one who needed a hearty breakfast and fresh air to face what came next. He stuck the rinsed dish in the dishwasher, closed it, and turned, drawing in a bolstering breath.

Nathan got a call in the middle of planting a kiss on Erin's lips while she was chewing on a mouthful of pancakes. He laughed and backed away, snatching up his cell.

At the serious frown on his face, everyone stopped talking and watched him, waiting for news.

He ended the call and stared at the cell. "I'm needed down at the river."

Erin slid off the stool. "The river? What's going on?"

Jack moved around the counter. "I'll come too."

Terra and Erin shared a look.

Nathan tucked the cell away. "I'm on the dive and recovery team."

Mackenzie gasped. "They found Chad Hastings?"

Nathan frowned. "I don't know . . . I can't say more."

"I'm going with you too," Erin said.

"No. I don't need an audience." But he eyed Jack. For moral support? The two had become fast friends.

And Alex? He'd been left out. He inwardly sighed. Like he expected to be included in their investigation.

But he pulled Terra aside. "I want to go too. Could you occupy Mackenzie and her sister?"

"You mean protect them?"

Was he making a mistake? Both sisters had in mind to pursue paths he disagreed with. "Yes. Are you up to it?"

"Owen's here. Gramps too. I have my trusty gun. No one will bother us here on the ranch."

"I'm more worried about them leaving."

"I'll do my best, but why do you want to go, Alex?"

"I . . . I need a break. I miss being in the field."

"I understand. Don't worry. Erin and I will keep them occupied. Keep them safe."

"Let me talk to Mackenzie about staying here while I go, but I wanted your agreement first."

"You have it."

Terra moved to the kitchen to scrape up the leftovers, and Mackenzie quickly took her place, dragging him by the hand out of earshot.

"You're leaving me?"

And just like that . . . all the dread, the pain of his words to her last night fell away. She still wanted him with her. Still needed him. He saw that much in her eyes. Or was he simply fooling himself? She dropped his hand.

He wanted to take it back. Grip her shoulders. He needed her touch again, but he refrained. "We still have a lot to talk about. A lot to work out. I'm worried about both you and your sister. This guy is dangerous. Please, just for a few hours, stay here. Keep Nora safe. You won't be alone. Terra is law enforcement. Her family—they all know how to protect you. That is, as long as you stay on the ranch. Can you do that for me?"

"Only if Nora will agree. I still have work to do on the system. Queries to analyze. I should have worked through the night."

"You can work from here, can't you?"

"Yes. As long as my access hasn't been discovered."

"It's a covert rogue access point, remember."

That earned him a smile. "Yes. And I also need to find that drone. I'll convince Nora I'm searching for it. You'd better get going. Nathan is leaving. Go with him. Trust me. I'll stay here and wait for you."

At her words, a fist squeezed his heart. "I trust you, Mackenzie." *Trust.* "And about . . ." Betrayal. Could he even say that word she'd used out loud? He hated the sound of it. He hadn't meant to betray her, but he'd known her reaction would be severe. Initially.

"It's okay, Alex. I was hurt, but you did what you believed you had to do. The only thing you could do, and you're keeping me in line."

He wasn't sure he'd done that at all, but he wouldn't argue. "You enjoy being on your computer, in your element, don't you?"

Something sparked in her eyes as she smiled. "While I enjoy navigating systems, stepping up to the challenge, there are other things I enjoy as well."

She winked and left him standing there as she turned and approached her sister, who had moved to look out the picture window with Erin.

Had Mackenzie been referring to their kiss? The thought stirred his insides, and he wasn't sure he appreciated the reminder, especially in the middle of this crisis.

He grabbed his oversized duffel bag—last night he'd tucked the drone tech that Keenan had sent him inside it—and rushed after Nathan and Jack, who climbed into one vehicle. Alex got into the back seat. Once they got to the river, he would call Lynch. Would Alex be completely shut down, leaving Mackenzie and Nora high and dry? He also had much more to report—everything he learned from Mackenzie and Nora after he'd already talked to Lynch.

On the drive over, Nathan stopped by the county offices to retrieve his diving gear. Equipment stowed in the back, he drove them to the location on Grayback River where the body was to be retrieved. Alex had been so absorbed in trying to unravel the convoluted threads, he'd barely noticed when they finally arrived. Nathan parked near the river next to other county and emergency vehicles.

Neither detective got out.

Instead, Nathan shifted in his seat to look back at Alex. "You've been lost in thought, man. Something bothering you?"

Alex was surprised at the question.

Before he could respond, Nathan added, "I'm asking as a friend. I speak for the both of us." He glanced at Jack, then back to Alex. "We don't have to be in detective mode all the time."

Alex liked the sound of that.

"And as your friends," Jack said, not sounding nearly as convincing, "we'd like to know what's really going on."

Alex wasn't sure what he could and couldn't say yet. He cracked his door. "We can talk later. I believe your recovery team is waiting for you."

While Nathan grabbed his gear, Alex followed Jack to meet up with Detective Trevor West next to another set of vehicles. Two other men were already getting on their dive gear, and Nathan joined them. All three county detectives were here, which could be considered a good thing. Not a lot of other demanding investigations. At least nothing more pressing than dragging a body from the river.

The recovery divers angled toward the rushing water. Alex

hung back, squeezing his cell phone. He finally lifted it to make the call he dreaded. The call that would reassure him or cost him everything. He hoped his agency saw things the same way that he did. That Mackenzie was as brilliant as they came, and he needed to see this through.

She was also determined and confident. And he knew that, deep down inside, she believed if she could fix this—catch this guy and turn the game around on him—that could redeem her from the damage she did in the past. It could free her.

But she could also end up making things worse. Others could die, and then she would truly never forgive herself.

He gritted his teeth, sent up a silent prayer, and stared at his cell to pull up the contact list.

Oh. Right. No signal out here in this ravine.

He had subconsciously sabotaged the call.

THIRTY

Mackenzie took advantage of the quiet at the ranch. Everyone was gone except for Terra, who was repotting plants on the porch. Staying behind to protect her? Nora was a mess, but Mackenzie had promised she would find the lost prototype drone before Nora returned from riding horses on the ranch with Erin and her mother. They hadn't gone trail riding because of the potential danger, but sticking close on the ranch should be safe enough, especially since Erin and her mother were both packing guns. If it had been any other time, Mackenzie would have taken a few pictures of Nora on a horse with the two armed women, and maybe laugh over it.

But this was no laughing matter.

If Carson had been in town last night, what would he have done? Come here with Nora? Or would he have whisked her away to safety elsewhere? Then again, would he have been at the Hanstech facilities trying to do damage control? How much did he know, if anything? Nora claimed she hadn't told him anything—but how could he not know that something was going on?

She needed to find out the cybercriminal's true identity.

That was the only way to stop what was happening now and prevent any future crimes. That was why she'd wanted a job with the DSS—to make an actual difference. To restore what was broken. But they rejected her. And with her hacking activity here, she would be ruined forever. But she refused to turn her back on this wrong that needed righting.

After all, in this case, Nebulous 2.0 had come back from the past to get revenge for what she'd done to him. He would probably lay this all in her lap so that she was charged with this particular cybercrime, of course, *after* he garnered the sensitive data he needed. And Mackenzie wasn't entirely sure Nora was correct in her assessment that the prototype drone was lost in the Montana wilderness. It could be more than lost. It could have been taken. That terrified her even more. In the wrong hands, who knew what would happen. And Nebulous 2.0 was definitely the wrong hands.

She had to bring him down. Somehow.

For now, Mackenzie worked off the assessment that the drone was within the nearest thousands of wilderness acreage. Nora hadn't given her any more details. How long had the prototype been missing?

Mackenzie eyed Terra on the porch. Shorts. Hair pinned up. Gardening gloves on. She paused to answer her cell. How long before the horseback riders would return?

Maybe she was fooling herself into thinking she was in the same league with Nebulous 2.0. But she'd brought this trouble to her family, and Rowan had been murdered. She couldn't let herself crumble now. She needed more answers. While she monitored the programs she'd deployed to destroy the malware Nebulous 2.0 installed, she needed to get back onto Knights Alliance and see if Julian left her a more detailed message. She could kick herself for not thinking of that sooner.

She shoved from the sofa and moved outside. Terra was up to her elbows in a huge pot.

"You enjoy playing in the dirt, huh?"

"I do. I love the outdoors. It's why I work for the forest service. You're welcome to join me."

"Um, no thanks. Actually, I was going to ask if I could borrow a computer. Laptop. Anything." Her iPad was back at the cabin. Worst case, she could hike back and get it.

Terra glanced through the open French door, though she probably couldn't see anything. "What happened? Did yours crash?"

"No. I . . . this is weird, but I need to use two at a time."

Terra's jaw dropped, then she clamped it shut. Then opened it again. "Well . . . I . . . I guess so." Terra angled her head. "Could I ask why?"

She really liked Terra, and her question seemed reasonable. "You can ask." She smiled. "But that doesn't mean I'll answer."

The woman's eyes grew wide. "Okay, then. Well . . ."

Mackenzie laughed. "I'm only teasing. I'm working on something, and if I were back in Michigan, I'd have multiple computers going so I could see the monitors simultaneously. Processing power, you know. And it's just easier and faster. If it's a problem, then never mind." She should have known she'd be asking too much. She turned to head back inside.

"No, wait." Terra followed her into the living area of the open floor plan. "I'm happy to let you use it. I have a personal one. But I'm not sure it has the capacity you need for whatever you're doing."

Mackenzie bit her lip. She spent so much time with geeks at the university where she taught, finding enough capacity was never an issue. "I guess we'll find out."

Terra removed her soil-covered gloves and set them on a table, then disappeared down the hall. Mackenzie sat on the sofa again and stared at her computer screen.

Terra returned with a laptop and handed it to Mackenzie. "It's all yours."

"Thank you." Mackenzie smiled. "I'll be done with it before you know it."

"I'm sure that's true, because I'm heading back outside." She started for the door, then paused and turned back. "Oh. The password is taped on the inside."

Old school. "Thanks."

Mackenzie set the laptop on the coffee table next to her own. Her heart sank when she opened the laptop and powered it up. Not a lot of processing power, but she would work with what she had. With the computers set up and running side by side on the table, she found the online gaming website for Knights Alliance and logged in, easily remembering the password she'd used repeatedly as a kid. She hadn't been on the game in well over a decade and was surprised she could still access her account.

She navigated the game and brought back to life her character, Freda, who bounced around in one spot waiting for Mackenzie to drive her actions. *If I were Julian, where would I hide the details?* Okay. Hmm. Maybe she should look for a castle. A stronghold. But which one? She hadn't played in so long . . .

Suddenly, a knight stood in front of Freda. Sir Galahad held his sword. He bowed.

She gasped.

What? How? He'd somehow programmed the game, his character, to deliver the rest of the message.

"How can I be of assistance, m'lady?"

She almost smiled at that. It felt just like old times. Mackenzie directed her character in conversation and movements. "I need your help. What can you tell me?"

"First, let's catch up. It took you long enough. I was starting to get worried."

Julian was good. Better than she remembered. He'd gone to so much work to program Sir Galahad's responses. She didn't want to catch up. She needed the details, and she needed them now. But she would have to play along to get the treasure she sought.

She groaned. "I'm fine. How are you?"

Please, please . . . just tell me the answers. I don't have time for games.

"Broken leg. But I'll live."

Broken leg? But I'll live? Wait. "Let me clarify. These responses are precoded responses. I'm talking to a program, aren't I? Julian is dead."

Like he would have thought to program a response to that. He couldn't have.

Sir Galahad stepped forward and held out his palms. "I'm not dead. I'm sorry if you thought that. So sorry. I've been waiting for days to hear from you."

"A friend told me you died."

"It must have been a hospital mix-up. I can imagine who arranged for that. And I'm surprised that I survived. As soon as I woke up, I refused an IV and meds. Too much could be tampered with. We both know who's responsible for my accident."

Julian had suspected it was Nebulous 2.0 all along. "You believe the hit-and-run was deliberate."

"Yes. I tried to warn you."

"I got the QR code, but if there was a hidden message, more details, I didn't see those in time."

"You didn't read the message inside the message."

"By the time I looked, it was gone."

"I couldn't risk leaving it up."

"What about now? Isn't it a risk being here—and now?"

"We never told Nebulous 2.0 about our gaming habits. If I'd left the QR code up too long, he might have learned that much."

Or had he already? Was she actually talking to Julian? It sounded like him. "How do I know it's really you? He could have discovered the QR code and known about Knights Alliance. After all, he knew you would be at the carnival trying to contact me, hence the hit-and-run."

"Good point."

"Well?" Mackenzie held her breath.

"Critical Alliance."

Relief whooshed through her. He remembered. They had always had a secret code between them—nothing too cryptic. Just a phrase that only they would know in case they needed to confirm their identities. She could only trust that Nebulous 2.0 didn't also know. Though she believed she spoke with Julian, she would look for tells.

"What more was on the message, Julian? I'm desperate. Things are bad. I think Nebulous 2.0 killed Rowan by tampering with his pacemaker. Last night, he hacked into Nora's car. Please help me."

"Don't worry. I only left you instructions to meet me here. You're here now, and that's all that matters. I've been waiting since I woke up in the hospital and could get on a computer."

"Can we back up? How did you know about his plans?"

Sir Galahad bounced around. Jumped high. Flicked his sword back and forth. Julian must have been typing or hesitant to share. Then, finally, the reply popped up. "I intercepted an encrypted message. Someone is trying to offload tech— classified drone technology—and destroy the facility where the tech is developed. I recognized his signature."

"It didn't take much for you to connect the dots and know it was Hanstech."

"He said he would come back for you. For us. Well, he got me . . . almost."

"And what about you? Do you want revenge for what I did? I talked you into going to the Feds. That decision changed my life in a lot of ways. Some not so good. I'm sure it was the same for you."

"I don't want revenge. I was young and reckless. We both were."

"But you're working on the dark web now . . ." *You're still reckless.*

"Let's keep this between us. But I'm working for the Feds."

What? "You mean . . ."

"I infiltrate and pass on intel."

Jealousy spiraled through her. She'd wanted that opportunity too—to work for the government and thwart cybercriminals. The DSS wouldn't have her.

"Which agency?"

"That's all I'm saying."

"That's fair. Did you pass on this intel to your agency?"

"I did. Months ago. The Feds weren't acting on the information fast enough, if they acted on it at all, and I couldn't wait for them any longer. I felt this was too personal to you, so I found you and handed off the warning. I couldn't risk any digital trail. The QR code was the only risk I took."

"And you paid a price. Thank you, Galahad. But Nebulous 2.0 is here in Montana. He physically threatened my sister. I feel like I'm in over my head." If she could admit that to anyone, it was Julian.

"Be careful. I'm not sure I should have warned you. It only sent you right into harm's way."

"You don't think he would have found a way to get me here? My brother's dead. I would have come for that. I can see my sister is traumatized. I just don't know what I should do next, beyond finding the missing drone."

"Not missing. I have the location."

She gasped. "You do? How?"

"It doesn't matter. But if he gets to it first, then he'll complete his deal."

"Do the Feds know this?"

"I don't know. But they have a man on the inside."

"I'm going to need those coordinates."

"Doesn't matter. You can't get to it."

"Just give me the coordinates. I'll worry about getting to it."

"This was never about the drone, Mackenzie. It was about protecting your family. Let the Feds protect their secrets."

Sir Galahad said the words, but the coordinates still came through. Mackenzie copied them.

"Those coordinates are in Indianapolis," he said. "And once we're done with this conversation, I'll delete our conversation in the gaming log files. It never happened. But if you need to connect again, I'll be watching and waiting."

Nora rushed into the living room from the sliding glass door at the side of the house, smelling of horses and tack. Her eyes were bright and contained none of the fear from last night. "Carson's here!"

Mackenzie stood as Nora flew by and headed toward the front door.

"Nora, wait." She wanted to follow her sister. She glanced at the screen, and Sir Galahad was gone.

"You wanted my computer so you could play a game while you worked?" Terra stood over her.

Mackenzie ignored Terra and rushed after Nora in time to see Carson getting out of his car, then catching Nora up in his arms.

"Protecting your family."

Wasn't finding the drone, finding the man behind everything part of that protection?

Mackenzie averted her gaze when the two kissed. She remembered the opened computers. She didn't need more questions from Terra. She headed back into the house, and Terra was at the kitchen counter.

"Thank you for letting me use your laptop. I'll just close out of my tasks." She hoped Terra hadn't read the conversation.

Mackenzie moved to the coffee table in the living area.

Terra washed her hands at the sink and said nothing. Maybe she hadn't heard Mackenzie. She wouldn't bother trying to explain that she wasn't actually playing a game. It was all too complicated. Mackenzie skimmed through the results of her counterattack and queries to search for additional nefarious code before she closed the tabs. She shut off Terra's laptop, closed it, and carried it over to the counter where Terra was looking at her phone.

Nora's and Carson's voices echoed from the front door, and they entered the house. Nora held his hand and brought him all the way into the kitchen to introduce him to Terra, who then offered drinks.

Carson declined.

Nora glanced at Mackenzie, and her smile said it all—her sister was in love and felt safe with her husband-to-be now at her side.

"I flew back on the earliest flight." He looked at Nora. "I want to know what's going on. Everything."

Nora offered a tenuous smile, then an apologetic look at Mackenzie. "We're going now. Carson is here, so I should be okay. I just want to go home and get into my own clothes."

"Protecting your family."

"Wait. I'll go with you, if that's okay." She rushed to the living room and grabbed her laptop and bag.

Arms crossed, Terra looked like a force to be reckoned with, and gave Mackenzie pause.

"What?"

"Aren't you going to wait for Alex? He's expecting you to stay here. You told him you both would stay here."

Oh. Right. "I'm sure he'll be fine with me going with my sister and Carson." She stepped closer and lowered her voice. "Terra, I can't let Nora go. I'm protecting *her*. I'll text Alex and let him know."

Terra pursed her lips. Mackenzie didn't need a babysitter,

though it appeared Alex had transferred his protection detail over to Terra for the time being.

"I'll text him too," Terra said.

She didn't trust Mackenzie to follow through.

"Okay. And thanks again for everything." Forcing a smile, Mackenzie left Terra standing in the kitchen and followed Nora and Carson out of the house.

She climbed into the back seat of Carson's car and listened to Nora telling him about her terrifying experience last night. He offered all the concern a man in love should offer. Then he glanced back at Mackenzie, a suspicious look in his eyes. Nora hadn't told him anything because she was afraid to put him in danger. Sounded like he was about to get the long story short.

"Okay, okay. But not here. I'll tell you somewhere safe. But first, please tell me you don't have to go back to Indianapolis."

THIRTY-ONE

Alex wished he could walk out of this ravine and get back to Mackenzie or even call in and check on her. But he'd asked to come along and here he was, the victim of his own bad decision.

The body had been recovered from the river and now lay on a tarp. Alex took one look at the man, then looked away. He didn't need to see more before memories rushed through him of the three men who died in the attack on the armored SUVs.

Alex couldn't hear much except the rushing river, but light, a reflection, caught his attention up near the top of the ravine. A UAV.

A search drone sent out by the county? He glanced at Nathan's vehicle, where he'd left the bag with his anti-drone tech. Now would be his chance to try it out. But first he needed information. He moved between the vehicles to Jack. Trevor was standing over the recovered body.

"There's a drone hovering over us. Watching. Is it yours?"

"Not ours." Jack angled his head up to the sky.

"Lots of people have drones, Alex. But you're concerned that it has something to do with the attack on Mackenzie, since it involved a drone?" Jack adjusted his sunglasses. "And the drone Owen shot down."

"I don't know what to think anymore," Alex said. "I'm getting paranoid in my old age."

"Good old age of thirtysomething?" Jack grinned and slapped Alex's back. "Come with me." Jack hiked back to the vehicle and grabbed a rifle with a scope.

"Are you going to shoot it down? What are the laws on those things, anyway?"

"This is a crime scene, and I don't appreciate the intrusion." Jack aimed his rifle at the drone. It suddenly veered to the right, then disappeared out of sight.

"Well, I guess they showed you," Alex said. He couldn't help but smirk.

"What's that supposed to mean?"

"I don't even know. But I brought anti-drone tech. If you don't mind, I'll grab my backpack and see if I can detect it out there."

Jack slowly looked at him. "You have anti-drone tech? Alex, what's going on?"

"What do you mean? Someone followed Mackenzie and shot at her. You know this. You have yet to find the shooter. I secured protective measures."

Alex made his way to Nathan's vehicle, opened the door, and opened his bag.

Jack stood behind him. "I wondered what you were carrying in that bag. Seemed kind of big."

"It's a radio frequency analyzer." He pulled out a large case and opened it. Popped up the antennas on each side. He turned it on, and the screen indicated the drone icon along with the distance from their location. "Looks like it's hovering."

"So this detects the radio comms between the drone and its controller? Can we find the controller?"

"That's what I'm working on. At least we know this isn't an autonomous drone."

"Say what?"

"This is being controlled by a human rather than AI."

"What else you got in this bag?" Jack held up what looked like a small rocket launcher. "Whoa, what's this?"

"An RF jammer to take out the drone."

Jack aimed it at the sky. "I can't see it. Point me in the right direction."

"Hold off," Alex said. "I want to see if I can find the home base where the controller is operating from." Alex pounded his fist against the seat back. "I lost the signal. The UAV could have gone out of range."

He ground his molars.

"Cool toys," Jack said.

"This tech is just what I could get my hands on quickly." Clearly, he needed something more sophisticated.

"The DSS provide you with the toys?"

Uh-oh. He wasn't prepared for full disclosure. Not until his superior gave him the go-ahead to share with the locals regarding his activities. "Not directly, no. I have a tech friend who helped find what I needed to protect Mackenzie. But obviously, there's more to it. It's not so easy."

"At least you can take out the drone if you need to. Maybe next time just pull out the RF jammer first thing."

"Well, I did manage to get the drone's model and digital fingerprint, or the MAC address. I'll send the information to my tech."

"The MAC address?"

"Hardware ID number. It should be associated with a specific Wi-Fi network. Not that we'll learn much from that, but it'll be useful if we need the information for prosecution later."

"I knew it," Jack said. "You're working. This wasn't a break for you at all. You came to Montana to work."

"You have me all wrong. This has everything to do with Mackenzie."

"Just tell me if what happened to Nora and her vehicle malfunction last night is related to the shooter and the drone that was watching Mackenzie." Jack pushed his sunglasses onto his head and squinted in the sunlight, but he still managed to drill his gaze into Alex.

Alex pursed his lips. He wanted to be transparent with the local law enforcement and with Jack and Nathan, his new friends. Forge a relationship of trust. But honestly, telling them anything could put them all in a precarious position. Now, what kind of friend would do that?

"I don't have the answer to that."

"Then just what *do* you know?"

Alex smiled.

Jack appeared stunned. "Why are you smiling? Did I say something funny?"

"Actually, yes. I mean, no. The truth is, I don't know anything definitive. And anything I could possibly say could bring trouble to you. All of you. And to your future wives."

"Is that supposed to be a snub of the county folks from the Feds? I'm former FBI. West is a former US Marshal. And Nathan, he's always been county. I'll leave it at that."

Alex turned serious and moved closer. "Not at all. I said those words as a friend. Not as an agent. I'm trying to protect you. But I might need your help, so I'm going to ask you to be ready."

Jack looked at him long and hard. "We've got your back, Alex, even now."

Trevor West approached, a grim expression on his face. "Am I interrupting anything?"

"Nope," Jack said. "What do you know?"

"Hildebrand, the county coroner"—Trevor glanced at Alex, gauging him, then looked back to Jack—"took a preliminary look. We'll need next of kin to identify the body, of course." Trevor rubbed a hand across his chin, then covered his mouth, as if thinking.

"That goes without saying," Jack said, "but you're pretty sure it's Hastings."

Trevor groaned and dropped his hands, hung his head.

Alex shifted to study the detective.

Still in his wet suit, Nathan joined them. He flicked his dark, wet hair out of his face. "What did I miss?"

"Nothing yet," Jack said, keeping his eyes on Trevor. "Come on, man, you going to make us drag it out of you?"

"I shouldn't. I really shouldn't. But you're going to find out soon enough. I don't know what kind of trouble this is going to bring down on us or this town. But keep it under wraps. If I hear one thing outside this group—"

"I'm losing patience, West," Nathan said through gritted teeth. "I just dragged a body out of the river. What's got you so upset?"

"Hastings wasn't his real name. He was a federal agent working undercover."

THIRTY-TWO

Finally, back at Stone Wolf Ranch, Alex hopped out of the vehicle. He'd put that phone call off too long, and now he had no excuses. He was actually surprised Lynch hadn't called him. He had three bars.

Agents might swoop down on Hanstech one way or another regarding what could be the murder of a federal agent. And Alex was exactly where he hadn't wanted to be. Caught in the middle.

Nathan steered away, and Jack got into his vehicle and followed him. Alex hiked away from the house and back toward the cabin where he'd been protecting Mackenzie. He should use his new drone detection device first before he made the call to make sure no one was using a drone to listen to his conversation.

He lugged the case out onto the table and turned it on. While it calibrated, he looked at his cell and noticed that Mackenzie had sent him a text. She could derail him, so he decided he would make the call to Lynch first. Alex tinkered with the device, which didn't detect a drone. Good enough.

On his cell, he called his superior.

"Lynch," the guy barked.

His attempt at intimidating Alex? Letting him know he was about to lose his job? If he was going down, he would go down fighting. He would lead this conversation.

"I'll get right to the point," Alex said. "There's a missing prototype drone. We can assume the cybercriminal has physically taken control of it and will deliver it to his contacts soon. Add to that, a federal agent was working undercover at Hanstech and is now dead. Sir, the State Department has a vested interest because it could involve espionage, possible stolen military secrets." *Shut up, Alex. You already tried to make your case last night.*

The line was quiet. He thought he'd lost the call, then glanced at it to confirm that, no, Lynch was still there. The man was probably chewing on the information and building up to an explosion. Alex braced himself.

"And you know this how?"

"The CEO of the company shared the information with her sister. I was present for the conversation. Sir, per my original call to you, I have a friend involved. I offered to help because of the time-sensitive activity. I felt it prudent to stay involved." He was repeating himself, but he wanted reassurance from Lynch. Maybe if he kept quiet, he would get it. He sounded entirely too nervous.

"You agreed to help, and before you knew what hit you, you were in the middle of an illegal and unsanctioned operation." Lynch groaned. "And I jumped in with you and told you to stay in it. Listen, Alex, I can see how this all happened. I don't know how the higher-ups will see it. I won't lie. Both our jobs are on the line now. But what you've learned so far could keep us out of trouble."

"Sir, that was exactly my thinking."

"I'm glad to hear it. We need to debrief. I need more details. In the meantime, and this sounds strange considering you're not currently working and your observation wasn't technically sanctioned, but I need you to stand down."

"Stand down, sir?"

"No further activity. No communication or involvement. We'll be seen as stepping into another agency's operations."

"The fact is that my friend and her sister are in danger and someone needs to—"

"Agent Knight, let me clarify, officially, you are to stand down and back off."

"And unofficially?"

"You know what's at stake."

Alex barely released his relief. Lynch didn't say more and instead ended the call.

What was at stake? His career? Military secrets? Mackenzie's life? He'd made the call and so what? He was still in a precarious position. He wanted to do the right thing—every time.

Serve his country. Respect his superiors. Answer to a higher calling. But what happened when the directives handed down were in conflict with that higher calling?

God, what should I do? What is the right thing for me at this moment?

What would he even say to Mackenzie? That he was headed back to DC and would leave her to finish this alone? Alex fisted his hands.

He stepped onto the porch, only to see Terra marching toward him.

"What are you doing here?" he asked, a new concern building in his chest. "Where's Mackenzie?"

"Check your messages much? She left with Carson and Nora."

His heart might have stopped. He struggled to breathe. "What? Why didn't you keep her here?"

"What was I going to do, tie her up? I told her you wouldn't be happy if she left, but Nora's fiancé arrived back from a trip. He flew in just for her because of last night. Nora wanted to go with him, and Mackenzie left too. She said she couldn't leave Nora alone."

He stared at the trees and shook his head. Scratched his temple.

"I don't know everything that's going on, and maybe your new girlfriend is just strange. But she was working on her laptop while she was at the house and asked to borrow mine. She started up a game on it! So she was working on hers and playing a game on mine."

He stood taller. "Did she say anything about the game?"

Terra's gasp was incredulous. "Why would she? It's a *game*. Alex, come on. What's going on?"

What's going on is that he was about to lose everything or save the day. But he definitely couldn't stand down. "Did they say where they were going?"

Terra shrugged. "I think Nora mentioned she wanted to go home. Mackenzie said she would text you."

He glanced at several texts from Mackenzie that had come through in a rush, explaining she was going with Nora and Carson. "Okay, yeah. She texted me."

But then another text came through. The last one he'd received from her. The one he'd ignored to call his supervisor. And reading it sent fear rippling up his spine.

Carson could be Nebulous 2.0.

THIRTY-THREE

Mackenzie tried to keep her breathing calm. Her hands from shaking. Carson might see. He might get suspicious that she had figured out his ruse.

The fact that the drone was in Indianapolis and Carson just got back from there couldn't be a coincidence. And after last night, Mackenzie wondered why she and Nora had so easily agreed to get into a vehicle that could be attacked by a cybercriminal.

Carson might not actually be Nebulous 2.0. He might instead be the insider working with the hacker. Carson parked at the Hanstech building. Other than security service vehicles, the parking lot was empty. Employees were encouraged to use the weekends to recharge and discouraged from working outside of official office hours. As a result, projects were less stressful and always completed early.

At least that's the mantra her father had pushed.

"You ladies can wait here or come in with me. I'm sorry I need to make this stop before heading home."

Relief swept through Mackenzie. She needed to get her sister alone to warn her.

"I need to get something from my office, so I'll go too," Nora said.

"Are you sure? I'll just be a second." Carson looked over at Nora, love in his eyes.

"I'm going too." Nora leaned over and gave him a quick peck.

Was he truly in love with her? Or was he just a great actor? Poor Nora. Mackenzie didn't know how to tell her, but she had to do it.

Carson climbed out, and Nora glanced back at Mackenzie. "Are you staying or coming too?"

"I'll come with you." If Carson was going to take only a few moments, then Mackenzie had to warn Nora quickly. They were in danger.

Mackenzie grabbed her laptop, hopped out of the vehicle, and followed Nora. She needed to get her sister alone. A simple text accusing Carson wouldn't be appropriate.

Nora and Carson headed down the long hallway to their offices. Carson winked and then took another hallway, where he stopped at his office door while Mackenzie followed Nora past the secretary's desk and into her office.

Mackenzie shut the door behind her and rushed forward. "Nora."

She swallowed the lump in her throat. This could be a total mistake, but she had to convince her sister to listen.

Nora sat at her desk and opened a drawer and searched it.

"Listen, remember last night. You're not out of danger yet."

"It seems surreal. I can't believe it even happened. I'm so relieved Carson came home. If only he'd been here last night."

Mackenzie searched for the right words.

Lord, help me! She glanced at the door. Would Carson come charging in at any moment? What did he have planned for them? Maybe he would continue with his ruse since he didn't realize Mackenzie had figured him out.

Nora lifted a prescription bottle and opened the cap. "I just want to forget."

That's what she'd been searching for in the drawer? Mackenzie stepped closer. "What is that? What are you taking?"

"Just Valium." Nora popped one of the pills, then returned the bottle to the drawer and locked it.

"This has gone on long enough. You know you've been scared for a long time. You told me everything last night, including about the missing—"

Nora's glare stopped Mackenzie's words.

"Nora, listen, I found the drone." Sort of.

"You found it?" She walked around the desk to be closer to Mackenzie. "Where is it?"

She could let Nora come to her own conclusion. Mackenzie reached for a pen and pad on Nora's desk and wrote down the information. "Here are the coordinates."

"Like that means anything to me. Where is this?"

Mackenzie released a slow, even breath to slow her pounding heart. "Indianapolis."

Nora frowned and stared at the paper. Mackenzie hoped she wouldn't have to spell it out for her sister, but if she didn't see what Mackenzie saw, then she was definitely in denial.

Nora looked at the door. Then she looked back at Mackenzie and held her gaze for a few long seconds.

"How do you know this?"

"My source."

"Your hacker friend? I'm not sure he's trustworthy."

"He has no reason to lie. So we need to look for the drone at these coordinates—or better, just send the Feds in to get it."

Her sister stumbled back against the desk, clearly shaken, then pushed away to stand taller. "I get it now. You're saying you think Carson is involved somehow."

What do you know about him? Where did he come from? How long have you been seeing him?

"I haven't said anything. *You* know what I know."

"Which is nothing. You don't know that it's there. You only have the word of a criminal."

And Mackenzie couldn't tell her sister that Julian was working for the Feds. She didn't know exactly what that meant, though she had assumed it meant he *was* a Fed, but maybe he was an informant for them instead. Either way, a sliver of jealousy slipped into her heart that he was working for them. That had been her dream, but she'd been rejected because of her past.

But Julian hadn't.

"We need to see if it's there, all the same. And . . . we have to be careful. Carson could be the cybercriminal stalking you."

"Why would he want to destroy his own company? I'm not buying your accusations."

"That's a fair point, but if he sells the tech to the black market, he stands to significantly increase his personal finances and destroy us at the same time." He would destroy Nora in one of the most painful ways possible—by shattering her heart. "I wish we weren't having this conversation. But we've known someone has been on the inside all along."

"Maybe he isn't the cybercriminal but has been pressured or threatened, like Rowan was. Traumatized like I've been, only he kept it from me the way I kept it from him, never letting on because I didn't want to put him in danger. Maybe he has been protecting me, Mackenzie!" Nora bit her lip as tears spilled over. She was searching for a way that Carson could be innocent.

"We'll find out, Nora. I hope for your sake, you're right." Mackenzie sat at the desk and opened her laptop, wishing it would all be so easy. "Let me show you." Mackenzie pulled up the forbidden servers. "I've deployed anti-malware algorithms to take down his cyberattack. It was scheduled to crash the entire system, but I'll stop it before it happens. I need to make sure that wasn't the only attack—and knowing Nebulous 2.0, it wasn't." Wait a minute.

All the windows from her previous session popped up, including the window to show the amplitude of nearby access points. Mackenzie stood and shared a look with Nora. "Something's not right."

"What are you talking about?" Nora said. "Why are you looking at me like that?"

"There's a rogue access point. A router here in your office." Mackenzie glanced around her sister's office. Could it be her sister? Her heart had jumped to her throat, threatening to choke her. She pushed down the rising emotions and searched the room.

"You're saying *I'm* the insider? Why would I give someone access to hack into my own company?"

Had Alex been right about Nora? No . . . "Not you, personally." *Lord, please don't let it be so.* "Are you sure that you haven't been threatened to cooperate? I would understand, Nora." And that made sense. All the threats and the fear to keep her in line.

Nora shook her head. "I swear, it's not me."

And something in Nora's eyes told Mackenzie she spoke the truth.

"Okay. Search your office for a device that shouldn't be here. Anything out of place."

Mackenzie stepped out of the office with her laptop, and the amplitude grew. Relief washed through her. Why hadn't she thought of this before? Mackenzie set her laptop on Maci's desk. She tried the drawers, but they were locked. The inbox held a stack of papers. Mackenzie rifled through them and found a phone beneath the stack.

"Maci!"

Nora stepped out of her office. "You found something?"

"Yes. Maci left her smartphone."

"She knows that's against policy. I caught her with it a couple of times, and she claimed she needed to allow the babysitter to text her. I didn't have the heart to fire her, and instead, I've been working on establishing a childcare center on campus. But with everything . . . I've been distracted."

"Well, this is clearly being used as a Wi-Fi router. Since the servers are down on the lower level, the connection is probably routing through another one somewhere too." If Carson was involved, he was either the insider or the cybercriminal, and he'd needed Maci's assistance. To direct the blame to her later? Mackenzie wasn't sure.

"I didn't see Maci's car in the parking lot." Nora hugged herself. She glanced around as though she could be overheard.

A little boy raced down the hall. "Cleo, come back!" Maci stopped short when she spotted Nora and Mackenzie standing at her desk. She looked at her cell, and unfortunately, her expression left no doubt of her guilt.

She took a few slow steps and lifted her little boy. A tear streaked down her cheek. Another step forward and she pressed his face into her shoulder, covering his exposed ear as if to protect him from the bad in this world. "I had no choice. He threatened my child. I . . . I was told to get the phone today, but I'm too late."

Mackenzie looked from Maci to Cleo. "*Who* threatened you?"

"I don't know. I got a text from an unknown number showing me videos of Cleo playing with friends, along with threatening messages saying that Cleo would be harmed if I didn't follow their instructions. I was terrified." The tears freely flowed now. "I'm so sorry."

"Take what you need from your desk, the office. Leave the phone and go directly to the police."

Mackenzie debated about whether or not to turn off the cell. Then again, if Maci had been instructed to retrieve it, then Nebulous 2.0 was done using it. Either that or he feared it would be discovered. She glanced at the camera in the corner. Was he watching them even now?

She turned off the cell.

"I'm scared." Maci's voice shook.

Nora stepped between them. "No police yet, Mackenzie."

Mackenzie eyed the boy. "This has gone on long enough. My career might be toast, and I might lose my chance at getting Nebulous 2.0, and Hanstech could be done too, but threatening a woman's child is going too far." Murdering Rowan had been going too far. Attempting to kill Julian had been too much.

It was all stepping over the line, but Mackenzie now realized the error in her thinking. She'd been arrogant, believing she should be the one to take Nebulous 2.0 down and do it alone.

"Maci, do you know who is behind this?" Nora asked.

Maci shook her head.

Nora appeared visibly relieved. "It can't be who you think, Mackenzie. He wouldn't need to use Maci."

"He could have done it to protect himself." She directed her next words to Maci. "I'll escort you to the door."

Mackenzie's pulse spiked. He could be planning to crash the system and was removing all evidence. She escorted Maci, who held her precious son close, to the front door and watched her climb into her older Ford Escort, then drive away. Maci had reassured Mackenzie she would drive straight to the sheriff's offices and speak to a detective about calling the FBI. Her model car was older and couldn't be digitally highjacked to cause her harm.

God, please keep them safe. Bring in whoever is needed to stop this. Forgive me for believing I would be the one to take Nebulous 2.0 down.

Mackenzie entered the building again, anger burning in her gut at the thought of someone threatening a small child. She found Tilden at the security desk. He hadn't been present when they arrived—possibly because he was checking the building and the grounds. Or taking a break? Where was his partner? She had never seen or met the guy.

Tilden.

He was here at night and on the weekends. She hadn't even considered him as a possible insider. Mackenzie rushed back to Nora's office and found her pacing.

Her face pale, Nora stopped in her tracks and stared at Mackenzie. "I went to Carson's office to face him."

"Nora, you didn't. Do you know how dangerous that was?"

"I didn't face him because he wasn't there!"

"What do you mean?"

"He's gone. I can't find him on the security cameras. I had Tilden patch me in, but I didn't say anything to him about what was going on. Maybe I should have." Nora stared at her desktop computer screen.

"Even on the lower level?" Mackenzie rushed around to look at the screen.

"Nothing shows up."

"He has to be down there. Let me look at the cameras. Maybe he looped them so his movements couldn't be tracked."

"I don't believe he's involved, Mackenzie. I can't."

"I understand." That didn't mean that he wasn't. Mackenzie skimmed all the security cameras and focused on those set on the lower level. "Wait . . ." *Oh no!* "I see something."

At the corner of the server rack, two legs—someone was sprawled on the floor. That's all the cameras could see.

Nora's hand went to her mouth as she gasped. "Oh no! Carson!"

Her sister raced around the desk to the door.

"Wait!" Mackenzie pulled her back. "You can't go down there."

"You're right. I'll call Tilden to check it out first."

"I'm not sure that's a good idea either." She couldn't let

Nora see her own fear rising. She had to stay strong and keep her sister strong. They would make it through this. "He could be involved. I mean, who else is here? Who could have harmed Carson?"

Nora nodded. "I'll call 911 instead." She lifted the handset to her ear, then pushed on the switch hook, searching for a dial tone. "The phones are down."

Terror flashed in Nora's gaze.

"Maci's cell." Mackenzie rushed to the secretary's desk and used the cell to call 911. She requested an ambulance too. Dispatch informed her that a call had already been made. She ended the call and stared at the cell.

Who had made the call?

Things were unraveling fast. How was it that Alex wasn't here with her when she needed him most?

Tilden suddenly appeared. Mackenzie moved in front of Nora as if to protect her. Just what did she think she would do? Her skills lay in the digital world.

"Ladies, we have a situation. I'm going to need you to step out of the building."

"Carson is hurt. He's down on the lower level," Nora said. "What do you know about it?"

"I saw it on the camera and called 911 right before the lines went dead. I don't know what's going on, but I'll get you to safety and then investigate the lower level. Danny isn't answering his radio either."

By the look on the man's face, she *knew* he was there to protect them and do his job. But could she trust her own judgment?

"I'm not leaving," Nora said. "I'm going down there to make sure Carson is okay." Nora rushed around Tilden, leaving Mackenzie and the security guard to follow.

Trying to stop Nora would be a waste of time, but before Nora could step onto the elevator, Mackenzie pulled her back.

"Let's take the stairwell. Now isn't the time to get stuck. I'm pretty sure Nebulous 2.0 was behind the elevator incident."

"And my car."

Tilden had already opened the door to the stairwell, and he led the charge. They took two flights of stairs, the sense of urgency unquestioned—Carson needed help. But concern squeezed Mackenzie's chest.

Was Carson behind the threats against her family and Hanstech? Was he Nebulous 2.0? And if he wasn't, who else was in the building?

At the glass-door entrance to the secured level, Tilden glanced at them before swiping his keycard. They rushed forward through the racks of servers, lights blinking with the silent alarm. Security cameras should have covered every area.

Tilden came to a halt. Nora rushed forward, but he held out his arm, stopping her. He took another step around the server rack. Nora and Mackenzie joined him to see Carson lying on the cold tile floor.

Tilden crouched and checked the man's pulse and nodded. "He's alive. I'll stay here with him. You ladies should go back up and wait for the authorities and the ambulance."

"I'm staying," Nora said.

"Who did this?" Mackenzie asked the obvious.

"He's diabetic and could have collapsed due to his blood sugar," Nora said. "I'm staying with Carson. I'll wait here for the medics. Or maybe we can all carry him up to meet them."

Mackenzie hadn't known that Carson was diabetic. Still, given the circumstances, she believed someone had caused him harm. And they could still be down here. She rose and rubbed her arms, looking around the room filled with servers and beyond to the next set of glass walls—the test drones.

Tilden stood and held his gun at the ready, angling his head left and right as if he sensed they weren't alone.

"Hello?" she said.

Tilden and Nora glanced at her. She moved around the rack of servers. "Come out and face me. I'm tired of this game."

"Miss Calhoun, what are you doing?" Tilden drew close, backing her up.

She glanced at Tilden and gestured to the other room.

He subtly nodded and crept forward, but she held him back. "I'll go. He's after me."

He shook his head. "You're not going anywhere. You and Nora need to go back up and wait for the police. While I hate leaving him here, maybe I should escort you up."

"You heard Nora. She's not leaving Carson behind." She pushed past Tilden, willing him to understand, though she wasn't sure if she was making the right decision. She knew for certain that Tilden was in danger too, and she couldn't stand to be the reason he got hurt. "I'll protect *you*."

What was she saying? But she couldn't help herself.

Whoever had been in this room had hurt Carson but hadn't been caught on camera. Maybe Mackenzie was wrong on all counts, and she was too arrogant to see. Too bent on making up for the past. All she knew was that she had to see the face of the man behind everything that happened years ago, everything that had started up again even before Julian tried to warn her.

"Nebulous! Don't be such a coward. Show yourself!"

She had tried to forgive herself. And she might have almost gotten there, pushing her mistakes far behind her, if only those same mistakes hadn't snuck back up on her to harm her father's company and kill her brother. Put others in harm's way.

Why, Lord, why?

Why had those mistakes found her again, come after her and impacted everyone, everything in her life? At least those she knew in Michigan, those she worked with, were safe and far removed.

Mackenzie nodded to Tilden. "Use your hand to get us in."

"I'm not authorized."

Nora stepped forward, but before she could press her hand against the biometric device, the doors whooshed open.

The three of them stood there, as if afraid to step into the room. Why had the doors suddenly opened? It remained dark, except for the dim light emanating from the running electronics and spilling from the server room.

Prepared to shoot, Tilden stepped into the dark room a few steps and was just turning back to them when he was Tasered—barbs attached to wires hooked into his back. Someone stood in the shadows against the wall. Nora screamed and jumped closer to Mackenzie.

"Stop it!" Mackenzie shouted as she rushed forward to Tilden's aide.

Tilden fell to the floor, temporarily paralyzed, stiff and gritting his teeth in pain.

She dropped to her knees next to Tilden. "Please, stop!"

She glanced up but still couldn't see the attacker's face—he remained in the dark as he held the Taser. She dug down deep, past the fear of facing off with someone who had been bent on revenge for much too long, storing it up inside until he had strategized on how to destroy her and her family. "Just . . . show yourself."

Their attacker emerged from the shadows, quickly moving in and relieving Tilden of his gun.

Mackenzie's heart stopped at the sight of someone she recognized.

THIRTY-FOUR

Grayback county vehicles crowded the Hanstech parking lot. Alex didn't know they had so many. But that couldn't be good. As soon as he'd seen Mackenzie's text, he tried contacting her to no avail, then Terra received a call from Jack that a 911 call had come in from Hanstech. Alex had hopped into the Mustang and raced here.

He swerved into the parking lot behind an ambulance, his heart thrashing against his rib cage. Of course, now was the moment the door of the old Mustang chose to be stubborn. Alex fought with it and couldn't get it open fast enough.

Finally scrambling out, he pushed beyond the sudden weakness in his legs and rushed between the haphazardly parked vehicles and up to a deputy.

"Special Agent Alex Knight," Alex said, flashing his credentials.

The man eyed Alex with curiosity, then said, "Deputy Whitehall."

"What's happening?"

"We can't get in," the deputy said. "I'm trying to contact the security guard who called me, but I'm getting no response."

Alex stalked forward to the glass doors, pulled out his gun, and aimed.

"Whoa, whoa!" Deputy Whitehall said, holding his own weapon. "Put your weapon away!"

"Their lives could be in danger, and we're going in. Back me up." Yep. Alex rushing in like a hero even though he'd been told to stand down if he wanted to keep his job.

Other agencies were on it. *Yeah, where were they?* He saw no one to help out the county. Bureaucracy was beyond frustrating.

Alex refrained from firing when he spotted movement in the lobby. Another security guard—not Tilden—unlocked the door and ran out. "There's a bomb! Get away and take cover!"

Alex grabbed the guard's arm, stopping him. "Mackenzie and Nora! Are they inside?"

He nodded. "You won't make it, man!"

He gripped the guy. "Where are they?"

"In the lower level."

Visions from Alex's past came crashing back as he rushed forward. The security guard and deputy pulled him back and away. He wouldn't be stopped this time and fought them off. He snagged the security guard's keycard, which was clipped to his belt, and dashed through the door.

"Stop!" Shouts rang out behind him.

"Mackenzie!" He sprinted through the foyer and to the corridor that would take him to the lower level.

God, please let this work . . . He was rewarded when the lock unlatched. He pushed through and bounded down the stairwell, knowing these could be his last breaths, his last minutes of life. Maybe he was crazy, but he couldn't live with himself if he stood by and let Mackenzie and Nora die.

An image of the Suburban exploding in front of him flashed through his mind over and over. Sweat beaded at his temples.

Lord, help me get to them in time.

He burst through the stairwell exit and into the lower level. Warning lights flashed on and off. He spotted a body on the floor. The man stirred. Carson. They'd gotten away from him.

Alex didn't have handcuffs, but he needed to secure the guy—if Carson, in fact, was involved. *If* he was Nebulous 2.0. Mackenzie hadn't given him enough information.

He pointed his gun at Carson. "Where are they? What did you do with them?"

The man groaned, frowning as if in pain. Alex had no time for mercy or compassion. He grabbed the man's collar and pressed the gun next to his temple—completely against protocol. "Where. Are. Mackenzie and Nora?"

Turning pale, Carson shifted away as if he would be sick.

Alex spotted red lights flashing along the servers. Too many of them. He couldn't defuse even one of the bombs. But he wasn't going to leave her.

"Your bombs are about to go off. If you want to live, I'll get you out of here, but you need to tell me where they are."

The guy was useless, and Alex was wasting time. He released his hold on the man and started searching between the server racks. "Mackenzie!"

They must be in the room with the test drones. He approached the door. This one required biometrics to open.

Suddenly Carson stumbled up behind him. Alex turned to face him and pointed his gun. What was he up to?

Carson slumped forward and pressed his hand against the biometric reader. "I'm not who you think I am," he said, his speech slurred.

The doors whooshed open, and Carson stumbled forward into the room and fell to his knees. Alex spotted a wide-eyed Nora on the floor next to Tilden, their ankles and wrists bound with plastic ties.

"Where's Mackenzie?" Alex searched and found a sharp object, then cut the ties.

"He took her."

"Who?"

"The guy behind everything. The cybercriminal." Nora hopped up and pulled Carson to his feet. "We have to get out of here before the bombs go off."

Alex turned to head back into the server room with the bombs.

"No!" Nora said. "Through the tunnel out the back."

Alex followed Nora, Tilden, and Carson through the maze of tables and shelves filled with drones. Wait . . .

"Which of these drones uses infrared?"

Nora barked a laugh. "All of them. Let's go!"

"If he took Mackenzie into the woods, I can use one of these drones to find her."

"There's no time," Tilden said.

"Mackenzie's life could—"

Carson stopped, causing Nora to release him. He reached for a small drone, along with the handheld controls. "Here. Take this and go find her. Don't worry about us. Head straight up the tunnel through the exit."

Alex hesitated, watching Nora and Tilden assist Carson. He wouldn't leave them behind either. "Here, Nora. I'll help Tilden. You hold the drone and controls."

She grabbed the items, then led the way through the tunnel. At the end, she pushed through the exit, which opened up into a loading dock.

A deep rumble rocked through his body, and the ground beneath him shuddered. "Go, go, go!"

They sprinted into the fresh air. A twenty-six-foot transport truck was parked a few yards away from the building.

"Behind the truck!" Nora shouted.

Alex wasn't sure the truck would protect them, but they continued forward, putting as much distance as they could between themselves and the building. He noticed a helicopter sitting in the grass about fifty yards away. Hanstech's . . . or someone else's?

They stumbled around to the other side of the truck and hunkered down as multiple blasts shook the ground beneath them, rocking the truck. Shrapnel flew through the air. Heat and flames exploded into the sky, no doubt destroying much more than the servers, the data, the drones.

Alex took the drone from Nora and leaned against the truck next to the security guard. Nora and Carson held each other. He eyed Carson—Mackenzie had thought he was the villain.

"You said the man who took Mackenzie was the cybercriminal. What else can you tell me?"

Nora closed her eyes, then opened them again. "William. His name is William."

William? He didn't know a William. It didn't matter. He looked to the terrain behind them.

Into the woods. To Tilden, he said, "Keep them safe. The ambulance is at the front, and I'm guessing a lot more police presence. I need to find Mackenzie."

Nora seized the drone from him and powered it up along with the controller that included a small screen. She gave him brief instructions. "I can search from here, and if she's out there, you can get her."

She sent the drone up and into the woods. Only the heat signatures of animals came up on the controller screen. The explosion had probably sent them running.

"Where could she be?" Alex asked. "Maybe she's not in the woods."

"That helicopter isn't ours," Nora said. "My guess is he wanted to take her on it, but she got away and ran into the woods. You were right to get the drone."

Nora and Alex gasped at the same moment. They spotted the heat signatures of two people. One figure was gaining ground on the other one.

"Where are they headed?" Alex asked.

"Toward the ravine," Nora said. "She might be trying to get to the zip line. She probably thinks if she could cross it, then she could disable it on the other side."

Desperation corded his throat. "He's gaining on her. She won't make it."

"Doesn't matter if she makes it. The zip line is down for the foreseeable future. She can't get across." Nora handed the controller off to him. "You might need this while you're out there. Now, go get my sister."

THIRTY-FIVE

ackenzie heard the explosion and stumbled. Her knees hit the ground, then she fell forward and sobbed into the pine needles. *Oh, God . . . Nora!*

There was no way Nora, Tilden, and Carson had made it out of there without a rescue. But Tilden had called 911, and she'd heard emergency vehicles. She had an ounce of hope.

God, please, please, please let them be okay!

Whatever had happened, Mackenzie had to survive so that William wouldn't win.

She pushed from the ground and started running again. How much farther was it to the ravine and the zip line? Taking it across then disabling it would get her to safety. William was a runner, and there was no way she could outrun him.

She wasn't sure how she'd gotten away from him in the first place. But there was no way she would let him take her away on that helicopter. No. Way. She shuddered to think of what he had planned for her. Initially, she'd escaped him because he didn't know which way she'd run, and he took off in the wrong direction.

The zip-line escape was a decent idea—though she really

didn't want to cross the ravine. And another issue was that it could have been dismantled after the accident. Her idea could be a big mistake. If it was, she would just have to find a place to hide in the wilds of Montana.

She tripped over a stone and fell to the ground again. Scrambling back to her feet, she approached the ravine and heard the roar of the Grayback River. She hoped and prayed the authorities were invading the woods. Nebulous 2.0 could be captured.

Finally.

But she couldn't know if she would be dead or alive when that happened. Catching her breath, she stood at the edge of the ravine. As she'd feared, the zip line had been removed.

She wasn't getting across. Footfalls pounded the ground behind her.

Hide. Move.

She dashed away from the ravine and dove behind a large rock.

"I see you, Mackenzie. You can't hide from me. You never could and you never will."

Gasping for breath, she remained behind the rocks. *Lord, what do I do?*

"I told you I would come back when you least expected it. It was worth the wait to see the surprise in your eyes."

Now she understood why he'd continued to pursue her romantically. She wished she'd thrown up on him during the octopus ride on their date at the carnival.

"*You* are Nebulous 2.0?"

"You thought you were smarter than me, even back then. Now you see how wrong you've been. And what were you expecting? A scrawny creature like Julian Abel?"

"I was expecting someone *else*. Not you."

"You didn't seriously think I would forget about you. Just let you go."

"Honestly, I had forgotten about you." *Why am I antagonizing him?* "I was trying to put my mistakes behind me."

Mackenzie remained behind the rock. If she tried to dash along the ravine's edge and then back into the woods, she doubted she would make it far. Time for a new tactic.

She slowly stood so she could see William over the rock.

An unfamiliar wicked grin spread across his face. "By mistakes, you mean turning over our scheme to the authorities. You wish you hadn't done that."

Acid churned in her stomach, but she stood her ground. "I wish I had never let you coerce me into committing those crimes in the first place. Look where it got me. Here with you." And most of her family lost to her forever.

His lips curled into a snarl.

Now wasn't the time to cower with fear. "You have the prototype drone and the data you can sell on the black market, so just leave now while you still can. The company will collapse." Though she hoped not, but better to convince him otherwise. "You got your revenge."

"Oh, I'm only getting started."

He had escaped the authorities for over a decade. Anyone who had waited so long for revenge would finish the job. Her knees started shaking at the thought. She had to hold it together a little longer and keep him talking.

Help would come. *God, please* . . . "Wait. You couldn't have hit Julian. You were there with me. Who are you working with?"

"You should already know I can be very convincing when needed."

William started toward her.

She backed away from the boulder, barely avoiding the ravine. "When did you become so physical? So violent? This is not who you were."

"When it became necessary." In a flash, William scrambled over the boulder, the only thing standing between them.

THIRTY-SIX

With a quick glance at the monitor, Alex saw William standing over Mackenzie, holding her precariously close to the deadly drop into the ravine.

Alex wouldn't make it in time to save her.

Come on, Mackenzie. Get away.

Lord, help her.

He continued his run toward the zip-line area and considered all his options. Depending on what William did next, Alex might still have time to ambush him.

Another glance at the controller screen, and he saw Mackenzie had broken free and scrambled away. Alex knew what he had to do. He sent the ten-pound drone diving toward William, then it slammed into him. Alex stepped through the tree line in time to see a tall man flailing his arms as he lost balance.

Alex rushed forward. Mackenzie reached for William.

"No! He'll pull you over with him!"

William fell back toward the ravine as Mackenzie tried to save him, and Alex dove forward, throwing his body over hers, preventing her from going with William.

But the man still had a grip on her. Or she had a grip on him.

"Hold on, Mackenzie. I got you." Alex groaned. She was slipping. "You have to let go of him."

"He isn't letting go of *me!*" Her voice echoed with the strain and effort. "But we need to save him."

"I . . . can . . . try . . ." Alex's muscles screamed, burning with the exertion. His palms were slicking, and Mackenzie's grip started to slip. He would lose her if he didn't do something right now. He would lose them both.

Adrenaline coursed through him as he crawled his hands along her arm to get a better grip and hooked his legs around the branch of a nearby tree. But he feared he couldn't save Mackenzie if she continued to clutch William's hand as he dangled hazardously over the ravine, the roaring river below, threatening.

Sweat poured over Alex. "Let's sling him toward the edge."

"I can't reach," William said. "Help me. I'm slipping!"

The fear and panic in William's voice knifed through Alex. Suddenly William slid from Mackenzie's grasp and fell, his screams of horror echoing against the rocky walls.

"No!" she shouted.

Alex instantly started pulling her now much lighter body toward him even as he watched William plummet into the river, shock rolling through him at the horror on the man's face. He didn't surface after hitting the water.

A sob broke loose from Mackenzie.

"I got you." He pulled her back up over the edge and then dragged them both a few feet away. He fell onto his back and gulped air.

Was it finally over?

He rolled to his side to see Mackenzie lying on her back. Tears streamed down her temples. "Are you okay? Did he physically hurt you?" Because William had already inflicted plenty of pain on her.

"I'm okay. Please tell me my sister is alive."

"And safe. I got down to the lower level in time to free her and Tilden, and they assisted Carson out. We got out before the blast. Nora used a drone to find you."

She closed her eyes. "It's over."

He brushed his thumb across her temples and cheeks, wiping away the tears. "There's still a lot to sort out, but if he was Nebulous 2.0, then yes, that part of it is over."

Would either of them be given a pass on the measures they'd taken to stop the cybercriminal? Would they have a chance to explore a relationship? He hoped so. With everything in him, he hoped so.

Mackenzie was traumatized, as he was, and now certainly wasn't a moment to kiss her. Except she opened her eyes and lifted her hand to his face and cupped his jaw. He saw the longing in her gaze, and he couldn't resist. Before they faced the chaos of the aftermath, he would have this one moment with her.

Alex leaned forward and pressed his lips gently against hers. She weaved her hands through his hair and pulled him closer. Emotions and warm sensations surged through him, and his heart soared. He liked this girl—really, really liked her—and needed more time with her.

Approaching footfalls drew him up and away from the kiss. Mackenzie sat up as well.

Nora rushed forward. "Oh, thank God!" She dropped to her knees and pulled Mackenzie into a hug.

Alex stood to face the contingent of law enforcement that Nora had led to the ravine.

Jack, Nathan, Terra, and Trevor stepped into view, along with a couple of others he recognized instantly as federal agents. He'd been informed other agencies were on it. *Now* they show up.

Let the games begin . . .

THIRTY-SEVEN

Back at the county offices in Big Rapids, Alex finished giving his statement to the federal agents. Mackenzie was around the place somewhere, and he intended to find her. The agents had found William's female accomplice, Anna Craven—a criminal for which a red notice had been issued by the International Criminal Police Organization, Interpol. William had met her on the dark web. She'd been apprehended at a warehouse in Indianapolis, along with the prototype drone, thanks to intel provided by Julian Abel. Anna was driving the vehicle that hit Julian and was also the one who shot at Mackenzie in the woods. Apparently, Anna had only been tasked with observing Mackenzie with the drone but was jealous of William's infatuation with her. In addition, the FBI had also taken into custody the individuals who'd arranged to purchase the classified prototype drone.

Nebulous 2.0 chose Indianapolis because he'd planned to incriminate Carson—who often traveled there to handle issues with his mother's care—and frame him if his plans went south. He'd also threatened to harm the zip-line employee's teenage daughter if he didn't cooperate by sabotaging the zip line to end the undercover federal agent's life. Maci's son's life had also been threatened. But Nebulous 2.0 had met his match in Mackenzie. Once she deployed countermeasures, he'd had to resort to plan B to take out the servers.

The woman was a genius. Alex had known that before this incident.

Stunningly beautiful. Compassionate. He wanted to catch her up in his arms and kiss her. Hold her and never let her go. But he was allowing his emotions, his desperation to get the best of him. He didn't want her to climb into her vehicle and drive home to Michigan without telling her how he felt. What he thought. Would she actually do that? He hoped she would stick around to support her sister through the chaos. But he simply couldn't know.

The biggest problem—he had been called back to DC without delay. SSA Lynch wanted him on the red-eye tonight. That was news he didn't want to deliver to Mackenzie in a text or even on a call. He had to see her face and make her understand.

Where was she?

Detective West sidled up to Alex. "I know this is probably not the right time, but I have something you might want to see."

"It's fine. They're done with me." *My career could be over too.* He followed Detective West down the hall. "Do you happen to know where they're questioning Mackenzie?"

West pulled Alex into his cubicle and sat down, offering him a chair as well. Then West gave him a warning look. "You know this could go either way for her. She was digging around where she shouldn't have been." He shrugged. "Or she could be seen as a hero, routing this guy out. They've wanted him for years, I hear, though I'm not sure I was supposed to."

"It could go either way for me too. I'm heading to DC tonight." *God, I don't want to go.* He had unfinished business with Mackenzie. He'd had to rush away from her all those years ago, and he didn't want that to happen again.

He'd been inexplicably drawn to her that first moment he saw her three years ago. And now, they'd had another chance, but the chaos of this world seemed bent on keeping them apart. If either of them was seen as anything other than a hero, then William would have taken even more from her—her future.

"Earth to Alex."

Detective West's words pulled Alex to the moment and the detective's arched brow.

West blew out a breath. "This is what I wanted to show you." He turned on his monitor. "This security footage is from a gas station at the corner of a state highway and forest road near Stone Wolf Mountain."

Alex concentrated on the video. West replayed it.

A woman dressed in all black—yoga pants, a T-shirt, and a cap—opened up the back of her car and shuffled stuff around. A sledgehammer was in plain view.

Alex memorized the license plate but asked, "Did you run them?"

"I did. The vehicle belongs to a Shelby Colton." West pulled up her address for Alex.

"Let's pay her a visit." Alex hoped that since the detective had seen fit to show him this much, he wouldn't mind him tagging along.

West nodded. "As long as you're free to go."

Alex stood and took in the busy county sheriff's office, which was filled with more personnel than it had probably ever seen, even during the incident surrounding Erin.

He was free, except he didn't want to leave Mackenzie. Then he spotted her walking down the hallway with Nora and Carson, heading toward the exits. She glanced over her shoulder. Was she searching for him? But her gaze never found him.

Disappointment landed in his gut. He should chase after her, but West had started walking. He turned to Alex. "You coming?"

He would catch up with Mackenzie later. Now was the time to solve the memorial vandalism. "Yes."

Twenty minutes later Alex was walking with Trevor up the steps to a second-floor landing, and they found Shelby Colton's apartment number. It was 8:30 in the evening. West knocked and held himself in both a compelling and intimidating demeanor.

The door opened, and a young, smallish woman answered with a tenuous smile. Her pupils spasmed, but she kept her cool. She was guilty alright. But was she guilty of vandalism?

"I'm Detective West, and this is Special Agent Alex Knight. Do you mind if we ask you a few questions?"

She stiffened and stood taller, then took a slight step back, bracing the door as if she would close it. "What's this about?"

Trevor hadn't given Alex leeway, but he was taking it. "We have video footage of you destroying memorial plaques at the Rocky Mountain Courage Memorial."

Next to him, the detective stiffened, but he didn't dispute Alex's words. Her response could tell them what they needed to know.

She moved to slam the door.

Trevor stuck his foot in the doorway. "Ma'am, I'm going to need you to come with me for questioning."

"Am I being arrested? Because I figure if you really had a video, then you would have led with that. I don't even own a sledgehammer."

Alex's heart jumped to his throat. They hadn't mentioned a sledgehammer. And that information had been kept out of the news for just such a moment.

Trevor pulled out his handcuffs and slapped them on her. "We have a video, and now with those words, we have our confirmation."

Trevor then informed her of her rights and tucked her in the back of his vehicle. As the three rode to the county offices,

Alex was itching to ask a million questions about why she would deface the memorial, but it wasn't his place to do so. Trevor had allowed him to come along as a courtesy because it was personal to Alex—and because he was a fellow law enforcement officer.

But that's where the courtesy ended. While the woman was being questioned, he found himself sitting in Trevor's cubicle. All Alex could think about was Mackenzie and his red-eye flight out to DC for debriefing. His time off had been cut short because of the chaos surrounding Mackenzie. He'd agreed to help her. He wanted to be with her. Strange that those actions were now pulling him away from her.

He didn't want to go.

Trevor marched toward him, his expression grim. The detective sat in the chair across from Alex.

"You're not going to believe this." Trevor ran a hand across his jaw.

West stared at the floor and shook his head.

"Well, what is it? Don't leave me hanging!"

He covered his mouth again as if measuring his words, reminding Alex of when he hadn't wanted to share about the undercover agent killed on the zip line.

"You thought it was personal, and it definitely is."

Alex said nothing. He gritted his teeth instead.

The detective scooted close to his computer, typed on the keyboard, and pulled up the video of Shelby in the room answering questions, tears streaming.

"You should hear this for yourself," West said as he hit Play.

"I recently learned who my father is," the woman said. "Was. He died fifteen years ago. And he has a memorial in his name. But he was *not* a hero. He left me and my mother to survive on our own. She died, and I grew up in the foster system never knowing who my father was."

Shock rolled through Alex. No. This couldn't be true. She must be lying. "Replay it."

Trevor replayed the video, and Alex watched it three more times.

She was telling the truth. Or at least she believed it.

"It started with Sheridan's plaque a few months ago," Alex said. "Why her?"

"I asked her the same thing." Trevor fast-forwarded the video.

"Because . . . I blamed her. He left my mother for her. Or so I thought. I found pictures of them together, but then I realized I had misunderstood their relationship. I'm sorry." She covered her eyes and sobbed.

"She looks like she's only nineteen, but she's twenty-one. She was definitely a troubled teen."

"And . . . my sister."

Trevor looked at him. "What are you going to do?"

"I'm going to bail her out." Alex stood.

"The fine is usually $400."

"How about just dropping the charges?"

"Good thing I haven't officially charged her." Trevor led him down to the jail cells.

"I can't believe you put her in a cell," Alex said.

"Sometimes kids need a little fear struck into them. I had the feeling that's all she needed. And if you think you can handle her . . ."

Alex had no idea. "I can." *God, help me.*

Alex couldn't just leave her here without at least talking to her. This was urgent, and he needed to deal with it and help her if he could. As for Mackenzie . . . *God, please let me talk to Mackenzie again. You know the time and the place.* He had no idea what that conversation would look like. Regardless, he hoped for her sake that there were no repercussions from the Nebulous 2.0 cyberchaos.

He paused outside of the entrance to the cells where Shelby was being held. "I need to make a call first."

Trevor crossed his arms and nodded. "I'll be waiting right here."

Alex stepped a few yards back down the hallway to make the call on his cell.

She answered.

"Hi, Mom."

"Hey, Alex. Are you okay? I heard the news about an explosion at Hanstech. A bomb or something. Did you hear about that? What is this world coming to?"

"Uh, yeah. I heard about it. Listen, Mom, I have some news for you. It's going to *feel* like a bomb." He squeezed his eyes shut. Should he open this door? But the door had been opened, and he had a feeling his mother was well aware of the past. He'd prefer that his mother be prepared to meet Shelby—Alex's half sister.

"Well, what is it?"

Moisture erupted on his palms. He didn't really want to do this now over the phone, but he had to leave town. This could be painful for Mom. But not telling her would be equally painful when she found out. Besides, Alex had a feeling he would need an entire family, his family—yes, that included Ron—to encourage and help Shelby, if she would accept their help at all. She needed love.

"I have a sister. She's here in town." He held his breath, waiting for her response.

Seconds ticked by, and he released it before she answered.

"I knew your father had an affair, yes, with Camille Colton, twenty-one years ago. I didn't learn about it until fifteen years ago, though, and we argued and tensions were high. Then he died in the avalanche. I'm sorry . . . I didn't think it was your business, but more than that, I didn't want you to be disappointed in him or hurt by it."

But I have a sister! He bit back his angry retort. "But you also knew he had a child with her."

Tear-choked words filled the line. "I didn't know, I swear."

Oh . . . Mom . . .

"What's her name?"

"Shelby . . . Shelby Colton. And she needs a family."

THIRTY-EIGHT

Mackenzie rode in the passenger seat of Nora's Lexus. It was already past 10:00 p.m. when they left Carson. Because of a severe concussion, he would remain in the hospital for overnight observation. Carson had apparently been conducting his own investigation, including tracking Nora for her protection. Carson had a degree in accounting and investment banking, but he also headed up the cybersecurity department for a company in the financial sector before coming to Hanstech. He discovered Mackenzie's rogue access point and went down to the servers to remove it when he came upon William, who Tasered him. When he fell, he struck his head on the corner of a server rack, knocking him unconscious.

Poor guy. She'd had Carson all wrong and should have suspected Nebulous 2.0 would be framing all sorts of people in his mad revenge scheme. She stared out the window and watched the dark forests of Montana go by. She imagined them during the light of day—blue skies and green trees and purple mountains, snowcapped at times.

Glorious.

Dad had been right to land here, but his dream had been

overwritten. She and Nora were now left to pick up the pieces and find a way to move on. Alex had never left her thoughts, but she had lost him in the chaos. He'd inexplicably walked back into her life during the biggest crisis she'd ever endured, and she feared he would walk right back out.

Again.

She needed to see him, tell him—before it was too late.

God, please . . .

Recent events had driven home the point that she shouldn't let anything stand between her and her loved ones. She'd allowed too many years, too many regrets to separate her from her family. Never again would that happen. She had already lost too much.

Alex—brilliant, good-looking, compassionate, and her hero—she loved everything about him. They'd connected emotionally, and she couldn't deny her strong physical attraction to him. After everything she'd experienced in life, she knew deep in her marrow that she shouldn't just walk away from him, or let him slip through her fingers for a second time—unless, of course, that's what *he* chose. And then Mackenzie would be alone again.

At least Nora had Carson, and Mackenzie was so very relieved that he'd had nothing at all to do with the espionage, stealing Hanstech's trade secrets to be sold to the highest bidder. William had created a business selling tech on the black market via the dark web. Even had a specialty website.

Nora had explained to the federal agents that she brought Mackenzie in as her own personal rapid-response team because of her cybersecurity skills. Nora had sounded proud of her. Among so many things, she was still trying to comprehend the admiration she'd heard in Nora's voice. As for the Feds, she had a feeling they would be watching her closely again because no one ever forgot what she did when she was a teen. And just as she feared, she could never completely outrun that mistake.

But she'd been instrumental in bringing Nebulous 2.0's activities to an end. And she would forgive herself for her past mistakes. With that acceptance, she believed the future was bright.

If only Alex . . .

Before Nora turned off the road to head to her house, Mackenzie needed to speak up. "Will you take me to Stone Wolf Ranch?"

"You're welcome to stay with me," Nora said. "We have a lot to talk about. A lot of catching up to do. I want time with you before you go back to Michigan. Maybe I can even convince you to stay."

Except Nora's future was up in the air as well. With an obliterated Hanstech headquarters, would her sister choose to stay in Montana?

"We'll have time. I want that too. But my stuff is at the cabin. I just want to crash." And wait for Alex.

God, please let Alex show up.

Nora steered up to the main house and stopped. Mackenzie must have been in a daze because it hit her. "No, wait, the cabin at the back."

Before Nora could correct her error, Terra and Erin rushed through the front door toward the car.

"I'll just leave you with your new friends. At least I know I don't need to worry. You're in good hands with them." Nora got out with Mackenzie. Her sister hugged her, then held her at arm's length. "Call me when you're ready to come over, okay? Or . . . just show up."

Mackenzie looked into her sister's eyes, tears surging. "I'm so sorry about everything."

"Shh. Let's let the past stay in the past. It's over and done with. You're here now, that's all that matters. Because of you, Nebulous 2.0 is gone."

Nathan and his dive team had recovered William's body

earlier in the day, not too long after he disappeared into the ravine.

Mackenzie couldn't find the words. It was like a dream, coming back to family—at least what was left of her family. And she wouldn't waste that gift from God.

She said goodbye to Nora. "Let me know how Carson is doing."

"I'll text you later with an update. I'll probably go back up to the hospital after I freshen up." Nora shook her head as if she was still trying to comprehend everything.

Mackenzie knew the feeling. Nora handed Mackenzie off to Terra and then climbed into her vehicle.

Terra pulled her into a hug, surprising her. "Come on in. I made a huge batch of pasta. I know it's late, but I bet you're hungry."

"I'm starving." And exhausted.

In the house, she sensed warmth and love as she watched Terra interact with her grandfather and brother, Owen, as well as Erin and her mother, Celia. Soon Jack and Nathan joined them. Mackenzie felt out of place and awkward. What was she even doing here?

They all had each other. Cared deeply for each other.

The family she never had.

She hoped for something like that with Nora in the future. Jealousy sliced through her, but she pushed it away. She couldn't stay in the past and mourn all that she had lost. She could, however, forge a new future with her sister. She would just have to work through what came next. She knew there would be more questions.

She'd settled onto the sofa, thinking she should return to her cabin. But it would be lonely without Alex, and really, she didn't need him to protect her anymore. So she didn't need to stay. She clearly hadn't been thinking right. She twisted and secured a pillow so she was lying on her side.

Whispered voices drew her attention, but she remained still. Did they think she was asleep?

"Where is Alex?" Terra whispered. "Does he know she's waiting?"

She didn't hear the whispered reply. Was Alex avoiding her? She felt foolish for waiting here for him, but exhaustion overtook her before she had the presence of mind to leave.

Someone shook her, and she startled awake. Erin stood over her. Behind her, Nathan.

"Oh, wow. I didn't realize I'd fallen asleep."

"Someone is at the door for you," Erin said softly.

"What? Who?"

Erin kept her eyes on Mackenzie as if to bolster her. "Someone official."

"Oh, great. Probably more questions." Or . . . someone to arrest her? She'd supposedly been cleared, at least for the moment. Light spilled through the windows. "What time is it?"

"It's nine in the morning. You slept through the night on the sofa. We didn't want to disturb you."

And no Alex. Disappointment raked over her.

Erin brushed her bangs down a little, then smiled. "You look fine."

If you say so.

Mackenzie plodded down the hallway to the door, leaving Erin and Nathan standing in the kitchen watching. Mackenzie opened the door, hoping that by some chance it was Alex who was standing on the other side.

But a man in a business suit stood on the porch. She didn't recognize him.

"Can I help you?"

"Miss Hanson, my name is Mike Powers. I'm with the DSS, Diplomatic Security Services. I understand that we talked to you three years ago."

Strange. "That's right."

"We're interested in talking to you again about a position with our organization."

"You must know about my background. That's why you didn't hire me before."

"We now feel we could use you. We're an elite organization, and we're interested in hiring the best. I want to warn you that others will be knocking on your door as well—though maybe not literally, like I am right now. We're in a time where we need the best cybersecurity experts we can get." He handed her his business card. "I'm in cybersecurity investigations, as they pertain to international terrorism, and part of a joint terrorism task force operation investigating and searching for the cybercriminal you took down. I was called to the area yesterday as part of the task force—but things obviously escalated before we took action. While I was here, I wanted to meet you in person and give you my card. I just missed you at the county offices. I hope you'll call me and we can schedule a time for you to come to DC for an interview."

She stared at his card. "How did you find me?"

She glanced up at him and read his expression. Oh. He had his ways. She wouldn't press. But maybe Alex had told him. She bit back the need to ask this perfect stranger if he knew what happened to Alex Knight. "I'll think about it and give you a call."

"I hope you do. I look forward to seeing you again." He turned and walked away to a rental vehicle parked behind a county sheriff's department vehicle.

She glanced at her cell and saw a text from Alex. It had come through sometime late in the night. Finally. But . . . just a text?

> I'm in the middle of crazy. I had to take the red-eye and fly back to DC for debriefing. I will call you later.

So, obviously he wouldn't be coming to the cabin because he wasn't even in town. Had he left without even gathering his things at the cabin? Maybe he hadn't had time to face her or say goodbye. Or maybe he hadn't wanted to say it. Could he have gone to the cabin expecting to find her, hoping to find her, while she was at the main house snoring away? Whatever had happened, they really were like the proverbial two ships passing in the night.

She'd come to the ranch expecting that he would meet her here. That he wanted to see her as badly as she wanted to see him. Maybe he did. He had put his career on the line for her, and she wouldn't forget it. But maybe he would quickly forget *her* now that he had returned to his job.

Whatever the outcome, she knew what to do next.

THIRTY-NINE

After arriving in DC last night, she thought everything today had gone as well as could be expected. She'd arranged to have lunch with DS Special Agent Mike Powers. His enthusiastic response should have made her happy. She'd informed him that she would be renewing her contract with the university soon if other opportunities were not made available. Bottom line, she needed to know if employment with the DSS would materialize.

Mackenzie felt like she had control over her life. Mere days ago, she'd had none, and this new twist of events reminded her of the octopus ride at the carnival the night it all started.

With William gone now, the metaphorical ride had ended with Nora asking Mackenzie to stay and help rebuild Hanstech with her and Carson.

For the first time, her family wanted her to stay.

For the first time, the DSS wanted her too.

Her dreams were coming true, but at the same time, now it was time to decide which path to take.

Her cybercrime past no longer overshadowed her hopes and dreams for the future. But now that she finally had the opportunity she'd wanted for years, she realized her heart was no longer in it. Turned out that being accepted by her family was a more important dream than working for the government. She'd had to come here and meet with Mike before she could know what her heart wanted.

She wasn't going to work for the DSS or the university because Nora needed her. Hanstech needed her.

And Alex? A pang shot through her heart.

His last text said he would call her later. "Later" to Alex could mean days or . . . never. But he might be in the thick of it, fighting for his career.

Because of her.

Her heart ached. Making matters worse, Mackenzie had found a bench to mull over her thoughts and noticed it was the very same bench where she'd sat with him three years ago.

She'd hoped to connect with Alex while here. But she had to admit it was a lost cause. She had to accept that.

Lord . . . what am I doing here?

She felt like such a fool—chasing after a dream that had died before it could come true. Chasing after a man she barely knew. She closed her eyes and allowed her foolish heart to remember their kisses. The way his intense gray eyes could see right through her. Thoughts of his nearness and the scent of him made her skin tingle even now.

She had lost her mind.

Alex, please, just call me.

She grabbed her cell and stared at his text from two days ago. She was in DC—she would make the call instead of waiting on him. That way she had done all she could not to miss this chance with him, though it was fleeting at best.

Should I call?

Or should I not call?

Her cell buzzed with a text, startling her. Palms slicking, she dropped the phone. She picked it up and brushed off a few blades of grass as she checked the screen. *Alex?* Her heart jumped right to her throat. Oh yeah. She had a bad case of Alex Knight in her system.

> I'd love to give you a tour of the city.

What did he mean? Her mind scrambled for a response, then she sensed a presence behind her. She slowly stood and turned around—no wonder she'd smelled his cologne. It hadn't been her imagination.

"How long have you been standing there?"

He rushed around the bench and pulled her close. "Too long," he said, his tone husky.

Alex pressed his lips against hers, and this time he thoroughly and deeply kissed her, answering all her questions and filling in every insecure place in her heart. She was breathless when he released her.

Then, as an afterthought, he asked, "What are you doing here? No, don't answer that. I'm just glad you are here."

She stepped back and composed herself, though he still held her hand and a spark of deep longing remained in his eyes. "What happened in the debriefing?"

His sleeves were rolled up, and he looked like he had been battling things out for a day or two. "I get to keep my job. Or I would keep it if I were staying."

"Wait . . . Are you leaving again?" To the other side of the world? But that wouldn't make sense either unless he was keeping his job.

Still, her heart sank, and she dropped to the bench. Alex sat next to her and draped his arm on the bench behind her.

He leaned closer. "I'm not staying here. I'm going back to Montana. I have a new sister who needs a brother. I'll explain later. But it's much more than that. I'm not letting anything, or anyone, come between us, Mackenzie. I want to get to know everything about you."

He cupped her cheeks. "If you're going back to Michigan, I'll make it work. That is, if you feel the same."

Mackenzie leaned forward and gave him a quick peck. "I'm staying in Montana to help Nora rebuild. And . . . I had hoped we could find our way back to each other."

He rewarded her with that dimpled, roguish grin, and her heart pounded with the promise of hope and a future devoid of past failures. "How about I give you another tour while we're here, and then we'll head back to Montana together?"

"Together sounds nice."

Alex stood and offered her his hand. Mackenzie smiled as they held hands and re-created their first date, and she knew in her bones that this would be the best date of her life so far and the start of an amazing life with Alex Knight.

Author's Note

My dear lovely readers,

I'm so thrilled that you joined Alex and Mackenzie on their adventure to find and stop a dangerous cybercriminal! If you're familiar with my books, you know I love to set my stories in stunning locations, so the romance and suspense are set against a backdrop chock-full of action and adventure. In *Critical Alliance*, I thought it would be fun to write about how technology and the digital world are encroaching on every corner of the planet, including the spectacular setting of Montana. It's true that for many years now, high-tech companies are relocating to beautiful Montana. Who can blame them?

As for my cybercriminal-turned-cybersecurity expert, I promise that I know nothing about criminal hacking. At least nothing more than I learned by reading several books for this project. And nothing more than I learned from an actual cybersecurity expert when consulting with her about every facet of the story. I have a computer science degree, but it's too old to be of any use to me other than to help me understand a little technical jargon. I'm sure my security expert was relieved that I could understand at least some of what she shared with me.

But here's the scary part—I had complete confidence that my expert would shoot down every one of my ideas for hacking crimes. Nope. She informed me that everything I had dreamed up, my hacker could do. I should say *can* do . . . in the real world. I don't know about you, but I find that disturbing.

On the video gaming, I'll be honest—I don't play games. I've never been interested. But my kids love them and seem to own every gaming platform created. So it wasn't hard for me to gather intelligence about how to include a video game in the story.

Again, thanks for joining me on this last installment of Rocky Mountain Courage. I hope you're eager to hop on the next ride with me in a brand-new series set in Alaska!

Blessings!

Acknowledgments

All writers need an extensive support team, or at least this writer needs one. I don't know what I would do without you, my dear friends and confidantes, really. God brought you into my life—I know he did! How can I ever fully thank you for your continued encouragement? For the times you've listened to my long rambling or incessant whining as I labored through yet another novel. Thank you for all the brainstorming sessions and the amazing fresh perspectives you've given me. You inspire me to keep writing, to keep answering God's call no matter how hard—Lisa Harris, Sharon Hinck, Shannon McNear, and Susan Sleeman. Thanks for your brilliant and unique suggestions—Chawna Schoeder, Michele Griep, and everyone in our Minneapolis Critique group, Lynette Eason, Lynn Blackburn, Patricia Bradley, and the BOLO Squad. Wesley Harris for always being quick to answer questions regarding police procedures!

A special note goes to you, Christopher, Rachel, Jonathan, and Andrew Goddard—for inspiring me with your love of video games. And thank you, Patric Gardner (my daughter Rachel's husband), who helped me untangle and understand video game chat rooms, where I hear people can meet their future spouses (I'm glad you found my Rachel). I wouldn't be writing or published if my husband, Dan, hadn't supported and believed in me. Thank you, my love!

Though I mentioned Shannon McNear earlier, I'm sending a special dispensation her way. I can't thank you enough for sharing your brilliant cybersecurity sister, Jessica Boyer, with me. Jessica—you must be the busiest woman on the planet. *Thank you* for taking the time to explain to this complete novice how the world of cybersecurity and hacking works. I couldn't have written this book accurately without your help! Obviously, all mistakes are mine alone.

I owe my deepest gratitude to my agent, Steve Laube, and my editor, Rachel McRae, who have believed in my stories! Much appreciation goes to my Revell team: Amy Ballor, Michele Misiak, Karen Steele, and the art design team.

Thank you all for making my dreams come true!

TURN THE PAGE

TO START READING ANOTHER

THRILLING STORY FROM

ELIZABETH

GODDARD

ONE

A family tree can wither if nobody tends its roots.

—Unknown

While death was no stranger to her, a courteous knock on the door to give warning this time would have been appreciated.

Willow Anderson had been blindsided. Hadn't seen it coming. Everyone faced death sooner or later. Reading obituaries and looking at tombstones were a part of her job, after all. Her life. So why had it come as such a surprise? Either way—warning or no warning—she had to face what had been left behind. There was no point in putting things off.

She stood at the edge of a cluttered desk and stared blurry-eyed at the stack of mail piled high. A fluorescent light in the corner of the office that had been converted from a warehouse flickered and buzzed, then dimmed, leaving her with less-than-adequate lighting. But she wouldn't be deterred and riffled through the envelopes in a daze, dropping each one on JT's desk as she went. Electricity. Water. Something from the appraisal district? Oh, look, JT won a free Caribbean cruise. Junk mail. More bills.

The next one looked like a check. She ripped it open. Sure enough, a check had been made out to Anderson Consulting for services rendered. Willow hung her head. Wait. Not Anderson Consulting. In her grief-stricken state, she'd read that wrong. The check had been made out to James T. Anderson, her grandfather.

Everyone had called him JT. Anguish gripped her. Had he really been gone two weeks? He'd been the lifeblood of this forensic genealogy business. How could she keep it going without him?

She let the remaining envelopes fall back to the desk, where they fanned out.

A stupid tear escaped. Raced down her cheek. Tonight she'd mustered the courage to return to the office and face what JT had left behind when he'd been killed. Willow could have let Dana Cooper, JT's assistant, take care of some of it, but she'd told Dana to leave the office alone. They both needed time to mourn. Besides, Willow wanted to be the one to go through his things, including the mail.

She crumpled a piece of junk mail in her fist. Maybe she'd feel less fragile if she waited a few more days. Except the bills couldn't wait until Willow had finished grieving. Nor could clients in any outstanding cases on which he'd worked.

I can do this. I have to do this.

What choice did she have?

The heat kicked on, reminding her of the chill in the air. She rubbed her arms. Only a corner of the warehouse had been renovated into offices for Anderson Consulting. The rest seemed like a waste to Willow, but JT had thought he'd gotten a great deal on real estate at the time. The vaulted space had given them room to spread out, but now it felt far too . . . empty. Willow would have to figure out what she would do with the business and the real estate it occupied.

With the mail spread out, an envelope from the Washington State Department of Health caught her attention. She tugged it from the pile. Hands shaking, she carefully slit the envelope with a letter opener and pulled out the official document.

Her grandfather's death certificate.

Air whooshed from her lungs. Willow sank into a chair.

He's gone. Really gone. She wouldn't hear his words of wisdom. His jokes and boisterous laughter, or warm and friendly banter. At least not in this life.

JT had been one of a kind.

She touched his name on the certificate and, for good measure, let the shock of his death roll over her again. That moment she'd first heard the news.

JT had been killed riding his bike. To think he'd taken up the hobby as a way of extending his life after being diagnosed with cardiovascular disease. No plan had ever backfired so completely.

Why, why, why? You weren't supposed to die yet.

Tension corded her neck. A sliver of anger cut through her that he'd died when he'd had so much life left in him. But trying to come up with answers when there were none was a futile endeavor. Willow forced herself to focus on the task at hand. At this rate, it was going to be a long night. She rolled her neck around to ease the stiffness.

The outer office door opened and closed. "Willow? You in there?" Dana called.

Great. She'd wanted time alone. "Yep. JT's office."

A few seconds later, Dana appeared at the door. Willow masked her irritation. The woman meant well. "You didn't have to come."

Dana dropped her designer bag in a chair and frowned. She

shrugged out of her sparkly jean jacket and stepped closer. "You didn't think I'd let you go through this alone, did you?"

"It's late. Don't you have a husband or something?" Willow forced warmth into her voice and then a half smile slid onto her lips. She was glad to see Dana after all. The woman knew what Willow needed. No wonder JT had leaned on Dana all these years.

"Stan is fine. On his laptop and watching television. He won't miss me." Dana leaned over the desk to look at the certificate. "Besides, he wanted me to make sure you were alright."

She slowly slipped the certificate from Willow's hands and studied it. "Are you sure you're ready to go through his things here? I can do this for you."

Willow covered her eyes. "I thought I'd accepted he was gone, but seeing his death certificate . . . it's so final."

"Oh, honey. I know it's hard." Dana rushed around the desk. After offering a comforting squeeze, she handed Willow a tissue, then snatched another from the box.

Willow wiped her eyes and blew her nose. "It's okay. I'm okay. I have to do this."

"I wish I hadn't told you about Mrs. Mason's call. But it was the only case he was actively working. You really don't have to get back to business so soon after your grandfather's death."

"I appreciate your concern." Willow touched Dana's arm. The woman had held her hand over the last two weeks—through the tragic news of JT's death, selecting a casket, and seeing him buried. In her fifties, Dana was more like an older sister or a best friend than a mother figure despite being two decades older than Willow. She was practically part of the family, though she had one of her own—a doting husband, two grown children, and four grandchildren who kept her busy outside of work.

Willow tossed the tissue into the wastebasket. "Decisions have to be made, and I'm the one to make them now. I need to call Mrs. Mason back and tell her that JT's gone. But I have to know what the case is about first. Maybe I can finish it up for him." If Mrs. Mason would allow her, and if Willow had the required skills.

Her grandfather was the talent behind their consulting business. Willow didn't want to ruin the reputation he'd garnered. She hadn't mentioned it to Dana yet, but she was seriously thinking about closing up Anderson Consulting.

"Dig into a new project." Dana gathered the scattered mail into a pile again. "It might help take your mind off things if you get busy again."

"Can you get her file?"

"I can do better." Dana smiled. "He videoed their conversation."

"What? When did he start doing that?"

"With Mrs. Mason. You were traveling, looking for the lost heir for that law firm. He came into the office one day with a GoPro camcorder, more than pleased with himself and anxious to try it on the next client."

Willow had missed spending the last few weeks of JT's life with him. She wanted more time.

While Dana sat down and started the desktop computer to bring up the video, Willow looked at the framed photographs on the walls. The floor-to-ceiling shelves filled with history books and dusty old journals. Curio cabinets showcasing collectibles and souvenirs. Her grandfather had provided an adventure as they traveled around the world conducting research about people's pasts. She'd watched as he'd used DNA and genealogy techniques for solving mysteries, such as identifying remains of World War II, Korean War, and Vietnam War servicemen. Even law enforcement entities had often contacted him for assistance. The list went on and on.

"Okay, here it is." Dana grabbed another chair.

Willow sat next to her friend. The video started up on the

computer screen. Her grandfather's voice boomed loud and confident. His boisterous laughter and warmth made the slender, sixtyish woman smile in return.

JT offered Mrs. Mason coffee and made her feel right at home. He had a way about him that made him personable. Everyone responded to his warmth.

He didn't have any enemies.

Or so she believed.

Willow paused the video. "He never met a man, woman, or child he didn't like." The words rasped out past the lump in her throat.

Dana sighed. "I'm sorry. I didn't realize that JT took up such a big part of the video. You don't have to do this tonight. We can tackle it later."

Shaking her head, Willow pressed play. "Tackling it later isn't going to make it easier for me."

As they continued watching the video, Willow smiled, her love for JT swelling in her heart. He propped his ankle up on his knee in a relaxed pose. His blue eyes were bright and intelligent. He acted like a man in the prime of his life, not someone in his late sixties, as he told a few jokes that made Mrs. Mason genuinely laugh. In fact, both Willow and Dana joined in the laughter, adding a few sniffles. Her grandfather was a force to be reckoned with. A pleasant, jovial force that the world would miss.

Then Katelyn Mason leaned forward and began her tale.

"I came all the way from Texas to speak to you about taking on a project for me," she said.

"A Texan, huh?" JT chuckled and winked. "I never would have guessed by your accent."

The woman actually blushed and smoothed out her collar. Was JT flirting?

"Let me ask you a question," he said. "Why Anderson Consulting?"

"I read an article about what you've accomplished. You've done the impossible."

Though JT kept a straight face, amusement and satisfaction glimmered in his eyes. "Tell me your story."

"Twenty-one years ago my baby girl, Jamie, was taken from me in the hospital. She was only a few hours old." Mrs. Mason hung her head for a moment, then raised her quivering chin to pin her gaze on JT.

Lines in his forehead deepened with his frown. "And the FBI? The police?"

"Failed to find her. It's a cold case now. Through the years I've hired private investigators. They have all failed."

"And why are you just now coming to me?"

"As I said before, I read that you can do miracles. I have . . . I have less than three months to live, so the doctors tell me." Her voice hitched. "I believe with every fiber of my being that she is still alive out there, and I desperately want to say goodbye to her. I want her to know how much I love her. How much I have always loved her. And I never stopped praying for her. I believe you, Mr. Anderson, are the one to finally bring my baby home."

JT cleared his throat. His tender heart must have flooded with compassion. Willow wanted to reach through the screen and comfort him. He got up and fiddled with the GoPro, his anguished face filling the screen. He understood the pain of losing a child. His daughter, Willow's mother, had been killed in a car accident along with Willow's father.

Mind racing, Willow shut the video off.

Less than three months to live. "When was this interview?"

"A month ago."

Mrs. Mason had less than two months to live then, if her prognosis was accurate.

But a baby stolen twenty-one years ago? How had JT thought he could help? He'd never done this kind of project, especially one with such a short deadline. Still, Mrs. Mason's desperate plea for help must have compelled him to take action. Willow understood why he hadn't been able to say no. She had to think, so she got up and paced the room.

"You should finish this one. Find that woman's daughter." Dana's voice broke the silence. "It would keep your mind off losing him."

"Mrs. Mason believed JT was the one to finally bring home her baby girl. That's what she said. JT was the one with the skills—the genius behind solving impossible mysteries."

"You're every bit as brilliant." Dana sighed. "Look, he's been training you since you were just a kid. Since your parents died. You know he meant for you to take over."

"Maybe so, but I don't have his knack for uncovering clues. Knowing which ones to follow."

Dana vehemently shook her head. "You're too hard on your-self."

She flipped through the manila file folder she'd retrieved from the desk drawer. Something flickered in her eyes. What was it? Worry? Frustration?

"Okay, what *aren't* you telling me?" Willow asked.

A smile quickly replaced the frown on Dana's face. "No clue what you're talking about."

"Right. I know you well enough to see something else is on your mind." Willow tried to snatch the file away, but Dana was quicker and held it close.

"Now I'm sure you're hiding something."

The woman buried the file back in the desk drawer already crammed with folders, then riffled through the same stack of mail Willow had been through minutes ago. "I can take care of these for you. You didn't have to come in tonight."

Willow crossed her arms. "You can't put me off forever."

"Okay, okay." Dana rolled her head back and groaned. "Be-fore he died, JT called Austin McKade to ask for his help on the Mason case."

Willow's stomach coiled. She pressed her hand against her midsection. She'd had a hard enough time getting over Austin without having to see him again.

"He did? But . . . why?" Did Austin even know about JT's death?

"It's an FBI cold case. JT had hoped Austin could get information so he wouldn't have to reinvent the wheel, so to speak."

Willow sank into a chair. "That makes sense. Total sense."

But she wouldn't put it past JT to have wanted to use the Mason case to his advantage.

This case might have been the excuse he'd needed to call Austin when he had other motives. He had an uncanny ability to convince people to go along with his wishes or what he believed was best for them. He had believed that Willow and Austin should be together. He just wouldn't let go of it. But JT couldn't have been more wrong.

Willow and Austin McKade had already crashed and burned, and those ashes would never be resurrected.

Elizabeth Goddard is the *USA Today* bestselling and award-winning author of more than fifty novels, including *Present Danger, Deadly Target,* and the Uncommon Justice series. Her books have sold over one million copies. She is a Carol Award winner and a Daphne du Maurier Award finalist. When she's not writing, she loves spending time with her family, traveling to find inspiration for her next book, and serving with her husband in ministry. For more information about her books, visit her website at www.ElizabethGoddard.com.

HIDDEN CRIMES. OPEN THREATS.
LONG-BURIED SECRETS . . .

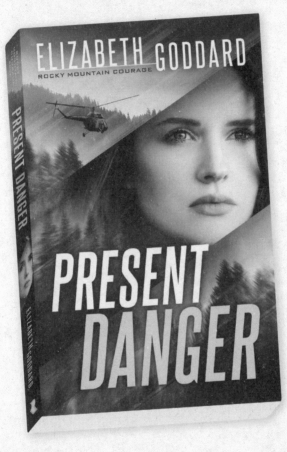

USFS Special Agent Terra Connors is called to investigate a body found in the national forest. As she's uncovering clues that show the victim may have been involved in criminal activities, the case takes a deadly turn that leaves her and former FBI Special Agent Jack Tanner fighting for the truth—and their lives.

Revell
a division of Baker Publishing Group
www.RevellBooks.com